The Long Battle

Book Five of the Sevordine Chronicles

by

Shawn P. B. Robinson

BrainSwell Publishing
Ingersoll, Ontario

ISBN 978-1-989296-63-9

Cover design and artwork copyright © Shawn Robinson
Interior Page Dividers designed from images downloaded from Freepick.com.

BrainSwell Publishing
Ingersoll, ON

Dedication and Thanks

To all my readers. I have so enjoyed sharing these stories with you and getting to know so many of you.
You truly are wonderful people, and I hope you all enjoy the series as much as I've enjoyed writing it.

This book is a work of fiction.
Characters and places and such are fictional. While there are some matters that are somewhat allegorical in nature, this book is fiction.
There! I said it. I said it without going on a rant about how dumb it is to have to say that about a fiction book. Are you happy? Is that good enough? Is that what you want? You've won! You got everything you wanted. I've told you the fictional book is fiction. Now you know! Because you couldn't possibly have known before this moment. You couldn't have figured it out on your own. We all need that extra help in knowing that fiction is fiction. That made up stories are made up. Arrrgghhh! At least I didn't rant again. I kept my cool. I'm a cool guy. A cool cat. I've got it all together.
Calm… I have my calm. Deep breath in. Growl out. No, that's not it… how did it go again?

Preface

The fifth book in this series was, by far, the hardest to write. Because it tells two different stories coming together as one, it made for a unique challenge.

But even so, I think it's my favourite of the five books, and I hope you love it as much as I do!

Enjoy!

Shawn P. B. Robinson

CHECK OUT THESE BOOKS BY
Shawn P. B. Robinson

Adult Fiction (Sci-fi & Fantasy)

The Ridge Series (3 books)
ADA: An Anthology of Short Stories

YA Fiction (Fantasy)

The Sevordine Chronicles (5 Books)

Books for Younger Readers

Annalynn the Canadian Spy Series (6 Books)
Jerry the Squirrel (4 Books)
Arestana Series (3 Books)
Activity Books (2 Books)

www.shawnpbrobinson.com/books

Table of Contents

1

Draydon and the Gratter

I lose my footing and crash down on the snow and ice. No, not snow. A quick look around tells me it's pretty much just ice down here. Snow is at least soft. The lack of it... well... that's why I hurt so bad now.

"You okay?"

I struggle to get my feet under me as I look up at Roran. We've only just entered the pass. I mean... like three steps in, and I've already hurt myself. This isn't looking good.

"Yeah, I'll be okay. That's one of the nice things about wearing leathers. It takes some of the impact." I examine his position up on a large boulder—the one I just jumped off. "I think you'd better find a different way down."

He smiles. "I'll be okay. I'm pretty steady on my feet."

A moment later, I'm pulling him off the ground where he hit. He's not happy. I don't blame him. He hit harder than I did.

Once the look of pain has faded from his face, we turn around and take in our surroundings.

We've entered the pass. It's our only way through to the Talic Region, at least our only way through from this area of the country.

The pass down south, Switcher Pass, is wide. In fact, there are no places in the pass where you can see the cliffs on both sides at the same time. Unless you climb a tall tree, of course. It's so wide that in most places, it would take you hours to get from one side to the other.

This pass is the complete opposite. We had to squeeze through a crack in the rock to get into it and looking ahead I see it's wide enough for maybe a dozen people to walk side by side in spots, while just barely wide enough for one person in other spots. And that's just from the bit I can see ahead as it's quite dark.

But of course, that's not the problem. I can deal with the dark. I can deal with tight spaces. And I can even deal with the ice, frozen down the sides of the cliffs on either side and pooling at the bottom.

It's the screaming that gets me.

Over and over, the familiar voice of the Talic Wolf screams out, "Give me the Princeling! Give me the Princeling!"

The creature is injured, or at least it was last I saw it. Its back legs didn't work. It was blind, and its body covered with burns. But I can't kill it. It's not some hesitation on my part. I'd gladly see that thing dead. It's just that I literally cannot kill it. My sword sliced right through its neck, doing no damage at all. That head should have rolled, yet it didn't.

That's the problem with enchanted creatures… they don't always make sense.

But for us, we have no other way forward. Since it's lost its sight and sense of smell, perhaps we can get past it, even in these tight spaces.

"Let's go."

Roran nods and follows. One thing about him, not much scares him.

He's smaller than I am by about a span, enough to make him have to crane his neck to look up to me when we stand close, but he's quite good with his sword and an excellent shot with his crossbow.

For the next in line for the throne, he'd make an excellent King, if it weren't for the political maneuvering that's cost him his throne. Now it falls to me. Neither of us are happy about that, but we're determined to do what's right.

We climb over a boulder, one not covered in ice, and slip and slide our way through the next little area. A few minutes later, we squeeze through a tight space where the cliffs come together and then slide down into the new area.

"If this pass is covered with ice like this the entire way, we won't make it through before we both turn eighty," Roran jokes. He's never been a funny one, but I smile back at him.

We move on like this for what feels like another hour before we come to some bare patches of rock, leading to more bare patches. Not long after that, we're walking normally again, but my muscles hurt.

The screams from the Talic Wolf haven't died down at all. I think they're getting slightly louder, though. It's strange that its voice carries so well.

Something catches my eye, and I stop. When Roran sees me, he whispers, "It's a gratter."

My heart feels like it's frozen in my chest, and I squint at it in the dim light. It looks like just a ball of fur. I try to keep my voice steady as I say, "I didn't think they looked like that. Relin told me they had a lot of legs."

He nods. "They do. And that one does have a lot of legs. That's just the way it sleeps. That's the best kind of gratter. A sleeping gratter. Don't wake it. We likely won't survive."

As we move, I spy out a few others, sleeping here and there. At one point, I see what I think might be a large pack of them, all sleeping together. I hope they're hibernating. I don't want to face one awake.

In time, as the Talic Wolf's screams gradually increase in volume, I see more and more of the creatures. I don't know how they sleep through the noise. It's really getting to me. But then again, I'm the one he wants, not the gratters. I doubt the gratters, as vicious and deadly as they are, would ever want to face off against a Talic Wolf.

By this point, Roran and I don't dare even whisper. All we do is signal to each other as we move along. We don't want to awaken anything.

Another ten minutes down the narrow path, winding our way along between the cliffs, one on either side of us, the gratters begin to thin out. I think we're just about out of danger, at least from them, when we come across three gratters, sleeping on the ground right in front of us. That wouldn't be a problem, of course, if there was lots of room to walk around them, but at that particular spot, there's barely room to get past the first two, and no room to walk around the third.

We squeeze past the first one, then the second. We manage to do this silently and without touching either one. But the gratter that now lies in front of us is spread out, rather than in a ball. It's actually on its back with its legs… six, no, eight… no… a lot of legs. I think I count eleven. All eleven legs stick up in different directions.

I'm not sure we can just get past this creature. I reach for my sword—not to kill it while it sleeps, but in case it wakes while we're climbing past it. As my hand wraps around the hilt, Roran grabs my wrist. He shakes his head, and I remember how much noise a sword makes as it's pulled from its sheath. It's not a lot, but it's likely enough to wake the one before us.

Roran goes first. He braces one foot on a boulder to the left of the gratter, then leans on me, using the boulder and me as support as he steps up and over the creature. I'm impressed that it works so well until I realize that it's going to be hard for him to do that for me.

As he quietly lands on the other side, I see he recognizes the same problem. He reaches across the creature and tries to support me as I do the same thing as him, but just as I step up onto the boulder, I come down hard, right on the belly of the sleeping gratter!

Roran grabs my arm and pulls. He's not a particularly strong guy, but he manages to get me off the creature. By the time I get to my feet, the gratter has flipped itself over. Its eyes are on me… all like… three hundred of those black, spider-like eyes, but it doesn't seem to be quite awake just yet.

I stand in horror as I watch it open its cat-like jaws and flex its shoulders. It's like the worst of every creature put all together into one beastly abomination.

Roran and I turn and run at the same time. The ground in this area is all stone, and it's fairly flat and completely clear of ice and snow. Gratters are fast, so by the time it fully wakes up, we want to be far away. Far, far away!

We race around one of the many twists in the pass, jumping over a boulder, and then ducking under a rock overhang. After a few minutes, I notice I'm no longer cold. At least there's that.

"Gratters are deadly!" Roran hisses unhelpfully.

"How do we kill it?"

"Don't know!" Roran glances back over his shoulder. "I think the key is to never have to fight one."

"We're past all that, Roran," I growl at him as I leap over a small crevice. "Berin killed one, right? So, it has to be possible." I focus on running for a moment, ducking to avoid hitting my head on yet another overhang, but then add, "You don't have any ideas how to kill it?"

"Nope. I don't think the problem is that they can't be killed," Roran gasps. He's in far worse shape than I am. I hope if we make it out of here, we won't have to run quite as much. "The problem is how fast they are. You can swing your sword, but you just can't hit it!"

I glance back and nearly fall over. I see the gratter. It moves like lightning—it was just a blur when I first turned around—but now it's sitting up on a rock, way up on the cliff, staring at us. It's like a furry spider with too many legs, a snout like a cat, dozens of eyes, and claws on the ends of its multi-jointed legs.

I don't think that creature should exist. And I certainly don't like the way it's looking at me.

We manage to find a bit more speed and rush along, but I see out of the corner of my eye, the gratter moving along the side of the cliff, its claws clicking along the rock wall in a manner that I'm confident will leave me with nightmares. If we survive.

I think it's trying to get in front of us, which I really don't like. Again… I think that creature should not exist. The word "abomination" keeps coming to mind.

As the screams of the Talic wolf continue to grow louder, I watch the gratter scurry down the side of the cliff. It's definitely trying to head us off. I don't know if it's planning on attacking right away or going to just get in our way, but I pull out my sword, careful not to hit me or Roran with it. The enchanted blade will cut through anything, and I don't want to continue this journey without a limb.

The creature reaches us faster than I would have thought possible, and I bring my sword up just in time, slicing where I think the gratter will be. Unfortunately, it dodges out of the way and comes at me again. I swing again, still running forward as best I can.

It dodges yet again, but then immediately comes for me, and this time I get it. My blade slices clean through it, two halves of the beastly thing falling to each side.

We come to a stop not only to avoid running into the body but to cover our ears as what's left of the creature lets out a cross between a growl and a cry of frustration. It's loud.

At first, I just hope it doesn't draw the attention of the Talic Wolf, although its hearing was destroyed in the fire all those months ago, but that worry quickly fades away as I hear a new sound. Behind us… a clicking sound… similar what I heard when the gratter came after us. But this one sounds like somewhere around a hundred gratters.

"Move!" Roran hisses, and we take off again.

The sound grows loud enough that I'm afraid they're already all around us, but as I glance back, I don't see any yet. My heart races, and all I can think of is that I don't want to face what's behind me, but I definitely don't want to run into this Talic Wolf! Its scream, "Give me the Princeling!" is enough to make me want to turn around and find a place to hide.

It doesn't matter, though, because any choice in the matter is taken from us when we round the next corner.

I come to a grinding halt, and Roran slams into my back. At first, he starts to holler at me to run again, but then he gasps.

As the sound of the approaching gratters grow louder, I stare into the eyes of five Talic Wolves, each one wearing a vicious smile, hungrily sizing up their next meal.

2

Draydon and the Chase

My breathing comes in ragged gasps. It's not all the running. I don't mind that. It's the wolves. The Talic Wolves. I've only ever met one before, and it was the most terrifying experience of my life. I remember its laugh, its voice, its penetrating gaze. I remember its mocking words, pretending to offer me comfort, care, and kindness as it prepared to eat me.

The only way to injure a Talic Wolf is with fire, and we have none of that. I'm also pretty sure they won't stand by while we take the time to build one.

But I guess none of that matters because at that moment, a hundred or more gratters come around the bend. Some stand on the rock floor, but most stay up on the sides of the cliffs. They swarm over one another, climbing past and onto each other, hissing, growling, snapping their jaws.

But their eyes are not on us.

The snarls behind me draw me back to the wolves. They're up on their feet now, backs arched, teeth bared.

And the two of us stand between five Talic Wolves and a hundred and fifty gratters.

"Maybe..." Roran begins, "... they'll fight each other and we can just, you know, walk away."

I picture that in my head, and a bit of hope rushes through my heart for just a moment, but then two wolves slowly walk around us and stand mere inches from the gratters. A quick look back and I see the wolves have intentionally surrounded us.

"They're ours," the wolf says in its creepy, hissing, high-pitched growl. If nothing else, that voice cuts to my soul. "Back away!"

Despite the cold, I'm sweating. And not just a little, either. My hands are shaking, and my teeth are chattering. But... again... not from the cold.

I've had nightmares of that day I woke up next to a Talic Wolf as it waited for the sun to set before it could eat me. Creatures that hunt only by day and eat only at night. I look around, desperate for something, anything. Any way that I can find to get us out of here. But these wolves are fast. There's no place to run.

If these were normal wolves, I'd expect the gratters to simply overwhelm them, but the gratters haven't moved—other than to snap their jaws and hiss.

Neither side budges as they size each other up until a gratter lunges forward. Before any other creatures can react, the Talic Wolf closest to it snaps its jaws around the gratters neck, and in a moment the many-legged creature goes limp.

The Talic Wolf spits out the gratter and screams, "GET OUT OF HERE!" and all the Talic Wolves howl. Terror overcomes the gratters, and they turn as one and race back the way they'd come.

"Well, at least we don't have to worry about the gratters," I say, trying to lighten the moment.

Roran frowns at me. "Not the time, Draydon."

I disagree. I think it's exactly the time for some humor. It's the only thing that I think can make this moment less terrifying, but I don't correct him. Not worth the argument when we're both likely to die.

The wolves all face us now. And smile. Wolves shouldn't smile, but these do. It makes it all that much worse.

The three wolves behind us part just enough and growl. I know what they want. They want us to run. Talic Wolves don't want to just eat their prey. They like the chase. And they've opened a path that leads directly to the screams of the Talic Wolf we met months ago. The one that cries, "Give me the Princeling! Give me the Princeling!"

"Run, little tasties," the largest of the wolves growls. "Run or we will eat you now!"

I know we'll never get away from them, but it's a chance, and that I'll take. Unfortunately, I hesitate for just long enough that one lunges at me, sinking its teeth into my arm, but only just enough to break the skin.

It pulls back immediately, though, and snarls. "Marked!"

The other wolves growl and begin to pace.

"Whose is it?" a different wolf asks. Their voices are all the same. High-pitched, airy, growls.

"It's the burnt one. It's his."

The same wolf that bit me lunges at Roran and breaks the skin of his arm. I think it's tasting our blood. "Royal blood. Both. The one is marked. The other… it may be marked too, but I cannot tell. It's from the same litter. Or… close to it. It's marked. Or its sire was marked."

I want to ask what all this means, but I know they don't care what we say. They just want to toy with us. Roran, however, has no such hesitation. "What does this mean? Does this mean you can't eat us?"

The wolves all laugh in that hoarse, scratchy way of theirs, giving us no more than a glance before the large one says, "Take them to him."

Something slams into the back of me, and I crash down on the ground with Roran right beside me. Before I can get back up, one of the wolves has me by the back of my armor. The wolves are big, but my legs and knees still drag on the ground as we move along.

I try to get my feet up under me, but as soon as I do, the wolf snarls, and I quickly figure out that he fully expects me to just accept my situation. When I let myself just be dragged, he settles down. I glance at Roran. He's in the same spot as me—carried by a wolf.

The sound of the screaming Talic Wolf grows louder and louder. I think we've nearly reached it. I don't want to face this thing again, but at least it might still be injured. That might give us a chance… but then again… there are the other wolves to deal with.

When we come around the next bend, I see it immediately. I had feared the Talic Wolf might have healed, but it looks like it hasn't. At all. In fact, it looks worse. Most of its hair is gone. It's still clearly blind. Its voice, although loud, is far scratchier than it had been. Both its hind legs still drag on the ground.

"Give me the Princeling!" it screams as it drags itself back and forth. I see a line on the ground where it's walked, chunks of fur and more just spread out in a line where it's paced back and forth.

It's insane. But not like Hob. He's a safe kind of insane. I think. Well. I'm not sure about Hob. But I am sure that this thing is entirely dangerous.

A large wolf approaches. This one's larger than any of the wolves I've seen so far. Its shoulders nearly reach the height of my own, and its head is huge. I think if it accidentally stepped on my foot, it would break every bone down there.

"Why are the prey not dead?" it hisses. Its voice is somewhat deeper than the others, but also much higher. Their voices… they're like nightmares.

"The prey is marked. It's the princeling."

The large wolf smiles, showing far too many teeth. "Which one is the princeling-prey? I will eat the other."

The wolves we came with shake their heads. "That one for sure," pointing its snout at me, "and the other one might be too. Same litter. Or close to the same. Royal blood."

The large wolf—I guess the Alpha—growls and shakes its head, looking quite disappointed.

I hate every moment of this. I glance at Roran. I think he's on the verge of tears. I expect I look the same. I feel powerless.

Without warning, the Alpha jumps backwards, twisting its body around and landing full-force on the injured wolf, slamming the smaller wolf's body down onto the cold rock. While the injured wolf still screams "Gives me the princeling!" the Alpha sinks its teeth into the back of its neck, and the injured wolf finally goes silent.

My heart stops in my chest. If they're killing it off, I guess that means they're going to eat us now.

When the Alpha stands, the injured Talic isn't dead. Instead, it pushes itself up onto its two front legs and begins to sniff the air.

The last time we saw it, its sense of smell was mostly gone, and that seems to be the case now, too. I know the wolves like a chase. Maybe they'll let this one chase us, and we can get away again!

My whole body lurches forward, and I hit the ground hard. The laughing wolves aren't going to just let us off easy.

I glance up just in time to see the injured Talic Wolf lunge for me, and I roll out of the way. Before I can get too far, Roran comes crashing down on top of me. I guess they want a show.

We both scramble out of the way as the Talic Wolf comes for us again. Although it drags its hind feet, it's still fast!

"I think it's following the sound we make!" Roran says as he jumps to the side. At the sound of his voice, the Talic Wolf lunges right at him.

"I didn't think it could hear!" I reply, which earns me a chance to dodge another attack from the wolf.

Roran points down the pass and grabs my arm, pulling me along. The other wolves seem content to watch the show, and now that we're being chased, I guess we can just run.

The injured wolf comes after us. I guess it's not just our voices, but maybe the vibrations of our footsteps… and voices… and anything. I guess it can figure it out and distinguish our steps from the other wolves, because they're running along, howling, roaring, and laughing. I think they're not just laughing at us, but at the wolf that's chasing us as well.

I feel bad for him for a moment, but then catch myself. Nope. I don't think I want to feel bad for the creature that tried to eat me and ended up injured when my friends rescued me.

We race along through the pass. It's no different here than at any other place. The walls of the cliffs are close on either side. There's a bit of snow here and there, but it's pretty much just rock floor along the bottom and rock walls on either side.

I see the occasional gratter asleep up on the side of the cliffs, one side or the other, but none move to follow us.

Roran, between gasps for air manages to say, "I think the Alpha communicated through the bite! How strange is that?"

At the sound of his voice, the injured Talic Wolf roars and picks up speed. I frown at Roran and put my finger to my lips. Footsteps are one thing, but the voice… that draws it in.

We run on to the sound of the one wolf screaming, "Give me the princeling!" and the other wolves laughing, growling, cheering, whatever they seem to feel like at the moment.

I know I can keep this up for a long time, but Roran isn't quite as strong right now. I've been wondering if that ring on his finger and fighting the enchantment has been sapping his strength.

After about an hour, I glance back. Something changed. I can't quite put my finger on it at first, but then Roran hisses, "They're not laughing as much."

I glance back again. The injured wolf seems just as angry and just as intent on eating me. The other wolves seem… hmm… the only word that comes to mind is subdued. For whatever reason, they're not as excited as before.

Roran's ready to collapse, and I'm feeling pretty wiped myself. But I don't think it's just that the wolves are tired. Nor do I think they're getting bored.

"Kill it soon!" one of the wolves screeches.

The other wolves join in, screaming, "Hurry! Hurry!"

I don't like this. Not only does it mean they want us dead soon, but I hear something else in their voices.

Panic. Fear.

Despite the fact that we need to be quiet, Roran asks the question screaming in my mind. "What can scare Talic Wolves?"

I don't really want to know the answer to that question. I know it's not gratters. I can't imagine it's giants, but if it is, and the Talic Wolves run away, then that's okay because I know my sword works on giants.

I can't imagine it's the Shaloomd. They're nasty things, but I would think Talic Wolves would eat them rather than be afraid of them.

That only leaves one creature that I can think of which might scare a Talic Wolf.

I dodge a large boulder and glance back to see all the wolves, aside from the injured one, have stopped—and I don't know why. I'm sure we're running into danger, but unlike the wolves, we have to keep running. I dodge around another large boulder as I push the thoughts down. I hope it's not what I think, because if it is, running is the last thing we should be doing.

We come to a halt and spin around. The injured wolf is still back there a little way. It's not moving too fast anymore.

The Alpha wolf bolts forward, right up to the injured wolf and hollers, "STOP!" but it moves forward slowly anyway, still screaming, "Give me the princeling!"

I turn and come to a halt as the Alpha sinks its teeth into the neck of the injured wolf again. I want to keep running, but something tells me what's ahead is far worse than what's behind.

"I won't stop!" the injured wolf screams.

Before it can continue, the other wolves attack it. It's hard to believe they'd kill one of their own rather than let it continue. Come to think of it, I don't know if they can truly kill the creature, but it doesn't matter. Regardless of what's ahead, we have to move on.

We turn back and slam into another large boulder, knocking us back onto our butts.

Only… it's not a boulder. And it truly is worse than a hungry Talic Wolf.

It's a Reber Troll. And it's not happy.

3

Draydon and the Beast

Troll to one side and Roran rolls to the other as a large fist comes down where we had landed only a second before. I feel the thud vibrate through the stone and scramble to my feet.

The Reber Troll is slow—that's one good thing—but there's a reason even the Talic Wolves won't come near them. We meet up on the other side of the troll and run down the pass. It's a little wider here than before, but it's still cramped.

I realize with horror that the boulders I've been dodging are actually more trolls. It's a wonder we got as far as we did without upsetting one.

I look back. The Reber Troll is on its feet, and its eyes are on us. I grind my teeth as it takes its first step in our direction.

A Reber Troll on our tail means the end for us. No city will welcome us. No home will open its doors to us. We are forever cursed.

We scramble around another Reber Troll, sitting on the ground, looking just like one of the many boulders in the area. I don't know what happens if you upset more than one troll at a time, but I doubt it'd be a good thing.

Reber Trolls are impossible to kill. At least, as far as everyone believes. Nordin is named Trollslayer, but I asked one of the men who worked with him about it. The guy laughed and told me it was just a joke, because no one can kill a troll.

Their skin is impenetrable. You can't stab it. You can't burn it. You can't bury it. You can't contain it. You can't hurt or harm it in any way.

The goal is simple: don't have anything to do with a Reber Troll.

If you annoy one—and it's not entirely clear how you annoy a Reber Troll—they will hunt you. Slowly, but surely, hunt you for the rest of your life. If you hide in a city, it will slowly tear the city down, brick by brick, until there's nothing left. No one can stop it; it just does what it does. When it doesn't find you, it'll leave the rubble and continue the hunt.

We round a corner, and I almost smile with relief, despite the circumstances. I don't see any trolls ahead. They're definitely hard to see up against the gray rock of the pass, but this area is clear of any bumps or boulders or rocks that could possibly be a troll.

We rush along and as we're about to turn another corner, I look back. Sure enough, the troll comes into sight. *"Scrape, thud… scrape, thud… scrape, thud…"* Its face is filled with rage as it slowly stomps forward, set on putting an end to us.

The pass near Sevord takes days to cross, but Relin thought this pass might only take hours. So far, we've been most of the day getting to this point, and night is setting in. If we didn't have a troll behind us, I'd suggest setting up camp, but instead, we run for another bit to get ahead of our pursuer, then stop to build a small fire to light one of the torches we brought with us.

Once it's lit, we carry on.

I see why no one survives the journey through the northern pass. Gratters, then Talic Wolves, then Reber Trolls. I'm not sure if there's anything worse ahead, but so far, it's not been good.

We're both exhausted, but as the night sets in, we push on, careful to watch our footing in the light of the torch. If we sprain an ankle at this point, I think any chance of survival will end there.

"Which one of us do you think it's after?" Roran asks, as he gasps for air.

I shake my head. "I don't see how it matters. It might be both of us."

Roran stumbles, and I help steady him as we move on. He grunts and adds, "It does matter."

"Why? For one, neither of us will leave the other. But either way, it's probably after both of us."

"No," Roran gasps as he falls into a coughing fit. We slow down as he tries to catch his breath. "It does matter. If it's after you, we have to kill it."

I laugh, but I'm not finding this funny. "If it's after you, we'll have to do the same thing."

He shakes his head. "No, you're the future king. We have to keep you alive or Parthun will rule."

"I'm not leaving you, if that's what you mean!" I say, feeling the anger build in me. "I'm not about to start my future rule by sacrificing my cousin."

"It doesn't matter what you want, Caric… or Draydon!"

I don't really have an answer for him. I feel like just screaming, "Well… it matters to me!" but I think that just sounds dumb, so I remain silent for a moment. When I'm ready to speak, I calm myself and say, "Let's walk for a bit."

As scared as we both are, we're ready to slow down. I hear the *"scrape, thud… scrape, thud… scrape, thud…"* of the troll's feet as it relentlessly continues the chase, but the sound is faint. We can't stop for a rest, but we can certainly walk for the time being.

Roran's breathing a bit better now, and he says matter-of-factly, "When we get out of the pass, we'll need to part ways for a bit and see which one of us it's after."

"Again, Roran, I'm not leaving you. If it's after you, we'll still stick together."

Roran frowns, but I see he's thinking it through.

He doesn't come up with anything, so I suggest, "I wonder if my sword can kill a troll. I mean, it cuts through anything."

"Maybe…" Roran says, and I can see hope is building.

"Scrape, thud… scrape, thud… scrape, thud…"

I feel a bit of a breeze, something I haven't felt all day since entering the pass, and I smile. The torch has also started to flicker a lot more. It likely won't stay burning once we make it out of here. I'm not looking forward to traveling across the Talic Region in the winter, let alone in the dark. Without a path, there are too many dips and holes and more to turn an ankle.

"At least we don't have to listen to the Talic Wolf scream anymore," Roran says, trying to lighten the mood.

I give a half-hearted smile, but I want to bring us back to the issue. "What do you think? You think my sword might work on it? I mean, it can supposedly cut through anything."

Roran doesn't answer at first, but after a bit, he slowly nods. "Should have tried that back when we first met it. The only way to test it out now is to get within reach of those fists."

I feel like I blew it, but then I catch myself. "No, that wouldn't have worked."

"Why not? How do you know the sword wouldn't work?"

"No, I don't mean that. I mean, if I had tried the sword on the troll, and I had killed it, we'd be in a worse spot."

Roran laughs, but not a happy laugh. "How could there be any worse spot than this?"

"I think the other trolls would have gotten angry, and we might have had dozens of trolls come after us. But if they didn't, I think the wolves would have resumed the chase. They only backed off because of the trolls. I think, for the moment, we're probably safer with a troll on our tail, rather than a pack of Talic Wolves."

"Scrape, thud… scrape, thud… scrape, thud…"

Roran gives me a look that suggests he agrees, but he doesn't like it. I don't blame him. I don't like it either.

"So, for now, we just have to keep ahead of the troll until we get the nerve to try my sword on it."

"No, we have another problem."

I don't like the sound of that. "What else?"

"How tired are you, Draydon?"

"I feel like I want to collapse. You?"

"Same." Roran glances behind us for a moment before adding, "We're going to need to find a place to sleep. So, we need to get far enough away from the troll that we can close our eyes for a bit. I don't think we can keep up the pace throughout the night. Or, at least I can't."

He's right. I know he's right. I just can't imagine getting far enough away from this thing that we could actually doze off. Maybe if we had horses, but not on foot.

We come around another bend, and a burst of wind blows out our torch, plunging us into darkness. As my eyes adjust, I see the exit. It's not much different from the entrance on the west side where we came in. Small, up a bit off the ground, easy to miss. "Another few steps, and we'll be one of the first, if not the first, to ever make it through here alive!"

"Well," Roran replies with a laugh, "let's just not die in the next few steps."

We move along, careful where we step, and scurry up the incline to the crack. Aside from this small opening, there's no way through from what I can see.

"Scrape, thud... scrape, thud... scrape, thud..."

We squeeze through. I suspect someone Rulf's size might have to pull his armor off to fit, and even then, he might not get his belly through.

On the other side, we half scramble, half slide down to the ground, and I look back to see the crack itself, from this side, doesn't look like much more than an indent in the rock. Aside from that, it's just a solid wall all the way up.

"How's the Reber Troll going to squeeze through that?" Roran asks.

As if in answer to his question, a large arm shoots through, swinging at us. We're well out of reach—by a long shot—but I still holler when it happens. I feel a moment of hope that maybe it'll be stuck in there, but then the arm disappears, and I see a foot in the crack. It sits there for a second, then moves up.

"It... climbing..." Roran says in shock.

I'm about to run, but I stop myself. I have to see if it makes it through. I don't want to be running from nothing. We back up, trying to stay a distance away as we hear the troll grunt, and the scraping sound continues.

In the dark, I don't really see it until it slams into the ground in front of the cliff. I feel the thud even from here, and we're quite far out by this point. A moment later, it pulls itself to its feet.

"Scrape, thud... scrape, thud... scrape, thud..."

"Time to run!" Roran announces, and we take off, heading east.

It's not as if we haven't run for our lives before, but, to be honest, it's getting a little old. I'd kind of like to have a life where no one or nothing is trying to kill me. But… if I'm going to be King, I guess that's not an option. Perhaps ever.

We do our best to watch our steps, but we still fall quite regularly. The ground here is, like most of the Talic Region, covered with rolling hills and thick grass. Even in the winter, the grass snags my feet, and I'm pretty tired of falling all the time.

We run like this for most of the night. I can't believe we still have this energy in us, but then again, when we're about to die, I guess there's a lot of motivation to keep living, and that seems to push us along.

By the time we see the first rays of sunlight, not only has it been a long time since we've seen or heard anything of the troll, but we catch sight of a small forest.

Without a word, we head for it. I think it's exactly what we need.

We enter the trees just as a light snow has begun to fall, and the wind dies down. We gather up some old, dry wood and set a fire.

"I'll take the first watch," Roran says.

"No need." As I lay out my bedroll on the soft ground, covered in pine needles, I wave my arm around. "It'll take a while for the troll to catch up, right? And when it finds the forest, how much noise do you think it'll make tearing down these trees to get at us? We can barely squeeze through some of these areas, and we've broken countless branches. We'll wake long before it reaches us. Let's just keep everything in our packs and be ready to run."

Roran nods, but he's not happy. He's taken this whole, "I have to get Draydon to the throne" idea very seriously. I'm glad about that, but he needs to rest too.

I eat a little, and drink from my waterskin, which is filled with icy, slushy water, and then both of us pack our waterskins full of snow, setting them down between us and the fire. I'm hoping the water will melt.

I then doze off to the sound of the popping and crackling of the fire.

4

Draydon and the Ring

When I awake, I'm shivering.

It takes me a moment to remember where I am.

It's dark. Not really dark, just dark like I'm in a forest. I smell smoke from a fire pit. Yes, that's it. I see it in front of me.

And I'm shivering.

I sit up as it all comes back. It's still daytime, I'm just in a forest. The light isn't coming through the trees all that well.

I think it's probably time to move on, so I turn to wake Roran, but he's gone. I panic at first, but then I calm myself. He's likely just out collecting wood or looking for food.

I get up and stretch, then look back to where Roran had slept. No, he's not just gone for food. His pack is gone as well! He's left me. He thinks he can lead the troll away!

I pack up as quick as I can, taking the time to shove a bit of food in my stomach and take a bit of water. I won't be able to catch him if I'm weak from lack of food.

I strap everything on, make sure the fire is out, and take off. But when I get to the edge of the forest, I stop and let out a groan. The light snowfall… it covered all the tracks.

I drop my pack and scramble up a tall tree at the edge of the forest, but when I get as high as I feel is safe, I still can't see him. Nor can I see the troll.

That's a pretty good sign the troll isn't after me.

I climb down and pull on my pack as I think it through. He wouldn't head back to the west. That's the way we came from, and he still needs to find the Spellcaster. That's what this whole trip is about, after all.

The Spellcaster is to the east, but he wouldn't head that way—at least not yet. His goal is to lead the troll away from me. To the north is, I think, a large lake, so that direction is likely out.

He's heading south.

I take off at a run, doing my best to keep my footing. My legs are sore from yesterday's journey, but it feels good to be on the move. And it helps warm me up.

When I reach one of the taller hills, I slow down at the top and try to catch sight of Roran, but still nothing, so I keep running. I don't know for sure that I'm going the right way, but this is the best guess I have.

I also don't know how long ago he left. The snow has covered his tracks, so I'm guessing he has a few hours on me.

Come to think of it, I also don't know how a troll tracks someone, but from what I hear, they just seem to know the direction to go. I gather it's part of the enchantment. Enchanted creatures rarely make logical sense.

The sun has nearly set by the time I catch sight of him, although I think I slept until about the supper hour. So, it's likely only taken me about three hours to catch up.

I see the troll before I see Roran. It stands out against the snow and grass. And it's big. Really big. In fact, now that I get a look at it while I'm not running for my life, it's a bigger troll than either of the ones I saw a few months ago. I guess from the fact that it's chasing Roran confirms that it's not after me. Roran must have already figured this out.

I turn to my right just a bit so I can run around the troll—a long way around. It's frustrating to have to do this, but I don't want the troll to focus on killing me as well. It's bad enough that it wants Roran dead.

When I catch up to my cousin, he not only looks exhausted, but his face fills with rage. "Draydon! I'm doing this to draw the troll away from you! You've gotta keep moving on. I don't!"

"How are you going to get the spell canceled?" I ask, knowing that doesn't have anything to do with this. I'm just annoyed at him for leaving me.

"What does the enchantment matter now? I've got a bigger problem. In fact," he says, looking back over his shoulder, "I've got a much bigger problem."

"Let's try to kill it."

He frowns at me. "You suddenly come up with a way to do that?"

"Well, no, but for starters, I think I should try my sword on it."

"Draydon, let's think this through…"

I ignore him and turn back. I'm not going to attack the troll head on. That seems extra stupid. I'm going to come at it from behind.

"Scrape, thud… scrape, thud… scrape, thud…"

When I get behind the huge, gray monster, I approach slowly. It doesn't move all that fast, so I don't have to do much more than jog to catch up. It likely only caught up to Roran because of how tired he is.

I come up behind it and glance ahead at Roran. He's still jogging away from the troll, but he looks back every few seconds. I draw my sword, but hesitate. It's one thing to talk about doing this kind of thing. It's another to try to defend myself. But it's a totally different thing to actually attack—from behind!

I work up the courage and approach. Strangely enough, the closer I get, the more the sword buzzes. I don't know what that's about, but I do know that enchantments work on a kind of power scale. For one enchantment to overpower another, it has to be stronger. If it's not, it might not do anything.

So, the question is: is my sword's enchantment stronger than the troll's enchantment?

For some reason, that buzzing makes me think it's not. I can't help but think the troll's enchantment is far more powerful.

I push myself onward and find the sword begins to shake in my hand as I get close, but I remember what Tilbur said about it. I can control the sword somewhat.

I focus hard on keeping the sword steady, and it calms down a little. The troll, however, grows more agitated the closer I get. It hasn't looked back at me, but something's really bothering it.

I raise the sword and plunge it into the back of the troll, using all my strength to drive it into the troll's flesh.

The moment the blade touches the troll's body, I hear a loud crack like thunder, and I feel like I'm floating on air.

When I hit the ground, I realize that was kind of true.

I lay there dazed for a moment, trying to make sense of what I see. It's cold. I see blue, and gray, I think. Sky. Yes, sky. And my fingers still work. So do my toes. I think I can move my body, but my head… it's killing me. Wait… fingers… I don't feel the sword.

I jump to my feet and immediately come crashing down again. My whole world spins.

"Draydon! Draydon! Are you okay?"

"Not sure!" I call out. I don't really even know from which direction his voice came.

I lean over my knees and close my eyes while my head settles. When I think I'm ready, I open them, expecting to see the troll and Roran a long way off by now.

Instead, the troll stands still, not far from me, eyes on me, face filled with rage. Every few seconds, it turns back to Roran, who stands on the other side of it, then turns back to me again.

"What's going on?"

"As best as I can tell," Roran begins, "the troll now wants to kill you as well. But it looks like it can't decide which of us to kill, so it's just stuck between us. While you were rolling around on the ground, I tried moving a bit. It always seems to center itself exactly between us."

I nod but then regret moving my head like that. "So we can survive as long as we stay away from each other."

"Yep, at least until one of us dies, that is. Then the troll will hunt down the other one."

I frown at that, but then ask, "Any ideas? Anything we can do to fix the problem?"

He shakes his head. "Nope. You've royally messed this up, Draydon. Now you're marked for death as well."

I focus on the troll and ignore Roran's grumblings. I'm missing something. Nordin was able to kill it… that is… if his nickname is right. I guess he could have used the King's sword which Parthun has right now. Maybe that did it. But no… he was serving with my father, General Geran, who carried the sword I carry now, so he must have used it, but… wait… I forgot already… my sword.

I pull myself to my feet and begin to search the ground. It's creepy seeing the troll move to center itself between us, but at least we can control the situation now.

"What are you doing?" Roran calls.

"Looking for my sword. I'm guessing I'll just be able to see the hilt of it sticking out, as the blade will have sunk right into the ground."

I move back to where I landed and take a look at where I attacked the troll. I think through the whole process of attacking and where my arm might swing if I landed in this spot… and I take a guess that it's back a little farther away from the troll. I head in that direction and find it, just the hilt sticking up, but it's there.

I pull it out of the ground, slide it into the sheath, and a possible solution hits me.

"Roran! I have an idea. You'll hate it, but it's a good idea."

He shakes his head at me. "What is it?"

"Your ring."

"The one I use to cancel my enchantment?" In order to see me, he has to move quickly to one side before the troll centers itself between us again. When he does, the look on his face is shock. "You can't be serious! If you pull that off me, I go back to being all crazy and submissive to Parthun. And you'll never get it back on me again. It took four people the last time."

"I think we can do this without taking it off you."

"How?"

I give a nervous laugh and call out, "I think you'll have to hold the ring on the troll. You'll have to grab his baggy skin with the hand that wears the ring."

"And what will happen then?"

"If it cancels at least a bit of the troll's enchantment, I might be able to kill it with my sword."

"Might?" Roran frowns again. He seems to do that a lot these days.

I shrug my shoulders. "I don't know what else to suggest. We won't know until we try."

"So, I have to somehow stand there with my hand on his belly while we check to see if it works?"

When he puts it that way, it seems like a really dumb idea. "No, that won't work, obviously. I'll get him to face me, and I need you to run up behind him, jump on his back and grip his skin as best as you can. Then I'll try to stab him with my sword. If the ring has dealt with the enchantment—at least a bit, anyway—it might work."

"And if it doesn't?"

"Um… well… I suspect we'll die."

He shakes his head, but then shrugs his shoulder. "Okay, Draydon. You're the future King. It's your call."

I slowly move forward. With each step, the troll steps back. It feels like the troll is trying to avoid me, but it's trying to keep itself at an equal distance between us. It must either not be smart, or the enchantment has a powerful control over it.

When I get nice and close, the troll takes a swing at me, and I jump back out of range. "Okay, this is it, Roran." I move around a bit to keep its attention on me and draw my sword, concentrating hard to keep the blade steady.

I can't see Roran at all on the other side of the troll, but he hollers out, "I'm going in!"

The troll lurches toward me and then roars as it spins around, waving its arms wildly. It looks almost like it's shrunk a little, and the roar has changed, a slightly higher pitch, maybe… and less full.

That's a good enough sign to me that the enchantment might be affected.

I lunge forward as the beast comes around, and I drive my sword into its side. Any other time I've used my enchanted blade, it slid in or out of whatever I wanted without much or any resistance at all, but this time, I have to shove with all my might, and even so, I feel a pushback.

The troll's roar changes again, and I hear the fear and pain in its voice. Letting go of my sword, I leap back out of reach of the huge fists as it comes around, then jump back in, shoving my blade once again.

The sword vibrates again, and I struggle to keep hold of it when I can get close enough to do so. Roran's started screaming out something or other, but it doesn't matter. I have to deal with this thing.

I give another shove, and the sword sinks deep in the troll, right up to the hilt, then I jump back. The huge beast stumbles a bit, back and forth. I see it turn to me, and its eyes fill with sadness.

The guilt just rushes over me, until I see the expression change. I think… I think it's… relief. And… I think it's mouthing the words, "Thank you!" to me.

I must be losing my mind, but either way, the troll collapses on its face, and Roran rolls off. He just lays where he lands, but his chest moves up and down really fast, so he's alive.

I can't take my eyes off the troll. It's hard to know what's happening, but something's changing. It's… the troll… it's morphing. The skin is shifting, but I struggle to focus on it. It's as if the whole thing has gone blurry.

When I finally recognize what's going on, the troll has shrunk by half, then half again, then again. Its skin changes from a grayish brown to… well, a dark brown.

Through his gasps for air, Roran manages, "It's a man!"

I step up to the man on the ground, pull my sword out of his side and sheath it as there's no blood on it. Roran then gives me a hand flipping the man over. He has dark skin, short, curly hair, and a fairly bushy beard.

"This was a man all along!" Roran says, "He was enchanted to be a troll! Who did this to him?"

I shake my head. As far as I know, trolls have been around forever. And they don't die because no one, aside from us and maybe Nordin, has killed a troll. "So, this man could have been enchanted as a troll for thousands of years?"

Roran nods. "That's my guess. Look at the markings on his chest. I don't recognize any of that. I wonder if he's from back before Sevord. Maybe from one of the tribes around here. This whole area was supposed to be dozens of different tribes until they joined together and formed Sevord. Only the Milterites and the Northern Tribes have retained any of their old identity."

"You okay?"

Roran's still breathing heavily, but he appears fascinated with this discovery. "Yeah, it's just that this took a lot out of me. And the ring…"

I rush over and grab his hand. The spiderwebbing through the ring has gotten much worse. I look into his eyes and see the conflict there. "We have to hurry. We have to get you to the mountain soon, before the ring stops working altogether."

5

Tilbur and the City

I ride quickly through the city as people rush to get out of the way. I'm not supposed to ride so quickly through the streets, but considering they're supposed to report this kind of thing to the Captain of the Guard… I'm not too concerned.

What I am concerned about, however, is the news I've heard.

I reach the castle gates and ride through at a gallop. Soldiers scurry out of the way and holler for the Nobles to move. Not many out today in the gardens—it's cold and miserable—but a Lord and Lady rush to get off the road.

On one hand, the news… it's making me want to shout for joy. This is one of the few times over the last dozen years that I've had reason to laugh—truly laugh.

On the other hand, I have to get ahead of this. When Parthun finds out, he's going to be enraged. I can't let him hear from anyone else but me.

I dismount and holler at a soldier to stable my stallion. He won't be pleased, but such disrespect to a soldier will help to give the impression that I'm taking this seriously.

A servant hesitantly approaches, bows, and asks, "How may I assist you, Captain Tilbur?"

I holler my response. "Inform King Parthun and General Corter that I request a private audience. Let them know this is of the highest priority!"

The man I just screamed at takes off at a run. He's loyal—Tereese tells me he works hard to send messages and more. He likely doesn't know I'm loyal to the throne as well. We've taken great care to keep many in the dark in case someone defects.

I move toward the throne room, but just before I reach it, I turn down a corridor. Parthun's quarters are back this way. He won't be happy with the intrusion, but… I need to tell him.

I reach his quarters, and the servant emerges, bows to me, and rushes off. The soldiers won't let me in until Parthun welcomes me, but I hear his sniveling voice call out, "Let the Captain in!"

I move past the guards, and they close the door behind me. Standing off to the side is Corter. He has a frown on his face. I know he's angry, but I doubt he even knows what he's angry about. I've often dreamed of facing him on the battlefield. He'll learn that his rank of General means nothing if he doesn't know the first thing about leadership or strategy.

Parthun sits directly across from me in a soft chair, eating what looks like a roasted turkey. His bloated belly is covered with scraps of food and the occasional turkey bone, and his chin drips either grease or gravy; I can't tell which.

The man sickens me in every way. It won't be long now…

"What," Parthun begins, food splattering every which way, "is this about? I am having my mid-day meal!"

I know he's not speaking of lunch. He's already had that. And it's too early for supper. I gather that means he calls a full turkey in the middle of the afternoon his "mid-day meal".

"I have received word, Your Majesty, of distressing news."

"More distressing than interrupting my meal?"

I ignore the question and get right to it. "Word has reached me that Caric… Draydon… Geran's son is still alive. He has been sighted by two different people, both loyal to you."

Parthun's mouth drops open, displaying far too much food, and the turkey leg in his right hand hangs just before his mouth. The look in his eye is… sheer terror. Until a moment ago, he believed only Lirnal stood before his claim on the throne, but with Lirnal currently taking up residence in the dungeon, he is hardly a threat.

But Draydon… the boy has a rightful claim to the throne. He could walk in and take the throne from Parthun, and no one could stop him. In fact, anyone who denied him his throne could be arrested. Even Parthun.

I glance at Corter. His face is angry, but his eyes keep shifting to Parthun. The man is useless. He knows he's mad, but he's not sure what to do with the anger.

"How…" Parthun manages through the mouthful, then spits it all out on the floor. He jumps to his feet, sending the tray and turkey crashing to the floor and points the turkey leg at me, brandishing it like a weapon. "How? How is he still alive? You said you killed him!"

"I gave you my full report, and two of my men gave you their reports."

"They were my men!" Parthun hollers, coming closer with his turkey leg. "My men! And they lied to me!"

I shake my head, trying not to look at the greasy, half-eaten leg in front of me. I have no respect for this man, but the turkey leg… it just puts it all over the top for me. "They did not lie to you. They gave you a true report. I found the boy we call Caric, Draydon, son of Geran, in a fishing village up the coast. I had no evidence to suggest that they were harboring him, just that he was there. I stabbed him in the belly with my switcher blade. The blade was even coated in poison to ensure a quick result. I saw the boy drop, and the men's report was accurate."

"But you didn't wait to ensure that he stopped breathing, did you?"

I stand up straight, hold my shoulders back, and answer. "No, I did not. Typically, a switcher does enough damage on its own, and the poison was what you gave me. The men even saw me coat my blade with it."

"Yes, and they spoke of the blood…" Parthun replies, eyeing me closely.

At that moment, I know my next steps. Parthun has lost trust in me. It's just a thread of doubt, a thread of distrust, but it is all a man such as him needs. I've seen what happens when Parthun begins to suspect a man. If I'm not out of the castle by tomorrow, I'll be dead.

"And what of the two witnesses who saw him alive?" Parthun growls.

"Dead," I say. "They won't tell anyone. Your orders, Your Majesty?"

"We need to kill him!" Corter shouts unhelpfully.

"Yes, General." I consider my next words. So far, what I have reported is true, but lies will be more effective now. "But I hear rumors that he has put forward a claim for the throne. If this is true, it will not be so simple." I can see from Corter's expression that he understands it will be difficult, but cannot comprehend why. I turn back to Parthun and give him what he wants. "I take full responsibility for Draydon's life."

"And how," Parthun screams, "do you think this can be dealt with now? Do you think he is such a fool as to leave himself unguarded? Do you think you can just walk in there with a hundred soldiers? A thousand? Now that word is out, how many will defect to that worthless arrogant churl's son?"

I almost kill him right there. Geran... Geran... I would have done anything for that man. He taught me everything I know. Everything I've done since the day he died has been for one reason and one reason alone, to make Geran proud. To call my brother a churl... But... Geran would tell me, "Look farther down the road, Tilbur. See the danger once we leave the forest."

"No, even an army would not be enough," I say. Soon, I'll have what I want, but Parthun will think it's his idea. "You need an assassin."

"And who would you suggest?" Parthun growls, stepping forward in a threatening manner.

I almost laugh. The pudgy man who can barely lift a sword is threatening me? I could break his... I focus. Now is not the time.

I shake my head slowly. "We will have to choose someone unusual. Someone who is loyal to the throne, but... different."

"What do you mean?" Corter asks.

Parthun throws up his hands and explains. "A regular assassin, Corter, would never get close. Draydon would not trust him. He would expect an assassin, so if there is any doubt, he will push the man away, keep him at a distance. We also can't send a friend, because without a Spellcaster nearby, I can't enchant anyone to kill him. So, we're left with trying to find a man who can get close but is not a friend."

Corter's eyes narrow. "So, we send... me?"

Parthun stares at Corter and shakes his head. "I don't know how you came to that conclusion. Do you really think you could kill him, Corter?"

"Of course! I would take a hundred men in there and run my sword through his chest!"

I close my eyes. One of the great things about Corter is his inability to listen to the basic details of a conversation. It helps at times like this.

Parthun turns back to me and drives his finger into my chest. "You will go!" I open my mouth to reply, but he cuts me off. "No excuses! You will go, and you will find a way to fix this mistake. You failed me, Tilbur! You failed me twice. First, when you let that brat leave the city and second, when you didn't confirm he was dead in Nimville!" Stepping in close, the snake hisses, "Don't return until you have proven yourself to me once again!"

I give a slight bow and walk out of the room, forcing down the smile that threatens to take over my entire face.

I'm already suited in my armor, so I rush to my room and pack for the journey. It doesn't take long. I've been prepared for a while now.

A quick stop at the kitchens for traveling food and to privately inform Tereese of the change in the situation, and I have all I need. I mount my stallion and head out. I can't waste any time. Parthun has a tendency to stew in his anger. He could send soldiers after me at any moment. I'd likely be able to kill them and get away, but I might not get out of the city.

As I head out the gate of the keep, I let the smile free. Now, I can truly show my loyalty to Geran. I don't know if he can see me, but if he can look back from the afterlife, he'll know. I will show my loyalty to Geran by serving his son. I will stand by Draydon with complete faithfulness.

I will make Geran proud.

6

———•———

Ellcia and the Northern Tribes

I lose sight of the approaching soldiers for a moment before they come back into view. From this distance, I can't tell how many, but I know it's a lot.

The wind coming off the ocean is bitter cold, and the waves crashing on the rocks are a constant reminder of how far I am from Caric… or Draydon. I have to get used to that. It's been a week since he left, and I worry about him constantly.

"How many do you estimate?" I ask Nordin.

"I'd say somewhere around four hundred, Lady Ellcia. Maybe more."

That sounds like a lot. I don't mean that I think he's wrong, I just think that sounds like a lot of soldiers to deal with. "What does that tell you?"

Nordin growls under his breath. "If I were to send four hundred armed soldiers, I wouldn't do it for a friendly meeting, my Lady."

"So, you think they're here to kill everyone?"

He shakes his head. "I don't. I think if they were to kill the entire farming community, it would devastate the food supply of the nation. There's no way Parthun could get enough experienced farmers up here in time to plant in a few months. The people would starve, and they might revolt—especially when they found out why they were hungry."

"So, what are they after?"

"Submission. I don't believe Parthun knows about us, my Lady. In fact, I'm pretty confident he doesn't and these soldiers don't either. They've traveled far to get here. They must have been sent before we reached the farming communities."

"Submission? So, they're just here to either scare us all into following Parthun closely, or they're here to set up a garrison to maintain control."

"Likely the garrison option, Lady Ellcia."

"Recommendations?"

I've learned quickly to turn to others for help. I've never been a leader, not like Caric... Draydon. Not like Draydon. He was always a natural leader. He just never knew it. I think that's one of the best things about him. He never sees himself as the one who should lead. He doesn't need the power. He just leads because it's the right thing to do.

Ah, I'm getting distracted again. I can't help but worry about Draydon, moving through that secret pass that no one lives through. I focus, awaiting Nordin's response. He's a good man with a good heart and a strong mind. He always has great advice, especially on military matters, which I really know nothing about.

"I don't think we can let them through. If we try to stand against them at the farming community, many will die. If we stay out of sight, they'll likely kill some people just to let everyone know they're serious. I recommend we ambush them."

"Could they be loyal? Should we give them a chance to swear fealty to Draydon?"

Nordin slowly shakes his head. "I don't think that's wise, my Lady, but I know ya're already planning on doing that."

I smile. He knows me well. I don't like giving orders, but Marleet's told me that this is what I'm supposed to do. Draydon and I are a lot alike that way. I can't dance around things. The reason I seem to be in charge is because everyone assumes I'm going to be Queen one day. So, if I'm to be a Queen, I need to act like it.

"Set up the ambush, Nordin, but I want to give them the chance to swear to Draydon."

"Yes, my Lady, but I insist that ya stay out of sight."

"Why?"

"Because, if they realize ya are in charge, someone as young as ya, they will know ya are Nobleborn, and ya will become a target. Most of these men aren't soldiers, they're ruffians, thugs. If I challenge them, I'll just be some tough old guy, but ya… they'll see ya as the real threat."

I don't like the sound of that, but it makes sense. I think. Not really sure, actually. But Nordin is an honest guy, and he understands these things.

I give him a nod, and he moves off. He's an older guy who struggles a bit with his knees, but he's tough. Working on a fishing boat for most of his life has left him strong. The men rush into position after a quick word from him. Those with military experience, which is pretty much every man and some of the women over the age of about thirty, respond without hesitation. Those younger struggle to understand the quick orders but fall in line quickly.

I move back up the beach, keeping low behind the rocks and boulders, careful to stay out of sight. One of our countless secret command posts sits just up on the cliff, within sight of the beach. Relin, the scary little guy who works with Nordin, established a bunch of them—I don't even know how many—in nearly every direction. And if things ever go sour with the war, we have plenty of hideouts.

I don't like calling it a war, but Hella, Nordin's wife insisted that we look at it seriously. Our Kingdom has been taken. We have to fight to take it back.

When I enter the command post, pushing back the dry, hanging grass in the way, the two sentries greet me with a "my Lady" and a quick bow. Once I'm inside, they take on a bit of a scary approach to the entrance. They peer out as if at any moment someone might try to attack, and they are the only ones who stand in the way.

I like these two. I think people should take their jobs seriously. The one on the right is a mother of two kids. She fought in the battle of Reber's Gate with Draydon's dad. She never met him, but said he was a lot like Draydon. She's from the farming communities.

The one on the left is a little too young to have fought in the war, but he's tough and loyal. He's been a farmer since he finished school at fourteen. Smart and focused, he likes to talk about just about anything, but right now, he's silent.

My scalp is cold with such short hair, so I pull my scarf a little tighter over my head as I watch everything unfold on the beach. Nordin's men stay out of sight—there are enough large boulders and more to hide behind. They've even set up what looks like wreckage of an old boat, and at least thirty or forty soldiers are in there.

When everyone's in position, Nordin steps out in front of the procession, and Parthun's men call a halt. I can't hear anything, but I know his strategy as he's explained it before. He speaks with them for a bit. They'll be rude and overbearing—I can see that even from this distance. Once they threaten him, he raises his arm, and our soldiers step out.

When they do, the reaction is quick. Many of the soldiers on horseback go for their weapons. Anyone who reaches for a bow or crossbow are killed immediately by our own archers. Surprisingly, about a quarter of Parthun's men drop. I feel anger build up inside at the sight. Not of so many of the enemy dying. I feel sadness for that, but I feel anger that so many have come here equipped with crossbows. Swords are common among soldiers, but crossbows… it means they plan on shooting fleeing people. And shooting a lot.

Those who are left slowly begin to dismount, a few at a time, and drop their weapons in a pile on the beach. They are then bound and led forward.

It's not until they're all out of sight that Nordin waves for me. When I reach him, he smiles. "Another successful defense of the free lands of Sevord."

"What have we learned, Captain?"

"Not much, yet. They tell me they have been ordered by the King to move up the coast to ensure the people remain loyal to the throne. Once we arrested them, their Lieutenant would not speak."

We leave a small group behind to strip the dead and collect the weapons and armor. I always feel strange leaving work for other people. I guess growing up as a servant has that effect.

When we reach the farming communities, which the people have recently named Freond, which they say means they are a friend of the throne, we move to the interrogation house. A couple loyal soldiers stand guard outside while dozens of Parthun's men sit in the snow, bound and well-guarded.

The door opens, and I find two men, both officers, bound and tied to chairs in the center of the room. Nordin enters after me, and I take my stand before them.

"My name is Lady Ellcia, daughter of Lord Rathar and Lady Shillin. I oversee this region, the area of Freond. I am loyal to the throne of Sevord, and loyal to the true heir to the throne." I've practiced all this repeatedly. Nordin and Relin helped me write it. I hope it's good.

"Parthun, King of Sevord, sits on the throne unjustly. Prince Draydon, son of General Geran, is next in line to the throne and has not only the legal right to that claim, but has the support of many Nobles in the Kingdom. I will not belabor this matter. The choice is before you." I focus on the man in charge. "Lieutenant, will you now renounce Parthun, Son of Trevolay as King of Sevord, and swear your fealty to Prince Draydon, Son of Geran?"

The man's face fills with rage, and I know what's coming next. Nordin and Relin have insisted that I not interfere when it happens—they knew it would. The Lieutenant makes a disgusting sound in his mouth and spits at me, just missing the bottom of my cloak.

I close my eyes so as not to see Nordin's response to the man, but I can hear it. Even Hella tells me that this is the way it has to be, but I... "Enough!" I say and open my eyes. Nordin simply steps back, and I find I cannot take more than a quick look at the Lieutenant. He's pretty beaten up. Nordin tells me the issue is not his refusal, it's his disrespect.

Nordin grabs the man, chair and all, and tosses him to the side where he lands and just... lies there. Or... sits. He's in a chair, so I guess he's sitting, but he's lying face down, groaning.

I turn to the next man, also a Lieutenant, but a bit younger. I stay back a bit in anticipation of a future spitting, and say, "Now you, Lieutenant, what say you? Will you renounce the imposter, Parthun, and swear fealty to Prince Draydon, Son of Geran, true heir to the throne?"

"And what if I don't?" he asks.

"You will be arrested for denying the rightful heir, and you will remain a prisoner. All your soldiers will be given the same option."

"Will you beat me like that?" the man asks with a look of disgust.

"No. He was not beaten for refusing me. He was beaten for his disrespect to the future Queen of Sevord."

I can't believe I said that. As soon as it comes out of my mouth, I regret it. I've just claimed Draydon as my future husband. I see Nordin shift on his feet, and I know I've said something dumb and impulsive, but the effect on the man is immediate.

As best he can, he bows his head slowly, "My sincere apologies, my Lady. I would never act with such disrespect, nor do I think my commanding officer would have had he known fully who you are."

I shake my head. "I told him who I was. I did not tell him Prince Draydon and my future plans because they were none of his business. He still acted with disrespect. Will you offer your fealty?"

He bows again and says with respect, "My Lady, I would be happy to, but not to suggest you would speak with any deception, but are you able to offer any proof of your claims?"

I smile. This is exactly how I would respond. "I admire your commitment, Lieutenant. Were I in your position, I would require proof as well."

I nod to Nordin, who brings forward Draydon's claim to the throne along with the support of the Nobles and others. The man reads it carefully, and, at the end, his eyes widen, and he looks at me. "I assume this means, my Lady, that Prince Draydon is not here?"

"True."

"Is Nordin Trollslayer here?"

I nod at Nordin, and he gives a little bow.

"Nordin…" he says in awe. "My father spoke of you. He said he served under you in the Battle of Reber's Gate."

"What's his name?"

"Frellin, Sir. Frellin, son of Vint."

"Frellin?" Nordin says slowly. "I don't… hmm… I'm sorry, I don't remember a Frellin. It was a long time ago." After a few seconds he adds, "I remember a Frell. He was tall and thin, had a big mustache that he was far too proud of considering how much food got caught in it. He was seriously injured near the end of the war, though. I went to visit him to see how he was on my way home after General Geran dismissed us, but he died from his injuries before I arrived."

The man nods. "That was him. He spoke of you a fair amount in his final days, and Nordin Trollslayer did come to see us, although I did not meet you." Turning back to me, he says, "I will swear. I trust Nordin's word, and because of that, I trust the word of every Noble on the list. I will swear to General Geran's son."

"Untie him," I order, and Nordin cuts the man's bonds.

When he is free, he drops to his knees and declares, "I now renounce any loyalty to Parthun, Son of Trevolay, and in place of this I offer my love, my loyalty, and my fealty to Prince Draydon and to his future bride."

My face goes red at the last part. I didn't want anyone to swear to me. That just seems weird. Really weird.

The other Lieutenant just groans and mumbles, face down on the floor. From what I can make out, he's not pleased with this other officer.

I turn to the young man. Well… he's much older than me. He's just young compared to Nordin and Relin and so many others around here.

"Tell me what you have been doing on the coast."

"Yes, my Lady. We were sent by Captain Frindor around two weeks ago. We've moved at a fairly steady pace up the coast for the most part, but we've stopped in each of the villages. Port was destroyed by Captain Frindor, but we searched the area for survivors. We then came to Grimmer and found them upset and angry, but also afraid. We had been ordered to add to that fear, and we did."

He doesn't go into detail about that. I'm curious, but at the same time I don't want to know. It would likely make me very mad.

"Deliver then was our next stop. They were not as afraid and far harder to break than Grimmer, but we did much the same at Deliver as we had at Grimmer. When we reached Nimville, we found the garrison had been killed, and the people had fled. I don't know any more than that. I am sorry to say we ransacked the village and burned all the buildings to the ground, but we found no people. Then from there, on to Shizzer."

"And your plans for Freond?" I ask.

"For the farming communities… or, I'm sorry, my Lady, for Freond, we were to scare the people into submission, but to be far less violent. Parthun is, I believe, concerned about food supplies if we damage the morale in this area."

"How many of the men," I ask, "are likely to swear allegiance to the true heir to the throne?"

He shakes his head. "I would say around half, my Lady. There are many more in our troop who would, but they would fear the King's wrath against their families."

That's good to know. I had thought I would release those who would not swear allegiance. Let them return to Sevord empty handed. But if I do that, the families of those who side with us will be punished or killed. So, all these soldiers who have arrived today must remain.

"And your name?"

"Frellson, my Lady. I was named after my father. The Mustache Lord of Haner."

"He was a Lord?"

The man's face grows pale. "Oh, no, I'm sorry. He was just called that. Well… I mean… not really. He… uh… was called the Mustache Lord of Haner because… well…" He frowns, drops his gaze, and looks genuinely embarrassed. "Actually, he just called himself that. He, you see… he loved his mustache. It was quite special to him."

I smile. "Well, isn't that… lovely?" I think that sounds like the right thing to say at a time like this. "Frellson, you are to report to Captain Nordin for your assignment."

He salutes to Nordin, and Nordin just waves him to follow. We leave the interrogation building, which is just a former abandoned house, and the guards outside head in to deal with the Lieutenant in his chair.

As we move through the soldiers, Frellson is right. Only about half are willing to swear allegiance. We have had to create a fairly large prison. At the moment, I think there's somewhere around a hundred in there. Those from this group who refuse to swear fealty to Draydon will nearly triple that number.

I leave the soldiers to their work and move back to the hall we have claimed as our residence. They're constructing more rooms and trying to clean it up to make it "worthy" of people of our status, but I'm just as happy to sleep anywhere. But, it's helpful, I understand, to give confidence to the people, and we do need a place to work, to plan, and from which to lead.

When I enter the hall, Marleet is busy giving orders. She's settled in beautifully to her role as "Lady Marleet". I still feel out of place as Lady Ellcia. I don't know how I'll take to being called Queen Ellcia one day.

The hall itself isn't all that big, nor is it fancy. I don't need fancy, but the fact that our residence is small and, as the farming community calls it, "ugly," really bothers the people.

In the corner, a raging fire burns bright, filling the room with heat and a nice glow. I've always enjoyed the smell of a wood fire.

Next to the fire is an old man. He doesn't do much, other than sit there, petting his hat. I'm not sure what's wrong with him, but he arrived on the fifth day after Draydon left with a note from Draydon attached to his arm. Every time I see him, my heart breaks for him, but bubbles over with pride for Draydon. Even when he's heading into danger, he's still thinking of others.

I stop that line of thinking. I can't think about Draydon right now. It pulls my mind to worry and fear and more. I have to focus on the task at hand.

Marleet, leaning over the table, smiles when she sees me, and I join her. She has a map laid out before her of the coast with all the villages.

North of Sevord City is our focus right now. We don't have to worry about Sevord itself right away, as Draydon is going to take care of announcing his claim to the Royal Court and to the common people, and we will likely send word there, too, in time. South of Sevord City, all along the coast, are other villages. Some are fishing villages and there are some farms, but most of those villages are industrial, producing weapons, armor, wagons, tools, and more. Although they are just as important as the northern villages, we've decided to take it one step at a time. For now, the northern villages remain our focus.

The largest communities are the Northern Tribes north of Sevord City, but we're here, so we just have to lead and protect. Just south of us is Shizzer, then Nimville. Nimville is empty as its people are here with us. Then comes Deliver, then Grimmer, and then Port. Port, of course, was destroyed by Parthun's men, but we still want to look there as there may be stragglers who escaped the soldiers.

In addition to that, there are some really tiny villages or farms between the ocean and the cliffs, and all those people need to hear from us. We've sent a team of four people south with letters from us to be read to them, stating Draydon's claim. My hope is that all the coastal peoples will get behind us, but secretly at this point.

Those who have gone south are going to visit each of the villages and each of the smaller communities, at least as they are able. They've also been ordered to stay out of sight of the main road. This group of four hundred soldiers coming up the coast is evidence of why that is so necessary. Frellson didn't mention catching a group of four travelers. I'm hoping that means our people weren't caught, unless Frellson didn't think it was worth mentioning the death of four men.

At that moment, Hemot walks in, and Marleet tenses. They haven't been getting along all that well. She adores him, that's for sure, but she's changed a lot over the recent months. Hemot has as well, but not at the same speed.

He approaches the table and smiles, but there's something bothering him. I think he hasn't read the letter yet. I wish he would, but he's Hemot. I'm the only one who knows what Draydon wrote in there. It might calm Hemot down. Or… then again, it might work him up.

I don't know. It's Hemot…

"Captain Hemot reporting for duty!" he says with a large, proud grin.

Marleet smiles at him and shakes her head. "You're not going to be Captain, Hemot. You're the Noble on this journey. Your job is to lay out the general plans and direction and give orders only to the actual Captain."

Hemot's face falls, and Marleet's fills with grief. "I'm sorry, Hemot. I can't do anything about that."

He frowns at me. "Can you?"

I shake my head. "You know I can't, Hemot. Despite the fact that Draydon left me in charge, I'm still just a Noblewoman. I might have a house and land and official status, but I doubt it's even been recognized by the Royal Court. And even if it has, I'm still just a Lady. Even if Draydon and I were married and he had taken the throne, I'm not even sure a Queen can give you what you want."

"But I'm a Noble!"

"Hemot, you're Nobleborn. You are a Noble, but not an official one. You have to be granted your title."

Relin walks in at that moment and bows to me, and says, "My Lady," then to Marleet, he says, "My Lady." Then to Hemot, he says, "Hemot."

Hemot purses his lips and nods back. "Relin."

Relin frowns. "That's Captain Relin in public, Hemot."

"Aaaahhhh!" Hemot hollers and throws his hands up in the air.

"What's wrong with him?" Relin asks.

I shake my head. "Perhaps you should call him 'Sir,' Relin."

Relin squints his eyes and says, "But I didn't think he'd been knighted."

I drop my head and rest my chin on my chest, doing my best to block out Hemot's complaining. Fortunately, Marleet steps in, tries to calm him down, then starts to tell him off. When she's done, he stands there pouting.

"So," I begin, trying to ignore Hemot's pouting, "Hemot will take the Geran south." We've been over this already, but I wanted to give the orders all in one place at one time.

The Geran is a small warship which Nordin captured just yesterday. He was able to do so with no damage to the ship itself, but half the original crew was killed. The other half swore allegiance to Draydon, aside from only two men. That gives us two warships in addition to our fishing vessels and Stevrick's shipping boat. We don't have much of a fleet yet, but Sevord itself only has around a dozen warships, so we have one sixth of the total fleet so far.

I'm not willing to send the large warship, the Nimville, away just yet as we need it to protect the farming communities, now called Freond, so Hemot and Relin are taking the newly renamed Geran out.

"Your mission will be to go ahead of the four sent out on foot and stop in at the fishing villages: Shizzer, then Deliver, then Grimmer. You'll read Draydon's claim and inform them that others will come as well. I wish for you to tell each of the villages that the four hundred soldiers whom Parthun sent north to scare the people into submission have either been killed, arrested, or sworn allegiance to Draydon."

The two nod. Relin seems unfazed by Hemot's outburst a moment ago, and Hemot looks like he's calmed down. One thing about Hemot is if he gets upset about something, he generally can move on quickly. This issue of having a title keeps coming up, though, but perhaps he can come to grips with it.

"Once you finish with Grimmer, you are to return to the port at Freond for further orders. Any questions?"

Both men shake their heads, and I'm reminded again that I don't like giving out orders. I had to do it now and then in the castle, mainly with Marleet or Hemot, but I hated it. Caric—I mean Draydon—was always officially in charge of our team, and he was good at it. Even though he hated it. Strange. The two people in the Kingdom who hate leading the most are about to become the King and Queen. Well, I mean, it'll be a bit before I'm a Queen. Draydon and I are both still seventeen. Far too young to actually marry, in my opinion. But Draydon will be King, hopefully before summer. We'll just wait a few years before we wed.

I shake my head and bring myself back to the moment. "We hope to see you return within ten days."

Relin bows, and Hemot salutes. I'm pretty sure no one is supposed to salute me, and a quick glance at Marleet confirms that.

They leave, and I'm left with Marleet. She's worried about Hemot, but I've talked to her about it. She just has to trust that he'll be okay. Hoping it'll help, I add, "He'll grow up in time, don't worry. He just never needed to in the castle. None of us really did, actually. As long as we got our work done, we could be as foolish as we wanted."

"I know," Marleet says quietly and gives me the slightest smile.

I examine my closest friend… well, closest aside from Draydon. She looks so sad and lost right now. I know she's a very different woman today than she was just a few months ago, but no one can change that fast. There's still the insecure, scared Marleet in there.

I used to envy her, actually. She's more than just pretty. She's perfect. Every part of her is perfect. I always felt ugly when I was around her. But I've come to see that's not what's important in life. It's not even really that important to her. Besides, I don't want to attract every guy— just one. And I've got him already. Everyone sees the way he looks at me, even when I shaved my head. I have nothing to worry about.

"And he'll be okay while he's gone," I add. "Relin will keep him safe."

"You think so?" Marleet asks. Yep, there's the scared little girl coming out again.

"I know so. Relin is about the toughest guy either of us has ever met. I think we can count on him to keep Hemot out of too much trouble. Besides, I don't know much about ships, but Nordin and Relin tell me the Geran is, in their words, 'a tough little boat.' It's not the biggest in the fleet, but that class of ship is fast, maneuverable, and carries a big punch in battle. The sailors and soldiers on board will also be armed to the teeth. I'm just hoping they can bring back some other ships with them."

Marleet smiles at me, and I know it's coming. Her voice comes out far too sweet and a little condescending. "Why, Ellcia?"

My face breaks out in a grin. I'm not going to let myself be embarrassed. I realized the other day that I've been trying to hide so much in my life about my feelings and thoughts. But I don't actually need to—not around Marleet, anyway. "I have plans."

"And what are they?" Her smile has grown. She knows. I can't believe she figured out what I'm trying to do.

"You know what I'm doing, Marleet. And it's not a bad thing."

She nods, and her face grows a little more serious, although she still smiles. "You're hoping you can present to Draydon a gift when he takes the throne. You're hoping to already own the fleet. And you're hoping to build him an army in case he doesn't have one of his own when he needs it."

I laugh. Another great thing about Marleet. She's able to figure stuff out now without having to have it all spelled out for her.

I like this new Marleet. A lot.

"But... something else is worrying you," Marleet says.

I frown and nearly break into tears, but I grind my teeth and take a deep breath. Maybe Marleet's not the only scared little girl in the room. "There's a lot that worries me, Marleet."

"Tell me about it."

"I'm worried about Granel and Tilbur and your parents. What will happen to them when word reaches the castle that we're all alive, and Draydon has put forward a claim for the throne?"

Marleet comes around to my side of the table and pulls me into a hug. If there's one thing I think I needed right now, it's this. After a bit of time, she steps back, but doesn't fully let me go. Instead, she just looks right up into my eyes and says, "Don't worry about Granel. He's a soldier, and my parents will find a way to keep him safe. Don't worry about my parents. They are well protected. Don't worry about Tilbur. He's a strong, powerful man, and a man with a lot of connections and influence. He's also very smart. When Parthun finds out that Tilbur didn't kill Draydon, Tilbur will find his way through that. If you can count on one thing with that man, it's that he already has a plan worked out in case this happens. Besides, everyone is required to get behind Draydon. It's not really a choice. So Parthun can't punish anyone for supporting the true heir to the throne, nor can he punish those who are related or connected to someone who supports him."

"Thanks, Marleet. That makes me feel better."

"And the other thing?" Marleet asks.

She knows me well. "The thing that bothers me the most is…" I pause for a moment. This is what's really tearing me apart. "It's Draydon. He's just gone through the northern pass. We're doing all this to put him on the throne, but he's traipsing through an unpassable pass! He's gone off to face Gratters and Talic Wolves and who knows what else! What if he doesn't make it? We won't know, maybe for months. There's no way we can get a message to or from him. In fact, years from now, we could be hunting for him, trying to find out what happened!"

She reaches up and wipes some tears from my face. I hadn't realized I was crying. "It'll be okay, Ellcia. You're just going to have to trust Draydon and Roran to take care of themselves. They're smart, strong, fast, and courageous."

She smiles, gives me another squeeze, then steps back. "This is how I do it. I focus on how each of us has a part to play in this matter. To bring down a tyrant, we all have to sacrifice. Each sacrifice is different, but every one of them is necessary. One of your sacrifices—what your part requires—is to accept the fear. You're just going to have to accept it, live with it, and focus on what you can take care of. Don't fight it. Just accept it's there and move on with it. Your fear simply means you love him. And that love is a good thing."

I wipe some more tears away. "You've really changed, Marleet."

As if to disagree, she gives me that silly little giggle and shrugs her shoulders.

7

Ellcia and the Ships

I scramble into my clothes, blinking hard to try to wake up and ready myself for whatever's going on. The horn blasts again. Whatever it is, it's an emergency.

Bang, bang, bang! "Lady Ellcia? Lady Marleet?" I don't recognize that voice.

"Yes, we are coming," I cry out. "What is…" I'm still not totally awake and obviously having trouble forming thoughts and sentences. The light coming in through the window is dim. "What is the matter?"

"Ships, my Lady. Warships from Sevord."

"I'll be out in just a moment."

I crash to the floor. My back aches, and the wind is knocked out of me. When I recover, I spin around and nearly scream at Marleet. She sits dazed beside me on the floor with a look that suggests she's not entirely awake.

"I'm sorry, Ellcia, I didn't see you there."

One of the downsides of the situation here with limited room in our residence is having to sleep in bunk beds again. Marleet, despite how much she's changed over the last few months, still hasn't learned how to wake up in the morning. That's the second time in the last few days she's dropped out of bed on top of me while I've dressed myself. Actually on top of me!

I scramble to my feet again and finish dressing. When I rush out of the room, Marleet's still on the floor in her nightclothes. She might be a while.

A few steps out my door, as I'm still pulling on my cloak, Lieutenant Frellson meets me. I remember now. It was his voice. Over the last few days, he's displayed competence in everything he's done and managed to convince Nordin of his complete loyalty. He's been given more and more responsibility.

"My Lady, three ships, two frigates and one destroyer."

Normally I just try to figure things out as I go, but I'm too tired at the moment. "I don't know what that means, Lieutenant. What's a frigate and what's a destroyer?"

"My apologies, my Lady. A frigate is a smaller warship. It's fast and maneuverable. A destroyer is larger. It's fast, but not quite as fast as the frigate, but it is more heavily armed. Captain Relin's ship is a destroyer."

"And what is Captain Nordin's ship?"

"He has what is called a Royal Warship. It's the biggest in the fleet, and there are only two of them." After a moment, he says, "We should stop here, my Lady."

I come to a halt and finally take a good look. In the distance, two ships are just visible in the light morning fog. One's definitely larger than the other. But those two aren't what worry me the most. The biggest concern is the ship close by, only minutes from docking.

Frellson stopped me at a good place. I can see everything clearly here, but I'm not likely to stand out. It gives me a chance to take it in without risking exposing my position.

My head is still a little foggy. I wish I had Nordin or Relin here by my side. Even Marleet, if she could think clearly early in the morning.

Now that I mention it, I can't think early in the morning. But at least I'm sharper than Marleet.

"Lieutenant. Nordin thinks very highly of you. What are your recommendations?"

He shifts on his feet, back and forth. I don't want to dump this on him, but I'm seventeen and have spent my life either working as a servant or running for my life. He's late twenties and has served in the army for somewhere around ten or eleven years.

"My Lady, I would recommend that you send soldiers to the frigate about to dock. They should know that my four hundred soldiers will have arrived by now. I can approach them with that number, and they might think we are merely approaching the ship to give a report. We might be able to storm the ship and capture it."

"There's a lot of 'mights' there, Lieutenant."

He shakes his head. "It's the best we can do."

"And the other two ships?"

"We will have to leave them to Captain Nordin. Once we capture this ship, we can join him, assuming he's seen them and is planning his attack."

I know he is. He's out there with that in mind—defending the farming communities. I nod at Frellson. "Do it, Lieutenant. You're in charge. Get me that ship."

He bows quickly and runs off. The rest of the soldiers will all be ready and awaiting orders, so I step back into the shadows of the building to stand by and watch.

A moment later, Marleet arrives. She has a crazed and confused look in her eyes, her shirt's on inside out and her skirt is on backwards, but the worst of it is her hair looks like it was sneezed out of her scalp. "What's going on?"

I bring her up to speed, and we watch matters unfold in the streets below us. Frellson leads around four hundred soldiers toward the dock, but another two or three hundred stand ready behind the warehouses and businesses along the beach.

By the time the boat has come to a stop, the soldiers are lined up in formation along the dock. A wave of panic comes over me. "This is a mistake," I whisper.

Marleet shakes her head. "Too late. If we try to stop it now, more people will die."

"But it's strange to have all the soldiers there, just waiting, isn't it? Won't that cause suspicion and put those on the boat on high alert?"

Marleet just shrugs her shoulders. No help.

On top of that, the men and women along the dock will have to run up the gangplank. If those on the ship knock it down, our soldiers will lose their means to board the ship. But even if they keep it up, there's only room for soldiers to stream onto the boat two at a time. The only way this could work is by sheer numbers, but many will die.

When the gangplank is just about down, I catch sight of Frellson, slowly, but purposefully, walking toward the boat from the beach, and I smile. A distraction. Those on the boat won't be looking at the soldiers along the dock, they'll be looking at the Lieutenant.

Once the gangplank is down, a dozen sailors, I assume one is the Captain, leave the boat and come down to meet him.

That makes things easier…

When the Lieutenant reaches the Captain, well short of the actual ship, he salutes, which seems to be the signal, and his men, who are positioned near the gangplank, just casually walk up the plank without the Captain noticing. By the time anyone reacts, at least fifty of our men are on board, yet the Captain still hasn't noticed what's going on behind her.

When she does notice something is going on, Frellson and the soldiers nearby capture the Captain and the dozen sailors with her while more and more soldiers file onto the boat.

I can see a lot of fighting on board the ship, and I watch closely to see which side is coming out ahead. It is as I feared. There's a lot of death, and the crew of the frigate will have to be overcome by sheer numbers.

I feel sick to my stomach watching it, but it all only takes a few minutes. When they're done, at least a hundred men and women are marched up the beach toward the interrogation building. I don't have Nordin with me, so Frellson will have to take care of that.

A boom, followed by another, then another, catches my attention. Out at sea, Nordin has arrived and engaged the remaining destroyer and frigate. His ship dwarfs each of the other two, but that doesn't mean much. They'll move fast and attack aggressively. Another dozen fishing vessels move out among the warships, Nordin's five and others we've collected along the way as we've built our navy. Captain Stevrick's shipping vessel also gets in the mix. We've armed it with a few cannons we pulled from Nordin's warship.

"Frellson!" I call out. I'm really short on officers at the moment, and I've learned that soldiers rarely manage well without an officer in charge to give them orders.

He leaves the sailors in the custody of his soldiers and reports to me. "Lieutenant. Take the frigate out immediately and assist Nordin."

"Yes, my Lady, but I have never sailed a ship."

"Then take someone who knows what they're doing!" I holler. "Just get out there right away!"

He calls out to his soldiers, and I watch them talking back and forth. After about a minute, he races off with a hundred or so men and women toward the docks.

"Marleet, let's go talk to this Captain. We could really use some more sailors."

Once I'm done with the sailors we've just captured, the vast majority of them have sworn fealty to Draydon. Unfortunately, the Captain herself did not. She yelled and raged at us, called us traitors and many worse things. I don't understand how someone can think we are the traitors, although maybe she doesn't believe Draydon is alive.

The battle at sea rages for another couple of hours. It's hard to believe it can take that long, but in the end, the docks are full with four warships and a dozen other vessels. None of the warships are in good condition anymore, and we've lost a lot of sailors. We also lost one of Nordin's fishing vessels, and they were only able to save one of his men.

I've ordered all available people to work on building new homes, barracks, and, unfortunately, prisons, along with storage and more. The farming communities have a lot of cut and dried lumber that they sell, but we're using it for needs in this area. I don't know how Draydon is making out with money, but we're kind of short on funds. I hope he doesn't mind sending money up this way to pay for it all once he takes the throne.

I look out over the carnage below at the docks and wait for Nordin to reach me. He's pretty banged up. I see a lot of blood, but he's bound it up with bandages.

"My Lady."

"Nordin," I say with a lot of compassion. It comes pretty naturally. I care a lot about this man. I care a lot about all these people. It's horrible to see his injuries. "I'm so sorry you have… I'm… I'm sorry."

"There is nothing to apologize for, my Lady. This is war. We have to retake the throne. Everyone here understands that. Victory will not come without loss."

I nod slowly. I still don't like it, but I know he's right. "I guess I should ask you for a report."

"Ya should, my Lady, but ya cannot speak to me this way."

I stop short and stare at him. I'm not sure what I've done wrong.

"If ya approach me with regret, or worse, approach the people will regret, ya will send them a clear message that ya are not committed to this path. Ya will lose us all. Ya need to move forward with confidence. It is difficult, my Lady, to sacrifice for what ya believe in. But for a woman of compassion such as yarself, it is far harder to order *others* to sacrifice for what ya believe in. But we all play our part. Yars is to lead. Mine is to fight."

I give him an appreciative smile. Closing my eyes for a moment, I take a deep breath and calm my heart. When I'm ready, I open my eyes and order, "Report!"

"The battle went well, my Lady. I believe ya are aware of some of the losses. In addition to what ya have already heard, each of the ships has sustained serious damage. The Nimville is no longer seaworthy, but I believe we can fix her up within a week, perhaps less. The other three are in rough shape, the best being the frigate which Frellson commanded as it came late to the battle and was less of a focus than the Nimville. The fishing boats are damaged, but aside from the one we lost, they are seaworthy. Stevrick's boat is in similar condition. We have also captured an additional eight hundred people."

A thought hits me. This matter hasn't come up, but an extra eight hundred… on the tail end of winter… that's a problem.

"Can we feed that many?"

Nordin purses his lips. "It's going to be a little more difficult. The fishing is poor this time of year, and we're running low on what we need. I recommend we send Stevrick north to trade for food and supplies."

"Send him out as soon as possible."

"I will do that, my Lady. With yar blessing, I will send him mainly for food, but also material for clothing, and any medical supplies. We seem to be in a constant need of all those things."

"Yes, that would be helpful. Now, for the eight hundred you've captured."

We head to the sailors, and I'm pleased to find that out of those we've captured, over seven hundred join us. I think in the end, we have somewhere around four thousand who can fight, or who can sail a ship. That's decent. It's far from a force to rival Parthun's troops, but it's enough to give Draydon an extra boost.

And when the time comes, I will be there with every last fighter I can scrape up from every corner of the land!

8

———•———

Hemot and Shizzer

What a load of rubbish! We're all Nobles... or at least Nobleborn, but Marleet is Lady Marleet, Ellcia is Lady Ellcia, even Relin is Captain Relin, but me... I'm... Hemot. Just Hemot!

I feel my chest pocket where Caric's letter... I mean, Draydon's letter sits. I haven't read it yet. I really don't want to. I know what's in there. He's pretty sure he's going to die while helping Roran, and he wants to make sure I'll take care of Ellcia for him. I know Draydon well enough to know that's what's on his mind.

He doesn't have to ask that kind of thing. I'll do whatever I can for her. Marleet and I will make sure we keep her safe. If we lose Draydon—I don't want to think of that—I expect Parthun will hunt Ellcia down next for no other reason than out of revenge and cruelty.

We will do all we can to protect her, that's for sure.

But I don't want to think of what could happen to Draydon. I need him alive. Nothing else will do.

I grip the wooden railing, twisting my hands back and forth across it, grinding my teeth. The teeth that belong to Hemot. Not Lord Hemot. Not Duke Hemot. Not Sir

Hemot. Just Hemot. Maybe I'm being childish, but it's really… annoying.

Someone comes up beside me as I lean on the railing, looking out over the sea. It's a good thing I'm able to hide my emotions so well. My face is unreadable. Stoic. No can know that I'm so angry. I need to act the part of a true Noble. I need to show them that nothing bothers me. That I can weather every storm. And I am a master at it!

"Why are ya so upset, Hemot?" Relin asks.

I spin around and give him the evil eye. I've never been good at that kind of thing, not like Ellcia. She can bore into your very soul with a simple look. I just hope that my evil eye is enough to let Relin know that now's not a time to mess with me.

Relin laughs. "What's wrong with yar eye? It's just… well… yar one lid looks like it's convulsin'. Ya dealin' with some seasickness? I thought ya'd be over that by now."

"It's not seasickness!" I growl. "I am over that." Spending two months on a fishing boat puts a quick end to seasickness. Standing on the deck of a frigate is easy compared to that.

"Then what's goin' on?"

"I'm just focusing on the mission, that's all."

"Ya're not still grumpin' about not havin' a title, are ya?"

I frown. "It's just…" I stomp my foot in a very Noble manner and add, "Who am I? I'm just Hemot. I'm nobody, Relin!"

"I've been a nobody my whole life," Relin says with a chuckle.

"No, you're the Hero of Reber's Gate!"

"Oh, we count that?"

"Sure!"

"Okay. Then that's all I have."

"Well, you were married, and you have kids, right?"

"Oh, right. The missus and I had three kids, raised 'em all, love 'em, proud of 'em. We count that?" Relin asks with a strange look on his face. "That's important stuff? That counts as something?"

"Of course! Isn't that your son over there hanging on... um..."

"Adjustin' the halyards. Um, Hemot? Ya really didn't learn any of the names of anything while working with us on the boats for two months?"

I ignore the ridiculous question and focus on Relin's son. "Yes, that's right. Exactly. He's a great guy. Grumpy at times, like you, but a great guy."

"So, that's important?"

"Of course it is, Relin!"

"Too bad ya don't have anything like that."

"I know!" I say, but I hesitate. He's up to something. Relin always is. He's sneaky that way. "Spit it out, Captain!" I say with as much authority as I can.

"Well, it's just interestin', that's all. It's interestin' to talk to the son of the Milterite Duke and find out he's a nobody. It's just interestin' to meet the young man who was raised as a servant in the castle, but trekked across the Talic, dealin' with Shaloomd, a couple Trolls, and faced off against a Talic Wolf and a giant, and to find out he's a nobody. It's just interestin' to meet the guy who helped deliver the missin' Prince to those who planned on restorin' him and find out that guy's nothin'. It's just interestin' to meet a guy who's run back across the Talic, runnin' from soldiers, makin' his way through Haner, through Switcher Pass, then managed to live in a fishing village for two months, then break into the castle, rescue the Prince and the highest young Lady of the court, then hide out on a ship, and is now the Nobleborn leading a frigate named after the greatest General Sevord and the Talic have ever seen. And to think... this nobody... he's won the heart of Lord Yune's daughter. I mean, Lord

Yune… he's not much to look at. I've seen turtles who can catch the eye of more women than that man. But he's a good man. A real good man. And his wife… wow. I mean… wow! And the daughter… she got her looks from her mom, that's for sure. She's about the prettiest thing I ever seen! But… I mean… I guess it takes a nobody to catch the eye of a woman like Lady Marleet."

I frown. I want to punch Relin. I hate how right he is, most of the time. Well, all the time. Now, he's just grinning at me, missing teeth and all. The Hero of Reber's Gate has won another victory.

"How'd you win the battle at Reber's Gate? How'd you get that title?" I ask.

His smile disappears. "Nunya business, Hemot!" he says and storms away.

"Strange…" I say quietly to myself. I'd really like to know that.

But for now, I have to get used to being Hemot. Besides, we have a mission to accomplish. Shizzer is not far down the coast from here.

The small fishing village of Shizzer is just ahead. I've never been there before, but I passed it on my way north to Freond.

The time on this boat, as short as it's been, has given me some good time to think. And I've come to a conclusion.

I've been a baby.

Not just about the title thing. Who cares if I'm Lord Hemot or just Hemot? None of that matters. In the end, I've been a baby about everything. It's time I grew up and stopped being so immature. Marleet's grown up. A lot. Much faster than me. And now I have a lot of catching up to do.

I need to stop sulking. I need to stop saying dumb things. Maybe even if I'm never to be Lord Hemot, I should learn to act like a Lord.

Come to think of it, I've seen a lot of Lords and Ladies. There are some who are like little kids who have been handed their titles and money and influence and power. And then there are those who act with maturity, kindness, wisdom. They're the true Lords and Ladies.

I smile. Regardless of my title, I'm going to be a true Lord.

"Are ya ready, Hemot?" Captain Relin asks. "Ya're the one who has to do this. I'm only the Captain. A lot of these people know me, but they'll take the word of a Nobleborn over mine any day."

"I'm ready, Relin. How long before we dock?"

"About ten minutes. 'Nough time for you to comb your hair."

I reach up and feel the mess on top of my head. Right… the hair. Marleet always reminds me of that.

I head into my quarters. Since there's no specific quarters set aside for someone like me, a guy who isn't involved in the actual sailing but is supposed to lead, Relin has given me the Captain's quarters. It's small, but comfortable.

I fix up my hair and grab the letter off the desk, the one that states Draydon's claim for the throne. Ellcia has also drafted up letters to the individual villages, and I'll read the one for Shizzer as well.

Just before I step out, I pull Draydon's letter from my pocket—the personal one he wrote for me. I almost shove it back in my pocket again. If he tells me he thinks he's going to die, I'll get all emotional and won't be much use out there with reading the letters I'm supposed to be reading.

It's almost time to read the other letters, but the personal one… the one written to me… Somehow, I know this is the time. This is the moment it must be read.

I take a look at the seal. It's not much. It's just some grayish wax that Draydon poured on there and then pushed his thumb into. It's the best he has until he gets an official seal. I remember watching Ellcia put some ointment on the thumb after. He should have waited for the wax to cool a little more.

I pop open the seal and fold open the letter. It's written in Draydon's fancy writing. He's a messy writer normally, but he has this neater handwriting—still terrible, but better—that he can use when necessary.

To Hemot, Son of Duke Berav the Milterite and Dutchess Hetaline. I, Prince Draydon, Crown Prince of Sevord and the Talic, future monarch of this wonderful Kingdom, do hereby now declare the following:

Hemot, Son of Berav, is henceforth granted the title and position of Duke with all the rights and privileges due to his position.

I, Prince Draydon, Crown Prince of Sevord and the Talic do also grant to Hemot any and all properties formerly belonging to Duke Berav or Dutchess Hetaline, kept in trust upon their death.

In keeping with Duke Hemot's new position, I hereby grant unto him the Dukedom of the Coast of Sevord, and he shall henceforth be known as the Coastal Duke.

But I, Prince Draydon, in granting this title to Duke Hemot the Milterite, do also declare that no title, no matter how high and lofty, will ever in my heart compare to the greatest title of all that can be given to the Duke. He is, first and foremost, my closest friend.

Sincerely, His Royal Majesty, Prince Draydon.

I stare at the letter in shock. My eyes water, and my bottom lip begins to quiver.

I purse my lips together and shake a little as the tears come down, and pace back and forth, shaking my head. Under my breath, I begin to mumble, "Stupid, nice, sweet Draydon, getting sappy and… sweet… and nice… and stupid… saying all those nice things, and making me a Duke… a real Duke… and making me cry. Making a Duke cry. That should be a crime. Stupid, sweet, nice Draydon. I should punch you in the face next time I see you for being so nice and sweet and stupid and…"

I look down at the letter. It's covered in tears, and I've crinkled the edges. I try to wipe my face with my sleeve, but this material of my tunic isn't all that absorbent, and the tears just wipe across my face. A moment later, I'm wiping my eyes and blowing my nose on my bedsheets. I think that might be gross later on, but that's tonight's problem. For now, I have a village to speak to.

I step out of the Captain's cabin, confident I can hide my emotions. Confident I can move forward with the dignity of a newly appointed Duke, friend of Prince Draydon.

"Ya look like ya've been cryin'!" Relin says with a laugh. "Did ya stub your toe again on the door? It's tricky, but ya'll get used to opening those things."

I shake my head and hand him the letter. He scans it, and his eyes bulge.

Handing the letter back to me, he begins to pace. He looks mad, but then I see tears streaming down his face and catch some of his mumbling. "Stupid, nice, sweet Prince Draydon, saying all those nice, sweet things about my friend Hemot, making him a Duke. Stupid, nice, sweet Prince Draydon. Next time I see you, I'll punch you in the face for being so stupid, nice, and sweet…"

A moment later, Relin has his arms wrapped around me, and he's crying on my shirt, mumbling something about how much he loves his new Duke. Try as I might, I can't hold it back, and I find myself weeping in his hair.

Not a great way to start out my new role as Duke, but one thing's for sure. At least one of those I lead cares for me.

When the boat shakes as it hits the dock, we push apart. The other sailors are all looking at us funny, but I don't care. I wipe away the tears, and Relin does the same.

"How do I look, Duke Hemot?" he asks.

I stare at his face in horror. There was a lot of dirt on there, and the tears didn't help the situation, just made it worse. I assume my face is just as bad.

A moment later, we're both in my quarters, washing our faces and trying to look presentable before we head out in public. When we're happy with how we look, we walk out on deck and then down the recently set out gangway.

A man and woman stand at the end of the dock. They're likely the leading couple of the village. I expect they own the inn, just like Nordin and Hella. Villages like this center around the work they do and the community they find, and an inn is where they find most of their community.

Relin has ordered thirty of our soldiers to move ahead of us, down the docks and toward the dozen soldiers standing on the rise. Those men belong to Parthun, part of the garrison. One of our Lieutenants will order them to follow him. I don't want the garrison around when the people hear word of Draydon. I'll deal with Parthun's men after.

Once the soldiers have moved on, we disembark. Moving down the dock toward the shore, I see both the man and woman's eyes flitting over to Relin, but he stays back. I gather they recognize him.

The man turns to me and cautiously says, "My Lord, welcome to Shizzer."

I half expect someone to correct him, telling him that I am not a Lord, but then I relax a little. If anything, that title comes short, but that's fine.

"Thank you. My name is Duke Hemot. I have been sent on behalf of Prince Draydon to the fishing villages along the coast. And I bring good news."

9

Draydon and the First Estate

It takes a week before we reach our first planned stop along the way.

My mind slips back, once again, to the man—the troll. It makes me sick to think that man was stuck in there that whole time. Which means… all the trolls are likely enchanted men or women, unable to free themselves. I wonder if he had a family. If he had a son, like me, who grew up without his dad.

When I become King, I want to find a way to free them all. I know that might mean killing them, but unless there's another way, we have to get them out—we have to free them. They all need to find the relief that I saw on that man's face before he died.

Since the ground was frozen, I used my sword to cut into the earth to bury him. It had not been a good burial, but it was the best we could do. I feel such sadness for him.

We walk close together as a couple of Shaloomd hover above. Neither of us is likely small enough to be carried away, but we don't want to be in the spot where the Shaloomd try.

"We have to use the road leading in," Roran says, pulling me away from my thoughts. "If we don't, they'll think we're thieves, and they can kill us on sight."

I nod. I'm glad Roran seems to know so much… about everything. Rulf taught him well.

The road into Lord Yune's estate is long. Judging from the ruts in the snow, it's well-used, too.

When we reach the manor house, a dozen or more people are at work outside, doing all sorts of things from shoveling snow—not that there's all that much of it to shovel—to repairing spots here and there. They actually don't look like they have much to do.

The house is huge. Like… castle-size. When I see the smoke billowing up from the many chimneys across the roof, I realize how cold I am, and we pick up our speed, heading for the front door.

Roran hasn't moved all that fast lately, despite the pressure to get to the mountains quickly. The ring isn't doing a great job anymore, and the fight with the enchantment has left him weak, frustrated, irritable—more than normal—and at times irrational.

But at least we're at our first stop.

Marleet gave me some pretty clear instructions on how I'm supposed to approach this whole arrival at the estate. They will welcome us and treat us well as guests, but they won't trust us and help us on our way unless we're careful to do exactly as she says.

When we reach the door, it opens for us before we knock, and we're welcomed in without challenge. Once inside, we're offered warm drinks and a chance to sit by the fire.

It's a little strange. No one has asked us what we want. They're just… being nice. I guess this is what Lord Yune's estate is like.

When the warm drinks arrive, I ask to speak with the head steward. The man bows slightly to me and then rushes off.

I sit and soak up the fire. A quick glance at Roran and I see my cousin has just about passed out. He's so tired. I would have carried him if I'd had the strength, but I'm not Rulf. I'm much bigger than Roran, but I still couldn't carry him for long.

I take a sip of the drink. It's chocolate! And it's fantastic. I've had hot chocolate before, but it was nothing like this!

I nearly gulp it down and then look enviously at Roran's. I wonder if he'll notice.

"Ahem!"

I spin around in my seat and then rise as I catch sight of a man dressed as a head steward. He's flanked by four soldiers, two on each side.

"Hello," I say. That seems a little dumb, but it's all that come to mind. I feel sleepy in the warm room.

"Hello, and welcome to the estate of the Lord Yune and the Lady Aldora. I am the humble head steward. My name is Cedrick. I understand you have requested to speak with me."

The man is of medium height, maybe a little shorter. He's thin, I would guess around sixty years old, but looks strong and healthy like he's used to hard work for long hours.

I nod. "I have to speak with you in private. I am willing to lay down my weapon and allow myself to be bound, if I can just speak with you in a whisper for a moment."

He furrows his brow at me and turns his head just slightly. "You have a message?"

I shake my head. "Not really." I know that's not an answer, but Marleet was pretty clear. I'm just supposed to say what I've said. I have to give the code, but I have to give it in secret, yet the soldiers won't let me approach the head steward while there's still a chance that I'm a threat.

Cedrick purses his lips. He doesn't look happy. But I get the impression that he's a man who rarely is.

"Bind him!" Cedrick orders.

I slip off my sword and set it by my chair, pulling out my knife as well and leaving it behind.

The soldiers bind my hands behind my back. The rope actually hurts. They're not gentle.

I take a look at Roran. They're obviously not concerned about him. I'm not surprised. He's out cold and snoring like an old man.

When I'm fully secured, one of the soldiers grabs me roughly by the arm and pushes me toward the head steward. When I get close, I say, "This is something for your ears only."

He nods at the soldier who backs away, and I lean in. "The Lady Marleet sent me. She said to tell you that we would like some gratter pie."

It's a strange code, but she explained that it was created because of how unexpected it is. No one could chance upon something like that.

The man's eyebrows shoot up, and he nods back at the soldier. "Release him and return his sword and knife. These two young men are to be trusted. The guard is to be informed that they should be protected as well as you might protect the Lord Yune and the Lady Aldora."

The ropes on my wrists come loose, and I say, "No, I'll get my own sword." I don't want them to accidentally touch the blade and lose a finger or a hand, nor do I want to risk exposing the fact that I have that blade to anyone who doesn't need to know.

"Wake the young man, and we'll take them to their quarters," the head steward orders.

When the soldier tries, Roran just pushes him away and continues to snore.

I smile at that. "He's pretty tired. Maybe I can carry him."

"No, young man, the guards will get him."

The larger of two guards moves over to Roran and throws my sleeping friend over his shoulder. A moment later, we're on our way through a large hallway to a set of rooms. "The young sleeping boy may sleep in here," Cedrick says, directing the guards to take him into a room, "and you, sir, may take this room here. If you please, I will leave you now to settle, and I will have a hot meal brought to you."

"That would be great," I say. "Thank you. Also, when you have time, I'd like to speak with you further."

"As you wish, sir. I will come back to visit you after your meal is finished."

I head into Roran's room first. The guard is stripping off his armor, but I let him know I'll do it. I doubt Roran wants me doing that, but I expect he'd prefer I do it than some stranger.

I get Roran's armor and weapons put away and leave him to sleep in just his pants. A small fireplace burns brightly on the other side of the room. I assume they weren't expecting us. Perhaps rooms like this are always kept warm.

I take a look around. It's fancy, that's for sure. I would say it's as impressive as Parthun's quarters in the castle. Maybe more so.

I leave Roran to sleep and head to my room, leaving my weapons off to the side. I don't want to take off my armor—I've grown quite comfortable having it on all the time—but I think I've grown so used to it, I'm afraid to be without it. I set it up against the wall and sit by my own fireplace. This room is just as beautiful and luxurious as Roran's.

I don't, however, have much time to think about it, because before I know it, I'm sound asleep.

I awake to the sound of someone in my room. I jolt forward and spin around in my seat, but it's not a threat. A young woman, not much older than me, stands at a table in the center of the room, setting down a tray of food.

The smell hits me before I can respond, and my stomach growls. The woman doesn't react. Instead, she continues to set out my meal.

I stand, and the woman turns to me and curtsies. "Your dinner, sir."

"Thank you," I say, and she curtsies again and heads for the door. "Wait."

"Yes, sir?"

"What about my friend? Did he get a meal? Is he awake?"

"No, sir. He is still asleep. The Head Steward has ordered us to put some bread, cheese, and water in his room, but we will wait until he awakes before we bring him a hot meal."

I nod. "Thank you."

She gives yet another curtsy and leaves. I check the food. It certainly does smell good. Before I dig in, I go check on Roran. A guard stands outside each of our rooms, but they don't stop or question me. Instead, each one gives me a slight bow. I don't think they're here to keep an eye on us. I think they're posted here to protect us.

Roran is still sound asleep. I decide to try to wake him as I'm sure he must be hungry, but I can't get anything out of him but a groan. I guess that's probably for the best. He needs his sleep.

Before I slip out, I check his ring. I haven't looked at it since the fight with the troll. It's turning black. The surface is still smooth, but with the black in there and white spiderweb cracks, it looks like it's about to break.

I pull the covers up around his chin and head back to my room. I want to eat properly, but I find I can't help but gobble everything down. To my delight, there's more of the chocolate drink. It's cooled somewhat, so I make the mistake of guzzling it, and the mug empties into my stomach.

Now I'm depressed. It's all gone.

When I hear a knock on the door, I call out, "Come!" just as I remember the Lords and Ladies in the castle did.

The door opens and Cedrick walks in. He's smiling, but it's not a friendly smile. I invite him to sit, and he stares at me for a moment.

Once he's made me sufficiently uncomfortable, he begins. "Now, Sir, I have called you Sir, but I do not know your name or your status. I know that I can trust you since you come with the backing of the Lord Yune himself—there is no way he would give up such a code without absolute confidence in you—but I would like some more information. You speak like a Lord when you call out, 'Come!' for me to enter the room, but you walk, talk, and act like a commoner. So, perhaps we could begin with your name."

I nod. I don't know how a future King should act in this situation, but I will not be bullied.

"Draydon. My name is Draydon."

The man nods. "Draydon. That is good information, but it tells me nothing."

I shake my head. "No, Cedrick, it tells you everything." I feel a little silly for pushing him, but I've known enough people like him who are used to pushing everyone around. Despite the fact that I'm grateful for the warm meal, I'm also still tired and a bit cranky. To help him out, I add in, "If that information is not enough to help you know what you need to know, I can let you know that my cousin in the other room is named Roran."

At that, his eyebrows shoot up. Neither name are common names. I've met a Draydon or two over the years, but I've never met or heard of another Roran.

"Roran…" His eyes unfocus for a moment as if he's trying to remember. "He did look like…" Cedrick looks right at me. "Was he… is he Prince Roran?"

I nod.

"Then you… the cousin… you're Prince Draydon."

I nod again.

"You're the next in line for the throne!"

I give a single nod.

Cedrick drops to his knees and bows before me. I don't like this kind of thing, but it's the way it goes for royalty. He simply says, "My future King."

"Please rise and take a seat, Cedrick."

He does, and I can see from his eyes that his mind is racing through every detail. After a moment, he bows his head to me and says, "What are your orders?"

Marleet gave me a lot of advice about how to proceed, and I take a deep breath. "I would like for you to continue to call me 'Sir' rather than anything that might indicate who I am. That goes for Prince Roran as well. We had hoped to stay here for no more than a day, just enough time to refresh ourselves and restock our supplies, but Roran is quite tired, and we've run into a bit of a problem. We might have to stay here a few days."

"Of course, Sir."

"I would also like to send word throughout the Talic of my claim to the throne."

"We can, of course, help you with that, Sir."

"We will also like to stop in at Lord Hemot's estate…"

"Oh, Sir, Hemot is not a Lord. He must be granted that title by the King."

I frown. Here I am trying to sound like I know what I'm talking about, but then I forget that little detail. "Well, that is something that will be addressed. We would like to stop in at Hemot's estate. And I would like them to work with you to spread the word."

"Of course, Sir."

"Are there people there we can trust?"

"Of course, Sir. The Milterite family is loyal. The head steward there is a good friend of mine. We meet often to discuss ways to improve the estates with which we have been entrusted."

"I would also like Prince Roran to be seen by a doctor, if possible. Is there someone here who could see him?"

"There is in the town nearby. I will send for him, Sir."

"And I need your word that you will not take the ring off his finger."

"Of course, Sir."

"That doesn't surprise you?"

Cedrick furrows his brow. "To receive an order, Sir? Of course not. I receive orders all the time. I never need to understand them. I serve Lord Yune. He is a wonderful, caring man, but…" Cedrick's eyes wander up to the ceiling for a moment, as if he's remembering a lifetime of odd experiences. "Lord Yune is, Sir, quite strange. Some of his orders are beyond my comprehension. I, however, follow them perfectly."

I smile. Yes, the little I know of him, Lord Yune is odd. "There is one more thing. Do you have any enchanted items in your care?"

"A few, Sir. What is it you need?"

I hesitate. I don't want to give too much detail, but Marleet says I can trust Cedrick. "Prince Roran has been placed under an enchantment. That is why he abdicated the throne. We have yet to release him from it, but the ring on his finger keeps it under control. Unfortunately, it is reaching its limit. I fear the ring will fail soon."

Cedrick nods ever so slowly. He scratches his mostly bald head and takes a deep breath before saying, "Well, Sir, we have an item or two that might help. Lord Yune has collected a few over the years. I have studied them a little, but I'm only guessing. Enchanted items are quite untrustworthy."

"We need to try."

"Have you tried taking the ring off and putting it back on?"

My mouth drops open. "No! We cannot do that. He goes mad if we take it off!"

"It might help. I can't promise anything, but we could bind him, gag him, and pull it off. Perhaps when it goes back on, it might start fresh."

Hope floods my heart. "Let's do that. In the meantime, go grab the items you spoke of."

"Of course, Sir."

With that, Cedrick rises, bows, and leaves the room. And I go back to bed.

I awake the next morning to a knocking on the door. I climb out of bed, still in my traveling clothes, and open to find that same young woman who brought me my meal yesterday. She leaves the food for me, and I ask about Roran. Turns out he's finally awake.

Grabbing my food, I head over. The guards give me a slight bow, and the one opens the door for me. When I enter Roran's room, he's sitting at the table, inhaling his breakfast.

"You must be hungry."

He laughs between bites. "You mean because I'm eating so fast?"

"That too. But you also haven't eaten in quite a while." I sit down and dig into my own breakfast. One thing's for sure, the meal yesterday and then again today is better than I've eaten for… well… maybe ever. Or at least since I was a kid.

When we finish, we have a seat by the fire. I don't say anything at first. It just feels nice not to be on the run.

Finally, when I think he's ready, I dive in. "So, we have a couple decisions to make."

"What are they?"

"First, I think we should stay here a couple days, just to help you recover. I've asked for a doctor to come and take a look at you."

"I'm fine. It's just the enchantment."

"Maybe so, but I still want a doctor to look at you." He's not impressed, but I'm not going to back down on this one. "Second, your ring. It's really in rough shape."

When I say this, he pulls his hand back and covers his fingers with his other hand. "And what can we do about that?"

"Well, I was talking to Cedrick about it."

"What? What gives you the right to tell him about this?"

"Roran, you've been getting more and more irritable the last while. The enchantment's taking over, or the ring is failing, or something. But whatever it is, we have to take action." I take a deep breath and continue on. "Cedrick has a couple enchanted items that might help. He thinks they might work like the ring, and I figured maybe you could make use of both at the same time. Together they might last longer."

"What are they?"

I shake my head. "Don't know. We'll find out when he brings them. But that's not the big challenge."

"What is?"

"He wonders if taking the ring off and putting it back on might help to… reset it or something."

Roran grinds his teeth and shakes his head. "You have no idea what will happen if that ring comes off!"

"No, but if we don't do anything, I think I'm going to find out pretty soon. He suggested that we bind and gag you, then pull it off. When we put it back on, we'll be able to see if it's better."

He grits his teeth, but nods. "That makes sense. I don't want to do it, but it makes sense."

I'm surprised by that. It doesn't make any sense to me. I'm only going with it because everyone seems to know more about enchantments than I do. "If that helps and the other items help, then we might have an easier time moving on from here."

"Okay, Draydon, yeah, I'll do that. When?"

"Let's go find Cedrick."

We wander out the door and ask the guards to take us to the Head Steward. The one guard goes with us, while the other remains. I assume he's guarding our rooms.

I'm amazed at the size of the place. I knew it was big from what I could see of the outside, but it just seems to go on and on and on! At one point, we pass the kitchen, which seems to be in full swing, even though I suspect we're one of the few guests in the house. I haven't seen anyone else, but then again, it's a big place.

As we move along, I see many people at work, cleaning, fixing things, decorating, repainting and more. I'd think that the place was under construction, but perhaps they're just trying to keep busy.

When we find Cedrick, he's directing a group of people to go shovel off a pond. I don't know what that's about, but it is what it is.

"Ah, welcome, Sirs. Thank you for stopping by. Are you enjoying your stay?"

"We are. My cousin just woke up, and we wondered if we could chat with you about what we were talking about yesterday."

He nods and smiles. I don't think he smiles often. It looks like it's enough of a struggle for him that I feel like I should congratulate him for a job well done, but I hold my tongue.

"I recommend that I bring the items to your rooms. I will attempt to be there within the hour, if that is acceptable to you."

"It is," I say.

He gives a bow, and we turn to leave. Since we have an hour, we ask the guard to give us a bit of a tour. He takes us through some of the boardrooms, the reception rooms, and more. Eventually, I ask why there are so many servants. I think there are more than in the castle, but the castle has a constant flow of visitors, so the castle should, I think, be a busier place.

"It's the Lord Yune. He provides employment for many people in the area. If they are out of work, and this time of year it is difficult to find work, he employs them. But the Head Steward does not allow anyone to have it easy. He works us all hard."

"You too?" I ask.

The guard nods. "When I am not serving as a guard, I often work in the kitchen during the winter or as a groundskeeper in the summer months. I am one of the ones who work year round."

"Do you know the Lord Yune?"

The guard shakes his head. "No, Sir. I have seen him once or twice over the years, but since the rebellion, he has not been here often. He would not likely remember me at all." Glancing at me, he asks, "Have you met him?"

"A few times, but I don't know him well. We're friends with the Lady Marleet."

At that, the man smiles. "I remember the young Lady Marleet running through the halls of the manor house years ago, when she was just little. Lady Aldora would chase her around. They were not here often, but they came. One time, they came with others. The King brought his son, Prince Roran, and General Geran brought his son, Prince Draydon. Those three were only four or five years old at the time, but they were a handful. Always getting in trouble." He pauses for a moment. "I had thought they were all dead. I am glad to know Prince Roran and the Lady Marleet survived, although I don't know why the Prince would abdicate."

We don't bother saying anything. I'm happy not to be known by anyone other than the Head Steward for the time being. It's no surprise that the guard thinks I'm dead. Word will go out soon in this area, but it's likely only along the coast at the moment.

When we return to our rooms, the Head Steward is only minutes behind. We enter Roran's room, and the Head Steward calls the two guards in and orders them to bind and gag Roran with his hands behind his back. They appear a little shocked at this, but follow orders.

Despite the fact that he agreed with it, Roran glares at me, but I just ignore it. I hope this helps.

When they're finished, the Head Steward explains, "This young man is under an enchantment. There is a ring on his finger that is suppressing the enchantment, but it is failing. We are hopeful that taking the ring off and putting it back on will help the situation. But neither of you are to speak of this event outside this room. Understood?"

The men give a deep bow to the Head Steward, and we approach Roran. When I grab the ring, he doesn't react at all until it's nearly off, at which point he grunts and screams and twists and more. The guards hold him in place, but he sure is a fighter.

I check the ring and break out in a smile. No spiderwebbing. The ring looks clear as glass.

"Try putting it back on him now, Sir," Cedrick shouts, doing his best to get above the noise of Roran's fit. At this point, Roran's not screaming anymore. It's more of a love-sick groaning. Like he's longing for someone.

I shake my head. It's Marleet. The enchantment made Roran fall in love with her. Poor Roran. To fall in love with someone as unreachable as her. She only has eyes for Hemot.

I have to work hard to get Roran's finger out again. As I get close, his groaning turns to screams again, and he shakes his head vigorously.

As soon as it touches his skin, however, he calms down. Once I get it on his finger, he relaxes. I take a good look at the ring. It's spiderwebbed again but with no streaks of black.

Cedrick pulls off the gag. "How is that, Sir?"

Roran's gasping for air, but he manages to nod and croak out, "Better."

"Is it all back to what it was when you first put on the ring?" I ask.

He shakes his head. "No. Just… better than it was a few minutes ago."

An idea hits me. "What if we leave it off for a longer period? Like a few hours. Will it completely reset?"

Cedrick shakes his head slowly. "I don't believe so, Sir. Enchantments don't really work like that. This ring may have been enchanted not only to stop other enchantments, but to fail within a certain amount of time. The ring will probably recognize our friend here, so it'll never fully go back to the beginning unless it's a new enchantment. I don't know if that's true, but it's my best guess based on what I've learned."

"Do you want to try it, Roran?" I ask. "You want me to take it off for a few hours?"

"No! Untie me. I want to stand up."

We pull off the ropes, and Roran jumps to his feet. It's good to see him with some energy again. I'm hoping this has given us a few more days. I also hope he's less grumpy now. The last few days haven't been fun.

"All right. So, that's a bit better, which is good." I turn to the Head Steward. "You have the other items?"

He grabs a large sack near the door and pulls out two objects. One is a medallion of sorts on a gold chain. The other is a large fluffy hat with flowers and, some fake fruit, and a squirrel.

It's a very ugly hat.

I turn to Roran to see him rolling his eyes. He mumbles under his breath, "And we know which one is going to work, don't we?"

We try the medallion first. It goes around his neck, and I see the relief flood his face. He smiles and says, "I think… that's good. I feel like it's pushed it back. I know the enchantment's there, but it feels far, far away!"

"Good," the Head Steward says. "Now let's try the other one."

I take the medallion from around his neck and throw on the big pretty hat. Roran looks quite unimpressed, but he has to admit that it works better than the medallion.

"All right," I say, forcing down a smile. "You can't wear that hat out on the Talic Region for no other reason than because the wind will blow it away. But who knows how long the medallion will work or if it'll cause problems if you're wearing it and the ring. So, while we're here, wear the hat. When we leave, put on the medallion."

Roran gives me the death look. I think he truly wants to kill me right now, but I think the real issue is he needs some relief. We can deal with the embarrassment of wearing that silly thing later. And when we're out on the Talic, the medallion will be an easy one to wear along with the ring on our journey to the mountains.

Over the next couple days, I watch Roran grow stronger and happier. His visit from the doctor turned out well. Roran appears to have no ailments, other than the weight of the enchantment. We're also eating well, which is nice after a long time of traveling through the pass and across the Talic.

To add to this, we lay out a plan with Cedrick for him to send out trustworthy messengers throughout the Talic Region and the Cities, informing them of my claim to the throne. We have letters already drafted up, detailing my claim and putting the names of Ellcia, Marleet, Hemot, Roran, Nordin, and Relin behind me. That gives me some clout right away, but puts Marleet's parents, Ellcia's brother, and Tilbur, who claimed I was dead, in a bit of a bind. But we have to take the risk.

I feel like it's wrong to put others at risk—like I should take it all myself—but the reality is, we all have to take part. So, I've tried to push my guilt and fear aside and move forward.

The letter lays out my claim for the throne and demands Parthun's support, calling people everywhere to be ready to gather when it is time to crown me their new King.

Cedrick has many men and women here he trusts, and sends out a dozen, six sets of two. I have fifteen letters in total, so that gives us more to work with. The six pairs of men and women are set to head to the three cities, along with all the villages throughout the Talic, and the mining villages.

My hope is by the time we return from the mountains, the entire nation, the Sevordine coast and the Talic will all be aware. I don't know if they'll all get behind me, but we have to start somewhere.

Two days later, while at lunch, I see we're ready to move.

"Let's head out tomorrow morning."

Roran nods his agreement. "That sounds good. I feel ready to go, and I've grown to like my new hat."

I laugh with him at that. I know he hates it, and he hates the snickering of the staff every time they see him, but we're at the end of the hat-wearing time.

I briefly wonder what would possess a Spellcaster to enchant such a hideous object, one that could never be hidden, but there's no way to know. Maybe some Spellcasters simply have a cruel sense of humor.

"I'll inform Cedrick that we're heading out, and we'll need our food supplies restocked."

Roran nods in reply and leans back in his chair. "How long do you figure it'll take us to get to the mountains from here?"

"I think if we push hard, we'll be a good ten days, if not a full two weeks. We have about a week to get to the mountain road, then we have to head south. I think three days to a week from there. I'm just not sure how far north we are exactly."

"Do you think…"

We're interrupted by a knock at the door.

I call out, "Come!" and Cedrick enters quickly, closing the door behind him. "Sir, we have a new visitor. I have not informed him of your presence and the staff has been warned not to speak of either of you."

"Who is it?"

My mouth drops open as he informs me, "Your uncle, Sir. It's Captain Tilbur."

18

Draydon and the Visitor

Ten minutes later, we're nearly at Tilbur's room. Although the majority of people in Lord Yune's estate can be trusted, the manor has a bit of an open door policy to those in need and, as such, over the years there have been many who have appeared as though they are spies for Parthun. At the moment, two men are in the house who might fall into that category. Because of this, we take a long way around, and since the Head Steward doesn't run, the "long way" takes a LONG time.

When no one else is around, we pelt the head steward with questions. It turns out that this is the prearranged safe-house for Tilbur, along with a few others. No King will force a search of a major Lord's residence without absolute proof of rebellion or criminal activity. Cedrick tells us that Lord Yune has messengers moving back and forth all the time, carrying coded messages.

When we reach the room, Cedrick knocks. Two guards stand outside. Both have guarded Roran or my rooms at times over recent days.

"Come!"

We enter to find Tilbur standing by the fireplace. His eyes are locked on mine, and his mouth hangs open. A cup of tea—I never took Tilbur for a tea drinker—sits in his hand and appears to be about to fall and shatter.

"Wha… how…?"

I laugh as the guard closes the door. "That's a bit of a story. I'm also wondering what might have brought you here."

Tilbur pulls himself back together and smiles, directing us to sit by him at the fire while Cedrick excuses himself.

My uncle stares at both of us for a few minutes. None of us speak. I stare at the man who treated me like I was worthless and someone to hate for eleven years. He stares at two young men he fought hard to keep alive for eleven years.

It's a lot to work through, and despite our previous conversations about things, I still struggle to feel anything toward him but disgust. Roran, however, due to different circumstances, has known only kindness from Tilbur.

"It's good to see you, Captain."

"It's good to see you, Prince Roran. And you too, Prince Draydon."

I smile and do my best to put things behind me. "We have a story to tell, and so do you. Who shall go first?"

"Perhaps this is a decision for the future King," Tilbur replies with another smile.

I see the tiredness in his eyes. I'm guessing he would be climbing into bed soon, if we hadn't shown up. "I'll tell you our story first, then, if you have energy left, you can tell us yours. Otherwise, we will wait for you to get some sleep. And please, call me Draydon. I'm still struggling with the titles and appreciate times of informality."

Tilbur nods. "I will call you Draydon. As for my exhaustion, I'm a soldier. I can push through a bit of tiredness."

I spell out the story for him of all that happened. As I explain that we have been sending out word about my claim for the throne, I get a twinge of guilt. I had been told by Tilbur and everyone that I should not reveal myself yet. That it would be dangerous to do so. Yet, I've decided to ignore them all and move forward anyway.

As we tell of the pass, he seems especially interested, although he's quite shocked by the story of the Talic Wolves and the fact that a troll had tried to kill us. And when we finish, he leans back in his seat as if he's trying to take it all in.

Finally, he says, "There had been rumors, stories, maybe even legends… many years ago, that the trolls were all from a cursed town up near where Milter stands today. The legend says that the people were wild and deadly killers. Assassins, murderers. One day, they upset a particularly powerful Spellcaster who cursed their entire village."

"So… that could be them?" I ask.

"Could be. Another legend says that the people were nice, trusting, giving, generous people who simply ended up in the wrong place at the wrong time, and then were cursed. It is difficult to know now, so many years after. But…"

"But what?" I ask. Even if I thought Tilbur was a terrible man all through my growing up, one thing I know for certain about him is he is a thinker. Out of General Corter and Captain Tilbur, Tilbur was the intelligent one. Everyone knew it, but Corter's birth order declared him to be the General. I think back to that conversation we overheard with Tilbur, Parthun, and Corter about sending out search parties for the Prince many months ago. Tilbur was clearly in control, pushing Parthun and Corter to do what he wanted.

"But…" Tilbur continues, "if they are people in there, then it might be worth trying to figure out how to cancel their enchantment. Typically, an enchantment ends with the death of the Spellcaster. But this might be different somehow." He turns to me and smiles. "Perhaps once the kingdom is firmly in your grasp, and you've established peace, this could be a task you set your heart to."

I smile back at him. That actually sounds quite interesting, but I say, "And your story?"

Tilbur leans forward and nods. He explains a lot of what has happened in the castle in recent months and what led him to have to flee. In the end, it turns out that as soon as he heard word that I had had been seen, he spoke with a few of the others who are loyal to the throne and manipulated Parthun into sending him out to kill me. No one stopped him, of course, as he's Captain Tilbur, a Prince and the First Captain of the Sevordine Armies.

When he finishes, I say, "I'm sorry I put you in this spot. I know you wanted me to keep hidden for longer."

He shakes his head. "No, Draydon, I didn't."

"What do you mean?"

Tilbur takes a deep breath and gives a tired smile. "Perhaps after I explain this, I should lie down. I haven't slept much in the last four or five days." He takes another sip of his tea, likely cold by now, and collects his thoughts. Finally, he says, "There was no way you could announce yourself while in the castle, that's for sure. You would be dead now if you had tried. But when it came to announcing yourself after that, you have to understand that we have been involved in kingdom politics for many years. We know what we're doing."

He laughs again and shakes his head. "We all knew you were afraid to take the throne. We knew you were not ready to lead because of that hesitation. We knew you wanted someone else to make the decision for you. So, we did. We felt the safest route for the moment was to tell you to hide. It would keep you alive, and we could continue to work towards you taking the throne.

"We were mainly doing this because you did not appear ready to lead. But, when you stepped back and evaluated the situation, you made a decision that was best for the kingdom, regardless of the pressure and demands we placed upon you. That, Prince Draydon, is the action of a King. When we heard you had gone against what we told you, I spoke with some of the others. They were thrilled, because now we know you are ready to take the throne."

I sit there for a moment, trying to take all that in. So… they wanted me to go against them. They thought I wasn't ready because I was too quick to follow. It seems really dumb, but this is the moment when I truly understand for the first time that a King's job is to lead.

How could I not have known that would be my job? Weird.

"But," Tilbur says, "I could really use some sleep. Will you still be here tomorrow, or are you heading out in the morning?"

I toss out my hope to leave the next day. This is more important. "We'll still be here. I wish to work out a plan with you for how to proceed."

Tilbur smiles again. "Yes, your Majesty."

With that, Roran and I leave Tilbur's room.

I have a lot to think about before tomorrow.

We've spent the day talking about how to proceed. Tilbur is quite pleased to find out that six teams have gone out into the Talic region to spread word of my claim. We've also planned for Tilbur to go out, as he can now publicly put his name behind me.

He explained this morning to us that this is an important development. Parthun will use this time well to spread lies, so if Tilbur moves through the countryside putting his support behind me, we might somehow manage to stay ahead of whatever rumors the King has come up with.

We've also spent time training. Tilbur is an excellent teacher. He's strict, focused, and very, very direct when he teaches someone how to use their sword, but I respond well to that. I don't like it when people try to convince me. I want to know what they want.

We focus a little more on how to control my sword, and we even spend time training Roran with it. Tilbur explains that it might transfer to Roran's line once I take the throne, but it is really hard to tell. Enchantments are strange. We won't know until the sword starts acting odd.

He wasn't able to give me any more information than that, as it's a mystery to everyone how a specific enchantment might work. Only the Spellcaster can know for sure, and they are rarely ever entirely truthful. Besides, that particular Spellcaster—the one who enchanted the sword— is long dead.

When we settle down for the night, I feel a lot better about everything. The plan is coming together. If all goes well, we hope to meet in Haner in four weeks.

11

Draydon and the Second Estate

We head out early the next morning. Cedrick has ensured our packs are full of food. Our clothes have all been cleaned and mended, and I feel rested. Cedrick has even given us an extra layer of clothing to help keep us warm. I have to admit, it's really nice.

We've given Tilbur four copies of the written claim for the throne. He's added in his support along with the others:

Tilbur, Son of Hartor, First Captain of the Armies of Sevord.

That leaves me with five copies to send out, which is plenty. The great part about Tilbur moving through the area is he has many contacts. Although he hasn't been able to meet with them in the cities for many years due to Parthun's control, he is childhood friends with some and has kept up the connection with others through mail or when they came to Sevord.

His focus will be the four cities, although he is hesitant about visiting Rainer, the City of Thieves. Unfortunately, he has as many enemies in that city as he has friends.

After a half day's journey, we reach our next stop. We don't actually have a secret code to convince them to trust us, but Hemot insisted.

We move down the long road onto the grounds, leading up to the large manor house. I'd say it's about a third or a quarter of the size of Lord Yune's estate, but I'm not even sure it's that big. It's huge, but Lord Yune is clearly far wealthier.

When we reach the front door, it opens for us, but unlike Lord Yune's property, there's no feeling of a warm welcome here. A man stands in the doorway flanked by six guards, three on each side.

"State your business, travelers."

"We are here to speak to the Head Steward."

"That is me. I am Herald."

"Thank you, Herald," I begin.

"No! I am the Head Steward to you. You will address me as 'Head Steward' or 'Sir'. You will not use my name."

I nod. Part of me wants to put him in his place, but then we'll have a fight on our hands. "Yes, Sir. I have two letters for you."

"Hand them over."

A soldier steps forward, and I give him two rolled pieces of parchment. The one is sealed with Lord Yune's Head Steward's seal. The other... well... Hemot doesn't have a seal.

While we stand out in the cold, Herald, or Sir, breaks open the letter from Cedrick. His eyebrows rise, and his mouth drops open. I don't actually know what Cedrick wrote. I've read Hemot's letter and told him what he was not allowed to say, but Cedrick wrote his own note.

Once the first letter is read, the second is opened. That one's from Hemot. He admits in there he has no way of proving that he is Hemot, son of Duke Berav and Duchess Hetaline, but he calls the Head Steward to take a step of faith on this matter and put his support behind Draydon.

The Head Steward finishes the second letter and lets his arms drop to his side. He stares at the floor for a moment before slowly raising his eyes to meet our own.

He looks at each of us and demands, "Tell me your names."

I glance at the soldiers, but the Head Steward merely raises his hands. "They can be trusted."

I look at Roran, and he speaks first. "I am Prince Roran, son of King Hartor and Queen Shalsee."

"And I am Prince Draydon, son of General Geran and Lady Tallia. And I have put forward my claim for the throne."

I don't really know what I expected, but I'm kind of disappointed when the Head Steward merely nods and waves for me to follow. The guards close the doors behind us and follow us through the manor house. In a few minutes, we reach a simple set of doors, and the Head Steward knocks.

From the other side of the door, I hear a loud, wailing noise, followed by a sad, mournful, "Come in… come in… to my den of doooooooom."

The Head Steward rolls his eyes and shakes his head as I hear a few of the guards snicker. I recognize the voice, but I just can't place it.

When we enter, I find a sparsely decorated room, spotlessly clean. In the center, a woman sits with her back to us. She's small, round, has gray hair, and weeps loudly. But… I don't think she's been weeping like this all along. I think it's for our benefit.

I force down a smile. It's clearly Borlynn, Hemot's nursemaid. She certainly does like drama.

"Wha… what… what neeeeews do you have for an old, grieving woman?"

"Borlynn!" the Head Steward begins in a scolding voice but is quickly cut off.

"Yes, that was my name… but now… now I wish only to be called the woman with a broken heart."

"Borlynn! Enough! Stand up and give me your attention. I have important matters to discuss."

Borlynn doesn't move, but instead asks, "More important than the grieving of an old woman with a broken heart who longs for her young charge, the one she alone was responsible for, the one she let fall to the clutches of yonder nothingness. You cannot, Herald, possibly know of my grief. Poor young master Hemot… forever lost."

The Head Steward closes his eyes for a moment and grinds his teeth. When he opens his eyes, he forces a smile and says, "Truly, my dear Borlynn, I cannot know your grief. But in the midst of grief, I think we must honor our dear Hemot by honoring those he claims are his friends."

Still with her back to us, she lets out a loud wailing sound and then says, "Oh, how I might honor Hemot! There is no way I can honor him aside from grieving for him for the rest of my miserable life! Oh, that perhaps I could…"

"Oh, come on, Borlynn! I just need you to tell me if you recognize these two young men as the ones who traveled with young Hemot and if the one is Prince Roran and the other is Prince Draydon!"

At that, she stands up quickly and turns to us. She points her finger at me and screams, "You!"

The guards grab her before she can reach me, but that doesn't stop her from screaming and swinging her arms at me. "You! You took him from me! You took him from the caves. I have cursed your name every day since!

Draydon, the stealer of Hemots! Draydon, the robber of my sweet child. Draydon, the corrupter of all that is good and kind in this world!"

"And this one?" the Head Steward asks as the guards continue to hold her back.

"That one! The one who claims to be Prince Roran, but no Prince would allow his cousin to steal my sweet Hemot! No Prince would stand by while his cousin kidnaps my sweet little child, a young boy, unable to defend himself from the lies and deceptions of an entitled Prince!" She lunges again at me, and I'm surprised to see the guards struggle so much with her! She's not a big woman.

The Head Steward grabs Roran and me by the arms and pulls us out of the room. Four of the guards come right away, while the other two push Borlynn back and then rush out, pulling the door closed and holding it tight against her as she screams for our deaths.

"Wow!" I say. I've never seen anything like that. I worry for Hemot when she finds he's safe. Come to think of it, I don't think I'm going to tell anyone here about the northern pass through the cliffs. If word gets to Borlynn, I think she'll try to take it, and, despite her passion and drive, I doubt she'll live.

I turn back to the Head Steward to find him on his knees before me. Four of the guards are as well, and the other two, as they hold Borlynn's door closed, have bowed their heads.

"Forgive me, Prince Draydon. I had to confirm your identity with Borlynn, as she was the only one here who can truly identify the two of you. I trust Cedrick's word, but these are dark times. Many are deceived, and many more go out deceiving. I offer you my allegiance and dedicate myself to the throne."

All four guards offer their allegiance as well, and I ask them to rise. When they're on their feet, I say, "Thank you, Head Steward and all of you. I am also dedicated to the throne of Sevord and dedicated to the people of Sevord. I am committed to ruling with strength and kindness."

The Head Steward smiles at me and says, "Please, call me Herald. And we should leave this area. Borlynn will not calm down for a while. She can be quite stubborn. Once, when young Hemot was only three years old, his mother, Duchess Hetaline, wanted to keep him up past his bedtime, but Borlynn nearly tore down the house to, as she explained, 'protect young Master Hemot' from a lack of proper sleep."

"Did Borlynn get what she wanted?"

"Oh," Herald says with a laugh. "Lady Hetaline never backed down. Borlynn lost that argument and sulked about it for a month."

We move down the corridor with Herald and four of the guards. The other two have remained behind, I assume to keep Borlynn from coming for our throats.

I briefly wonder if she and Hob would make a good pair. I'd love to see her trying to control him as he cartwheels around the room.

We reach a small, comfortable receiving room with a fire burning in the large fireplace. Herald invites us to sit as the guards take up positions by the doors.

When I notice Herald hasn't taken a seat as well, I invite him to, but he looks uncomfortable with it. I think maybe that's not something most Head Stewards do with royalty. Cedrick might have been an exception.

"Listen, we would like to stay here for the night. We will head out first thing in the morning, but we wish for you to send out six messengers, if you can spare them, in pairs to spread word of my claim for the throne throughout Sevord."

Herald's face breaks out in a grin. Unlike Cedrick, it looks like he does a lot of smiling. I glance at the guards, and they all smile as well.

"Of course, Your Majesty. The Milterite family's estate is behind you. Do you have letters?"

I hand three letters to him. That leaves me with two. I don't know what I'll do with the last two, but I wanted to have more than I'd need.

"They will go out tomorrow. I will send those I trust, and they will spread word. Are there any places in particular?"

"No. I have others from Lord Yune's estate traveling through the area, and Captain Tilbur is as well."

"Tilbur…" Herald's face fills with confusion, and his eyes drop to the floor. "Ah… yes… that makes sense. I knew there was someone high up in the castle who was loyal and fighting hard against Parthun, but I did not know who. I had wondered if Tilbur was the one, then I heard many things about how dedicated he was to Parthun and discarded that possibility. But he must have been loyal all along." Looking directly at me, he says, "Captain Tilbur was close, very close, with your father, General Geran. Geran was a strong leader, and Tilbur was his muscle. There was little Tilbur could not do—physically, as well as politically and militarily. He's a solid fighter. At least he was the last I saw him."

I smile. "He's still a big guy."

"Yes, he was the largest of the brothers," Herald says with a smile. "In time, we learned much of the six sons. King Hartor was the one with the most integrity. General Geran was the best leader—by far, and the most brave. General Lirnal was the most sacrificial. Parthun was the most devious. Corter…" At this point, Herald laughs. "Corter is not one who is spoken of often. He holds the rank of General right now, but he is certainly the most incompetent General you could imagine. He has no idea what's going on. Just spends his time drinking or… well… who knows. And, of course, Tilbur. He is physically the largest and strongest. He's a great leader but struggles with anger and rage."

Herald smiles at me as he continues. "Your father and Tilbur were close. Your father saw great potential in Tilbur, despite his anger. They worked together closely, and, if I recall correctly, Tilbur was named a hero of Reber's Gate."

I don't actually know anything about that battle. Everyone talks about it, but it's a total mystery to me.

"A lot of people were named heroes there," Roran says.

Herald laughs. "Quite a few, but it was a major battle. It lasted weeks, and if we'd lost, we would have lost the kingdom. We were outnumbered, outmatched, and the enemy managed to bring in a troll—how they got it to fight for them is anyone's guess—and we all thought we were lost."

"You were there?" I ask.

He nods. "So was Duke Berav. He wasn't a Duke back then. He led the Milterite division. We served side by side and, after the war, when he was named a Duke, he asked me to be his Head Steward. I couldn't refuse. I moved my family here right away and have been here ever since."

"Your family?"

"My wife runs the hospitality division: kitchen, cleaning, decorating, and more. My oldest son oversees the guard. And my youngest son serves as the groundskeeper. My daughter is the only one who has left. She married one of the guards who works for Lord Yune, and her daughter works in the kitchens, serving food to guests."

I nod. Once again, I see a life I envy, a life I can never have. So many seek power and authority and want to rule, but all I ever wanted was a simple life. And Ellcia.

A yawn forces its way up. We haven't traveled far today, but I'm still tired. "We'd like to have a meal and settle down for the night, if we could. We hope to set out at first light."

Herald smiles. "Of course, Your Majesty. I will speak to my wife about bringing a meal for you soon, and I will plan on seeing you off tomorrow."

That night, I sleep well. I'm excited about getting to the mountains.

12

Ellcia and Shizzer

It's been five days since Hemot left. Marleet is pretty worried by this point, but I keep reminding her that we all have a part to play. It's something I've heard a lot from her since we got her out of the castle.

Fortunately, we have something to distract Marleet right now. And truthfully, I'm grateful for the distraction as well.

"My name's Gerbin, and this is my dear wife, Verral."

I've sent for Nordin. He'll be thrilled to hear they've arrived, although I had hoped they'd stay where they were.

"So, this is the entire village of Shizzer?" I ask. There's a lot of them. I don't know how it compares to Nimville, but... that's a lot!

"Yes, my Lady. Once Duke Hemot informed us of Prince Draydon's claim to the throne and killed the garrison of Parthun's soldiers, we packed up and came right away. Of course, we were already prepared as Nordin let us know a little of what was going on. This is everyone, except for those who are bringing up the four fishing boats. They're taking their time because we're concerned they'll be threatened by

Parthun's navy if they're not fishing. It will be difficult for them to explain why they're traveling north."

"Duke Hemot...?" Marleet begins, but I raise my hand to signal for her to leave it. I haven't told her what was in the letter. I'm glad to hear Hemot finally read it.

"Yes, my Lady," Verral says to Marleet. "He's an unusual-looking man, but handsome in his own way, and we are proud to have met the Coastal Duke."

Marleet smiles at Verral and says, "I look forward to speaking to him again."

Verral bows to Marleet and smiles sweetly at her. "He spoke about you, Lady Marleet."

She opens her mouth to ask about that, but I cut her off. I have lots to do, especially now that I have another few hundred or so people to feed. "Gerbin, Verral, I will send one of our ships to meet your fishing vessels. I ask that you write a letter to them to help them to know they can trust our people, and our ship will escort your fishing vessels here to the Northern Tribes, the place we have named Freond. This is where Duke Hemot has been staying while in this area for the last while."

Gerbin and Verral's eyes light up, and they look around in awe. Whatever happened in Shizzer, these people are not Draydon's people, despite the vow of fealty to him while Hemot was there in their village. These people may serve Draydon, but they love Hemot. He's managed to impress himself on their hearts.

I send them on, and assign a few soldiers along with Frippolee's wife, who turns out to be quite an organized woman, to see to the needs of the people of Shizzer. As they settle in, I come to find out they brought with them every scrap of food they could carry, which turns out to be a lot. The main path moving north up the coast isn't overly smooth, but it's good enough for the wagons filled with preserves, salted meats, and more.

Shizzer also, unlike Nimville, has livestock—and a fair amount. We now have increased our source of milk and meat, and once the fishing vessels get here, we'll have another four fishing boats. This is not a good time for fishing, but whatever we get is better than what we have without it. The last thing we need is to run out of food. If that happens and Parthun arrives, we might as well surrender.

To add to all this, the people of Shizzer have arrived with tents. It sounds like they are content to continue living in them, but I've ordered more people, including the people of Shizzer, to focus on construction of new homes. I hope this doesn't mean no one leaves when all this is over. I think it's best if the people go back to their villages, not remain here, but that's a worry for another day.

Ten days later, the horn blares just after the evening meal. It's not a surprise this time, as I'm standing with Frellson, talking about security matters. I guess, growing up as a servant, I thought I knew what hard work was, but I clearly didn't.

I mean, I did work hard as a servant, cleaning, arranging, working in the kitchen, but as long as we got our work done, we could sneak out, we could play games, we could do just about anything we wanted. And we rarely had to work past the dinner hour. There were other servants who did that.

But now, I'm hard at work from sunup to sunset. There's rarely ever a moment when I can just sit and relax. Both Marleet and I have lost weight, not because we're trying to, or want to, but because we're always on the run. Hella tells me stress can do funny things to the body. And after only a short time of carrying this stress on my shoulders… I feel… old.

It's like my body has aged. I'm afraid by the time Draydon sees me again, a lot of my hair will have grown in, but I'll be nothing but skin and bones, with gray hair and wrinkles upon wrinkles. He was fine with the bald head. We'll see how he feels about me if I age fifty years in the next couple of months.

Marleet tells me I don't look that bad, but then again, I'm telling her the same thing, and she has these hideous bags under her eyes, and at times she slurs her words.

I've stood in this spot for about an hour, looking out over the water as I deal with one matter after another. I'm on security, oversight of the army and navy, and working with Frippolee to ensure the farming communities don't get overlooked. Marleet is on housing, construction, and food supply. I think I've missed something, but I just don't know what else to do. I need Draydon. And Roran. The two of them would be indispensable. I'd even settle for Hemot, the Coastal Duke. He's the least organized thinker in Sevord, but a lot of these people will only listen to a Noble as long as we're around.

But the ships… the ships approaching in the distance. They're what's most important right now. I don't know if there's another battle on the horizon, but I'm glad we have Nordin's Royal Warship, the Destroyer, the two frigates, and all the fishing boats. Because whatever's coming—it's too far away right now to see for sure who or what all we're up against—but it is a lot of ships.

There's no need to signal Nordin. He's within sight. I see his warship, which had been moving north, turning around. I've already given the order to launch every ship we have docked, and Nordin will coordinate the defense.

I try to count the ships coming in. There's a lot of them, and a greedy part of me hopes in this we might double our fleet.

And, fifteen minutes later, it's clear they're not here to attack. I'm pretty sure the one ship is the Geran, Captained by Relin with Duke Hemot in the lead. The other boats… fishing boats.

Marleet's beside me, giggling in a way that throws all her maturity out the window. As she bounces on her feet, she grabs my arm and starts to chatter about Hemot and how happy he'll be now that he's a Duke. I'm just hoping that when he returns, he'll take on some of the load we're carrying, and he won't distract Marleet from her duties.

When Hemot comes in, Nordin's ship comes with him. The Geran, Hemot's ship, is packed full of people. I can't see how that boat is still afloat. The fishing vessels are also packed. I make an attempt to count, but quickly give up.

The original docks of the farming communities are often full, but I've begun construction on more in anticipation of this kind of thing. At the moment, we can handle all the new arrivals, plus Nordin's warship with a little extra space, but the rest of our fleet sits out, anchored offshore.

As I stand on solid ground, just before the main dock near the Geran, I wait. No one disembarks, which is a little weird, at first, until I see Hemot step down the gangway. When his feet hit the dock, all the people cheer, and he waves at them. Once they've calmed down, I see him holler something at them, then wave for them to follow, and he comes toward land.

When he reaches us, Marleet runs into his arms, and they hold each other, talking really fast and overtop of one another. I don't bother interrupting for the first bit. They won't even hear me unless I yell and maybe smack one or both of them in the arm.

They pull away eventually, and Hemot looks at me a little funny. Nordin's explained to us how things should work. Despite the fact that Marleet is likely the highest-ranking Noble among us, since Draydon put me in charge, the others need to treat me that way. Unfortunately, now that Hemot's been made a Duke, Draydon and I both knew he'd struggle with the new arrangement.

So, technically, he needs to give me a little bow to keep the formality.

I wait, but he kinds of shifts on his feet for a moment, glancing at Marleet. She gives him a little nod, which I take to mean that he still needs to give the bow, but I think he takes that as a sign that he should wait for me to bow.

I nearly growl out loud at this. I don't really care about the formality. I don't need a bow. But Nordin explained that we need to maintain order, and the matter of who is in charge is crucial to this. And I know the people he came with are watching to see how this interaction goes.

"Hemot!" I hiss. "We agreed in public to follow the rules of honor! Give me the bow and then I can ask for your report!"

Hemot frowns at me, glances at Marleet, who gives him another little nod, which I think he takes again to mean that he should stand his ground, and says, "I'm not sure if you're aware of this, but Prince Draydon gave me the title of Duke and declared me to be the Coastal Duke. All this land falls within my Dukedom. So…" The look he gives is pretty clear. He's waiting for me to bow to him so everyone lined up behind him on the dock can see that he's truly their Duke.

I'm too stressed to deal with this kind of thing right now. I open my mouth to tell him off, but Marleet speaks up.

"Hemot," she says kindly, "you are now a Duke, appointed to that position by the Crown Prince. It's official, and your position is powerful. But you hold that position at the pleasure of the royal throne. And… think about this. You're expecting your future Queen to bow to you?" She steps closer and gives a kind smile. "If you're expecting the future Queen, the wife of the man who gave you your position, to bow to you, you're creating a problem. The next time you see Draydon, he might be King. Will you also expect King Draydon to bow to you as well? And how do you think he will feel about you pushing Ellcia, his future bride, to bow to you?"

Hemot's mouth falls open, and he shakes his head. "Oh, no… I'm sorry!" He turns to me and shakes his head. "I'm sorry, Ellcia… Lady Ellcia… I didn't see it that way." I see he's about to bow, but then he stops. "Wait, if I bow, will that make them think I'm not a good Duke? Will it threaten my Dukedom?"

I'm out of patience with him. "Hemot!" I hiss. "Bowing to me will not threaten your Dukedom. Not bowing to me will threaten your Dukedom, and everyone standing behind, all those in your Dukedom, will think you are a dumb Duke! You don't want to be a dumb Duke, do you? Now, bow and get it over with!"

He gives me a deep bow—far too deep, actually, considering his position—but it's better than the stubbornness from a moment ago. The people behind him are clearly pleased with this—most people like knowing there's a certain order to the Nobility, but I can see them straining to look at me. I know what that's like. They're all wondering who could make their Duke bow like that.

I wave for the people to come up off the Dock, and I stand on a rise, a little above everyone, hoping my voice will carry. The weather has warmed a lot with the coming of spring, but the wind has also picked up.

I turn to Hemot and ask, "Have they all given a vow of fealty?"

He nods. "They have, my Lady."

Before I can continue, Marleet interjects. "They gave a vow of fealty to… Draydon… right?"

"Oh, yeah. Of course," Hemot says. "I thought about asking them to give their vow to me since I'm their Duke, but Relin told me not to do that."

I close my eyes and spend a moment thinking about how grateful I am to Relin, but then open my eyes and ask for his report. He tells me the people are prepared to sleep in tents, and they have brought food and many supplies with them. In addition, some of the fishing boats are deeper sea boats, able to fish farther out.

I think about that and realize how much of a help that is. Nordin has spoken about how they are over-fishing this area.

When Hemot's finished, I address the people, welcome them, and call for Frippolee and his wife to process our new arrivals.

When I finish, Marleet squeals with joy and runs off into the crowd of people, up to a ragged old couple. They scoop her into their arms and hug her. I think I hear her call them Gramma and Grampa, but I must be hearing things. I'm pretty confident her grandparents aren't alive, and they certainly wouldn't be dressed like that.

Once the people have all moved on, and Marleet and Hemot are off taking care of things, Frellson approaches me. "My Lady, we have gained another three hundred and fourteen people, many of whom will be capable of sailing ships or serving as soldiers. I expect many will be capable of construction as well. We have also gained 13 fishing boats, bringing your Navy up to six warships, twenty-two fishing vessels, and one shipping boat."

I smile. At this rate, it won't be long before I own the sea. That'll be the perfect coronation present for Draydon.

I watch Stevrick's boat pull away. He's a good man. Loyal, competent, and focused. But he's right. He and his crew need to return to Sevord. They can explain their absence at this point without too much trouble. He's managed to fill his hold with supplies for Sevord City, such as lumber, tools, and material from farther north.

He also has a plausible story to report, in case he and the crew are questioned, which will help. They will act shocked at the thought of any rebellion and insist that they only met people who are entirely loyal to the throne. If questioned about the ships, they will explain that the original warship only followed them for a time, then stopped. It had originally been called the Dauntless, but he will explain how once it stopped, they no longer saw any sign of the Dauntless. As for the other ships, he will mention he saw some frigates and a Destroyer, but his focus was primarily on trade and on remaining loyal to the throne.

Everything they have to report will actually be true, on one level or another.

Their return will have three purposes. First, they will help to put aside some of the suspicion growing in Sevord, which will be helpful. Second, Stevrick and his crew will be able to see their families. Third, every member of the crew is committed to spreading word of Draydon's claim to the throne. Which, unfortunately, will create new suspicion.

It is likely that few people in the city know what is going on outside in the nation. Parthun is quite good at keeping people in the dark. They will circulate and post letters declaring support for Draydon and announcing that Parthun is expected to present himself to Draydon at Haner on the first day of Spring.

The last thing we can do is leave Parthun free to rule in his city, unopposed.

13

●

Draydon and Milter

ell, now we're stuck on this path!" Roran growls.

"I'm sorry. I just couldn't see any other way!" We're coming up on Milter, the main city of the Milterites. Well… city… town, I guess. More than a village, maybe. It's… small, but spread out. And it doesn't look very nice.

Tilbur had warned us to avoid the Milterites for now. They would come on board with the change of leadership just fine—when that day came. Milterites are stubborn, aggressive people. And their lands are generally avoided by everyone except those who have to go there.

We were supposed to take a path heading south before we reached Milter, but unfortunately, we never saw it. I'm guessing it was covered in snow, so we just kept going. Roran was sure we missed it, and truthfully, so was I, but I didn't see what we could do about it. The snow in this area is a lot deeper and trekking on an unused path or across the hills of the Talic would be slow-going at best.

"Should we go back?" I ask.

Roran shrugs. "I've heard nothing but bad about entering a Milterite village. They don't like outsiders—

117

well… I think they like them, but not for kindness. They like beating them up. They're fighters and proud of it."

"Can't a King do anything about it? I'd have thought someone would have stepped in."

"Well, here's the thing," Roran explains as we approach the town. "They pay their taxes, they never rebel, and if the nation goes to war, they are the first to show up and often volunteer to take the first charge. They're loyal people who never cause trouble outside their region."

"Well…" I begin, unsure of what to ask.

"That's the thing. What they do here in their towns is under their law. As long as they don't violate the King's law, if they haven't done anything the King won't allow, then they haven't done anything the King needs to address. No King will send out an edict saying, 'No beating people up.' It's just kind of assumed that towns will take care of that kind of thing on their own. But Milter… doesn't."

I shake my head. One of the downsides to my sword is its ability to cut through anything. It means I can't really use it to defend myself because it will either kill anyone who comes at me, or it'll slice their sword in half, which makes my sword a target. Who wouldn't want to steal a sword that can cut through anything?

By this time, we've entered the town. Everyone looks at us—either staring or glancing at us now and then. Most people smile, but it's not one of those friendly, "I like you" smiles. It's more of a "hungry" kind of smile. The town is fairly large—I'd say three or four times the size of Nimville—but I can easily see the other side. We just have to make it that far.

As we walk, the people continue to watch us, but I think that's it until I notice the crunching of feet on the snow behind me. I glance back to see a half-dozen men following not far behind.

Ahead is what I think might be their town square. It's a larger open area with a statue in the center. The statue is, of all things, a troll. An ugly troll. It's only about a quarter of the size of a real troll, but there's no doubt that's what it is. I suspect it's made of brass or something. It looks solid and sits on what might be a granite base.

Compared with the town, which is average at best, that statue seems out of place. I would guess it would take quite the craftsman to create it.

When we're nearly at the statue, Roran jolts to the side and slams into me. I grab him and steady him on his feet, but he's dazed.

"Whatcha doin'?" a man screams, coming up to Roran, grabbing him by the cloak and giving him a shake. "Messin' with ma kid?"

"I… uh…" Roran's pretty shaken.

I try to make sense of what's happened, and I catch sight of a kid standing not far away with a big smirk. At his feet is a ball. I check Roran again, and he seems to have his balance back, but the side of his head is red and puffy. The kid kicked the ball at him.

"Hey, we don't want any trouble," I say, but the man turns to me and glares.

He waves at the men behind us and says, "Well, ya got trouble. Ya messed with ma kid."

"Hey, we didn't do anything. Just walking," I explain.

"No, ya did everythin'. Ma kid kicked his ball, and ya pal here stepped in tha way."

I personally think that's very dumb reasoning. It's like complaining that someone hurt your hand when you punched them. But I hold my tongue on the matter. I know the guy has just found a way to pick a fight.

"What do you want?" I'm feeling pretty angry. He's just… I don't know… some people are just mean. Some people just want to cause conflict. I want to tell the man there's enough problems around that he doesn't have to create new ones, but I know it'll make things worse.

The man moves to give Roran a shove, but Roran knocks his hands back. The man's face immediately fills with rage, and he screams, "He attacked me! Did ya see it?"

Hands grab me and the next thing I know, I'm pinned up against a wall while Roran is dragged out into the middle of the street. They start to hit him, over and over, kicking, punching… I don't want to watch, but then I feel like I don't want to turn away from him. I don't know what the right thing to do is.

I struggle hard against the guys, but another two men come and join in. They haven't taken my sword. If I can get it out, I can put a stop to this, but I'll end up killing a lot of men. Roran's sword and knife and pack lay on the ground not far from me.

I drop low and then kick up as hard as I can. My shoulders connect with the chins of two of the men, and they go down, and then I push back the other men while I go for my sword. Before I can get it out more than a little, they grab me again, and my sword slides back into the sheath.

Another three men come along and hold me tight. I can't move. I can barely breathe.

The men have stopped beating Roran now. He's still moving, and I'm grateful for that, but he's definitely beat up pretty badly.

A man steps forward, pulling a black cloak over his shoulders. When it's fully on, I see he's wearing a judge's raiment, and my heart races. He stops in front of the troll statue and raises his arms like he's trying to get everyone's attention.

This can't be happening!

The Judge drops his arms and asks for the story, but I remember the guy—he knows exactly what happened. He was one of the men following behind us with a big smile on his face.

The man whose son kicked the ball into Roran's head gives a tearful story of how his son was just trying to play, and Roran stepped in to cause trouble. When the dad came to rescue his son, Roran hit his arms.

The surrounding men are snickering. I don't understand why they would even go through this sham of a court case.

"Do ya have anythin' to say for ya'self?" the Judge asks.

Roran shifts on the ground, but doesn't respond. He looks like he's barely conscious.

"Nothin' to say in ya defense?" the Judge asks. "That's as good as an admission of guilt."

"He's not guilty!" I shout. "You can't do this!"

The Judge smiles at me and says, "Yes. I can." Turning back to the people, he declares, "It is ma judgment that this boy be hanged at first light. Until then, he will be retained in tha pit."

The men drag Roran away as I struggle. I still can't break out of their grasp.

"As for you," the Judge says, "has this young man committed a crime?"

The two men I hit with my shoulders a moment ago complain, but the judge asks, "Were ya restraining him at tha time?"

I'm surprised to see them admit they were, and he declares, "It is written that a man restrained may defend himself with any and all means." Turning to me, he adds, "Since you are friends with tha culprit, you are hereby banished from this town henceforth."

With that, the Judge simply pulls off the robe, tosses it to a boy who runs away with it, and then the Judge walks through the doors of what looks like a tavern. I jerk to the side, and a few minutes later, I'm tossed out of town into a snowbank. Roran's pack lies beside me, along with his sword and knife. I shake my head. I guess someone liked his crossbow enough to keep it.

I pull myself to my feet and stare back into the town. What a horrible place! I get images in my mind of razing that town to the ground when I become King, but I know that's not the way.

A few men watch me from the town. I'm guessing they're hoping I'll return, and they can throw me in the pit as well, but I'm going to have to take a different approach.

Hefting up Roran's pack and weapons, I move off down the road. I have until tomorrow morning to get Roran out of there.

Once the road curves a bit, I set Roran's pack down, up against a snowbank. I plop down on the road beside it to think things through. I'm hoping Roran is conscious, although I'm sure he's uncomfortable. I'm also hoping no bones are broken. Both for his sake and because when I get him out of there, we're going to have to run.

I also think that I'm not going to get out of this situation without bloodshed. I don't want to kill anyone, but I can't see any other way.

I briefly consider letting them know who I am and demanding they release him, but I don't think they care who sits on the throne. They'll obey the throne, but Parthun or I likely makes no difference. So, I can't count on loyalty.

I decide to wait until dark, which isn't that far away, considering the time of year. I do my best just to keep moving and stay warm until the sun sets, then leave Roran's pack and sword on the side of the road. I set it out in a way that it's going to be easy to pick up in case we come out in a rush.

When I get to the edge of town, I find a few guys moving back and forth along the road. I'm not surprised.

They likely expect me to come in to try to rescue Roran. I move off the road to the north just a bit, then make my way in.

I think to myself that I've outsmarted them, but then it hits me. They're looking for reasons to hang people. They likely want me to sneak into town. If they catch me after I've been banished, maybe they can hang two guys instead of one.

For a moment, I wonder where the pit is, but I hear a crowd of men laughing and jeering not far away. I move in that direction and find about thirty guys circling what I assume is Roran's prison. They're throwing stuff down in there, and I hear Roran yelling at them. I hope that's a good sign. I hope it means he's okay.

I take it all in and realize I'm in a lot of trouble here. I can't defeat thirty guys—even with my sword. One of them will get past my blade and then I'm done.

My only thought is to draw them away.

I frown. I know how to do that, but I don't like it.

I circle around the area, careful to avoid any men in shadows who might be on the lookout for me. I see a couple of men here and there and take the long way around.

When I get to the far side of the pit, I move along until I find a shop that doesn't appear to have an apartment or living space in it. I quickly search around and find another one in the same area and grab some lanterns hanging nearby. A moment later, I throw a lantern through a window of each shop.

As I move back, I realize the problem. As soon as the men arrive to put out the fires, they'll see the broken windows and know right away that this is arson. On top of that, two buildings separated from one another is a sure sign that someone did it on purpose.

I only have minutes to spare.

I hide behind a pile of snow as men rush by to respond to the fires I set, then bolt down an alleyway. When I get to the pit, I find only two men guarding Roran.

I don't have much time, and I act without thinking.

I run up behind the men and shove them into the pit, hoping they'll be injured enough to give me time to get Roran out.

I grab a rope that's tied off to a large post nearby and throw the end into the pit. "Roran!" I hiss. "Roran!"

The rope begins to shake and move, and I wait. I see a hand coming up and nearly scream when I see one of the men. He grabs me and yanks as hard as he can, pulling me over the edge and into the pit.

A second later, I hit hard, knocking the wind out of me. On the side of the pit, I see the other man I pushed, holding his hand over Roran's mouth, and a knife to his throat. While I struggle to catch my breath, the man lets go of Roran and scrambles up the rope. A few seconds later, the rope itself is pulled up.

"That didn't work," Roran says with a bit of a chuckle as he holds his side and drops to the ground.

"No, it didn't." I move over to sit beside him. "I pictured it going better than that. I guess I thought the pit was deeper."

I look up. Sure enough, the edge is not all that high up. I don't think I could jump and reach the top, but it's not much farther than that.

A snowball hits me in my face, and Roran tells me this is what they do. I can only hope they don't do it all night.

An hour later, the rest of the men return. The fire is out, I gather, but they're angry. The Judge leans over the wall and screams, "Guilty! Hanging!"

"Well, at least I didn't have to endure a long, drawn-out court battle," I say with a smile.

For the next couple hours, we huddle together while the men of the town throw snow, ice, and less pleasant things at us. At one point, a shoe hits me in the back of the head, and I hear a faint voice call out, "Anyone seen ma shoe? It was right here on ma foot just a moment ago!"

When they finally grow tired of harassing us, they stand above us and laugh and chat and go on for another hour or so. I think it has to be nearly the middle of the night by the time they finally head to bed. A man is left to watch us, but it's not long before he drifts off.

"Okay," I whisper, "Plan B."

Roran rolls his eyes. "Really? You have another plan?"

"My sword."

"You gonna fight your way out tomorrow morning?"

I shake my head, stand up, and quietly draw my weapon. I drive it into the stone wall and start to work on cutting my way through. In a few moments, I've sliced through the stone and the frozen dirt, doing my best to catch any pieces and set them down gently.

Roran moves to help, and that's when I see he's hobbling. He focuses on moving all the large chunks away.

Although my sword easily slices through everything, that doesn't mean I can remove the pieces. The sword cuts straight. And a straight cut into a wall of dirt doesn't do much good for us. I manage to find a system where I cut in, then cut on an angle, allowing me to pull out chunks.

It's slower work than I'd have thought with an enchanted blade, but we're making progress. After a bit, I begin to angle upwards. I don't know which way I'm going. I hope I don't end up in a house—under someone's bed or something. That'll be hard to talk our way out of. Or in the middle of the street where we can be seen. I'm hoping for an alley. But that's unlikely.

When I reach snow and see light, I cut my way through and find we ended up in the street. Poking my head up, I see the guy left to guard us. He's facing us, but sound asleep. I climb out and pull Roran up behind me.

Quiet as we can, we move out of the street, back to the east. I try to reach the same spot I came in. I doubt any guys are guarding the road now that I've been caught, but it's not worth the risk.

We scramble up onto the rolling hills of the Talic region and make our way around toward the road. When we reach it, I feel relief flood over me. I want to cheer for joy, but then I hear a bell go off in the town. They've discovered the empty pit.

We take off running, and I grab Roran when we reach his pack. We both work to get it on him, and his sword strapped in place, then before he can take off down the road, I pull him toward the snowbank. "We can't take the road!"

Up the hill and over the top, we run as fast as we can across the snowy Talic region.

"What's wrong with the road?" Roran calls out. "It'd be a lot faster!"

"It would," I call back. He's fallen behind a bit, but I don't want to slow down. We need to move fast, and he'll have to push to keep up. "The people of the town have horses. They'll likely search along the roads first. Horses will never make it through this snow. Wait!" I say, a little unsure. "I actually don't know if horses can travel through this. I hope they can't!"

"Not all that encouraging, Draydon!"

"No, I guess not." With a laugh, I add, "All I can say is, I hope they don't catch us."

We push on as hard as we can. When I look back, I see the faint light of the town, and I think I can make out torches moving along the road. They really want to hang us!

We push on for much of the night. We can't run with the snow so deep, but if we take it slow, we can keep up the pace. At the first rays of sunlight, I catch sight of a forest, and we head that way. The wind is cold, and I could use a fire and a meal.

When we reach the trees, the sun is up. We find a nice spot, then quickly set some snares. I'm not good at it at all, but Roran actually knows nothing of this kind of thing. Rulf never taught him. We set five in various places throughout the forest, doing our best to remember where, then go light a fire. I would have lit it before we set the snares, but the risk of it spreading was too great. I don't care to lose my shelter, nor do I care to announce to the town where we are. A forest fire won't go unnoticed for miles around.

An hour later, we're warm and spread out in our bedrolls. If we can sleep, maybe we'll wake to a rabbit or two in our snares. A warm meal would be nice. And the more we can preserve the food from Marleet's estate, the better.

14

Frindor and Yune's Men

The anger boils inside.

It always boils. Every day. Every hour. Every second.

"WHAT DO YOU WANT?"

"My apologies, Captain Frindor…"

"I care nothing about your apologies!"

He wilts under my gaze. I like that. If there's one thing I enjoy in life, it's seeing men cower before me.

I'm not mad at this man for coming to give me a message. He's only doing his job. But it makes me feel good. And my anger has been my greatest weapon in life, helping me to fulfill my goal of destroying Geran's legacy.

"What is the message?"

"My Lord, King Parthun has ordered you to the throne room. He wishes to speak with you."

"What about?" I know that's not the right response, but what is this guy going to do about it? As Second Captain, I report directly to General Corter, now that Tilbur is gone. Even if someone did report me to Corter, the man likely wouldn't understand the accusation.

The man shrinks back in horror. Oh… the smile. I'm giving that smile which I'm told terrifies people.

"He…" the man begins. "King Parthun… there's… two men. Lord Yune's men… they're… he… King Parthun needs you, My Lord."

"Well, that was certainly incoherent," I growl, but then I wave the man away.

As he scurries off, I turn to make my way to the throne room. If Lord Yune's involved, I never know what to expect. The man is… devious… strange… I don't know. He's just never what I expect.

When I enter the throne room, I'm shocked to see what lies before me. I don't show any shock, of course. I'm good at hiding my emotions.

I walk farther into the throne room, soldiers stepping out of the way of the temporary Captain of the Guard, the Second Captain of the Sevordine Armies. I know it's not respect, but fear, which is exactly what I want. I don't care about respect. But to scare people… that's where it's at.

Corter is here, doing what he does best… missing the point of everything. His eyes dart every which way as if he's trying to convince everyone that he's constantly on guard, constantly aware, constantly knowing exactly what's going on at all times. A soldier comes up behind him to give him a report, and he jumps. I barely contain my scowl.

Parthun, the man I've reported to for years, sits on the throne. He looks vaguely irritated.

But it's Lord Yune whom I find surprises me. Not that he's in the throne room. He's often here. But his two guards—the ones I've bribed—kneel before the throne. It's not a kneel of respect, but of punishment. I don't know what this is about… but then again… it's Lord Yune. He's up to something. He always is.

"Frindor!" Parthun hollers, ignoring my title yet again.

"Yes, Your Majesty."

"Lord Yune has been telling me he has caught his servants relaying information to his enemies."

I give a slight bow of my head and ask, "Do we know to whom they relayed the information and what the information was?" I know they don't suspect me, or I wouldn't be standing here. Parthun doesn't care, actually, but he'd have to arrest me just to prove to the Nobles that he will respond.

"Noooo," Lord Yune says in his long, slow drawl. "These men have serrrrved my familyyyy for many yearrrrs, but I have caught them receivinnnng a bribe."

"Did you catch those from whom the bribe was received?" I ask.

He simply shakes his head. "I have brought them here to Parrrrthunnnn to ask for his judgmennnnt."

"I see." I'm glad about that. I don't want to lose any men. Finding men with the devious qualities I seek is sometimes difficult. "And what, may I ask, Your Majesty and Lord Yune, do you wish for punishment?"

Now, this is going to be interesting. If Lord Yune wants a simple execution, then I don't mind the hanging, but it's boring work. I'm hoping for something else. Something I've always wanted to do.

Parthun leans forward. "I am willing to hang them—what are their names, Lord Yune?"

"Dennerrrr and Billoooot, Parthunnnn."

"Denner and Billot. Yes, I am willing to order their execution for today at noon, if you so desire, Lord Yune."

Parthun hates Lord Yune, and I can see it in his eyes. I see the same hatred I feel every single day toward Geran's line.

Lord Yune bows low before Parthun but says, "Thank youuuu, Parthunnnn. But I do not feeeel that hanginnnng is the proper responsssse. I would prefer somethinnnng more terrifyinnnng, more horrifiiiic, somethinnnng which will send a messaaaage, somethinnnng…"

"Yes, Lord Yune," Parthun says, the exasperation clear in his voice. "I understand. What do you have in mind?"

I rarely struggle to force down a smile. I think I might get what I want!

"I wissssh for Tilburrrr's Drop. I wissssh for Tilburrrr's Pit."

I hear the Nobles in the room gasp, but I cannot keep the wicked smile from forming on my face. Ever since I first heard of Tilbur's Pit, I've wanted to see it, but I had no reason. Now I can actually throw two men in.

Denner and Billot cry out, "No, our Master! Please, Lord Yune! We have been faithful. It was just this one time. We grew greedy. Please, Lord Yune, show us mercy!"

"Quiet, swine!" Parthun screams. "I officially condemn these men to Tilbur's Pit for their crimes against the Sevordine Nobility."

I move forward and grab the men by the backs of their shirts, pulling them to their feet. They're both larger men, but their spirits are broken. They don't fight me.

I'm kind of disappointed at that, actually. I wouldn't mind pushing them around some more.

"Parthunnnn," Lord Yune says.

"Yes, Lord Yune?" Parthun replies, the frustration coming through clearly in his voice.

"I doooo not want them injurrrred. I want them to haaaave the fuuuull experience of the piiiit."

Parthun nods at me. "Ensure they are safe until they enter the pit."

I nearly growl as Lord Yune points at two of his soldiers, and they join me. I'd still be able to beat these men, but Yune's soldiers will report back.

The two men I bribed struggle, but they don't accuse me. I nod at one of my men, and he comes and gags them. I don't need them shouting out any accusations.

As I drag them out of the throne room, Lord Yune attempts to spit on them. Unsurprisingly, everything he does is slow, and his saliva ends up not gaining any distance. He wipes it off his chin as his men stumble past him.

Once out of the throne room, four of my men join me. They grab Denner and Billot and push them along. They're rough with them, but not enough to cause Yune's loyal soldiers concern as they follow along.

We make our way to the dungeons. I watch to make sure my men are careful not to injure Lord Yune's men. I don't need Yune as an enemy.

In the dungeon, we move past Lirnal's cell. Now that Tilbur's gone, I might get a run at that man. That'll be fun.

We move farther down the hall. There's another pit here. The giant spawn is in that one. It's different from Tilbur's Pit, but the oversized child should be suffering in there.

At the end of the hall is a large door, solid wood, steel bars running left to right and top to bottom. I call ahead to open it, and the men guarding the door laugh, while Denner and Billot let out moans.

We enter and then I order, "Close it."

The door slams closed, and it's the nine of us in here. Denner and Billot, my four men, Lord Yune's loyal soldiers, and me. I want to start beating these two—that'll be a lot more fun than simply throwing them in—but I can't. Not with Yune's two loyal soldiers watching me.

Before I can push them both in, one of Yune's men speaks up. "They should be lowered in. Lord Yune will not want to risk them dying when they land.

I growl at them, but they stand their ground. If Lord Yune wasn't so influential, I'd throw those two men in with Denner and Billot.

Instead, I tie a rope around them and lower them down. Once they reach the bottom, I just drop the rest of the rope in.

"Happy?" I ask Yune's two soldiers sent to observe.

The one man nods, and I order the door opened.

That was far less exciting than I had thought. I figured I'd get to beat the men and then throw their bodies into the hole. Maybe once Lord Yune's men are gone, I'll come back and pour some oil down there and follow it with a torch.

15

———•———

Ellcia and the New Arrivals

M

y Lady, this can't be good."

I examine Relin's face. He looks irritated, but I think it's genuine concern. I know where his loyalty lies—there's no doubt in my mind. He is entirely committed to Draydon. In fact, he's more committed to seeing Draydon take the throne than I think Draydon is. I know both Draydon and I would love nothing more than to run away and hide from all this.

"But they are just more refugees," I reply.

"Are they?"

I shake my head. I don't really understand what he's getting at.

"My Lady…" he begins slowly. I can tell when he's about to explain something to me that seems obvious to him. That's one of my problems. I don't easily see these little maneuvers and threats. To me, I see a problem, I solve it. That's life. But Relin… I don't know how he earned the title of The Hero of Reber's Gate—not "a" Hero, but "The" Hero of Reber's Gate—but regardless of the details, every day I spend with him lets me know this man is dangerous. Not dangerous to me, nor to Draydon. This man is dangerous to everyone who threatens his future King.

136

I take a seat and point at the chair across from me. It's inappropriate for him to sit with me while we discuss matters—the rules of court require that he stand while I sit, if I so desire. But I don't care. I'm tired. I want to sit. And I won't make him stand.

He sits, awkwardly, on the edge of the seat as if he'll need to jump up at any moment. When he speaks again, he lays it out. "Everyone who has arrived so far has come from a village. They are people who have spent their lives together. They know everyone and are related to most. That's why a lot of our people marry someone from another village. Too many in the village itself are cousins or uncles or aunts or nieces and nephews. And we tend to know the surrounding villages quite well, so, those of us from Nimville know the people from Shizzer and Deliver. In fact, my sister and her children arrived with those from Shizzer. And we know the people from Grimmer to an extent, but we barely knew the people of Port at all."

I nod. "Continue."

"We also know a lot of the independent people around, but not all of them. Some of them only show up now and then or never show their faces in the villages ever. In fact, there are those who only deal with people in Sevord City. So, some we never actually meet unless there's a crisis like a major fire. Once, years ago, a family died—all except their little son and daughter. The two children were less than five years old, but they managed to survive, and no one even knew they were alone until they were both adults, and someone happened to stop by."

"That's terrible!"

Relin frowns. "Yes, but that's not the point."

"What's the point?"

"The point is, all these people who have shown up today... we don't know them. And we don't know how many are independents from along the coast."

"Who else could they be?" I ask.

He nods slowly. "Who else indeed…" then stands and moves slowly to the door.

"No, wait! I really mean that! Who else could they be? I really don't know."

"Oh, I thought…" He looks at me awkwardly for a moment before saying, "I'm sorry, my Lady. I don't know who they are. That's the problem. They could just as easily be people from Sevord. Not all look like farmers, my Lady. Some carry themselves like soldiers. Others carry themselves like they're used to slinkin' in the shadows. What I'm saying is, we need to watch these new arrivals closely. Any one of them could be here to kill ya or the Lady Marleet or Duke Hemot."

I hate what he just told me, but I know he's right. As of the last two days, there have been families showing up, groups of people showing up, individuals showing up. All of them have stories. All of them swear fealty to Draydon. But if a man has no integrity, his sworn oath means nothing— and it never will.

We head outside. I don't plan on speaking with this new group—Nordin and Frellson are taking care of these people. It's a unique group, as they are all on horseback. Some of the groups had a mixture of those on foot, those with wagons, and those on horseback. One man even showed up riding what he called an oss-stretch or something like that. It looked like an emaciated, overly large, novelty chicken. He even had large socks on its feet and legs and a scarf around its thin neck to keep it warm in the cold wind.

Relin points to two of the men riding into town. "See those two? The ones near the back. They're soldiers. No doubt about it."

I examine them as best I can from a distance. They sit straight in the saddle, ride comfortably, and as they move, they seem to be looking at everything, taking it all in. The looks on their faces are not expressions of curiosity or wonder, but of searching for something—or someone. They do look familiar, though. I just can't place them.

What's strange about this group, too, is it's all men. None of the groups so far to arrive have been all men or all women. Every group's been a mixture because they're all coming from farms or from villages.

One of the two men in the back, the ones Relin identified as soldiers, looks in my direction, and his mouth drops open. He slaps the arm of the man next to him and points, and the other man calls out, "My Lady!"

Both men dismount and lead their horses toward me, smiles on their faces. When they come close, Relin steps in front of me and growls, "State your name and yar business!"

The older man stops, gives a small bow, and says, "I'm sorry, Sir, I…" He focuses in on Relin and whispers, "The Hero of Reber's Gate!"

Relin shakes his head and growls again. He hates that title. "I ordered ya to state your name and business. I won't ask again. Ya take another step, and I'll show ya how I earned that title!"

Both men give a respectful bow. "I apologize again, Lieutenant Relin. My name is Denner, and this is Billot. We have come to offer our protection for our Lady."

"Lady Ellcia is not yar Lady," Relin replies with a snarl.

"Lady Ellcia?" Denner's eyes shift to me, and he bows deeply. "My deepest and most sincere apology, Lady Ellcia. I did not see you. I caught sight of the Lady Marleet behind you and could see no one else. We serve her father and mother and have been sent here to protect the young Lady."

I turn around and see Marleet standing around ten paces away, dealing with what looks like a conflict between two of the dock workers. She'll be happy to have an excuse to get out of there.

I call for her, and I see her tell the two men to wait. When she gets about halfway to me, she stops, her face lights up, and she runs in a most unladylike fashion, squealing out, "You've come!"

The men bow low to her, but she just charges into them, embracing both. As I watch the three of them together, something clicks. I'm pretty sure I remember them from the castle. I think they helped us get around a bit. And… in the throne room. They put on quite the show.

When Marleet pulls back from her hug, she turns to Relin. "Relin, would you deal with the two dock workers? They're having a disagreement about a shift schedule, and they won't listen to the dock manager."

Relin growls, turns toward the men, breaks into a run, and screams out, "Ya pull me away from Lady Ellcia for some petty disagreement?"

The two men spin around and take off at a run with Relin close on their heels. For an old guy, he can move. I feel bad for the men. I fear what Relin will do when he catches them, and he will catch them, that I know for sure, but I can't deal with everything.

"Tell me how my mother and father are! And what brought you here?" Marleet asks Denner and Billot.

Denner smiles and says, "Your parents are well. They have taken every precaution to protect themselves against assassination, but the threat is real. However, they have been concerned for your safety, so they arranged to accuse us of betrayal, which allowed them to sneak us out of the castle."

My mind spins with that, but Marleet just giggles. I've heard that Lord Yune has his ways of getting things done, and he tends to always win.

"Excuse me," I say.

Both men bow to me, and Denner respectfully says, "Lady Ellcia."

"I would like to hear a report from you about the situation in the city at your earliest convenience."

They both bow again but turn to Marleet. "My Lady, when would you like us to give this report to the Lady Ellcia?"

"Right away, please."

I find that a strange interaction, but then again, I remember that these men are bound to Marleet's family. Their loyalty will need to be to the throne, but they will always seek permission from Marleet's family first.

We move off to the hall we use for meetings, or as the people call it, "Lady Ellcia's Residence," and we settle inside. It's warmed up a lot outside, as it often does this time of year, but there's still quite the chill in the air, so the warmth of the fire is welcome.

I take a seat in the chair that's been set for me when I give rulings and more. I hate it. It's comfortable, but it feels like a throne. Relin tells me there's a reason it feels that way. It's because the people see me as their ruler until Draydon returns.

I first require a vow of fealty from each of them to Draydon, which they happily give and even inform me that they've already given such a vow before Lord Yune. When they finish, I explain the arrangement in Freond and how I have been appointed to lead in this area and lead among the Nobles, such as Lady Marleet and Duke Hemot.

When they tell us of what is going on in the city, I'm pleased to hear that the Royal Court knows very little of what's happening here in the north. There is suspicion that we have a bit of a navy as some of Parthun's fleet has not returned to Sevord, but no one knows anything for sure.

Parthun himself, however, has grown erratic and paranoid, threatening Nobles and has arrested countless people. He knows Draydon is alive, but believes Tilbur is going to assassinate him.

Lord Yune, of course, knows we've headed north. He had hoped we would settle in with the northern tribes, but Denner and Billot traveled the coast in case we stopped at a point earlier. Even on their journey here, it was a while before they learned anything of what was going on.

"How did you arrange to leave the city?" I ask.

"The Lord Yune," Denner answers, "accused us of betrayal and brought us before Parthun, insisting that the only punishment worthy of our crime was Tilbur's Pit."

I shiver at the thought. Everyone knows Tilbur's Pit is a death sentence, but not so simple as a hanging or any other form of execution. It's a pit in which criminals are thrown. Most break bones when they land and simply moan until they starve to death. Those who survive the fall often battle it out in the darkness throughout a series of caves with solid stone walls. It's nothing but a nightmare.

"How did you survive?" I ask.

Denner and Billot both smile. "Tilbur's Pit is not a punishment, my Lady." He pauses and says, "Although I know you to be trustworthy, I must inform you that this information is incredibly secret. No one can know this."

I smile. "You don't have to worry. The only one I will tell will be Prince Draydon."

He smiles and bows. "As I said, Tilbur's Pit is not a punishment. It is a shallow pit. The pit opens to a single cave which is cut through the rock, leading out of the city. The pit is only used for those to whom Captain Tilbur wishes to provide a means of escape.

I close my eyes and try to take that in. Tilbur's Pit has always terrified me. I vaguely remember other children telling me scary stories about it. And all along, Tilbur was using it to rescue people.

As for Draydon, both Denner and Billot are surprised he's not here, and they both wonder where he could have gone. Aside from south, the only options most people would be aware of would be to head north, which leads to people outside the nation. Those farther north are often less than friendly to the Sevordine Royals. The other option would be to try to circle the cliffs to reach the Talic Region, but that journey is dangerous, the land is desolate, and it's really far. Few people have made the journey as there's a lack of water, food, or anything up there.

When I'm finished speaking with the two men, Marleet comes close and gives them each another hug, then tells them she wants to introduce them properly to Hemot. The three head out, leaving me alone to think through all I've heard.

It's a lot to take in, but I am glad to know what's going on back home. Parthun is a dangerous man. It's difficult to predict what he might do, as he is very devious.

The door opens, and I turn to look. I don't know the four men standing there, but that's no surprise. Thousands of people now call Freond their home.

I stand and smile. "How may I help you?"

"My Lady," the man in front says with a kind look in his eye. "We have come to petition you for living quarters."

I shake my head. "I'm sorry, but I do not personally assign anyone living quarters. That is something Frippolee and his wife arrange."

The men bow, and the one in the back closes the door. Something's not right. I don't understand why the guards allowed these four men in this room without following them in.

They each take a few steps toward me and add, "Yes, my Lady, we understand. But we are simple men. We do not believe he will consider our needs." They've all taken another two steps. This is all wrong. "Would you, my Lady, speak to him on our behalf?"

I take a step back and am about to call out for help, when the men lunge for me. I barely get out a squeak before a hand goes over my mouth, and I hit the ground, my head crashing against the floor. Lights flash before my eyes as my world goes dark.

I awake to a splitting headache, and a groan escapes my lips before I can catch myself or even make sense of what's going on. I'm cold—very cold—and my hands are bound behind my back. My whole upper body swings back and forth, and my legs feel numb.

I hear voices. I can't see anything. Something's over my head, and something else—something gross—is packed in my mouth.

I try to squirm, but someone has a good hold on me. I hear their voices, laughing, but they're also gasping for air. They're running.

I bounce along on someone's shoulder. I'm guessing he's one of the men who attacked me a moment ago. I squirm and shift, trying to knock myself off onto the ground, but something slams into the side of my head.

"Quiet!" someone orders. I don't recognize the voice, but I guess I only heard one of those men speak.

I hope someone knows where I am and is coming after me. I think through what this could be about. Kidnapping of a royal or noble is usually for money or pressure. Draydon doesn't have any money, so it's pressure. They want to force Draydon to do something. That means these are Parthun's men.

And the fact that the man told me to be quiet might just mean he finds me annoying, but it could also be that noise will help other people find me.

I scream as loud as I can inside the bag over my head. Another fist slams into my temple, but I just let loose again.

The man carrying me picks up speed, but it's not because of my screaming. Something else is going on.

"Run!" someone hisses.

"I'm trying!" another man replies.

"Not hard enough!"

"You wanna carry her?"

With my splitting headache, bouncing around, slung over a man's shoulder, this is no fun at all. My head feels like it's about to explode, but then the man drops me. No... that's not right. He doesn't just drop me. He's fallen.

"Grab her!" a man hisses. I think that's the man who spoke to me back in Freond. "They're almost here!"

I'm hoping rescue is on the way. It's likely Hemot, Nordin, maybe Frellson, and a bunch of other soldiers. If they catch us... oh... I so hope they catch us.

I scream again, but I can't help but think no one can hear me, other than the men who kidnapped me. The gag, the sack over my head... it'll muffle all the sounds.

I struggle and squirm as I'm lifted into the air, but it's not enough. The man who has me is strong. I don't think I'm making it easy on him, but I'm certainly not making it hard.

I hear them now... not the men... but whoever is chasing us. It's a strange sound. I think... it's women. No... children. No... men... boys... girls? I don't know.

"Over here!" one of the men growls.

We shift direction, then shift again. I feel branches scraping across my back, and something across my side. We're in a forest. The forest is just to the southeast of Freond. It's big, so we could already have traveled far.

I squirm some more and scream as loud as I can. Twisting hard, I manage to shift off to the side, and I fall for a moment before they catch me, and then back onto the shoulder I go.

I hear more of whoever's chasing me. It's not just men or women... it's a lot of voices. It's a crowd.

The men carrying me... I hear their breathing... they're not just out of breath. They're scared. Really, really scared.

"Down here!" a man whispers.

A new voice breaks out of the crowd chasing us. A woman cries. "I see them! Over there!"

The crowd breaks into a roar... they're angry, that's for sure. I hope it's not at me, because they don't sound like anyone could stop them from anything they wanted to do.

"RUN!"

I feel myself crash down onto the cold, frozen ground. No one touches me for a few seconds, then multiple hands grab me again, and I squirm and twist and scream.

I feel hands on my throat, and I do my best to pull away. Smelly hands. Whoever has me, stinks.

The rope around my throat loosens, and the sack comes off.

Faces... all around me. I don't recognize any of them, but they look wild... enraged... hungry...

I pull back, but there's more of them behind me. My hands come loose, so do my feet, and I scramble up. My head hurts too much, and the world spins. I fall, but hands catch me.

"My Lady!" one of the women screeches. Her voice... it's like she's trying to cut through to my soul with that... that shrill voice! "My Lady! Are you injured?"

"I'm... yes." I touch the back of my head where I hit the floor in the hall. A glance at my fingers reveals blood.

Some of the faces I recognize. They're the people… they're my people! From Freond! One of them… oh… it's a young woman I worked with in Hella's Kitchen.

"Help me to my feet," I order.

Far too many hands grab my arms, the back of my cloak. One person even tries to grab my neck, but someone slaps his hand away. When I'm on my feet, despite the fact that I'm a lot shorter than many people here, I see there has to be a hundred or more surrounding me.

"The men…" I begin.

"Don't worry about tha men who kidnapped ya, my Lady," an older woman with few teeth says with a shake of her head. "Our men are dealing with them."

"I need them alive."

The woman gives me a strange look, then nods. "Well, that's gonna be a problem, but I'll see what I can do."

She hollers out, "Someone go make sure they don't kill 'em all. The Lady wants to kill 'em herself."

I shake my head. "No, that's not it. I need to find out who sent them."

"Don't you worry about that, my Lady. They'll get that information out of 'em."

"Will they still be alive after?"

The woman gives me another strange look. "They kidnapped Prince Draydon's bride-to-be." She shakes her head. "I don't think any of those men will live to see tomorrow. They'll spill all their secrets just to put an end to what your people will do to 'em."

I try to protest, but they just keep smiling at me, and some even pet my hair. I'm having trouble speaking. My head spins, and my thoughts are slow and confusing.

I think it takes about an hour to get out of the forest, and once we do, I find a cart waiting for me along with somewhere around a thousand people. Some of my soldiers are here as well. I see many more racing in our direction.

When I get into the cart and can sit again, I find my mind clears a bit. Someone comes up into the cart next to me and begins to tend to my wound. Someone else wraps a blanket around my shoulders. I didn't realize how much I was shaking from the cold until I feel a bit of warmth.

When we reach the hall, a fire roars in the hearth, and a hot cup of tea sits ready for me. A moment later, Marleet, Denner, and Billot, along with Hemot and Relin, burst into the room. I don't really feel like being touched by anyone right now, but Marleet and Hemot wrap their arms around me and hold me. I want to push them away, then I think about how much I appreciate the warmth and snuggle in.

When they let go, I ask, "How did you find me? How did… the people…" It's still hard to speak.

Marleet's face brightens up. "It was Hemot!"

I turn to Hemot and examine him for a moment. I have a bit of trouble believing he was the one who managed to send a mob of villagers to my rescue. But then again, perhaps anyone else who tried to rescue me would send soldiers.

"How did you do it?" I ask.

Hemot smiles in his awkward way and then shrugs his shoulders. Sometimes he's quite willing to brag. Other times, not so much. This is obviously the "not-so-much" moment.

Instead, Marleet explains at high-speed. "Your guards were killed. They were found behind a pile of wood not far away. Frellson was the senior officer in the area, and he sent out search parties immediately, but then Hemot showed up, and the people had gathered. A lot of them! Everyone was upset."

"What did Hemot do?"

Marleet smiles again and says, "He just called out for everyone to head off in every direction as fast as they could until they found you."

I open my mouth to say something, but then find I have no words. It was definitely a Hemot-type-plan, but it was brilliant. I smile and say, "Thanks Hemot."

A noise outside catches my attention, and Relin leads two men into the room. I try not to look at their hands. I wish they'd washed before they came in. I'm guessing they're some of the men who found the guys who kidnapped me.

"My Lady," the one man says and bows low before me. "We found the men and interrogated them."

"Are they still alive?" I ask.

The men look at their hands for a moment, then put them behind their backs. "I'm sorry, my Lady. They did not survive the questioning."

I close my eyes and try to calm my heart, but can't. Instead, I open my eyes, do my best to give a gracious smile and nod for them to carry on.

"They were sent by the traitor to kidnap you. They did not know why, but they suspected it was so Parthun could use my Lady against Prince Draydon. They informed us there are other men down the coast with a small boat, and I sent around three dozen men to find them."

I close my eyes again and try to think about how to proceed. I'm still so shaken by all that's happened.

"Thank you," Marleet says. "The Lady Ellcia appreciates your loyalty and your kindness. We are forever grateful to you and the people of Freond for your kindness towards us in this difficult time."

The man gives a shy smile as if he's just received the greatest compliment of his life and bows before both he and the other man leaves.

One thing's for sure, we are not as safe from Parthun here as I would have hoped. That, and Parthun definitely knows I'm up here. At least if the men down the coast are caught, we'll be able to keep the traitor from knowing what all is going on up here amongst the Northern Tribes.

For the time being, anyway.

"I disagree!" Marleet snarls.

I've rarely seen Marleet like this. Now that I think of it, this is definitely the angriest I've ever seen her. In fact, I didn't think she could get this mad!

She comes close and pokes me hard on the shoulder. "You think you can just throw people around like they're just a means to an end? You think everyone should just obey you? You really think Draydon is going to let you boss him around when he's King? You think you can run the whole country? How long before the people see that you're willing to sacrifice any of them just to accomplish your goals?"

She spins around and storms across the room. Relin stands near the door, pretending like he doesn't hear anything, while Nordin has the most intense look I've ever seen on anyone's face as he aggressively tackles a hangnail. Hella's here as well. She's… dusting. She wasn't dusting a moment ago. Now she's wiping an imaginary mark off the wall. Oh, and now she's using her own spit to scrub away at it.

Marleet comes at me again, this time her face is beet red. Her hands shake, but she stops a few steps before she reaches me, crossing her arms and pursing her lips. After waiting just a moment, she says, "If you do this, I will never speak to you again."

I shake my head. If I hadn't just been rescued from a nearly successful kidnapping, I would feel more compassion. But I simply don't. Marleet won't carry through on her threat. That I know for sure. And this is the right thing to do.

"Marleet," I begin.

"Lady Marleet!" she growls.

"Lady Marleet." I take a deep breath and try to calm my irritation. I'm not mad. I'm just irritated. Very irritated. So irritated it feels a lot like being mad. "Lady Marleet. It doesn't matter what you say. This is the decision I've made, and I stand by it. Hemot…"

"Duke Hemot!"

"I'm sorry, Lady Marleet. Duke Hemot, the Coastal Duke, is assigned to the Geran. He is going to act as Prince Draydon's emissary to the Southern Coast. He leaves tomorrow at dawn. This is not up for discussion. This is a decision that has already been made."

"You don't have to send him!"

"I don't," I admit. "I could send any number of people, but the risk is the same. However, if he is to function as the Coastal Duke, as we expect him to, then he will need to be heavily involved in this mission." I step closer to Marleet and put my hands on her shoulders. She doesn't pull away. She's just scared. "The southern communities need to know they have a Crown Prince ready to take the throne from the tyrant, Parthun, and they need to hear this from their Duke. Marleet…" I come closer and lower my voice. "Hemot is capable of far more than any of us give him credit for." To be honest, I'm not sure I believe that, but I hope it's true.

Her bottom lip quivers. "But it'll be really dangerous. And he'll be gone a long time."

I nod. "It will. And he will. But we are all risking our lives. We are all committed to this, even to the point of death. I've committed myself to that point. I know you have. Hemot hasn't said it, but he would die a thousand times over for Draydon."

She wraps her arms around herself and almost seems to shrink before me. In a small voice, she asks, "Then why can't I go with him?"

"Because I need you here. I desperately need your help."

The door opens at that moment, and Hemot comes in. He stomps his feet to knock off some of the slush, swinging the door closed behind him. Marleet turns and walks to the fireplace, stands in front of it, and pretends to warm herself. I catch sight of her wiping tears from her eyes.

"Hem… Duke Hemot," I say, remembering the title. It's strange to call him a Duke, but I'll get used to it. "Thank you for coming. I have an assignment for you."

Hemot smiles. I know what he's thinking. He's hoping it's something dangerous. In his most formal voice, which sounds like he's mocking me, but… he's not. It's just Hemot. He's doing his best. In his most formal voice, he says, "Yes, Lady Ellcia. I am forever at your service," following it up with a deep bow.

"I'm sending you south again, but this time you'll go to the Southern villages. Prince Draydon and I planned this before he left. You are to reach all the major centers to spread the word and seek vows of fealty, then order them to assemble at the capital, two weeks before the first day of Spring."

His eyes nearly pop out of his head. "Wow!" He lets out a laugh and glances at Marleet, seemingly unaware of how upset she is. "We'd love to do that!"

Marleet spins around and points her finger at him. Raising her voice, she snarls, "Really? Do you know how long it'll take you? You'll have to go far out to sea to get around Sevord City. You won't be able to take a fleet with you, so if you go down, you'll have nothing but lifeboats. If you're attacked, no one will come to rescue you! Do you have any idea how dangerous it's going to be? And we have no idea how the Southern Coast will take to you. They might arrest you and hang you for treason! They might skin you alive! They might hand you over to Parthun!"

The more she speaks, the bigger Hemot's smile grows. Turning back to me, he says, "This sounds great! We'll do it!"

Marleet turns back to the fire with a frustrated groan, but Hemot doesn't appear to notice. He tries to make eye contact with Relin, Nordin, and Hella, but none of them will meet his eyes.

"We?" I ask. "Who do you mean? You don't know who I'm sending you with."

"Well, me and Marleet, of course," Hemot replies. "I mean… if you're sending me away for that long, we'll need to go together. I had to spend three months apart from her a little while ago. I'm not doing that again. She almost ended up married. I can't risk it."

I catch sight of a small smile on Marleet's face. She turns to him, and in Hemot style, he completely misses the expression on her face and even the tears on her cheeks. Stepping up next to her, Hemot slips his arm around her waist and says, "When do we leave?"

I shake my head. Why is it so difficult dealing with Hemot? "I'm sorry, Duke Hemot. The Lady Marleet must remain here. This is a trip you will have to take alone." I move up close to them. "I know this will be hard. In fact, I don't expect we will meet again until the day we all arrive at Sevord, but this is necessary."

Hemot frowns as Marleet just wraps her arms around him. I can't believe I'm sending him away on something so dangerous. In that moment, I realize for the first time that if he gets hurt or… worse… I… I could be sending him to his death. This could be our last time together.

Hemot looks down at Marleet. She looks so small and so much like the little girl I grew up with, not the young Noblewoman I've come to rely on over the recent weeks. And what's even stranger is that Hemot looks old and mature.

I think maybe I need some sleep.

"Can we do this?" Marleet asks in a small voice.

Hemot nods. "I think so. I don't want to, but… this is the cost of putting Draydon on the throne. We all have a part to play, don't we? Isn't that what you keep telling me? Maybe this is our part."

Yep. At the moment, Hemot's the mature one. I definitely need some sleep.

Turning to Relin, I call him forward. "Relin, you'll take the Geran under Duke Hemot's lead."

I feel like I should say more, but… to be honest, that's it. I turn it over to Nordin, as he understands all of it a lot more than I do. I've only been out to sea a couple times before, and even then, it was well within sight of land. And, aside from waves, we faced no danger—well, aside from canons that one time.

I leave them to their discussion and take a seat. With the heat of the fire and the quiet conversation, it's not long before I'm sound asleep in my chair.

16

Draydon and the Mountain

e haven't found rabbits for a few days. I wish we still had Roran's crossbow with us. Plenty of birds around, but they're hard to catch.

We have a lot of traveling food left, but we also have a long way to go. I think we've almost reached the Spellcaster. It's only taken us eleven days, but once we deal with him, we'll have to travel back to Haner. That's a six-day hike. We have enough food for about three. My hope is we can get out of the mountains and reach the area of the Talic where groves of trees pop up here and there. If we can, we should be able to find some food.

Otherwise, we'll starve.

Roran's cuts and bruises from Milter have healed up somewhat, although he still looks pretty beat up. We could use some medicine, but we just simply have none. I'm hoping he doesn't get an infection.

"Where do we head up?" Roran asks.

I point to a section a little farther on. "Right over there."

It's hard to know for sure where we came down, but I'm pretty sure that's it. When we came off the mountain, I was distracted by some big things. On top of that, it was still late summer or early fall. So, there was no snow in this area. But I'm pretty sure that's the spot.

"Check Hob's bracelet," I say.

Roran pulls it out. It's not much to look at—just a gold bracelet with some jewels on it. I'm guessing it's worth a lot, just from the standpoint of the gold and jewels, but I've never had an eye for that kind of thing.

The bracelet is small, and just barely fits over Roran's hand, but right now he holds it. As he does, a small diamond shaped section, attached to the bracelet by a gold chain, jumps up and points east.

That's the direction of the Spellcaster.

We head up the mountain at the point where I think we came down months ago. We check the bracelet often in this area, as I'm afraid that the Spellcaster will go through one of those doorways and disappear, ending up anywhere in the world. I don't want to get to the cave and find he's been gone for hours or more.

Climbing the mountain is, of course, much harder and slower going than coming down a few months ago. We drink a lot of water in this area, which is too bad because if we need more, we have to melt it, which is not easy without a fire.

When we settle in for the night in a cave, we pull out some of the wood we've brought with us and light a fire, warming ourselves and melting some snow for drinking water.

"So, let's talk it all through," I say. We've gone over most of this a couple times already, but there's one part— the actual killing part—that I don't think I want to do.

"All right. Here's what we know," Roran begins. "The Spellcaster is the only one who can cancel the enchantment. If he won't do it willingly, the only option is to kill him. I think we're both pretty convinced he won't cancel it, and even if he does, he might try to enchant us both at a later time."

I frown. Not because I disagree, but because I agree with it all and don't like any of it.

Roran continues. "We know your armor protects you from enchantments, but I don't have anything like that, so he could enchant me like he enchanted Marleet, Ellcia, and Hemot. If I'm enchanted, you will have to move quickly to kill him before the new enchantment I've been placed under makes me do something to stop you."

"But," I say, raising an idea that hadn't hit me until now, "you have the ring and the medallion. They seem to cancel enchantments, so whatever he puts on you might cancel right away, or at least be easy to overcome."

"But if it overloads the ring and medallion, and they fail, you might be in a lot of trouble. What if he gives me super strength or something?"

That's a scary thought. "Can he do that?"

Roran shrugs. "Some Spellcasters obviously made the trolls, and they're super strong. What if he does something like that to me? If the ring and medallion fail, you'll have to move fast!"

He's right. Because whatever happens, I can't hurt Roran. Doing that will kind of throw away the entire reason we're here.

"Wait," Roran says. The look on his face suggests he's deep in thought. "You said he knew Marleet was there when you guys arrived, right?"

"Yeah."

"Well, he didn't even know who the rest of you were. Maybe he didn't know you were even there until you spoke."

"Okay." That's good information, but I'm not sure where he's going with this.

"I just assumed that the Spellcaster would know we were coming, but maybe he has no idea. Especially with you, with your armor. In fact, even if he now has some spells or something set to warn him of our presence, your armor might hide you and my ring and medallion might cancel what it's doing. We might be able to surprise him!"

"Oh, that's good," I say. "That'd be really good." I smile at Roran. I'm pleased with that possibility. "Okay, so we will stick to the plan of sneaking in, but we will be as quiet as we can in the hopes that he won't know we're coming. We'll go in and try to force him to cancel the enchantment, but if he doesn't, we'll have to kill him."

We agree. At first, Roran had seemed totally against the idea of trying to get the man to cancel it, but the closer we get, the more he realizes we would rather not have to kill the man. We're just not sure we'll have a choice.

The medallion has helped a lot, but the power of it, just like the ring, wanes in time. The colors in the medallion, which used to be bright red and blue and yellow, are now dull and look washed out. The ring itself has spiderwebbed even more than it was before Lord Yune's estate, and the black streaks are all back. I don't know how long we have until they both fail completely.

Roran's doing well. A few bouts of anger and irritation here and there, but overall, okay. I wonder if having both items protecting him might be helping enough that even though they're failing, he can manage better.

After we've eaten, we climb into our bedrolls for the night. I think it's going to be cold.

And it is. I wake up a few hours later. The fire is just about out, and I'm shivering. This far up the mountain in the middle of winter is not a warm place! Even in this cave, it's absolutely freezing!

Roran's doing his best to pull his blankets close. He's shivering as much as I am.

"You want to use more wood?" he asks.

"We'll need it for the trip down. We don't have enough to use more now and still survive the return."

"If we freeze tonight," Roran says, "there won't be a next time."

He's right. And I'm so cold. I think freezing is actually a real possibility. Without the sun, this is bitter!

"Let's do it."

With my blanket still around me, I pull out a few of the small logs I have in my pack. The only reason I have room for firewood is because we've eaten a lot of our food already.

I get the wood placed on the coals of the fire and try to bring it back to life. It's cold enough, I think the fire is really struggling to catch, but I have a bit of oil and add it in—just enough to get it going.

The fire burns brightly and we both warm up. When we go to sleep, we remain sitting, leaning against a rock, side by side, hoping the warmth of our bodies helps get us through the night.

The next morning, the fire has just enough heat to help melt some more water for us to drink so we don't have to dip into our waterskins at all. We pack up, cooling off the last of the unburnt logs, hoping that what little we have will help. I'm not looking forward to a night with no heat!

When we exit the cave, I'm shocked by the temperature! There's no wind, which is really nice, but the snow feels odd—extra crunchy under my feet. And the air… any exposed skin feels like it freezes instantly. We ensure that our ears and hands and more are covered and resume our journey up the mountain.

The sun hasn't crested the peaks yet, which means we don't have the sun's warmth, but it also means we don't have the light reflecting off the snow. That's been one of the difficult parts of this journey so far. Moving across the Talic Region with the glare of the sun off the snow has given me a headache just about every day.

We push on for the entire morning and into the afternoon before we find the cave. The bracelet has been a great help, but the snow up here is deep. I'm so cold. I just want off the mountain!

No, I just want to be back at Marleet's manor house. That's what I really want. I want to warm myself by the fire and eat warm food and have a warm drink and…

I hit the snow hard and scramble back to my feet. Roran's staring at me. I'm not sure if he's laughing or smiling, as I can only see his eyes with the scarf covering his mouth and nose. Even if I could see the rest of his face, it'd probably be frozen in place, so it wouldn't matter.

"Daydreaming?" Roran asks in his muffled voice.

"Yeah."

"Thinking of warm things? Like a fireplace with a hot meal and maybe some of that chocolate drink?"

I laugh and nod. "You got it."

"Me too. I almost fell back there because of it." He holds up his hand with the bracelet. "It says we're on the right track."

"Good. I hope it's not much farther."

When we reach it, I don't recognize the cave at all from the outside. I'm not even sure I looked at it as we left, but I recognize the area, and when we step inside, I remember everything, including the turn not far away.

"It's warmer up ahead," I say. "Around this bend it's not so windy. We can light our torch."

When we get the torch lit, we carefully move forward. We've decided that when we see his light from his workshop, we're going to set our torch down. We don't want to give him any warning at all.

The way through the caves here is simple—there are no turns, but it is far. When we came through here the last time, I was leading an enchanted Ellcia and Hemot. I'm glad Roran's enchantment doesn't make him hug me all the time.

"Wait!" Roran signals me to hold and steps forward a little. Turning back to me, he tells me to hold the torch back around the last bend. When I do, I see it as well. Light ahead. Hard to see with the torch in hand.

We get a little closer, walking as quietly as we can, and set down the torch, careful to keep it in a position where it will continue to burn. I don't want to be left without a light in these caves. We also shed our packs and extra layer of clothing. It's warm enough in here that we don't have to worry about that kind of thing. What we want is to be light on our feet for what's coming next.

17

Draydon and the Spellcaster

pproaching slowly and quietly, I smell something similar to what I smelled the last we were here. I think that was the potion that put the others under the Spellcaster's power.

I grab Roran's arm and point to his head. That was the signal we arranged to ask whether it was affecting him. He nods, letting me know it is, but signals that he will be okay.

We reach the Spellcaster's lair and peer around the corner. Sure enough, the man is here. He's sitting in a chair with his back to us. I wonder if he's sleeping.

When I hear a page turn, I realize he has some kind of book in front of him. So far, I believe we've come in unnoticed.

I nod to Roran, and we quietly take a step out, but I feel something snag on my ankle and a loud crashing sound nearly makes me yell. The Spellcaster jumps to his feet, spinning around, terror on his face.

"You!" he screams. "Caric! Draydon! Whoever you are!" He takes a quick glance at Roran and bares his teeth. "You're mine! I own you, but... something... something's stopping my spell!"

Roran charges forward, but trips on the same wire that caught my foot. Some kind of alarm or something. It's definitely effective.

Roran goes down, and I pull my ankle out of the tangled mess at my feet. Leaping over Roran, I go for the man. Despite his age, he moves fast.

I draw my sword and run after him. This little cave is small, but it's big enough for him to scramble around to get away from me.

I see what he's after—he's heading for a shelf. I didn't quite remember this detail before, but the man had waved a tiny wooden statue at the wall, opening up the doorway through the rock.

I see the statue, and he's almost there!

I jump and grab the man. My sword clatters to the ground, slicing through whatever it hits and lodging in the rock wall not far away.

The Spellcaster twists around in my arms and slaps me in the face, but before he can hurt me too much, I roll and do my best to throw him away from the shelf.

I scramble toward the rock wall and grab my sword, then run to the shelf, bringing my blade down on the statue. When I hit it, slicing it in two, I'm blinded for a moment by a bright flash that sends me staggering back.

I can't see a thing, but I crash into something behind me. I'm guessing it's another shelf as I hear tons of glass— likely bottles—crash to the ground.

I hear grunts and another crash. Roran… he's back on his feet.

Blinking rapidly, I try to get my sight back. I'm starting to see clearly again, although I'm dizzy. Roran's wrestling with the Spellcaster. The man's fighting hard, but Roran's teeth are bared, and he looks like he wants to… well… it doesn't look good.

Roran pulls out his knife and drives it into the man's chest, but the response is not at all what Roran wanted. The Spellcaster just laughs and pushes Roran back. Pulling the knife out of his chest, the man leaps on Roran and starts screaming, "What's stopping me? What are you using? What's in the way of my spell?"

As I pull myself to my feet, trying to get my balance back, the man slaps and hits and bites as he searches Roran, checking his hair, his ears, and more. In the end, he grabs Roran's hand and screams, "My father's ring! You're using my father's ring against me! How dare you!"

He grabs it and pulls, but Roran makes a fist and fights back. I stumble toward them, but whatever happened when I cut that statue has really thrown me off.

The Spellcaster releases Roran's fist and grabs his face, one hand on each cheek as he chants, louder and louder. I don't understand the words, but I know it's not good. I reach the man, grabbing him by the back of his cloak, and try to yank him off, but the man swings his fist around and connects with my jaw, sending me back into the broken shelf behind me.

I recover faster now, but I'm too late to stop the spell. I hear the ring shatter—it's loud and there's a sound like a rushing wind as it breaks.

Roran screams and struggles, but not as hard as when we took off the ring a couple weeks ago.

"What?" the Spellcaster growls. "Something else? Something else holds me back! What is it? What are you wearing? What are you wearing? WHAT ARE YOU WEARING?"

He goes at Roran, trying to pull his armor off. Roran's eyes are unfocused as he swings his fists at the Spellcaster, but not hard, and even if he manages to connect, it certainly won't stop the man.

My ears ache with the sound of the ring's destruction, but I charge forward again.

"The medallion! That was mine! How dare you…"

I crash into the Spellcaster, and we roll on the ground. My back hits something hard, but I concentrate. It can't actually hurt me while I'm wearing my armor.

The Spellcaster gets on top of me, but I get my legs in between us and kick with all my might, sending him crashing into his chair, breaking it into pieces.

Leaping to my feet, I go for my sword. Terror floods my heart as I realize it's not in its sheath. I lost it… when I fell… after destroying the statue.

I rush over to the area by the broken shelves. I don't see it at first, but then I catch sight of the hilt, sticking up in a pile of broken bottles. I grab it, sliding the blade out of the floor, and rush back toward the Spellcaster, shoving it back into its sheath. I've learned to keep it there to protect myself, and only draw it when I need it.

The Spellcaster is back on Roran, who looks like he has no idea what's going on. The man's trying to get the medallion, but Roran, despite the confusion on his face, fights as best he can, trying to keep the chain around his neck.

I wrap my arms around the Spellcaster and pull him up, throwing him against the wall. When he spins around, his face is red, and his teeth are bared, but I slam my shoulder into his chest, stunning him while I draw my blade.

A moment later, my left fist grips his cloak, while the tip of my blade hovers close to his heart.

The Spellcaster's face breaks out in a grin. "Caric," he says in a sweet voice, "you don't actually think a knife or sword can kill me, do you? Didn't you see what Roran's blade did… or didn't do?"

He laughs at me and touches the blade of my sword to push it away, but instantly yanks his hand back, blood on his finger. "How…" His face fills with shock. "How? How is this possible? What… wait…" His eyes widen, and he cries out, "Astamatiti? Your father's… I thought it was lost!"

I bring the blade in closer. He can't stop me. The slightest movement forward with the blade will kill him. And there's no spell that will work on me.

"And yet…" the Spellcaster says and smiles. "And yet… Here you have Astamatiti, the sword you know can kill me, and yet…" He laughs again. "I know you, Caric. I have learned about you since you came to see me last. You are kind. You are careful. You have a conscience. Not like many men. You have a conscience that stops you from doing things…" He laughs again. "Things like this."

The man's gaze shifts, and he says, "Roran, do you remember who I am? You remember you are not to harm me, right? You remember that you must obey me, right?"

Roran's voice comes out weak, but clear. "Yes."

"No, Roran!" I call out. "Fight it! You still have the medallion. Fight it!"

I know I can drive the blade into the man and put an end to it. I know I must. But… I just can't. When I think about it, my arm won't move. I don't want to just stab him.

I feel Roran's left arm slide around my neck, and he slowly pulls back. He's choking me, but I manage to say again, "Roran! Please! Fight it!"

"I'm trying, Draydon." His voice is just above a whisper. "I just can't stop my arm."

The Spellcaster is laughing now. Hysterical laughter. "Kill him, Roran! Kill him! He won't hurt you. I'll take care of you. Kill him!"

I try again to drive my sword forward, but I hesitate yet again. The blade just sits there at his chest. It's gotten close enough at times to have cut his cloak, and I even see a little blood there. But I can't…

"My left arm is yours," Roran says, squeezing his arm tighter around my neck.

"Yes," the Spellcaster says. "And your right arm. Now draw your knife and find a spot on Caric that does not have armor."

"No," Roran whispers. "My left arm is yours. My right arm… it's mine!"

That's when I feel Roran's other hand on the elbow of my arm holding the sword. He shoves as hard as he can, and the blade drives through the Spellcaster's chest and right into the wall.

Roran lets go and collapses behind me. I rush to him and grab his shoulders. "Roran! Are you okay?"

He doesn't respond at first, and I shake him. "Roran!"

His eyes are closed, but a smile breaks out on his face. He lets out a little laugh as tears stream down his cheeks. "I'm free!"

"It worked?"

I look back up to the Spellcaster and pull back in shock as his body disintegrates into dust and ash, leaving my sword stuck in the rock wall.

Turning back to Roran, I see his eyes are open now. "It's not there. I don't feel it. It's not telling me to give up the throne. Not telling me to love Marleet. Not telling me to obey Parthun."

Okay, the Marleet part was weird, but I let that go. "You're really free?"

He stares directly into my eyes. "It's gone. It's fully gone."

He sits up and pulls the medallion off, letting it hit the floor of the cave. Standing up, he stretches his arms out and spins around, laughing. "I'm free!"

But then I smell smoke.

I turn around. All the books on the shelves have a small wisp of smoke drifting up from them. A few seconds later, one of the books bursts into flame, followed by another, then all of them.

"We have to get out of here!" I holler above the noise of the raging fire and shattering bottles. "He's set some kind of spell to burn this place down."

I grab the medallion and shove it in my pocket, then grab my sword out of the wall, and we start toward the exit. Halfway there, I stop. "Just wait a moment."

I rush back to the chair and slice it into a few pieces. "Grab them!" I order, then cut up one of the shelves that's not burning, filling my arms with wood.

As we run out, we're choking on the smoke, but we have firewood for tonight. That'll be a lot nicer than freezing.

Once we have our extra layer of clothing back on and our packs on our backs, we take our torch and move back through the cave. The smoke still makes it hard to breathe, but it's easier the farther we get from the flames. I'm guessing this cave is not only the route to get out but also the only route for the smoke to take.

When we round the bend near the exit, the wind blows out our torch, and we rush out to the mountainside, breathing in the fresh, but cold air. We take the time to load up the new firewood in our packs, and with smiles on our faces, start down the side of the mountain.

We've accomplished our mission. Now, all we have to do is take back the throne of Sevord.

18

Draydon and the Return

We awake the next morning, cold and ready to move on. We've made it most of the way down the mountain, and the temperature wasn't quite as low last night as the night before. Plus, we had plenty of firewood.

But it's still cold.

Roran, however, is happy. I'm not sure he's stopped smiling since we left the cave.

He actually wants me to throw away the medallion. He thinks I'm holding on to it in case he needs it. Truthfully, there is a bit of worry in me that there might be some of the enchantment still holding on, but the main reason I'm keeping it is it seems like a medallion like that could come in handy one day. Maybe not today, but something that cancels enchantments? That's worth keeping!

We make sure our fire is out, not that there's anything around here that it could spread to, and move out of the small cave we've used for the night.

When we get to the bottom of the mountain, we head north. Something inside me is curious about the caves where my Uncle Lirnal and the other rebels stayed for many years. I wonder if it's completely cleaned out or if some people have moved in there. I can't help but think the cave system is going to be used for bad stuff if it's not watched closely. It's quite the network, perfect to hide an army of soldiers, or an army of thieves.

But that's something to worry about another day.

We spend the next few days traveling north. We pass the giant I killed months ago, and I try to ignore it. Although, it's interesting to see that it still looks almost the same. I guess no animals will eat it, and for whatever reason, it just doesn't seem to want to break down.

When we eventually reach the road to Haner, we turn west and make our way along that route. We haven't seen a single person so far, but that's not surprising.

Few people travel this way. These roads function as supply routes to the cities, for trading and export of the copper mined in the mountains. But, from what I remember in my studies, supply from the cities to the mining villages is rare as the villages are fairly self-sufficient. Trading happens only two or three times a year. And export of the copper happens all at once, now and then.

So, aside from if we meet one of the men or women spreading word of my claim on the throne, we might not see anyone until we get to Haner.

At night, we stay in forests when we can find them. That's given us some more food, which is great as we've run out of traveling food. We now have nothing to eat if we don't catch anything. That's a dangerous spot to be in because winter is not as good a time to catch rabbits, as we've found. Or, we're just not as good at setting snares as Rulf. Either option is possible.

The skies have been relatively clear of Shaloomd, which has been great. They typically only take really small people who are alone, so we're not in much danger, but Roran and I still walk close together if a Shaloomd does show up in the sky. They tend to circle above us for a bit, then they lose interest, and then we don't see another one for hours.

When we finally catch sight of Haner, it's nearing the end of the day, so we settle down in a small grove of trees. I set the snares, hoping we'll catch something. We still have hours to walk tomorrow morning and perhaps hours after that before we can eat.

Since Roran has been released from his enchantment, we've taken time every night to practice at least a little of swordplay, if we can find sticks. We avoid using swords. Neither of us wants to get cut up.

That night, we practice for about an hour. It's fun, lots of fun. And Roran's pretty good. He's been training with Rulf since they escaped from Parthun eleven or twelve years ago.

Interestingly, though, I'm actually nearly as good as him. I've been told I'm a fast learner with the blade, which makes me feel pretty good. Besides that, Kings have traditionally been expected to be solid fighters. If they're not, they're thought to be weak in all areas. That's one of Parthun's problems. People fear him because of his cruelty, but no one will expect him to be a solid King for no other reason than I doubt he's sparred with a sword for years.

We doze off that night, feeling quite warm. This grove of trees is mainly pine. It gives some really good cover from the wind, and soft ground to sleep on. We just have to make sure nothing catches fire other than what we want to burn, and we're all set.

The next morning, we've caught a small rabbit and a squirrel. It's plenty for what we need, and we cook it up as quickly as we can. We're excited to get on the road. It's time to make my move for the throne!

"Oy!"

I'm prepared for it this time. I've met Lumber before. I think he's a good guy, good heart, just doesn't always seem to know what's going on.

"Oy! Carrot!"

"It's pronounced Caric," I say with a patient smile as Roran snickers beside me.

"Caric?" the guard says slowly. "Are you sure?"

I don't know how to respond to that, so I just stare at him. What does he mean, am I sure that this is my name? Who doesn't know how to pronounce their own name?

Unfortunately, he just stares back at me, so I eventually say, "Yes, Lumber, I'm sure that's my name."

"It's pronounced Lum-BARR," he says.

I nod, but then he adds, "Or… wait… no, I'm sorry. You're right. It's Lumber. Sorry, sometimes I have to think back to how my mom pronounced it. I'm sure she had it right."

Well, that explains that.

"What are you doing here?" he asks.

"We're here to see Lord Hillbin."

"Lord Hillbin? What does the Portly Lord want with you?"

I smile. So, I'm not the only one who thinks he's portly. "I don't think I can tell you that, Lumber. I wouldn't want to share any of Lord Hillbin's secrets."

Lumber nods slowly and just stands there, examining me for a bit.

We've reached the city, but Lumber's the lead guard on the east gate. I've met him twice before, once fleeing the city from a Talic Wolf, and the second time entering the city fleeing from Captain Frindor. It's nice to use this gate under different circumstances, but I just don't know why this guy has to be so difficult.

"The last time you came through, you were armed and coming from the mountains. And this time, you're doing the same thing. Are you part of the Rebels?"

"The Rebels left the mountain a long time ago. We didn't come from them. We had another appointment to the east of here."

"Maybe you're a thief."

I close my eyes for a moment in frustration, but then see an opportunity. "If that's possible, why don't you take me to Lord Hillbin and ask him to use the Raker on me again, this time to ask me if I'm a thief?"

Lumber shakes his head. "No, I've taken four people to him over the last couple of months for different things. He's told me I'm not allowed to bring people to him anymore for the Raker."

I can't help myself, so I say, "Well, Lumber, then that's a good lesson to learn, isn't it?"

"Yes, don't take any more people to Lord Hillbin for the Raker."

"No, I don't think that's the lesson. The lesson is that you shouldn't be too quick to…"

"Nope, I'm sure it's that I shouldn't take anyone else to Lord Hillbin for the Raker."

I take a deep breath and look at Roran. He has a big smile on his face. I don't think it's just the post-enchantment-removal smile that he's been wearing for a bit. I think he's enjoying himself.

I decide to focus in. "Can we pass through into the city, Lumber? Lord Hillbin will want to see us right away."

Lumber ignores me and turns to Roran. "You… I remember you. You didn't come through the last time, but you did go through the time that you were trying to escape the Talic Wolf. I think… hmm…"

I don't like where this is going. If Lumber wasn't the lead guard at the gate, I think I'd just grab Roran and move on, but we can't enter the city without this man's permission. If he says no and we run, any number of things could happen to us, but we might never make it to Lord Hillbin's house.

Lumber steps closer to Roran. I glance around at the other guards. Some stand back, but two stand between us and the city.

"Yes… I remember you. You ran out while the Talic Wolf was screaming for the Princeling. That other guy… he's not Prince Roran, but maybe you are. Maybe you're him. Maybe you're the one the wolf was after."

We've actually come here to announce who we are, so in a sense, it wouldn't be bad for Lumber to find out who Roran is, but the problem then is, we still have to make it through the city. And Parthun has enough assassins in his employ that we might not reach our destination.

"So, here's what I'm thinking. I checked before to see if the other guy was Prince Roran. I find out he's not, and the real Prince Roran has abdi… abdorn… abnickl… has given up the throne. And now, we find out Prince Draydon is alive. So, I'll ask you now." Lumber leans in close, puts a finger on Roran's chest, and screws up his face before he asks, "Are you Prince Draydon?"

Roran's face fills with a bit of shock, then confusion before he laughs and says, "No, I am certainly not Prince Draydon."

Lumber doesn't do anything for a moment, but then lets his hand drop to his side. I think he's seriously disappointed. I also don't think he'll ever quite understand that he asked Draydon if he was Prince Roran, and he asked Roran if he was Prince Draydon. This is going to confuse him for years to come.

"Okay. I… uh… guess that's okay then. What are you going to do in the city?"

"We're going to meet with Lord Hillbin," I say.

Lumber's face fills with such sadness that I actually feel bad for him. He's so sad, if circumstances were different, I might give him a hug. One of the other soldiers steps up to him and pats him on the back.

I figure maybe we can do something for him. I know he's loyal. He's just not tracking with what's going on. I can't hold that against him.

"Lumber, it's really important that we meet with Lord Hillbin. Perhaps you could escort us there and then Lord Hillbin might allow you to remain while we conduct our business, which will give you the chance to take part in something really important to the nation. And… you might find out why we are here."

Lumber gives a half smile but shakes his head. "No, I can't do that."

"Why not?"

"Because Lord Hillbin isn't in the city. He won't be back for at least a couple more days."

19

Draydon and the King of Haner

"What are we going to do?" Roran asks.

"I'm not sure. I guess I had just assumed he would be here." It turns out Lord Hillbin is back in Sevord City. He went for the royal wedding and simply hasn't returned. In speaking further with Lumber, I found out that when he says that Lord Hillbin won't be back for at least a couple more days, he doesn't mean that Hillbin will get back soon, that's just what they say from the moment Lord Hillbin leaves the city. So, he's been at least a couple of days away from returning for many weeks.

I briefly consider heading to his house, anyway. I remember Clarice is there. He seemed loyal—in fact, I'm confident of it. But he might have gone with Lord Hillbin. He might also not have the authority to do all I need. I need a guard set up, one I can trust. I need messages sent out throughout the nation, once again, by people I can trust.

I figure maybe I could just go in and take charge, but I find sometimes I can do that, and sometimes I can't. And I don't always know which time is which.

"Well, we have to do something."

I want to snap at Roran for that. Of course we have to do something! I mean, we can't just live on the streets. Well, I guess we could. We have bedrolls and stuff, but we'll get robbed and maybe beat up, I expect. From my experiences with Rulf, I think I might be a very beat-up-able kind of person.

On top of all this, neither Roran nor I thought to bring any money with us. I mean, none at all. So, we can't even buy food. I just assumed Hillbin would feed us. I really didn't think ahead.

I calm myself down before I say something to Roran that I'll regret. The only realistic option I can think of is to head to the Horse and Bow. I turn to Roran and say, "Follow me."

When we get there, I've already brought Roran up to speed. I'm hoping we can slip in discreetly, not draw much attention to ourselves, and maybe stay at the inn for the time being. I think the safest place in the city is Hillbin's residence, but until then, I guess I'll have to remain hidden.

I swing open the door and find the familiar tavern smell of food, drink, and sweat. It's dark in here, but I tried to shield my eyes from the sun a bit before going in so I can adjust quickly.

Unfortunately, the room goes silent when we step in. It's not our armor—we don't look like much. It's not our bearing—I was raised a servant, afterall. It's obviously something else.

"It's him! It's… them!"

I look at the man who said that. His mouth hangs open, and he looks so shocked I fear he may never recover. The men around him react in a similar way.

Behind the bar stands Phil. He's wiping a dish with a cloth. No… wait. His mouth is open, and he looks as shocked as the other guy. He has a cloth in his hand, just no dish. He's so shocked, he's wiping an invisible dish, inside and out. How weird is that?

Laanna is here as well. She's smiling at me and gives a little flirty wave. One thing's for sure, I'm not going to let her flirt with me this time—especially when Ellcia's not here.

I hadn't really expected this kind of response. They obviously know who I am, but I didn't want to announce myself here.

I nod at Phil, unsure what else to do, and it seems to be all he needs. He sets his imaginary cup down along with the non-imaginary cloth and comes around the bar. "Ya Majestuh…" He stops, clears his throat, and puts the effort in, speaking slowly to enunciate his words. "Your Majesty. Welcome back to the Horse and Bow. I did not expect your return, or we would have…" He stops and looks around. I don't think he knows what he could have done differently. "Well, we would have done something. I'm just not sure. Laanna would have figured something out."

"Thank you, Phil," I reply with a smile. "Does everyone here know who I am?"

He looks around. "Yes, Your Majesty. They are all loyal and…" He turns and looks at a short, broad-shouldered man sitting at one of the tables. The next thing I know, the man is pinned up against the wall by three large, burly men.

"Are you loyal to the throne?" the one large man growls.

"Yes, of course! Of course I am!"

Phil nods at the commotion. "We just don't know that man all that well. The others, of course, are well known to us. They are all loyal."

The man who had been pinned up against the wall crashes to the floor at my feet. He kneels before me. He's short, but his arms suggest he's a blacksmith. The muscles just bulge and make his shirt look like it's being punished for just existing. His hands are coated with black dust, and I recognize the smell. Yep, a blacksmith.

Phil hollers at him, "What's your name?"

"Ennen," the man replies, voice shaking.

Phil leans in and orders, "You will be the first to declare fealty to our future King!"

"Of course I will!" He looks up at me and says, "Prince Draydon, I have been loyal to the throne my whole life. Please, Your Majesty, do not take this display as anything to suggest my disloyalty. I offer you my loyalty, my love, and my fealty."

Unfortunately, it turns out this man feels that such a declaration must be followed by a kiss on the hand. After he stands, the next man comes, offers me the same declaration, with a similar kiss.

As this continues, for far too long, I think about how disgusting it is for me that these men and women kiss my hand, but then, I also consider how much more disgusting it is for each successive kisser. I mean, it's like the last one to kiss my hand will more or less be kissing every person in the room. Uuuggghh!

While they line up, even the large cook comes out of the kitchen, although he struggles to get to his knees before me. I almost tell him to remain on his feet, but Roran puts his hand on my arm and shakes his head. I guess these things need to happen properly.

The last one to come is Laanna. I think she's thinking the same thing about my multi-kissed-hand, because after she offers me her fealty, she looks at my hand with disgust. Out of kindness, I simply take her hand and pull her to her feet. The look of relief on her face is strong.

But… now I have a problem. I glance at Roran for some help, but he just shakes his head and shrugs his shoulders. This is not how we imagined our stay in Haner. As another Prince, I think he's supposed to be one of my advisers, but I guess if he doesn't know what to do, he can't just make something up.

I turn back to the people in the room. I don't want to pretend I know what I'm doing when I don't, but then again, I do have to make a decision. So, I make it.

"Listen." Everyone leans forward in anticipation. Clearly, the word, "listen," is a fantastic way to start a speech. "My friends. I have come to Haner to make my claim for the throne. Word has been sent throughout Sevord and the Talic, and this city is where I will reveal myself. I had planned on doing this at Lord Hillbin's residence, but he is out of the city. I have come here because I know of Phil and Laanna's loyalty."

I decide to do it, even though it wasn't what I wanted. Taking a deep breath, I dive in. "I wish to make my claim here in the Horse and Bow. I wish to declare myself now, and I wish for all of you, my loyal friends, to stand by me now and establish my first court as the future King of Sevord and the Talic."

The men begin to cheer and holler and stomp their feet. I wonder what people outside must be thinking, but when I glance back, I see they've barred the door. I guess they know this is secret on some level.

"Do any of you have military experience?" Just about every man in the room, and some of the women raise their hands or nod their heads. "Were any of you officers?"

Phil and the cook both nod. "We were Lieutenants, Your Majesty."

"Then your rank and status have been reinstated and you are both now my Lieutenants. Prince Roran is my Captain. The rest of you are my guard. You are welcome to continue your employments and trades, but I ask that you dedicate as much time to this task as is possible."

The men and women bow their heads to me. I don't like ordering people around like this. I think I'd rather ask them what they think, but... I have to lead.

Turning to Roran, I say, "Secure the Royal Residence. Work with your Lieutenants to ensure the building as well as the area is well guarded. And please assign one of your trusted soldiers to keep a record of all that happens so that no one's loyalty will go unrewarded."

"Yes, my future King," Roran says and bows to me.

We have planned this all out ahead of time. Roran was really helpful with this, but I had expected to do this in the Lord of the city's hall, not in a smelly tavern.

Roran sets to work while Laanna starts pulling out a chair from a table. The next thing I know, a couple of men have smashed the legs off a table and set the tabletop down on the floor. The chair is then set on it along with a blanket to cover it, and a cushion is set on the seat.

One of the men, waves me over and I sit on what I guess is my new throne. The tabletop gives me an extra few inches of height off the floor, but is kind of wobbly. But still... I guess it does make it look a little fancier. One thing's for sure, they're doing the best they can, and that, I appreciate.

Roran's talking to Phil and the cook. I think I hear that the cook's name is Garb or something like that, but Phil doesn't always put the effort into pronunciation that he should.

I sit there while Laanna fetches me a drink of some kind. When she comes, she places her hand on my arm in a very flirtatious manner and gives me one of her smiles. "Laanna," I say quietly, but firmly, "I don't think it's honoring to the Lady Ellcia for you to touch me like that."

Her face turns red, and she backs away. "I... I'm sorry, Your Majesty. I... just thought... I mean..."

"It's okay, Laanna. I'm just entirely committed to the Lady Ellcia. I would never want to entertain anything that would be disrespectful to my commitment to her."

She smiles at me, but much more sheepishly this time. "I'm sorry. Sometimes I… I just kid around."

A few minutes later, Roran stands before me. I stare at him in a bit of confusion. The room has been mostly cleared, with tables and chairs pushed to the side. Men and women stand on either side of the throne like Lords and Ladies of the court, but no one seems to know how to stand or if they're standing in the right place.

To be honest, I don't know either. But I think I know how to connect with them.

Before I ask Roran for what it is he has to say, I quiet the room by raising my hand. "My friends, please understand. My parents were killed when I was but a child. Parthun, who was Regent at the time, saw fit to convince me as well as other children that we were servants in the castle. As such, I have grown up working hard, serving, dusting, cleaning toilets, and being yelled at for leaving spots on windows or dust on a mantel. I do not know how a Royal Court should look, so however you stand, is fine with me. I care nothing that you are not wearing the robes of Lords and Ladies. If you look at my outfit, I am dressed in traveling clothes and old, worn armor. My shoes are in need of repair, and my legs are tired from walking. I am a commoner in all ways, but by birth. You are my people. Do not feel uncomfortable in my presence. I am your King, but I will also be a friend to my friends. Please, I see you struggle to know how to stand. I don't know how to stand in a Royal Court either. So, relax."

I turn to Roran and ask, "Yes, Captain Roran."

Roran just beams at that. He explained to me a while back that he was looking forward to being a Captain. We weren't sure if he should be my first General or how this should work, since it's such an unusual situation, but we'll figure it out.

"Your Majesty, a guard is being set up, and I have sent word throughout the city that you are here and are making your claim for the throne. The Nobles in the city and the Business Leaders have been invited to come."

I nod. We have prepared all this, so I respond with what needs to be said to declare that I will be different from Parthun. "Yes, but please do not turn anyone away. I have lived as a commoner most of my life. Nothing has changed in my heart. The common people are my friends. If they wish to see me, then please welcome them."

I hear a bit of a quiet murmur throughout the room. I think they're unsure how to respond, but they're pleased.

Roran bows and pulls away. Now, I talk to the people.

An hour later, the first of the Nobles arrive. Since Lord Hillbin is out of the city, anyone who comes will be a minor Lord or Lady at best. Roran explained that this creates both an opportunity and a challenge.

The opportunity is that these minor Lords and Ladies will be unsure of how to react, fearful of Parthun, unlike a major Lord who has more influence and power. But they will also be quick to get behind me in the hopes that this might increase their standing in the future.

The challenge, however, is two-fold. First, I have little to no proof that I am Prince Draydon. Second, Roran explained that the major Lords and Ladies are gifted politicians. They know how to act and react in various situations. Minor Lords and Ladies, however, are often lacking in that regard.

"Get out of my way!" I hear someone holler outside.

The scrape of steel against a scabbard catches my attention, and my heart jumps in my chest. This can't be good.

"Ya wo' co' in withou' the King' permissio'!" Phil hollers back.

"You are nothing, swine! I will have your inn torn down, and you will be put in the stocks!"

I want to run out there and help, but I have to let my officers deal with matters. Roran stands by me and gives me a slight shake of the head as if to confirm this. I wonder why he doesn't go out, but then, perhaps Phil needs to establish his position as well.

"Di' I hea' ya co…"

"Speak clearly, swine!"

I have to admit. Although I don't like whoever this is who's shown up, he's got a point. Phil needs to put in the effort.

"Ahem! What I was saying is, did I hear you correctly that you are suggesting you will burn down the King's residence?"

Hmm… I think to myself, that's a good point. The other guy obviously thinks it is as well, because there's a long silence.

Finally, I hear some mumbling from outside, but I can't make out the words. They're obviously speaking quietly.

When the door opens, a man steps in and announces, "Lord Vickor of Haner wishes an audience with Prince Draydon, Rightful Heir to the Throne."

"Granted," I say. "Please send my new friend in."

Roran gives me a look that tells me what I just said was a little weird, but… I've never been normal.

A man strides into the room, obviously convinced of his own self importance. When he sees me, his face fills with contempt and disdain.

It's easier to see now in this room since someone opened the blinds and washed the windows clean. We also have many lanterns at full brightness, which is nice.

When he reaches the center of the room, he gives a proper bow, and then waits. I let him stand there for a moment or two. I don't really like the way he treated Phil.

Finally, I say, "Welcome, Lord Vickor." He smiles and opens his mouth to respond, but I decide to interrupt. "I am concerned about what just happened outside. I heard yelling and someone disrespecting my Lieutenant, my guard, and my current residence. I hope the matter is resolved."

Lord Vickor stares at me with a look of worry, mixed with hesitation. After a few moments, he says, "Nothing to worry about, Your Majesty. It was merely a misunderstanding. But it is resolved now."

"Good," I reply. "Circumstance has led me to this place to make my claim, and I am grateful for the loyalty of Lieutenant Phil, Lieutenant Garb, and the rest of my court. Their kindness will never be forgotten."

Lord Vickor slowly nods. He looks like he's reconsidering every decision he's ever made in his life. Finally, he says, "Thank you for welcoming me into your court, Your Majesty. May I presume I am speaking with Prince Draydon?"

"You are. And I have made my claim for the throne of Sevord." Now, it's time to make a connection with the man. "And you are the first Noble to come to me here in my residence."

Hearing this has clearly pleased Vickor. "I am grateful then to be the first of your loyal subjects."

I don't correct him on that. It's a common thought among Nobles that they are the people, they are the nation, they are everything. So, no one else's loyalty means anything in their eyes. But I let it go.

"I wish to bring you a gift," Vickor says.

Now, that excites me. I'm not all about money, for sure. That's never been a big pull for me. But, as King, I kind of need a bit of a treasury. I will have to pay my guards and pay for things I need. If I just take what I need from people, I move from benevolent royal to cruel tyrant in no time.

He hands over a gold necklace, and I nearly groan, catching myself at the last moment. A gift like that is something I have to keep. But I need cash.

I accept the gift from his hand and place it around my neck. On my wrist is the bracelet Roran wore. We agreed that I would wear it. If someone puts an enchantment on me, it will instantly point in the direction of the Spellcaster, thus letting us know if some spell has transferred to me.

I glance down, and the bracelet hasn't shifted at all. "Thank you, Lord Vickor. I would like to ask you to be open and honest with me. You are the first of the Lords to come. I wish, of course, for your vow of fealty to me. However, I know there is a question that you likely wish to ask."

Lord Vickor gives a small bow. "And what question is that, Your Majesty?"

"The question is simple. How can you know for certain that I am Prince Draydon? Under different circumstances, this wouldn't be a question anyone would ask, but the fact that I have taken up residence in a tavern and not at the castle in Sevord, raises this question immediately. Is that true? Please be honest."

"I'm certain some may question this, Your Majesty."

I smile. "Do you question it? I promise if you are honest, I will not be upset. In fact, I will welcome the question and seek to answer it. But if it is not something you wish to know, then please say so."

Lord Vickor stares at me for a moment as if he's trying to evaluate the risk of asking such a question. But then again, if he doesn't confirm my identity, he's risking his life.

"I would recommend that you prove it for those who do doubt you, but I have complete faith in you!"

Somehow I doubt that, so I decide to play his game. "Thank you, Lord Vickor. Then if the next Lord or Lady would like me to confirm it for them, I will do so."

His face falls for just a moment, and he hesitates. Finally, he says, "It is true. I have had some doubts. Concerns, more than anything."

"How can I convince you fully, Lord Vickor?"

"Well, if you had a high-ranking Noble to stand behind you, that would help, Your Majesty."

I hand him the letter, and he nods. "That is certainly helpful, but someone present would be better."

"Certainly," I say. "What about a member of the royal family? Would you recognize any of them?"

His eyebrows shoot up, and he smiles. "That would do wonderfully. And I certainly would. I would recognize King Parthun, General Corter, Captain Tilbur, or Prince Roran."

I turn to Roran, who's standing off to the side. As is typical of many Nobles, Vickor did not notice anyone other than me in the room. "Prince Roran, would you step forward and support my claim?"

Roran steps to me, bows, and turns to Vickor. "I place my support behind Prince Draydon, rightful heir to the throne. I can say with confidence that this in him. I have known him since I was an infant."

I still see doubt in Lord Vickor's eyes. The problem with Roran is he abdicated. He is recognized as a Noble and certainly is a member of the Royal family, but the abdication is a pretty big mark on his record.

"What else do you need, Lord Vickor?" I don't want to spend all day with this, but Roran assured me that the first few Nobles and leading businesspeople are crucial to this stage.

"Perhaps..." he begins, carefully, "to state your claim on the Raker."

I expected this, but I wanted him to ask for it. Unfortunately, such a request assumes that I'm lying.

"Of course, Lord Vickor. I would be happy to do so, and I commend you for requesting this. The future of our kingdom is too important to risk on the word of a young man sitting in a tavern. You have done well to ask for this."

Vickor is clearly surprised by this and relaxes immediately.

"Lord Vickor, will you select two of your men to go with two of mine to fetch the Raker from Lord Hillbin's residence?"

Ahh, there we have it. The look on Vickor's face tells it all. He doesn't have two men. He is certainly a minor Lord.

"Or perhaps you wish to go yourself."

He nods. "I would like that, Your Majesty."

"Excellent, then I will send three soldiers with you as your guard to assist you in this. I think it is also helpful that you go yourself to give greater credibility to this action." I turn to Roran and say, "Write up a letter to be sent with Lord Vickor informing the Steward at Lord Hillbin's house that Prince Draydon requests the Raker be sent with his friend and ally, Lord Vickor."

Lord Vickor smiles and gives a bow.

Before he leaves, I add, "Also, Captain Tilbur has put his support behind me. I hope that he can do this in person one day soon."

Lord Vickor reacts to this. "Your Majesty, the King has sent out word that Captain Tilbur should be killed on sight. He has declared him an enemy of the kingdom due to his intention to kill Prince Draydon."

That doesn't surprise me. Word of Tilbur's support for me must have reached Sevord, and Parthun will certainly want to discredit him. "I declare here and now that Captain Tilbur is not an enemy of the kingdom. In fact, I have met with him recently, and he has given me his full support. His name, written on this letter, is written by his own hand."

"Yes, Your Majesty," Vickor says, and then requests permission to leave to retrieve the Raker. I give it with the request that he move with haste.

Once he's gone, I call for my scribe. I don't even know who that is until Laanna steps forward. Roran, in setting up my court, had about a hundred little jobs to do. My job was simply to be the face of the kingdom.

I ask Laanna to write up a notice to be sent to all four gates, stating my presence in the city and ordering Tilbur to be received with honor when he arrives. I include that King Parthun's order that he be killed on sight is to be rejected. I know this is a bold move, requiring each soldier to choose now to follow me, but it's all I can do. I have her write up letters to be sent to the three other main cities in the Talic, and Roran sends out riders right away.

We're still kind of short on money, though, so the next four businesspeople who come in, one a merchant, two traders, and an owner of many rentals in the city, all offer financial gifts. None of it is all that much, but it's far more than we started with. Interestingly enough, what we had in Marleet's pack months ago when we last traveled through this city was about a hundred times what we have in my entire treasury now.

But over the next hour, the lineup continues, and the gifts pour in, all visitors trying to earn a bit of favor with their new King. I invite many to return for a dinner, which I hear Lieutenant Garb putting together in the other room. It smells delicious, actually. My hope is to announce myself using the Raker at a meal with Lord Vickor and the others.

Another few minor Lords and Ladies come through as well. Their gifts, like Vickor's, are items which cannot be used to purchase food, horses, or pay wages. At the moment, I think we have enough money to pay my guards for about an hour and a half. None of them have complained yet, though, so I just have to push on.

When Vickor returns, the meal is ready, and I invite all the businesspeople and Nobles to join me, along with anyone else who is not on guard duty.

It turns out a lot of the people in Haner are excited, not only because there's a new King, but because he's set up his temporary residence or "castle" as many have taken to calling it, right in the center of their city. However, Roran tells me that few of the people will ever come to see me because they feel they never have anything worthy of a Royal's attention.

Somehow, Phil and Laanna manage to turn the common room into a banquet hall, fitting somewhere around seventy-five people, I think. It, unfortunately, stinks in here with so many squeezed into such a small area, but the smell of the food is balancing it out. Somewhat.

Once everyone who felt up to it has toasted to my health and safety and all sorts of boring stuff, we dig into the meal. People laugh and talk, and I do a lot of nodding. I don't understand much of what is said. Roran sits not far from me, and Phil, Garb, Laanna, and the blacksmith, Ennen, who swore fealty to me first, sit around, along with many others.

It must be a strange sight for most, considering Garb is one of my main Lieutenants, my First Captain is a sixteen-year-old, and a blacksmith is welcomed at my table. But on the other hand, I suspect many see opportunities for advancement.

When the time comes for me to give a speech, I stand and raise my hand. I'm actually quite nervous, but Roran has given me instruction on how to speak with confidence and deal with my fears.

The room goes silent, everyone waiting for me. "Thank you, one and all, for your support and kindness to me. I am here to put forward my claim to the throne. It is direct and clear as I am second in line, next to Prince Roran, but since the first has abdicated due to many circumstances, I am stepping forward. As the son of General Geran, I stand before General Lirnal, King Parthun, General Corter, and Captain Tilbur. As such, my claim is solid.

"However, with you, my friends here today, I wish for no doubt to be present in our midst. I will ask for your vows of fealty before you leave, and you are free at this point to either give them or withhold. Once I take the throne, however, there will be no choice left in the matter."

Roran has actually written this speech. He says it's balanced in its authority and kindness. Continuing, I say, "But in order to remove doubt, I wish to draw your attention to the centerpiece."

In the center of the main table, Phil and Laanna, or someone—this has been a whirlwind of a day for me—has set up a display with carvings and candles and more. I suspect if it were spring, it would be filled with flowers, but in mid-winter, that's not an option. In the middle, up high enough for many people to see, sits the Raker.

It's just a small statue, made of bronze, of a woman in a dress, holding a flower. But the Raker is nothing so simple as there is a powerful enchantment attached to it. If you lie while holding it, I'm told an invisible rake comes along and rakes your body. Over and over. Until you die. And apparently it takes a full day.

So, using it is a risk, for sure. Because at the end of the day, there's always a fear in the back of my mind that says, "What if something I say isn't quite true?" Like, what if I claim to be the Prince, but I happen to say that I'm Caric, which is not truly my name, but it's what I've been called since a little child? The last time I used that name with the Raker, it was fine, but now I'm not using that name anymore. What if I slip up somehow?

I force myself back to the moment as I realize everyone is staring at me. "As you can see, Lord Vickor has graciously retrieved the Raker from Lord Hillbin's residence." I look around the room. "Is anyone here able to confirm that this is indeed the Raker?"

Roran told me this is a crucial question to ask. He said there was no worry in this regard. Plenty would confirm it, as many would want to say they've seen it before as it's a famous little statue in the city.

About thirty people stand up and nod that they do, in fact, recognize it and can confirm that it is indeed the Raker. "Is their testimony accepted by all who are present?"

Everyone nods their agreement.

"Then I will take the Raker in my hand now and declare that I am Prince Draydon, rightful heir to the throne of Sevord and the Talic."

No one says a word at this. Even Phil and Laanna look at me like I'm crazy. They knew this was coming, but the Raker is not something to use if you aren't forced to do so.

I'm about to ask someone to hand it to me, but then I remember even Lord Vickor carried it in a bag, unwilling to touch it. So, I wander over to it and casually pick it up.

Returning to my spot, I hold it in my hand, then pass it back and forth from hand to hand, settling it in my right hand. Roran explained this was to prove that there was nothing between my hands and the Raker.

Finally, I say in a loud voice, "I declare here in your presence that I am Prince Draydon, rightful heir to the throne of Sevord and the Talic. And I wish for each of you to support my proper claim."

When I'm done, I set the Raker down on the table, and hold my hands up again, just to confirm that there was nothing stopping my hands from connecting with it.

I nearly run as the room breaks out in a roar! I see Roran jump to his feet and go for his sword, but he hesitates. It's not anger or threat, but… cheering. I see now that there was an element of doubt in the minds of many people, but no longer.

Phil, Garb, Laanna and everyone else moves to the side of the room as the people quiet down. I take my place near the bar, which is one of the few places without tables or chairs. Setting my eyes on one man in particular, I call out, "Lord Vickor, do you have any doubt anymore?"

"No, Your Majesty, Prince Draydon. I do not."

"Then will you, as the first to visit me of the Nobles of the City of Haner, offer me your fealty?"

Lord Vickor comes to me and, dropping to his knees, which is clearly something he's not used to, says in a loud and confident voice, "I, Lord Vickor, Lord of the North of Haner, offer my love, my obedience, and my fealty to the future King of Sevord, Prince Draydon. May you rule with the wisdom of King Hartor, and the strength of General Geran."

I almost cheer with everyone else. That is certainly the best vow of fealty I've received so far.

The rest come forward, one after another. The personal vows would not, of course, be necessary if I were to take the throne in a typical manner, but since the circumstances are so different, Roran has explained to me that this will help to secure my rule.

When the hour is late, and everyone is tired, they file out of Phil's tavern. I'm exhausted, but as of the end of tonight, I am, for all intents and purposes, now the King of Haner.

<h1 style="text-align:center">20</h1>

Draydon and the Assassins

I didn't sleep well last night. Both Roran and Phil insist that I wear my armor all the time, except during what they refer to as the Royal Bath. I'm assuming when that happens that I'll be able to order everyone out of the room. They don't seem to think I need privacy for much else.

I wave at the people assembled outside the tavern. The plan is for me to do this four times a day: morning, noon, mid-afternoon, early-evening. Before I step out, Roran has the area scoured for possible threats. He's concerned about an assassination plot. I agree with him. It's just a matter of time. Since I'm wearing some kind of fancy robe over my armor, it's possible an assassin might try to shoot me in my heart, which would be about the best of all possibilities. My armor would stop that without any trouble at all.

I head back in to meet with the next group of people. I didn't mind this kind of thing yesterday, but now that I realize my life could end up being not much more than meeting with people and receiving gifts from them, I kind of long for the fishing village again. At least there, I felt like I was doing something useful.

I dread all the compliments and praise heaped upon me.

But the good news is, now that word has spread about my declaration while holding the Raker, no one doubts who I am, nor do they doubt my claim.

I've sent out word to the other cities. I have informed them that Haner has shown loyalty to the throne and supported their future King. I have also informed them that I expect them to send delegations immediately to offer their support and fealty. My letters did not allow room for them to refuse.

Roran says that when the Rebel armies came through before, the other cities were approached gently on the matter, and they struggled to get behind him. He believes their fear of Parthun held them back, and since Roran's delegations were gentle, they were not afraid of him.

Lord Hillbin was the only one who supported Roran's claim to the throne, and even then, Hillbin had some trouble keeping people in line. Roran hopes this approach will be better. Not that we might rule with fear, but because the people fear Parthun so much, they won't get behind anyone who does not appear stronger.

I don't want to start out my rule with demands, but I think I have to approach every situation a little differently. The cities need to know who their King is, and an expectation of fealty will hopefully give them confidence that I not only plan to lead, but I also plan to remove Parthun.

In time, I will send a letter to Sevord.

It turns out the treasury is growing quickly. The gifts come in more generously now that people are convinced I'm the King, and Phil had some money set aside for him and Laanna in case the tavern needed to close, or for major repairs. I hate to take all he has, but this is the risk. If I become King, all debts can be settled. If not, it will devastate many.

But with more money, I can actually pay for things we need, such as horses and outfits for the messengers to the other cities, Royal Robes, and to start caring for the people in the city who are in need.

My thoughts are interrupted by a strange request. "The people are requesting a parade."

I stare at Roran like he's nuts. A parade? I get it, Royals and important people like to parade around and some people like that kind of thing, but... really? How boring and obnoxious is that? I'm supposed to walk down the streets, waving to people, and they just... look at me?

"It's part of what royalty does, Draydon," Roran says with a smile, as if he can read my mind. "You're going to have to get used to it."

"What about security? We're still pretty sure Parthun's men will make an attempt on my life, right? So far, I'm not traveling far from the tavern. If we move through the streets, anything could happen."

He nods and shrugs his shoulders. "I agree. But I also agree with Phil that this will be worth it. The people really need this, and it might help to establish your control of the city. Delegations from Morgin and Leito likely won't be here until the day after tomorrow at the earliest, and Rainer's delegation will be after that. It's probably a good time to go out and walk among the people."

I don't like the idea. It's actually not the security issue that's big for me. The big issue is that I don't like making a show of myself.

Again, I long to be a fisherman. This life leaves me feeling so lost.

The parade is announced just before noon, and we have a quick meal. By the time I finish eating, I can already hear the crowds cheering outside.

When I step out, the screams and cheers are enough to make my face break out in a large grin, despite how embarrassed I am. I wave at the people and walk down into the street. A path has more or less been laid out for me. I'm not sure how Roran arranged this, but he seems to be managing. He's good at figuring out who can do what.

On that note, I miss Ellcia. She's about the best problem solver I've ever met. I wish she could be here with me now. Not just to solve problems, but I'd like to walk this road with her. The entire journey, actually.

I move along for a bit, waving at people, smiling at them. Royals never approach commoners, so I make a point of doing just the opposite. Now and then I go and take the hand of a woman holding a child, or some old man missing most of his teeth.

At one point, I experience the shock of my life. I've just spent the last couple of days receiving gifts from people. Someone would give me an item or a bag of silver or something, and I'd thank them, hand the gift to Laanna or Phil or Roran, then take the next gift, hand it off.

So, when a young woman hands me her baby, my heart fills with dread thinking, "Oh no, now I have a kid to worry about," and without thinking, I thank her, then turn to hand the baby to Roran for him to put with all my other gifts. Fortunately, before Roran takes the kid, I realize that's not what's going on. So, rather than send the baby into the treasury, I smile, tell her the baby is beautiful, and hand the child back.

My heart is racing after that one, both because of the shock of what I was going to do with her child, but also because of the fear that I suddenly had a child at seventeen, and that if I could get a kid that easily, I might suddenly have a hundred kids by the end of the day.

I feel so lost.

"I'm glad you didn't kiss the baby," Roran says to me when I move back to the center of the road. "If you'd kissed him, you'd likely have to kiss all the kids."

"That's a lot of babies," I say.

He shakes his head. "Nope. I don't just mean babies. You'd likely have to kiss every parent's child. That could be babies, toddlers, children, teens… you might even have an old man come up to you and ask you to kiss his fifty-year-old daughter." He smiles. "Or son. We'd never get back to the tavern."

I don't reply to Roran. I hope he's joking. I can't imagine having to kiss everyone who happens to have a parent nearby. I don't really like the idea of kissing strangers, let alone thousands of them.

The parade goes on for a long time, with Phil leading the way. I'm glad I'm wearing extra layers of clothing as it's really cold.

When we reach the City Square, Phil takes me on a circle around the outside. I wave at people, take their hands, hold their babies for a moment and try to remember not to keep the kid. We passed Lord Hillbin's residence a little while ago. I kind of wish I was there. Phil has a nice room for me and all, and it's more than I need, but the tavern is kind of cramped and smelly for much of what I'm doing.

When we complete our circle and come around to head back to the tavern, I feel a sharp pain in my chest as I go bowling over, crashing into the ice and snow-covered ground, coming to a stop against the frozen fountain.

The entire square fills with screams as people rush about, and I feel something else slam into me. I concentrate on the pain, pushing it away, reminding myself that it's not real, as I struggle to catch my breath. Someone's here… I try to focus.

It's Laanna. She looks terrified, but she's checking my chest. I catch my breath and the last of the pain fades away.

"I'm good. The armor took it all. It just takes me a moment to work through it."

Relief floods her face, and I sit up, catching sight of three crossbow bolts on the ground next to me. I'm about to stand up when I slam back down again, and I hear Laanna scream.

I see black and flashes of light as my head hits hard against the side of the fountain. No armor there.

When my vision clears, Laanna is holding her arm, and a crossbow bolt sits on my chest where it hit me. I twist her towards me and see blood on her arm. The last shot went clean through her arm before it hit! I look at the angle it would have come from and see a window in a tall building. It's all dark, but I know where at least one of the threats is.

"There!" I holler, pointing up at the third floor of a stone structure.

Four of my guards, along with Roran, run into the building as others gather around me. I hear more screams as what looks like about thirty men come rushing out of another building, charging towards us. Each one has a sword in hand, and most of their faces are covered.

I don't really know what it is that comes over me, since all I want to do is run, but I call out, "To me!" and my guards line up, Phil on one side, Garb on the other, and the rest spread out to my left and right.

A quick glance around before the fight begins shows me that I only have about a dozen guards with me to fight against the thirty coming against us. Laanna's on the ground, injured and unable to fight, but she has her knife in her good hand. I need Roran here now, but he and four others are in a building, likely unaware of what's happening out here.

We're outnumbered against a bunch of what I expect are trained assassins, and we're about to die while five hundred commoners watch and scream in panic.

When they reach us, I don't hold back. It's not just my life on the line. This is the kingdom. If I don't take the throne, if Parthun manages to kill me, if the Royal line cannot stand, a tyrant will rule, and countless lives will be lost under the reign of a madman.

I briefly consider focusing to make sure my blade does not slice through anything, but every second I hesitate could result in the death of one of my soldiers.

I attack with all I've got, and with Astamatiti, assassin after assassin falls. I don't know how many I've killed, but I use every skill and all my focus just to go after the next, and the next.

Some of my men have gone down, and Laanna's screaming behind me, but she's not in danger at the moment. I force myself to focus not on loss, but on winning. I must survive, so the kingdom can survive!

The pile of bodies around me grows, and I have to step back to keep from tripping, only to see bodies of my guard on the ground as well. Two more down, another one of my guards gone, another assassin… it just goes on and on.

But I holler out and attack with a new fury, determined to make it through one more threat. I feel a sword blade strike my belly, but I just ignore it. I'm safe. I take that man down, and another two come at me.

What I don't see, however, is the man coming from the side. He slams into me, and I go crashing to the ground, my sword clattering across the stone ground of the City Square.

I punch and kick at the man, drawing my knife, but he knocks it away as three men rush up behind him, all assassins. All three are ready to strike.

I can't move with the big guy on top of me, pinning me down, and I watch as the man above me brings his blade toward my neck. My only hope is that one of my guards is still alive, but to take on four?

A rock hits the man in the side of the head, and I look to see weeping Laanna, struggling on the ground with her good arm, looking for more stones. A moment later, she has a chunk of ice, and she screams as she throws it, hitting another of the men in the head.

They laugh as they raise their arms to block her projectiles and come at me again. I squirm and fight, but to no avail. I'm not strong enough.

They seem to decide there's no more time to waste, and the man with the knife raises his arm to strike, ignoring the next piece of rock or ice that comes his way.

But his blade never reaches me, because he lifts right up into the air, and then slams down onto the ground.

The one man continues to hold me as the others rise and charge a large brute of a man. He brings his fist down onto the one, driving him to the ground, and the other, he finishes off with his sword.

The man on me reaches for his knife, but the new arrival grabs his arm, and the knife drops to the ground. A moment later, the last of the assassins is unconscious.

I scramble to my feet, glance back at Laanna to make sure she's okay, then turn to the man who's just saved my life.

He's tall, built like a mountain, balding head, and has a mean, cruel look on his face.

"Tilbur!" I holler, and rush into his arms.

He doesn't seem to know what to do with this. I doubt he's hugged anyone in many years, but after a moment, he embraces me back.

"You made it! Just in time!"

I spin around to take in the scene around us. The people are all there but cowering in fear. I see some guards from the city trying to make their way through the crowds to me, but none of my own guards are still on their feet.

I check on Laanna, ripping off a piece of my cloak to help me bind her arm. She takes the cloth and waves me away. She's upset. Really upset. It's not the pain. The look in her eyes…

I move to the closest of my fallen soldiers. He's dead. Another one, he's gone too. The assassins did their work well. I come across another. It's Garb. That's why Laanna screamed like she did. I shake my head and close his eyes before moving on to the next. This next one's alive, but barely. I call out for a doctor. It's just Tilbur, Laanna and me in the Square, aside from all the people, but they all stay back. Certainly someone around here knows what to do, because I certainly don't.

Tilbur comes up and sets to work on the guy. I guess that makes sense. A soldier should know at least a bit of how to respond to an injury.

I continue to make my way along as Laanna gets up and runs to a large man on the ground. I dread reaching that point.

The next man is alive as well. As best as I can tell, he's just unconscious.

When I reach Laanna… and Phil, there's only about four so far who have made it.

I crouch next to Laanna and check her dad. Relief floods over me as I see the rise and fall of his chest, and his lips move just a little. He's alive. He's injured, that's for sure, but he's not bleeding badly. His eyes flutter open for a moment, but then close again. There's a gash on his head. He won't be up for much for a while.

I hear some grunting and arguing coming from behind me, and I turn to see Roran and the four guards with him leading two bound men from the building. They're dressed like the other assassins were, but their faces are uncovered. Crossbows are strapped to the backs of two of my men.

When they exit the building, Roran looks around in shock. I'm guessing he knew nothing of what was going on out here. He stares at me, and I nod back. His face fills with a bit of relief, but it's all too much.

Two people, a man and a women approach, bow to me, and offer their services for the wounded. Another two come forward, and tell me they're morticians, prepared to deal with the dead.

The crowds, however, seem to be just coming out of their shock. A woman screams, "They tried to kill Prince Draydon!"

I want to sarcastically tell her she's a little late on this new revelation, but I hold my tongue. Another man hollers out something about, "How dare they attack our future King!" and others scream out similar thoughts.

Then, something happens that I don't expect. The crowds charge toward Roran.

I rush to his aid but can't get through the angry mass. When they move on, Roran and my guards are left behind. Roran's climbing to his feet, and the four others are back against a wall.

The assassins are… gone.

I don't know what just happened, but Roran points through the crowd. The people, they're angry—really angry. I see a rope go up and over a wooden beam running between two buildings. Then another rope, then two more.

By the time I realize what's going on, the two assassins Roran captured, along with the two unconscious assassins dealt with by Tilbur, rise into the air on the ends of the ropes.

I holler and order and scream for the crowd to stop. I try to tell them that we need to question them, but no one hears a word I say. They're too worked up.

I turn away at the last moment. I don't know what else to do. Again… it's just too much.

I'm expecting Roran to take charge of the situation—it's kind of his job now, but he just stands there. While the action was going on, he went after the assassins. But now he's lost, looking around at the bodies.

"Tilbur!"

"Yes, Your Majesty!"

"We need to get off the street. We've been staying at the Horse and Bow, but it's far, and we have injured. Options?"

"Lord Hillbin's place, Your Majesty. I recommend we take our wounded and dead there."

The crowd has calmed and returned to circle around me now. I want to yell at them, but Tilbur comes close and puts his hand on my arm. "Careful, Caric… Draydon. What they did was wrong, but they acted out of a love and passion for you. This is one you'll just have to accept."

I frown at that, but I know he's right. "Get us to Hillbin's house."

Tilbur goes into action, ordering men out of the crowd to help carry the bodies. The two doctors and the two morticians join in. I'm about to try to help as well, but Tilbur and Roran refuse to let me. Instead, they lead the way, with Laanna and me following, and the others of my guard either carried or stumbling along.

I glance around. Lord Vickor along with some businesspeople I recognize are in the crowd. They look horrified. I think they're in shock.

I get that. This is terrible.

We reach Hillbin's residence, and the guards part without question. I guess that means they recognize me. Inside, I find Clarice running up to us.

"Hello, my Lords and your Majesty, my name is…"

"Clarice. I remember you." I don't say this rudely, but there's no joy in my voice.

He appears shocked that I know him, but he smiles and bows. "I am unaware of what has happened, but I heard the crowds. I see you have wounded. Please, this way."

He takes us to a side room big enough for the doctors to work on those who need the help. Laanna stays there to get her arm bandaged and to be by her father.

Before we leave that room, I announce, "Thank you all for your brave service. I am honored to have men and women like all of you by my side." At that moment, I notice that the blacksmith, Ennen, sits in a corner with a nasty gash in his side. Any question of his loyalty vanishes immediately. I give him a smile and a slight bow of my head. He dips his head in return.

I don't know what else to say, so I move on. In another room, we leave the bodies. I almost just walk out, but I stop instead and bow my head for a moment to honor them. I don't even know all their names, but Garb is there. I can't believe he's gone.

When we leave that room, there's only Tilbur, Roran, and another man named Yeorg, in addition to Clarice, who's patiently waiting. Yeorg was knocked out in the fight but has come to. Despite the trickle of blood down the side of his face, he refuses to leave me.

I can't believe we're down to four. At least some will recover.

Clarice orders a guard to retrieve another doctor and to assist with the morticians as needed. He then bows and invites us to follow him. We move down the hallway. I remember this from last time. We're nearly at the receiving room, just before the ballroom. We pass a stairway leading up, and a quick glance lets me know things have changed up there since the last time I was here.

Before, I didn't go upstairs, but I saw it was poorly cared for, and unopened crates were piled up against the wall. Now, the crates are gone, the wall looks repaired, and a painting hangs up there. On top of that, I smell paint. Fresh paint.

We enter the receiving room, and I'm shocked to see everything's changed. Tilbur grunts, and I look back to see he's pleased. When I turn around again, Clarice is staring at me with a smile.

I smile back quickly, trying to show the enthusiasm I'm obviously supposed to show… but it's hard after what's just happened. To give myself some extra time, I step out into the room and slowly try to take it all in.

Colors. Banners. Lots of blue and purple. A large crest… the Royal Crest. Oh, that's it. The blue and purple. That's my family's colors.

"You've… been preparing the place for my arrival!" I say in shock.

"I have, Your Majesty. I did not wish to be presumptuous, but I assumed at one point you would move your residence to this place as it is the best in the city, so I have prepared a proper royal receiving room, as best as I am able, and the banquet hall has been turned into a throne room. It is far from what you will find at the castle, but I have tried to make it a place which you can call your home. Upstairs, I am renovating the area, and you have a place to stay in the guest room."

"Excellent," I say. "As you have noticed, we were attacked in the Square. I have lost many guards, and many are injured. I just have Captain Tilbur, Captain Roran, and Lieutenant Yeorg." At that, Yeorg's eyebrows shoot up, but I don't have time to work through this. That's his promotion. I hope he's up for the job. "I need my court transferred from the Horse and Bow to this place. Do you have guards and servants who are able to do this?"

Clarice smiles. "Yes, Your Majesty. When I heard you were in the city, I not only began the renovation, but I also hired extra security and servants. Each one is fully trusted by Lord Hillbin, whom you must know is loyal to you."

"I do know that, Clarice. And I know of your loyalty."

He smiles and bows. "Please, if you wait here, I will see to this matter of the transfer and return, so I may lead you into your throne room."

He rushes back to the door, and I look back to see him give detailed instructions to two men. They move off, and Clarice returns.

"Through this way, Your Majesty."

We move toward the doors to the banquet hall. No, to my new throne room. That's strange. I'm impressed with the receiving room as it is. It's set up beautifully.

But that's nothing compared to the throne room itself. The area is huge. I remember that from before, but now banners, blue and purple material, and new tapestries have been placed around the room. Some of the blue and purple material hangs from the ceiling in what I can only describe as waves hanging down. It looks amazing!

But on the far side of the room, near where Lord Hillbin's desk used to be, is a throne. It's built up on a small platform with three steps leading to it. Well, I shouldn't say that. It's being built there. Two men scurry around, doing their best to finish it off.

"Ahem!" Clarice says, and the two men jump, spinning around.

"He's here!" one of them hisses. "We didn't finish in time!"

The way they move… these two men… they're like… scared mice! Fast, jumpy… strange!

The men bow, but then realize they're too far away for that to make sense, so they run towards us, which they then regret because both Tilbur and Roran draw their swords.

About halfway through the room, they stop, one of them bows, the other curtsies, then that man looks confused, and then bows. "I'm sorry, Your Majesty," the older man says. "We've never met royalty before."

I wave for Tilbur and Roran to put their swords away and walk over to the men. "Please, show me what you have built."

At that, they nearly giggle with delight. And, strangely enough, they grab me by my hands, one on each side, and pull me over there. When we reach it, they jump and run and laugh as they show me how they built the throne. I don't know an awful lot about carpentry, but I know enough from assisting the castle carpenters to see they've done a fantastic job. Under the throne is actually a secret door which allows me to hide something or even hide myself if the situation requires it.

"How long before it is finished?" I ask.

"We only need minutes, Your Majesty."

"Then I will wait. I would like to see you finish it, as this is a historic moment."

The older man's eyes bulge, and the younger man's mouth drops open. "I didn't think of that…" the old man says under his breath.

They set to work and finish the last of it, after which Clarice calls in two women who cover it with pillows and more, and another woman quickly tacks everything down so the cushions don't move.

When they finish, they all stand around, waiting for me to climb the steps. Oh, how I wish Ellcia were here. I don't want her to miss this. This is…

My mind goes to others. I am to be the future King. I have to remember others. Not just my Ellcia. Not just my friends.

"I cannot sit on the throne just yet." The carpenters and the three women, along with Clarice, look disappointed. Roran and Tilbur look… well… bored.

"What do you need, Your Majesty?" Clarice asks.

"I will not sit on the throne until the Lords and Ladies of the city are here, along with the leading businesspeople, and my entire court." Turning to the five who put the throne together, I add, "And I would like these five to be present as well, since they have prepared my throne."

The looks on their faces let me know this was the right move. I'm determined to be a King of the people, not a King over the people.

While word goes out, sent by Clarice, we explore the rest of the house. It's not large, at least by the standard of Lord Yune's or Hemot's estates, but it's plenty big enough for us. There's a room which has been prepared for me, along with a room for Lord Hillbin, and one for Roran and Tilbur to share. The rest of my court will have to squeeze in here and there, but it's better than what we faced in the tavern. Far more space.

Clarice tells me that Lord Hillbin should be back soon, although it is difficult to know for sure when he will arrive. There has been no communication coming through that way, and Parthun is likely quite paranoid by this point. Anything could happen.

When everyone has assembled, and all my injured guards are present as well, with one of them still unconscious, I nod to Lord Vickor, who is the highest Lord in the city at the moment, and move up to the throne.

I feel anxious. Really, really anxious. It seems like such a big deal. The one in the tavern was a mess compared to this one. When I sit down, the weight of the room lands on my shoulders. It's really happening. Although I'm not officially King, sitting in the throne helps to establish my claim. I can see that clearly now.

And when the room breaks out into applause, I can't help but smile.

Soon I hope to have the first delegation from the other cities, and once I have at least one more city behind me, I'll send word to Parthun.

There's no way I'm heading to Sevord for this. I'll never make it alive. Parthun can come to me. I already know what I plan on saying in the letter.

And I have no intention of being polite.

21

— · — · ● · — · —

Draydon and the City Nobles

The first delegation from another city enters my throne room.

This is a tricky one. Roran and Tilbur and I have talked at great length about this. We've even brought in Clarice. He's not a Lord and not involved in politics, but he and Lord Hillbin are close, and he's quite aware of the ebb and flow of the Nobility.

This first meeting is a turning point. Because it is the delegation from Leito, Lord Barton himself.

All in all, it's not his title that sets him apart. It's his history. He and his city, Leito, supported the rebels. Well, not the rebels. The "rebels" were actually those loyal to the throne. They just rebelled against the one who usurped the throne. And Lord Barton supported them, which should mean he'd support me in an instant. But when Roran tried to take the throne, Lord Barton did not get behind him.

Barton steps before me with two other lesser Lords standing just behind him. They all give a bow, although far less than what I've seen offered to royalty in the past.

We've decided that the best course of action with Lord Barton is strength.

"Welcome, Lord Barton," I begin without a smile, "although I am curious what to expect in our meeting." The

211

court is filled with the Nobles and businesspeople of Haner. I informed them prior to Lord Barton's arrival that his city, Leito, had not supported Roran as the rightful heir and, as such, I am disappointed in him.

Since the incident in the Square, no one in Haner questions my right to the throne. In fact, many in the city are volunteering to stand with my guard to help protect the King. And the Lords and leading businesspeople do not appear impressed with Barton.

"Of course, my Lord," Barton says, avoiding use of either "Your Majesty" or "Your Highness," both of which would be more commonly used for one of my position.

"My Lord?" I ask. Turning to Roran and Tilbur, I ask, "I don't believe I am a Lord. Is there any record of such a title handed to me?"

Roran and Tilbur both shake their heads. Captain Tilbur steps toward Lord Barton and says, "No, Your Majesty. It would seem silly to give you such a title when you are the rightful heir to the throne."

I nod. "True. That is very true, Captain Tilbur. Thank you." Turning back to Barton, I say, "I'm not very interested in taking my time to work through this matter. Not with you, considering your reluctance to support the son of King Hartor as he made his way to the throne."

"Oh, Your Maj... uh, Your Majesty." When he finally says it, he sounds like he's admitted defeat. "There were extenuating circumstances."

"Of course," I say, raising my hands. "And I am a patient man. I have decided that I will be a kind, caring, and compassionate King. I am a King of the people." Lord Barton shifts on his feet. It is often thought that kind Kings are easily controlled. "But... there will be a unique aspect to my rule."

"And what might that be, Your Majesty?"

"It is simple. I will show kindness and compassion to many, but to Lords who either stand against me or will not support me, I will simply remove them."

His mouth drops open, and he stares at me.

This is all hard for me to do. I'm generally a pretty polite guy, but I know I must be forceful with this particular man. I lean forward as I continue. "I don't know why you suddenly pulled back your support at the time it was most needed, but I will assume then that you are not a loyal or reliable Noble. As such, I will require that you convince me of your loyalty."

"How, Your Majesty, might I do such a thing?"

"Leito will take its place as the second city to stand behind their future King."

I just leave it at that, and Lord Barton doesn't appear to know what to say. Tilbur explained to me that the Nobility likes to play their little games and rarely do they enjoy directness. They would prefer that I dance around the issue and hint at this or that while they also dance around and hint at matters of their own.

But that's not for me. Not at this point, anyway. I doubt it ever will be. The delegation from Morgin City is expected within the hour, and I want Leito's support before I meet with them.

"Of course," I add, "you have two other options."

Barton merely gives a slight bow in response.

"Option number two. You could postpone your support and be the third city to throw their support behind me. That would be unfortunate, but quite realistic considering the representatives from Morgin City should be at the northern gate of the city by this point, from what my messengers tell me."

"And option number three?"

At this, I stand. I'm not good at this kind of thing, but we'll see how it goes.

In a shout that matches the looks of anger on the faces of all the men and women in the room staring at Barton's delegation, I holler, "Or you could tell me right now exactly what caused you to pull your support for Prince Roran!"

Barton gives a quick bow and then says, "I, Your Majesty, appreciate your candor. It is often uncommon among the Nobility. I am reminded of…"

I turn to the right. "Captain Tilbur and Captain Roran, remove this man from my court. The moment I am declared King, send a letter out to remove Lord Barton from his position of Lord of the City of Leito and to remove his title from his family."

Tilbur moves forward without hesitation. He spent a lot of time scaring me with his mean looks and huge, intimidating size. Barton, having the build of a Noble, shrinks back before him and immediately cries out for mercy. I don't respond at all as Tilbur drags the man to the door.

When they are just about out, Barton hollers, "Your Majesty, I have wronged you. I will tell you everything."

"Hold!" Tilbur stops at the sound of my voice and releases Lord Barton. When Barton returns to his spot, Tilbur stands behind him, letting out just the slightest growl every few seconds.

I have to stifle a laugh, and I manage it by pretending to take a drink from a cup that's already been emptied. It was good, too, whatever it was. I hope someone refills it. I guess I could request that, but I don't want to be a bother.

"Your Majesty." Lord Barton shifts on his feet and glances at the others around him. Aside from Roran, Tilbur, and myself, he is certainly the greatest Noble in the room. It must be difficult for him to be treated this way. From the way he's looking at all the others, I know he wants to speak with me in private.

"You will speak here, Lord Barton," I say, with an emphasis on his title. "These are those who have stood for Sevord and the Talic. They have stood against a cruel and vindictive man who has lied and murdered his way onto his throne. They have nothing but courage, faithfulness, and virtues unseen in even those of high Nobility, and I will remember their loyalty. I would show more patience with you, but to hesitate to support me is to offer your continued support to Parthun. Since these are my loyal friends, everything you say can be said in front of them. I trust them. You should too."

Barton gives me a bow and, to his credit, gives a bow to those standing in the court. "Yes, Your Majesty. Please, be patient with me as I inform you of why I hesitated to support Prince Roran. I do not deny it. As a man who supported General Lirnal for years, I pulled away at that moment."

"Go on."

"The one who was known at the time as Regent Parthun simply reminded me of a story, Your Majesty."

"And what story might that be?"

"The thief who wanted too much."

"I am not familiar with that story, Lord Barton," I say with a frown. "But you must understand, I don't believe Lord Grindor is far behind you."

"Yes, of course, Your Majesty. It is an old tale more common in the Talic than in Sevord itself. I am not surprised you have not heard it. Truthfully, I was surprised that King… that… Parthun," he says carefully, leaving off the title, "knew of it."

He steps forward and begins. "It is a story of a young boy who was a thief. He stole at first because he was hungry, using what he found to feed his mother, his sister, his younger brother, and his aging grandmother. He hated to steal, but he could see no other way.

"But one day he stole not just food and a little money, but he stole a gold statue, selling it later that day for a lot more money than he'd ever seen before. He used the money to purchase a better home for his family. Then the next week, he stole not just a statue, but jewels, and more, using that to purchase an even larger home. In time, he found he not only stole for what he might use, but he stole because he enjoyed it.

"But his deeds could not go unseen for long, for a man approached him, telling him that he would like the young boy to steal something more precious. He would like him to steal the crown. Such a theft would bring the boy great respect among the thieves of the world, but would also provide him with enough money to live richly for the rest of his life.

"The boy could not resist. In fact, he agreed right away, and the man helped him find a way into the castle to steal the crown. Since the boy was such a gifted thief, he had little trouble sneaking in and taking the crown from the table beside where the King slept that night.

"He slipped out of the King's chambers unseen and returned nearly all the way to where he needed to meet the man who hired him, but the alarm sounded. He reached the door, but it did not open. He scrambled to a window and called through the bars to the man, 'Please open the door.'

The man assured him he would, but he must hand over the crown first. The boy gladly did such a thing, tossing the crown down to him, but when the man caught it, he laughed and ran away.

"The boy was then, of course, caught, hanging from the window, crying for the man to come back. When they brought him to the King, His Majesty was enraged as he was a powerful King, unforgiving toward those to harmed him. He ordered the boy beaten and hanged, and his family arrested and thrown in prison."

I sit there, waiting for more, but when nothing else comes, I say, "That's a terrible story."

"It is, Your Majesty. But do you see why I could not support Prince Roran?"

"If I understand it correctly, the threat is that Parthun will punish anyone who seeks more than what they have now with death and imprisonment of their family."

Barton slowly bows as if to let me know I understand.

"Then you must decide if you will take a risk." He doesn't reply, but his face shifts to the side a bit as if he's trying to understand. "Lord Barton, the moment I set out to find Prince Roran, Parthun sent assassins after me. And the moment I learned of Roran's abdication and when I decided to pursue the throne to save Sevord from a tyrant, I knew I was in danger. Everything I have done since I began to move against that man has nearly cost me my life. In fact, an assassination attempt that cost me the lives of many of my guards and friends took place just the other day. I am no stranger to risk or threat to myself or those I love. And just as I take risks, you must as well."

Barton's face falls.

"I do not ask anything of you that I do not risk myself."

"I risk my children's lives," he says. "To ask a father to do such a thing… it is unthinkable."

"Lord Barton, I do not ask you to risk your children's lives for nothing. I ask you to protect them so they can grow up in a nation where they will be safe from a man like Parthun. You may feel you ease the threat of death now, but it will always hang over your head. You would be better to throw your support behind me and then protect yourself and your children by locking yourselves in your residence than to remain under Parthun's thumb. Because he will surely kill you if you ever challenge him."

Barton doesn't say a word. He has remained unconvinced.

"Lord Barton, do you know why Prince Roran abdicated?"

"No, Your Majesty."

"Then let me tell *you* a story."

I take the time to lay it out for him, all that happened. I even try to use the same tone of voice he used when telling me the story, to help drive it home. I lay out how Roran was enchanted to abdicate, but we are unable to prove it. I lay out how he was even enchanted to refuse to draw his father's sword, which would have canceled the enchantment, and how the enchantment led to his engagement with the Lady Marleet which was designed to lead to her and Prince Roran's death.

"So, you see, Lord Barton, no one is safe. Nothing is sacred. Parthun will even enchant people to do his will. This is the life you have before you. But it is also the life you have lived for the last eleven years. It is time for this to change, and it will not change unless I risk my life and the lives of those I love. And it will not change unless you risk all you have. This is our only hope."

He nods, but he says, "May I ask you a question, Your Majesty?"

"Please do."

"I see Captain Tilbur is with you. He has been declared a traitor to the throne. It has been announced that he has set out to murder you."

"And who sent out this word?"

"Parthun, of course."

"Does Captain Tilbur appear to be a threat to me, or does he stand by my side?"

"He is at your side, Your Majesty."

"Then you know Parthun has lied, correct?"

"It appears so, Your Majesty."

"Then what was Parthun after with this lie?"

He stares at me for a long time before he nods. Finally, he says, "Yes, I see. He was after the death of a man who wished to give his loyalty to you. And he will be after my death as well. And the next man's. And the next." He nods again. "If we allow this tyrant to rule, we have only ourselves to blame." Raising his voice, he calls out, "I, Lord Barton, pledge my love, my loyalty, and my fealty to Prince Draydon, future King of Sevord, and I pledge the support of the City of Leito to Prince Draydon's claim."

The crowd cheers, and I decide to do something a little unusual. I climb down from my throne and go to Barton. I take his hand and whisper, "I understand the fear. Let us get this in writing, then you must go home and set your guard. You must protect yourself, surrounding yourself with those loyal to you. Quickly."

We move to a table where a letter has already been drafted up. Barton signs three of them, and he leaves my throne room immediately. I send an extra dozen guards with him to walk him to the gate. I hope it's enough.

When I return to my throne, it's not long before Lord Grindor from Morgin City arrives. He's a much happier guy than Barton, but I see the fear in his eyes. I decide to go right to it.

"Lord Grindor, I am aware that you might hesitate to support me, although I am confident you know I am the rightful heir. If you are hesitant, I wonder if it is because you have received threats to yourself and your family. I have recently learned that one such threat went out in the form of the story of the thief who wanted too much."

Grindor's eyebrows shoot up at this, but after a moment, he slowly nods. "So, I was not the only one, then."

"No, Lord Grindor, you were not. How does knowing that the sitting King is not only not the rightful heir but is also sending out death threats to anyone who does not support him… how does that affect you?”

“It affects me a lot, Your Majesty, for I fear that is not the kind of King we want.”

I give a slight bow. This one's going to be a lot easier.

The Nobles from Rainer are next. In one sense, this will be easy. They won't refuse their support, not now that I have the support of the three northern cities, Morgin, Haner, and Leito.

But it's also going to be difficult. Rainer is called the City of Thieves. The Nobles are puppets. Lord Dimtor, the Lord of the city, has no power or influence. The real power belongs to a man named Farnum. He's a crook, a traitor, and a scoundrel.

Lord Dimtor is just outside the throne room, waiting to enter. He has two others with him, minor Lords from Rainer, but the guards on the gates of the city have sent word that Farnum, the man who actually runs Rainer, is also here in the city.

When I heard that, Tilbur smiled at me and asked to be excused from the throne room. I let him go, but I have no idea what he's up to. That smile though… it makes me think he's found an opportunity he's been waiting for.

I invite Lord Dimtor in and welcome him. I ask him for his support, letting him know what he doubtless already knows, that the other cities have thrown their support behind me already. He readily offers to stand with me, but I can see it's an empty promise. He doesn't speak like there's any chance he'll have a say in the matter. For now, though, I have his support and his signature.

With the letter of support from Ellcia, Marleet, Hemot, Nordin, Relin, Tilbur, and Roran, along with the letters from Morgin, Leito, and Rainer, and a declaration of Haner's support as the place where I have taken my stand, I now have all I need to demand Parthun come to me.

I read over the letter we've written:

To the Royal Court at Sevord, Capital City of the Kingdom of Sevord and the Talic, to the throne currently occupied by Parthun, Son of King Trevolay and Queen Marlina, Third in Line to the Throne of Sevord:

I, Prince Draydon, son of General Geran and the Lady Tallia, First in Line to the throne of Sevord, future King of Sevord and the Talic, address he who occupies my throne.

Your presence, Parthun, son of Trevolay, is required in the Talic, at the City of Haner, as of the first day of Spring. If you fail to arrive by that point, you will be considered a traitor to the throne and the order for your execution will be assumed. Any man or woman who then carries out the execution will receive the gratitude of the throne and be rewarded accordingly.

Regarding General Tirnal, second in line to the throne, and loyal servant of the Kingdom, I require his presence and expect Parthun to arrive with General Tirnal. It is, as future King of Sevord and the Talic, my personal belief that General Tirnal is held without cause. If he arrives unharmed, then such a show of good faith will be taken into consideration. If he does not arrive safely, then I will consider such injury to be evidence that he was, in fact, held without cause and will pursue an appropriate investigation and trial of any involved in his arrest.

Upon Parthun's arrival, I, Prince Draydon, will expect a public recognition of my claim and my right to the throne, along with a public transfer of the Kingdom and my crowning as King of Sevord and the Talic.

I, Prince Draydon, also humbly request the presence of all the Nobles of Sevord and the Talic. Your presence at such a momentous occasion in the course of our history will be appreciated.

Attached to this letter are letters of support from the following:

Lady Ellcia, daughter of Lord Rathar and Lady Shillin

Lady Marleet, daughter of Lord Yune and Lady Aldora

Duke Hemot the Milterite, son of Duke Berav and Duchess Hetaline, newly appointed as the Coastal Duke

Nordin Trollslayer, Lieutenant of Reber's Gate

Relin, Lieutenant of Reber's Gate and Hero of Reber's Gate

Prince Roran, Son of King Hartor and Queen Shalsee

Captain Tilbur, Son of King Trevolay and Queen Marlina, Fifth in Line to the Throne of Sevord and the Talic

Lord Barton, and the City of Leito

Lord Grindor, and the City of Morgin

Lord Dimtor, and the City of Rainer

Lord Vickor, in place of the Portly Lord, Lord Hillbin, and the City of Haner

By order of the Crown Prince, Draydon, Son of Geran, this letter is to be read in Sevord City Square and posted in the Square for all to read in addition to being read in Parthun's presence.

Signed, Prince Draydon, First in Line for the Throne.

I'm pleased with that letter. There is so much more I could say, but much has been said. I especially like the demand for Parthun's presence, but the request for the Nobles. It sends a clear message that he is no longer worthy of respect, and the day has come for Parthun's removal.

I have also written a second letter, but this one will go in secret. I give it a quick read-through.

To Captain Granel, Son of Lord Rathar and Lady Shillin.

I, Prince Draydon, son of General Geran and the Lady Tallia, First in Line to the throne of Sevord, future King of Sevord and the Talic, send this letter with my utmost kindness and respect.

As of the day this letter is written, you have been declared Third Captain of the Armies of Sevord, under Prince Tilbur, First Captain of the Armies of Sevord, and Prince Roran, Second Captain of the Armies of Sevord. In addition, Captain Frindor has been placed as Fourth Captain, under your command.

All command of the armies is now placed under your authority with the order to bring the Armies of Sevord to Haner to assist in the legal transfer of the Kingdom to my name, and from this point on, you will only accept orders from Captain Roran, Captain Tilbur, or Prince Draydon.

You have also been granted authority to remove any officers under your command if it is in the interest of the

Kingdom to do so. Your soldiers are to assist Parthun and all the Nobles to reach Haner by the first day of spring. If any Nobles refuse to attend, they have my blessing to remain behind.

If Parthun refuses to attend or does not appear in your judgment to make attendance in Haner on the first of Spring a priority, you are hereby ordered to bind him, throw him over the back of a mule, and bring him to Haner.

A letter has, at this same time, been sent to Parthun, Son of King Trevolay and Queen Marlina, demanding his presence at Haner as of the first day of Spring to meet with me for the transfer of the throne to my name.

Signed, Prince Draydon, First in Line for the Throne.

I smile at the part about the mule. I'm kind of hoping, actually, but Tilbur assures me Parthun would never let it come to that.

I had wanted to include a demand that Rulf be freed and brought as well, but both Tilbur and Roran resisted such a move. Rulf is actually held on a crime. To demand General Lirnal's release is one thing, since there are no proper charges. But to demand the release of a potential criminal is another matter.

Besides. Rulf is likely still happy where he is. Laying in a mud pit is kind of… well… heaven for one with giant blood. On top of that, Rulf could get out anytime he wants. No one could stop him.

But these letters will anger Parthun. And not just a little.

"Send them!" I order, and Roran gives me a smile, taking the letters and heading out. He and Clarice will ensure the right messengers are sent.

It's late now, and I want to sleep. I have a quick meeting with Lieutenant Phil, who's back on his feet now, although a little unsteady, and with Laanna. We address a few matters of security and of schedule. I just... it just... there's so much... hmm... One thing I don't like is there is so much "boring" to this job!

But I head to bed after and fall asleep immediately.

22

• — • — • — • —

Draydon and Those Whom We Trust

I awake to a terrible pressure on my lungs… can't breathe. Something's over my face. My nose feels crushed. I struggle… can't move.

I twist and shove and do all I can to get up. A crash sounds at the end of my bed, and I hear footsteps.

I gasp for air as the pressure leaves my face, my chest, my throat. I'm coughing, gasping, confused. I just want to get away.

Someone grabs my arm. I see blond hair, and for a second, I think it's Marleet, and I wrap my arms around her. She's come for me. She found me. I hope she brought Ellcia. I need her.

"Draydon! Draydon! Talk to me!"

I twist to see Roran on the bed with me. He has a wild look in his eyes. I look back at the woman in my arms. It's Laanna. I let go immediately, careful not to hurt her arm.

"What… what happened?"

Roran shakes his head. "They got past us. I don't know how, but they got in your room."

I climb to my feet. My throat hurts, my nose aches, I'm still having a bit of trouble catching my breath. I hold the bedpost as I stand and take in the room around me.

Tilbur has two men, bound and gagged, on the floor. Phil is here as well, sword drawn, and an angry look on his face. Lieutenant Yeorg stands by the door. Yeorg appears shocked and uncomfortable. I have to remind myself that he's never served in any kind of military.

I clear my throat and call out, "Find how they entered. Tilbur, question them. Get all the information out of them that you think you can. If they cooperate, we'll offer some kind of leniency. If they do not, we won't."

He nods and yanks one of the men to his feet. Phil grabs the other, but with his injuries and age, he's not as strong as Tilbur. The man struggles up as Phil pulls on the back of his shirt.

Once they're out, I check myself. My nose is bleeding. That doesn't surprise me. I think they had a pillow over my face, and I can't help but think they punched me once or twice. I see a hole in my nightclothes where they tried to shove a blade into my heart. Tilbur was right. Sleeping with my armor under my shirt is the way to go.

The men are gone now, and Lieutenant Yeorg and Roran search my room, trying to figure out how the men got in. Laanna finds me a cloth with which I can wipe my nose, and then we both join in on the search.

The window is sealed. In fact, it opens outward and the snow on the windowsill is undisturbed. They didn't come in that way. There are no holes in the wall, and even if they wanted to come in through the wall, Roran and Tilbur's room is on one side and Phil and Laanna's room is on the other. The floor is solid stone, and the ceiling is unbroken.

"How did they get in?" Yeorg asks.

"They were already here," I say. "When I went to sleep, they were already in the room. I can't see any other way." Turning to Roran, I say, "We'll need a guard posted on my room at all times, whether I'm in here or not. And we'll need to do a search of my room before I come in."

He agrees. Unfortunately, that's two more guards full-time outside my room. This whole "King" thing is quite expensive. Fortunately, this evening we received a large gift from Lord Yune's estate. That will carry us through for months. I hope.

I have trouble sleeping after this, but I manage by staying in Roran's room, sleeping in Tilbur's bed. Tilbur is occupied with the two men.

When I arise the next morning, Tilbur waits for me in a small room we use for meetings with him and others. He looks pleased.

"Does this mean the men talked?"

He nods slowly. "I was afraid they would be Parthun's men. His assassins will not talk. When you tried to get the crowd not to kill those men in the Square, I knew even if you kept them alive, we'd gain nothing from them. These men, however, work for Farnum, the criminal that runs Rainer."

"How do you know?"

"Criminals like these men will not die for a cause— unlike Parthun's men. They live or die based on fear or profit. I just put some fear in them and let them know that talking is of greater profit than not."

"What did you offer them?"

Tilbur leans toward me. "I let them know that the only way to live is to be useful to me."

"So you let them go?" I ask, shocked.

He laughs. "No, useful in giving information, not moving around freely. If I release them, they'll just find the next criminal who will pay them to kill people." He takes a deep breath and leans back in his chair. "They were sent by Farnum to kill you. This is partly due to an arrangement

Farnum has with Parthun to remove threats to the throne. They did not tell me this, but I am aware that Parthun has this agreement with the criminal Lord. But the other reason they tried to kill you is Farnum sees his fortunes have changed and doesn't like that. In my search of the city the other day, I found out Farnum has settled south of here in a fairly affluent section of the city."

"What can we do about it?" I ask.

Tilbur puts his hands up and gives one of his dangerous smiles. The kind that always scared me growing up. "Leave it with me."

"Then take care of it," I say, and Tilbur gets up and moves out of the room.

There's a small prison not far away. I expect the men will be moved there. We've also begun construction on a guardhouse next to Lord Hillbin's residence—or I guess my residence. I'll still need to talk to Hillbin about all this when he arrives. Clarice says he will be happy with all we've done, but it still feels weird to take over someone's home.

Anyway, once we have the guardhouse built, we'll have room to expand our security. I've hired a fairly large force, and it's been made clear to all that the way to advancement comes down to one thing: loyalty.

It's helpful to have both Clarice and Phil here. They know many of the people already. Otherwise, I could be appointing traitors and assassins as my personal guard.

Speaking of Clarice, he's just entered the room. He gives a deep bow and asks to speak with me.

I invite him to sit, which is not typical. Rarely will a steward sit with a Noble, let alone a King.

He slowly lowers himself into the seat, but once he's settled, he smiles.

"Your Majesty," he begins in a quiet voice. He takes a moment and looks around, over his shoulders, and around the room once again. When he's finished, he leans in. "Your

Majesty, for Lord Hillbin, I always maintained a connection with the common people of the city, keeping some of them on my payroll."

"For what?"

"Information, Your Majesty. I simply want to know what is going on in the city. If people are upset, I find out and bring that information to Lord Hillbin. If people are pleased with some change or movement in the politics of the city, I bring that information as well."

I like the sounds of this. I'm trying to stay in touch with the people, but the busier I get, the easier it is just to connect with the Nobles and major businesspeople. I fear that in another week, I won't even have time for the businesspeople.

"What have you heard?"

Clarice's face turns sour, and I think I see grief in those eyes. I fear the people are already turning against me. Tilbur talked to me yesterday about personal insecurities that can creep up in my role and how to deal with them, but nothing he said helps at this moment. I feel like a fake. I feel like they've found me out. I feel like I'm a failure at everything.

Before he can tell me what he's learned, I ask, "Are they upset at me?"

"You, no, Sire, not at all. You, they love. I would recommend more contact with the people, but the recent assassination attempts suggest such a move to be unwise. The people, however, love you."

That makes me feel a lot better, but then I remember Tilbur said I should not feel insecure about the possibility of their dislike for me, nor should I relax in their love for me. This is complex.

"What I have heard, Your Majesty, is terrible news. I cannot confirm anything, just that I hear rumors. Many rumors. All about the same thing. Similar rumors all coming from different places. Which usually means it's true."

"And what do the rumors say?"

"They say that Captain Tilbur is meeting with Farnum, the criminal Lord from Rainer. They say he is creating an agreement with him. They say that he is the one who let the assassins into the Palace to kill you."

I pace back and forth, clenching my hands and releasing them. Roran leans against the wall, punching a cabinet now and then.

Part of me isn't surprised. Tilbur has always hated me. On top of that, he always had a reputation of being what they called the Fist of the Kingdom. If something needing punching, Tilbur usually did it. I was always outside of the politics, but from what I heard, when it came to killing anyone, Tilbur was the guy for that as well.

He's a brutal, cruel man.

But then again, I had started to trust him. And many people trusted him. He was said to be loyal.

And... he didn't kill me when he had the chance. Why would he do it now?

Roran starts punching the cabinet again. He grew up seeing Tilbur all the time, too, but his experience was positive. Tilbur was always kind to him. Like a proper uncle. He cared for Roran and provided for him as much as he was able.

So, for Roran, this is an even greater betrayal.

"But, maybe it's not true!" Roran growls, but I can tell he believes it is.

"That's what I thought, but Clarice came to me again. He just received word that one of Farnum's men was overheard in a bar, bragging about Tilbur's involvement."

"What can we do about it?" Roran asks. "Tilbur is not like a regular soldier. He has a lot of connections even in your own guard, knowing a bunch of your personal guard for years. This isn't a small issue. He's a deadly swordsman, and he's kind of… you know… strong. Not like Rulf, but I don't know any human man who could take him. You'd almost need to shoot him from a distance before he knows what's happening."

"Well, I'm not going to assassinate him," I say.

"And if he assassinates you?"

I don't have a response to that. In fact, I don't think there is any response I could give that wouldn't sound ridiculous. The truth is, I don't want either option.

"So, then we're back to the same question. What can we do about it?"

"We wait," I say. "We wait and see. We watch him and see what he does." In response to Roran's frown, I add, "I don't know if there's much else we can do. We could challenge him on it, but if he's innocent or guilty, he will respond the same. And if he's innocent and takes offense at the accusation, which I would expect he would, we could lose him and turn him against us."

Roran steps forward and smiles. "There is one thing we could do."

"What's that?"

"We could question the assassins. If they give us different information, then we would know he's filtering what he tells us. Or adjusting it to make him look good."

I nod. That's it. That's what we can do.

We move down the stairs, and I call my personal guard. The bunch of us set out immediately for the prison. The walk there takes a bit longer than it should because of the interaction with people. They've stopped just standing back and are now willing to approach me. I like the interaction, but right now it's a bit of a pain.

When we get to the prison, I enter and ask to see the prisoners brought there by Captain Tilbur. The man behind the counter is tall, well built, and has a fair amount of gray hair. He has a tough look about him, and his smiles seem to be something he needs more practice at.

"Yes, Your Majesty, of course. But I am not sure who it is you might be asking for."

"The prisoners. There were two men questioned by Captain Tilbur."

The man shakes his head. "No, we have no new prisoners as of the last two days. The last man to come in was for theft. Could that be the man you are seeking?"

"No," I say as I glance at Roran, then back at the guard. "Thank you. We will move on then."

We return to Lord Hillbin's residence… no, the Palace. I have to remember, that's what everyone calls it. I guess that's what it is now. I expect when I travel, this will now be my Palace in Haner. I'll likely have to set up something in the other cities as well.

When we arrive at the Palace, I ask Phil if he knows anything about the assassin's whereabouts. At first, he just looks at me funny. "I thought you knew, Your Majesty."

"Knew what?"

He frowns. "They never made it to the prison. They died."

My mouth drops open. "What? How did they die?"

Furrowing his brow, he says, "I assumed Tilbur did it. They were quite beat up."

"Where are their bodies?"

"I think they're already gone. Likely on their way out of the city. I checked them myself. They were definitely dead. In another hour, they'll be buried, or at least in a burial tomb, until the ground thaws."

"Thanks Lieutenant," I say, and Roran and I leave him.

"Well, that's certainly suspicious," Roran whispers to me when we're out of range of Phil.

I grind my teeth. I can't believe he lied to us about keeping the men alive. When we enter the Palace again, Tilbur's back, but just for a bit. I try to catch up with him to ask him about the men, but he's gone again before I can speak to him.

I find Clarice and ask him to keep me updated with anything new he hears. This is going to be a difficult one for me to deal with. Potential betrayal in my own house, before I even fully take the throne!

I ask Clarice for some advice, but he has no idea what to do. He tells me that he can pick up information, rumors, or the morale of the people, but he's never been good at dealing with any of it. I don't want to go to Phil because that will divide my people. I still don't really know if Tilbur's untrustworthy. But it sure looks like it.

I set about my day's work, meeting with people, entertaining, and more. Today, I'm even asked to pass judgment on a matter between a man who owns a small factory and Lord Vickor.

I can see right away that Lord Vickor believes he has the judgment in his favor without question. I can also see that the man who owns the small factory is sure he's about to lose everything he's ever owned.

The only thing is, it's clear that Lord Vickor is not acting properly. But I don't see that anyone has broken any laws. Nor is the judgment clear in one person's favor or the other.

So, in the end, I split the decision right down the middle, much to the disappointment of Lord Vickor and the relief of the factory owner. I also take a moment and chastise Lord Vickor for the way he's treating people. He just stands there with a look on his face like he can't believe something like this might happen.

The factory owner heads out, likely to tell his family they can still eat and his seven or eight employees that they still have jobs, but Lord Vickor remains. I wait until the other man leaves and ask, "Is there a problem?"

"No, of course not, Your Majesty. I am just surprised that you ruled against me, a man you've called a friend."

I nod. "I have been doing some reading, Lord Vickor. It appears that King Hartor was here about twenty years ago. He was only just new to the throne, and he made some very unpopular decisions. It turns out he ruled based on justice, not giving way to friends or family, but choosing to support those in the right."

"I see, Your Majesty," Lord Vickor says, but he is clearly unimpressed.

"Good. I'm glad you see, Lord Vickor. Because I hope that you are my friend. Because if you are, I hope that you can make it through this disappointment. You see, if I start my rule by showing favor to one person or another due to friendship or status, then I will be a wicked, corrupt King my entire rule. I will be just like Parthun." I pause and lean forward. "Lord Vickor? Do what is right and honorable, and I will always rule in your favor."

"Yes, Your Majesty."

I excuse him, and he heads out. He spends a lot of time here. I think he's actually taken over one of the rooms, claiming it as his own. I didn't think he could do that in my Palace, but I'm still learning how this works.

I continue through my boring meetings, one after another, smiling until my cheeks hurt. When I'm done,

Tilbur is back. He seems satisfied with something, but he's not saying what just yet.

We eat our meal with Lord Vickor present. Come to think of it, he's always around! I'm beginning to wonder if he sleeps here at night, somewhere in the building, but I'm not sure how to ask him that question without appearing… rude.

When we finish, Tilbur asks to meet with me, and Roran comes along. When we get into our meeting room, he sits us down and begins.

"I met with Farnum. He wants to meet with you in person."

"Is that a good idea?" I can't imagine how this could turn out well.

"I don't think it's a good idea," Tilbur explains, "but I think it's necessary. I don't think we have a choice. There's no doubt he's behind the second assassination attempt, and I suspect he was involved in the first on one level or another. This will simply continue unless you either promise to submit to him or you gain control over him."

"Well, I won't submit to a criminal," I explain, "but I don't see how to gain control of him. I'd actually like to arrest him."

Tilbur shakes his head. "That is something that you might manage once you are King, but not now. It would be too costly. You would lose just about every man and woman you have standing with you. If you anger Farnum now, every other person in the city will avoid coming to your aid."

"So, how do I gain control over him?"

Tilbur shakes his head. "I don't see any way at this time. I just recommend you meet with him and hear what he has to say."

"We can't meet him here," Roran says with shock. "If word gets out that we're welcoming Farnum the

Murdering Lord of Rainer, Draydon will always be seen as crooked."

"No, not here. Not in his headquarters, either. I recommend you meet with him in private in a small, out-of-the-way tavern to the south of here. There's a room in the back big enough for a couple of us and a couple of them."

"So, my guard will not come?"

Tilbur shakes his head. "No, if you leave with them, people will notice. You have to sneak out secretly."

The distrust that I held for Tilbur my entire life, along with this matter of the assassins… it weighs heavily on me. I'm not sure I can just overlook it all, especially when he's asking me to meet with a man who's already tried to kill me. "Tilbur," I begin, trying to sound confident, "do you really think that's a good idea?"

The rage flashes through his eyes… the rage I grew up seeing. But, with effort, he forces it down. "I think, Your Majesty, the only option you have is to meet with him. I'll remain nearby. I've faced enough men like him in my time that I'm not too worried."

I can't exactly tell him that Farnum is not the one I'm worried about. Well, of course I'm worried about Farnum. He's the stuff of legends. And, of course, the recent assassins… but I'm mainly worried that Tilbur has different plans for me than everyone else.

I study him for a moment. It doesn't make sense. If he wanted me dead, he could just kill me. But then he would be blamed. What does he have to lose if he's blamed for my murder?

Parthun… that snake will turn on him, throw him in prison for murdering me. That way, Parthun will be seen as the hero. Besides, right now, Tilbur is trusted by Lord Yune and others. If my murder doesn't go as planned, he will have no one on his side.

But then again… if I'm wrong… and I can trust him…

"How can you ensure my safety?"

Tilbur shakes his head. "I can't."

I'm guessing my reaction to that lets him know I'm not on board with his whole approach to… you know… dying.

He shakes his head again and raises his hands like he's trying to calm me. "Draydon, listen. I can't guarantee anything. I tried to keep your father and mother alive. I tried to keep King Hartor and Queen Shalsee alive. I tried to stop everything from happening. And look where we are now. Any way we look at it, I can't ensure anyone's safety. But I do know what I'm doing. I was second Captain after Corter under King Hartor, but I was always the one the King turned to, functioning as First Captain since Corter is inept in all he does. And I served as your father's right-hand man for years. Now, I've been first Captain of the Sevordine armies for eleven years. You need to know that despite all you've seen, I'm quite good at what I do. I can't ensure your safety, but very few things get past me these days."

Roran pipes up at this point. "Except for those two men in Draydon's room."

The rage flashes again, but Tilbur calms down. "True. Except for those two men."

"What happened to them, anyway?" Roran asks.

Tilbur's face remains expressionless as he says, "They talked."

"Can we ask them some more questions?" Roran asks casually.

"All right, out with it!" Tilbur says, slamming his fist down on the table.

"What do you mean?" Roran spits back. "Out with what?"

The two stare each other down. It's kind of ridiculous, actually. Tilbur's like a mini-troll, and Roran's not an overly big guy. I guess I take after the tall men in the family. Roran certainly does not. An image of Tilbur picking Roran up and... eating him... flashes into my mind. It's rather terrifying.

"Calm down!" I slam my fist onto the table to get their attention. I can't help but think I made a much smaller bang when I hit the table than when Tilbur hit it.

"What do you mean, out with it?" I ask Tilbur.

"I mean," Tilbur growls, looking at each of us in turn, "something's up. There's something on your mind, and you're not telling me what it is. I know the two of you went to find the two men I questioned. I'm guessing that means you assumed they were still alive."

"Well, you told us they were," Roran says.

"No, I told you I offered them life if they told me what I wanted."

"But they told you what you wanted," I say. "And... they're not alive."

Tilbur growls again. "If you don't trust me, I will not be able to serve you, Your Majesty. I did offer them life. I offered to keep them alive if they told me what I needed. Then, when I was leading them to their cell, they tried to get away. That wasn't part of the agreement, and I killed both of them."

"Why did you kill them?" I ask. "Why not just capture them again?"

"I made a judgment call," Tilbur says with a growl. "It was nothing more than that. We got all the information out of them that we needed." He stares at me, his eyes boring into my own. "But that's not what's wrong, is it? You're upset. Something has shaken your trust in me. And it's not the killing of those men." He leans forward, and I instinctively move back. "What happened, Draydon?"

I feel like running away. I also feel like just telling him anything he wants. I feel… interrogated. And still… as always… I feel so lost.

I almost spill it all out, but he'll just deny it. He'll just have another explanation. And, I always have to remember one thing: I'm the future King. Not Tilbur. Me. I must always remember that. Even when Tilbur gets like this.

Ignoring his question, I ask, "How will you try to keep me safe?"

Tilbur frowns at this, but he answers anyway. "I will position men in places where they can get to you quickly. I will also work out escape routes and observe who comes and goes, ensuring Farnum doesn't pull anything we can't handle."

"Anything we can't handle, or anything at all?" I ask.

Tilbur shakes his head. "There's no way to stop him from trying something. He will. There's no doubt about it. But we can protect ourselves from at least some possibilities."

"Will you be with me?"

"I can, if you need me there, but I would prefer to remain outside the meeting. I recommend Roran."

The last of my trust melts away.

I give a quick glance at Roran. I'm the only one who stands in the way of Parthun's claim to the throne, but Roran will always remain a thorn in Parthun's side. In one move, Tilbur can take us both out of the picture. And he, conveniently, won't be there.

I shake my head. It's time to push back and see what Tilbur does. If he insists that we both be there…

"I'll go, but Roran will stay."

Roran reacts to this, but I put up my hand, and he holds his tongue. Tilbur, however, simply says, "No. He will go."

"Why?"

"You can't go alone."

"Agreed. I'll take Phil."

"Phil has no voice in the Kingdom."

"He won't be there to speak. He'll be there as my second."

Tilbur merely shakes his head.

I purse my lips and give a firm nod back. "Phil's going."

Tilbur grinds his teeth again, but accepts it. "As you wish, Your Majesty." He then spends the next few minutes laying out his plan, going over escape routes, pointing out spots I can run to for safety where there will be backup, and more.

As I walk through it all, I think about how Roran would certainly be a better option as my second. He's fast, I know what to expect from him, and he's a solid fighter. Phil is a solid fighter as well, but he's rusty. To add to that, he's injured, which slows him down considerably.

Once Tilbur finishes, Roran asks, "When is the meeting?"

"I would recommend tonight, after dark. It would be best not to give much notice."

Despite my doubt in Tilbur, I nod. "Set it up."

23

•——•—•—●—•—•——•

Draydon and the True Lord
of Rainer

The innkeeper leads Phil and me toward the back room where we're to meet Farnum. Both of us wear hoods. I'm obviously easy to recognize now, but Phil is actually the bigger issue. He knows all the innkeepers in Haner. He tells me this particular man is decent, but easy to upset. And when he's upset, he's petty and cruel.

The door we come to is typical of rooms like this in inns. Just a boring door, out of the way, usually open when no one's in there. I would have liked to have arrived before Farnum, but the door's closed. I assume he's already here.

When we enter, the room is relatively dark. I have to admit, I expected a bit more light for a meeting, but perhaps he doesn't want me to get a good look at him.

I step in, with Phil right behind me. Phil's a big guy, not Tilbur big, but big enough. Unfortunately, he's nothing like the thug standing behind the criminal Lord.

"Please, have a seat, Your Majesty," Farnum offers with a large smile. Immediately, I notice he has a nice voice and a pleasant way about him. I think if circumstances were

242

different, I'd like him almost right away. I suspect that's one of the things that makes him so dangerous.

I pull out my chair and sit without a word. It's not that I'm trying to be tough, I just really have no words to say, and I'm nervous enough that I fear my voice will come out shaky.

He sits and waits, staring at me. I just remain silent, which seems to amuse him, but agitates the man standing behind him in the corner.

"No words for me, Your Majesty?" Farnum says. "Well, let me introduce myself. I am Lord Farnum. I am the true Lord of Rainer, and, to be honest, a greater influence in your future Kingdom than you might be aware."

I nod. "I suspected as much. I suspect you are behind or involved in not just one, but both assassination attempts on my life in recent days. I also suspect you have been involved in much of Parthun's rule and even the rebellion in which King Hartor and Queen Shalsee were killed."

"Your parents were killed in that rebellion as well, were they not?" Farnum asks, avoiding my question.

"Yes, many people were murdered during that time, and," I add, despite the fact that Tilbur recommended I not provoke the man, "the time of reckoning is yet to come."

Farnum laughs. "Oh, I expect if you do manage to take the throne, Parthun will see the gallows."

I don't give any response to that. I'm actually not sure what I'll do with Parthun when the time comes. I've been all over the place with ideas. But as for Farnum, Tilbur advised me to be confident, yet not anger him at all. Despite my distrust for Tilbur at the moment, I think that's probably wise advice.

If I can force myself to take it.

Ignoring his statement, I ask, "Why is it you asked to meet with me, Farnum?"

The lack of title has an obvious effect on both Farnum and his bodyguard, but Farnum himself pulls back his expression. "Ah, informality. I see. That's fine. Well, Draydon…"

"You may refer to me as Your Majesty."

"Yet," Farnum says, "you will not give me the respect I deserve."

"You are incorrect," I say. I know I'm pushing it, but this guy is responsible for just about all the serious crime across the nation. And he's been doing it for years. "You are most definitely incorrect, Farnum. I'm giving you far more respect than you deserve."

The man behind Farnum moves forward, but Phil gets to him before he reaches me. Farnum's on the move as well, his face contorted with rage. I slip off to the side and give him a shove, sending him into the wall, but in a moment, he's back up again.

Out of the corner of my eye, I see Phil and the thug going at it. The big guy is fast and strong, but Phil is holding his own. Farnum, although shorter than me, is built much larger than I am, and as with most people, likely has a lot more experience than I do.

He lunges for me, and I drive him back quickly. He has a knife on him, but he doesn't go for it, so I don't draw my knife or sword. Either he doesn't want a fight that might lead to death for him, or he wants me alive.

A loud crash next to me pulls me from my focus, and I see Phil go down. Before I can turn and give my full attention back to Farnum, lights flash before my eyes and all goes dark.

Cold… so cold…

I shiver all over. My fingers and toes feel numb, and my ears ache. My back is colder than my chest.

I work hard to get my eyes open, sending shooting pain through my throbbing head. My teeth chatter faster than I would have thought possible.

I apply a little technique someone taught me a long time ago. Not sure who… maybe my dad. But whoever it was, it works. I relax my muscles, and the shivering calms a little, easing the pain.

Lifting my head, I take in the room. It's fairly bright in here, with nothing covering the windows. And it's cold, seeing there's not even glass between us and the bitter winter weather. It's daytime—likely early morning. I'm lying in a light layer of snow, and I might be naked.

I twist around to see I'm still wearing my undergarments, which is a relief, but that's not going to do much to keep me warm. The rest of the room is empty, other than an old table and a chair not far from me.

I try to sit up, but can't make it, and a groan escapes my lips before I can hold it in. Footsteps draw my attention toward the door, and the thug from last night pokes his head in. He sets his eyes on me, then says in a deep voice, "Hey boss. The princeling's awake."

I hate that name. Princeling. It's like… I don't know… it just seems demeaning and embarrassing.

A moment later, Farnum walks in. He has a smug expression, and he takes the chair.

"Ah, it's good to see you're awake, Draydon." He smiles. "You don't mind if I call you Draydon, do you? I mean, it's not like you're going to be King now. I just wanted to let you wake up before I killed you. Are you finding the accommodations to your liking?"

Anger floods my heart, but I calm myself and decide to be confident. I laugh and shake my head. "That's the way the Talic Wolf spoke to me when I faced off against him months ago.”

He looks at me in surprise. “So, he really was after you! Interesting!”

“Yes, he was. And, as you can see, I’m still here. I’ve also faced off against a troll after enraging it. And, again, as you can see, I’m still here.”

“And then after a Talic Wolf and a Reber Troll, neither of which could kill you, I easily accomplish it.”

“That remains to be seen,” I say, with a lot more confidence than I feel. “I’m not alone in this city.”

“Oh, of course not. You think you have a lot of allies. Well, let’s consider this for a moment,” he says with a laugh. “You have the staff at Lord Hillbin’s residence, or as you call it, the Palace. What do you think they will do? You also have your guards, or should I say your carpenters, masons, millers, roofers… all those you put armor on and called them soldiers. They don’t know the first thing to do in response to a missing Prince.”

“I have Captain Tilbur and Captain Roran, neither of whom will let you away with this. And I have the heart of the people.”

“Oh, the heart of the people, you say?” He laughs quite hard at that one, and the thug joins in with a witless chuckle. “What do you think about that, Bilt?” he asks the man behind him.

“I think he might be wrong, Lord Farnum.”

Farnum smiles at me in a kind way, which is infuriating. “Do you know how many people saw us carry you in here, Draydon? It’s no secret among the people where you are. That was hours ago. And yet, where are Tilbur and Roran?”

Despair floods my heart. What if I am actually alone? What if they can’t come for me? What if the people won’t actually stand up for me? What if nobody finds me?

"Besides," he says, "what do you know of both of them? Have you not heard the rumors about Tilbur?"

I don't reply to that one. If what I've heard is true, I don't know if I can trust my uncle.

"And what of Roran?"

I furrow my brow at that one. "Roran is like a brother to me!"

He gives a smile, but it's like he's talking down to me more than anything. Leaning in, he says, "You thought you could trust Tilbur, yet he led you into my trap. You don't think we planned this? And now you're relying on him! And you also rely on Roran, but what do you know of Roran and Tilbur's relationship?"

My mouth drops open, and I gasp. I want to remain confident, but I know Roran and Tilbur are close. I've known that for months now. Tilbur raised Roran in a lot of ways. He did all he could to protect and care for Roran. And now, Roran has to take second place to me. I figured Roran would be angry if Tilbur betrayed me, but if Tilbur can't be trusted, how can I trust Roran? Have they been working together this whole time to take me down?

"But none of that matters, Draydon," Farnum continues. "Just because the only ones you can trust are back along the Sevordine coast, doesn't mean we should sit here and mope! Let's enjoy ourselves!"

I growl at him, doing my best not to shiver, laying here bound, nearly naked in the snow.

"Oh, I'm sorry, Draydon. I guess that's not fair. You have nothing to enjoy. So, mope all you want. But, while you mope, I have something to discuss."

"And what's that, Farnum?"

"Your chance to get out of here."

"And what chance is that?" I ask. "I seem to be unable even to stand up, and I'm slowly freezing to death."

"True. It doesn't look good for you," Farnum says with a smile. "And even if you do get out, you can't trust those who stand with you. You are in a pathetic situation." He leans toward me, and his smile grows. "But I can change pretty much everything."

"What can you change?"

"I can change your standing in the Kingdom. I can change your security situation. I can't change Tilbur and Roran's trustworthiness, as I don't believe either of them can be bought, but I can remove them. I can even put you on the throne. I can have Parthun taken out, and someone else blamed, and you can simply walk back home and climb those marble steps to your rightful place in Sevord and the Talic."

"And what will that cost me?" I don't care for this conversation at all, but I'm kind of stuck here. I'm not even curious about what he has to say, but I *am* cold… so, so cold. Talking helps distract me from the knowledge that I can't feel my fingers or toes.

"Nothing, really. I don't want money. I don't want fame. I don't really want anything."

"Other than?"

"Other than your vow of fealty to me."

I close my eyes for a second in disbelief, and a laugh escapes my lips. How could he ask for something like that? "That seems like a lot, Farnum."

"Well, it's all perspective. Tell me, Draydon, why is someone like you going for the throne?" Before I can answer, he goes on. "You see, I'm a bit of an expert on people. I study them. I understand them. And you, my friend, are not someone who wants to be King. I can see that. You don't desire power. You don't desire wealth. You don't desire much of anything other than that girl with the shaved head and your little friends. So, why are you going after the throne?"

"Because," I say, lifting my head and staring directly into his eyes, "Parthun should never be allowed to rule. He's vicious, corrupt, and wicked to the core. I will take the throne not because I want it, but because he should never be allowed to continue his reign of cruelty."

"Exactly," Farnum says with a look of satisfaction and leaning back in his seat. "You are doing this for the nation. Which is where I come in. Right now, Parthun and I have an agreement. He doesn't bother me; I don't bother him. It's been quite freeing after Hartor's restrictive rule. I've been able to grow my empire and establish myself across all the cities, especially in Rainer. So, I like having Parthun on the throne."

"What does that have to do with me?"

"You see, Draydon, I want more." He laughs as he glances back at Bilt, who offers a deep chuckle in reply. "If you will agree to serve me, I will allow you to rule the country any way you wish. You can care for people, you can build whatever you want, you can go to war if you like, you can do all you wish. All that you desire to do to care for the people of Sevord, you'll be able to do, and Parthun won't get in the way anymore. You can be the King you want to be. You just have to serve me if I ever, which I likely won't, happen to send you a note requesting some small favor. Anytime I want anything, you just have to give it. Doesn't that seem worth it if it puts you on the throne?"

To be honest, it kind of does. I think about how I could take that throne and do all the good I wish to do. It wouldn't really cost me anything, just a little thing here or there. If that's what it takes to free an entire nation from under the control of a man like Parthun, isn't that the right thing to do?

I so badly want to say yes. I almost do. But... I can never agree to this. "There's two problems. First, your little things that you ask for will be the very things that corrupt the Kingdom. Second, if I agree to serve you, I instantly corrupt myself." Again, I raise my head and stare directly into his eyes. "I won't do that, Farnum. I'm going to take the throne, but I won't take it your way. I'm going to claim it as the rightful heir, and I will claim it with my heart committed to the nation, not to you."

Farnum smiles. "I know, Draydon." He shakes his head. "I know that. I knew you wouldn't take it. You're too good. You won't corrupt yourself when you're trying to do good. It just seems wrong to someone like you. But," he says, raising his hands as if admitting defeat, "I had to try. You can't blame me, can you?"

I almost feel like answering. He has a way of making me feel like he's on my side. I just know he's not.

"Although I knew my first approach wouldn't work, I still felt compelled to try. What I'm going to do instead is jump right to my second approach."

"Torture?" I ask. "It won't work. I won't give in. I'll die rather than corrupt myself."

"No, no, no," Farnum says with a laugh. I can't help but notice Bilt has a look of disappointment at hearing there will be no torture. "I know that won't work. It would likely be my third option, but I'm sticking with two approaches. After that, I'll just let you die."

"And what's your second approach?" I say with a growl. "Get on with it."

He smiles, that irritating smile that seems to draw me in and make me want to trust him. And then he says one word. One name. And it's all it takes to make my heart go as cold as the icy floor beneath me.

"Ellcia."

I stop breathing. I want to pretend like I don't care about her to distract him from her, but I just can't do anything other than lay there, paralyzed with fear.

"Yes, I see that's gotten your attention... Ellcia... Ellcia..." He leans back in his seat and puts his hands behind his head. "I've never seen her, actually, but my men have described her to me. Pretty, right? Quite pretty. That other one, Marleet, is also quite pretty, but you only have eyes for the brunette. They tell me even with a shaved head, she's still attractive, although she's certainly lost that glow that she had before."

"Out with it, Farnum!"

"Well, I wonder to myself..."

"Out with it! I don't care to hear you circle the matter like a Shaloomd looking for its lunch. Say what you mean!"

He drops his hands back to his lap with an amused expression on his face. "Okay, I'll be direct. If you don't swear yourself to me, I will send four of my best assassins to see her. They won't take the risk of anyone stopping them. They won't bother trying to get close or to make it look like an accident. They'll simply put a crossbow bolt through her neck, then slip away while everyone's screaming." His smile grows. "I have a sneaking feeling you picture her as your future Queen. If you don't swear to me, I'll order her death right away."

My heart races in my chest. I can't. I just can't. I can't swear to him, but I can't lose her. I can't give up who I am, but how can I take the throne without Ellcia?

"I wo..." I begin, but I choke up, earning me a smile and a slow, deadly nod from Farnum.

"You don't need to lose her, Draydon," he says, his voice filled with compassion. "You can save her. You can have her. What's one little sentence... one little promise to save her life?"

Through clenched teeth, I manage to say, "I won't. I won't corrupt myself... or the throne. I won't do it."

"Even if it means losing that young lady?"

I can't answer with words. I know I don't have it in me. Instead, I squeeze my eyes shut as tears stream down my cheeks, and I give a single nod of my head.

I've just signed her death warrant. I've just agreed to let a man kill the woman I love. All I have right now is hope. Hope that she can survive this. If she doesn't survive… no… I still can't give in. I can't. How many will pay the price for the kingdom? Even my Ellcia…

"Very well. I will admit, I'm disappointed, Draydon. I guess I just have to stick with Parthun on the throne. But before I kill you, I have an item of interest."

He reaches back and pulls something forward on the table, something I couldn't see from this angle on the floor. When it comes into view, my heart drops. It's my armor. Of course it's my armor! I'm not wearing it anymore. They've obviously got it. So, even if I manage to get out of this, Farnum will still have my greatest defense.

"I've heard of this," he says, poking it with his knife. "Your father wore it. When Parthun killed him, I had hoped to get the armor and sword, but when I found his and your mother's bodies—you were there, by the way, do you remember?"

I just stare at him. There's no way I'm going to give him the pleasure of letting him know I don't. Besides, I'm still working through what I've just done.

"Regardless of whether you remember, I can tell you what happened. You sat there in the corner, crying. I guess you just hadn't been killed yet, actually. Unfortunately for me, your father's armor and sword were already gone. I figured someone else had stolen it. Now, all these years later, how it came to be in your possession is a mystery to me."

I still don't say anything. He'll get nothing more out of me.

"Of course, I was quite angry, and figured I'd at least help to end Geran's line. I sent my four brothers to kill you, told them to throw you out a window."

I'm actually quite curious about this. I don't remember a thing from that day. Not even a flash of memory. It makes me sick to think of my parents lying there, betrayed, dead, but I want to know what happened to me after this.

"As soon as my brothers moved toward you, you stopped crying, balled up your fists, and screamed, 'I'm the son of General Geran! You'll never take me!'"

At this, both Farnum and his thug break into laughter again, the thug chuckling along in a way that suggests he knows it's time to laugh, but doesn't know why.

But then Farnum's face grows serious. "My brothers never survived the experience."

Now, that makes me smile. "They couldn't stand against a six-year-old?"

He shakes his head. "Oh, I don't think you did anything but run and hide. While trying to find you, they met up with someone else. As far as I can tell, it was only one man—I saw him running from the scene. Don't know who he was, but he killed all four of my brothers. Which is saying something! My brothers weren't the smartest guys in the world, but they were solid fighters. Isn't that right, Bilt?"

The thug nods. "Right. Not bright like me."

Farnum shakes his head. "No, they were certainly brighter than you, Bilt."

The thug nods again. "Right. They're bright like me."

Farnum's eyes drop with a look of defeat, shakes his head, and then he just carries on. "Anyway, I didn't really care about my brothers. They were helpful, but also a threat to my position as the true Lord of Rainer. So, whoever it was, did me a favor, but then again, I also swore I'd find him and kill him one day. The problem with your father and with King Hartor is they had this nasty habit of instilling loyalty in those around them. So, it could have been any soldier. Anyone who loved your dad or uncle enough to risk their own life."

He turns back to the armor. "But… none of that matters now. I have what I wanted. Your father's armor, as ugly as it is, is now mine."

He gives me a smile and then grabs something else off the table. "I also have this."

He holds my sword in its scabbard above me. It's scary. Not just the sword, but a sword which can cut through anything. Having that held above my head… even in the scabbard… terrifies me.

He slowly draws it out, and I see nervousness in his eyes. When he speaks, he sounds anxious. "I really have it. I… really have it. Astamatiti. It's finally mine." Turning to me, he smiles and says, "This sword has been a legend for centuries upon centuries. Even before it was tied to the Royal line, stories were told of it. If all the stories are true, then what you think you know of it is nothing compared to what it can do."

I hold back a smile of my own. I'm guessing he doesn't know what it means for the sword to be tied to the royal line. It means he can probably get away with using it… for a little while… but if he keeps it too long, it'll turn on him. Maybe he'll have hours. Maybe days. Who knows, maybe longer? But there will come a time. Enchantments always have a dark side to them, and to mess with a sword enchanted to cut through anything seems foolish, at best.

"Now, there's something I've wondered for many years," Farnum says.

"Me too," Bilt says.

Farnum frowns and closes his eyes. When he opens them, he snarls, "And what's that, Bilt?"

"Well, I just wondered if everyone has eight toes, or just most people."

Farnum stares at his bodyguard, lips moving slowly, as if he can't quite figure out what to say in response to that. Finally, he says, "There is just so much wrong with that question." Turning back to me, he says, "I've always wondered if Astamatiti can cut into this armor."

Truthfully, I've wondered that as well, but I've never tried. I didn't want to take the risk of damaging my armor.

Farnum grabs my leather armor off the table and throws it around the back of the chair, then pushes the chair up against the wall. With a big grin, he drives the sword into the center of the armor, and I watch with fascination as something I didn't expect happens.

The sword doesn't go in, but it also doesn't not go in. I can't quite make sense of it, but it's like the sword has gone through it but also won't penetrate it. A gasp pulls my attention from the sword and toward Farnum. The look on his face... something's happening.

My blade... somehow, I know it's already turning on Farnum. This one act was far too much. A moment later, it happens.

The sword swings around, pulling Farnum with him, and plunges right into Bilt's chest. I turn away, unwilling to watch, but I hear Bilt's body slump to the ground.

"NO!" Farnum hollers, and footsteps sound outside the room.

The door opens and three men run in, all roughly the size of Bilt, all with that same vacant look in their eyes.

The largest of the three takes in the situation for a long time, then asks, "You killed... Bilt?"

Farum shakes his head. "NO! The sword killed him!" He growls at me and adds, "Did you know this would happen?"

"The sword…" the large man continues, "… killed him? But… you hold the sword."

The two men behind the big guy in front growl, and a moment later, all three men charge Farnum. I roll to the side, despite how numb I feel, anxious to avoid getting stepped on or fallen on. As I struggle to get away, I catch glimpses of Farnum easily taking down all three men with Astamatiti.

When he's done, he comes over to me again. "Those were four of my best guards! A little dim, but solid fighters! I can't replace them! You did this!" By this point, he's screaming at me. "Did you know? Did you?"

I shake my head and defiantly say, "No, Farnum, but I knew it would turn on you, eventually. I just didn't know it would turn so quickly! Sorry you lost your men, but it serves you right!"

Farnum snarls at me and raises the sword high, ready to strike.

When the blade comes down, I just resign myself to the fact that this is the end. I didn't want to die, but at least I stayed true to myself, and to Ellcia. At least I didn't corrupt myself.

The blade slams into my side, and I cry out. It hits me again, and I holler. The pain is intense. I wish he'd just strike the final blow, but I know he wants to torture me.

He drives it into me again, and I groan, but this time I can't help but look down. My body… it's in one piece. I'm… I don't even see a single cut.

I watch the blade hit me this time, and again I cry out, but the blade just pushes in my skin. It hurts, but it doesn't cut, nor does it hurt as much as it should, considering how hard Farnum is striking me.

"Why? Why won't it…" Farnum's face is filled with shock, mixed with rage.

I want to answer him with something really snarky, but I can't think of anything. I'm just so shocked myself that I'm not dead. All this time I've been scared of cutting myself with the sword, but maybe it's enchanted not to hurt me. Or maybe someone else can't use it against me? Or…

The sword lunges around toward Farnum this time, and his face fills with dread. It almost cuts right through him, but he ducks and manages to keep hold of the blade.

Rushing back to the table, he slides it into its scabbard and drops it. He slumps forward, hands on the table, trying to catch his breath.

When he turns around, I see nothing but hate. "It's just as well. I think I'm quite happy to have you freeze to death, rather than kill you outright." A vicious, seething smile fills his face and he adds, "But we can't have you calling for help, now, can we?"

He pulls a couple rags off the table, then comes close to me. He shoves the one in my mouth, and the other he ties tightly around my head, holding in the rag. The one in my mouth tastes disgusting, and it gives me the gag reflex, but I do my best to hold it in.

"Bye-bye, Your Majesty," Farnum says, and then drives his fist into the side of my head.

Everything goes black, and the only thing on my mind in that last second is Ellcia. My chance to save her life is now gone.

Movement…

I feel hands roughly toss me around. Yelling. Arguing. Orders given.

I land in the back of a wagon, and it takes off. More yelling. We're moving fast. I struggle, but strong hands hold me down. I'm not bound like I was before, but I can't move.

I squint in the light, and my head aches, but I can't do anything but wait it out. The more I struggle, the harder the men above me hold me down.

"Out of the way!"

That's the first words I can make out. Someone's hollering at people. Farnum's likely in a rush to get me out of the city before he's found out. He might be after ransom, but who would pay for me?

It gets dark, and I'm shifted around again. I can't move… back and forth I rock as they roughly toss me around until I pass out again.

"Draydon! Draydon!"

Someone strikes me, and I struggle to protect my face. It comes again, but I can't stop it. They hit me twice more.

"Draydon! Draydon!"

My eyes focus on Roran. "What? Why'd you hit me?"

"Trying to get you to wake up."

I start to focus. I'm still mostly naked, but I'm propped up in front of a large fire. Someone's holding a blanket behind me.

I crane my neck one way to see Clarice. His face is filled with both worry and relief. The other way, it's Tilbur.

Clarice I trust. Roran and Tilbur… not at all.

I turn back to Roran in time to see him give Tilbur a slight nod. They're up to something.

A mug lowers down in front of me, and I see it's Phil. "You're okay?" I croak, my voice scratchy and thin.

"They knocked me out quite good, Your Majesty," Phil says in his slow attempt to speak clearly. "When I awoke, you were gone."

"How'd you find me?" I ask Phil.

"I didn't. They did," he replies, pointing at Roran and Tilbur.

I don't really want to hear from them, but I'm not sure there's much choice now. I don't see how I can move forward without them, but I also don't see how I can move forward with them.

Roran sits back. I notice he avoids sitting between me and the fire. It feels far too hot on me, but with the blanket behind me and the fire in front of me, they're clearly trying to do the same thing for me that Tilbur did when they fished me out of the river in the castle just a month or so ago.

"When they moved against you and Phil," Roran explains, "Tilbur and I rushed in as quickly as we could, but they had an escape route already planned out. They slipped past us."

"How'd you find me in the end? This is a big city."

Roran looks up to Tilbur, who steps just within sight, still holding the blanket. "I sent out word to all my contacts that we needed eyes on you immediately. Any word, any rumors, anything. It turns out an old lady saw someone carried into an abandoned house down in the southeast corner of the city. She didn't see a face or anything to let her know who it was—she wasn't even sure it was a person, but it was all we had to go on."

I nod. "And Farnum?"

"By the time we got there, you were in the house alone, tied up on the second floor. Much longer, and we would have lost you."

I take a look at my fingers. They all ache, but I can move them. My toes too. I hope that means I won't lose any of them.

"We got you in a wagon and back to the Palace."

"I remember being thrown around a lot," I say with a frown. I'm not in the mood to be polite.

Tilbur grimaces. "I'm… uh… no one's ever accused me of being gentle."

"So, back to Farnum, do we just let him go?"

Tilbur growls. "Never! I thought we might be able to put him off for a bit, but he has shown his hand. He wants you dead."

He hands the corner of the blanket to someone else. I glance back to see it's Yeorg. That's good. I was afraid it was Laanna. I'm not really dressed to have a woman walking around.

"If we had an army at our disposal," Tilbur continues, "I'd have sent a legion after them. Farnum and a few of his men were seen fleeing the city not long ago. I sent six men after him, armed with crossbows, but I don't think they'll catch him. At this point, we'll have to wait until you have a bigger armed force to work with. Until then, I've put out a bounty on his head."

"How much?" I ask, quite curious.

"Five hundred gold for just his head and two hundred gold if it's still attached to his body." Tilbur smiles. "It's an effective way to ensure he doesn't get away during transport to us. I've also offered whoever brings us his head honors from you when you take the throne."

I nod. Not much else I can do. I'm not sure where we'll get five hundred gold, and I don't know what this "honors" thing means, but I'll learn, eventually. I gather I'll have to honor whoever it is by a ceremony or give them some title like Farnum-slayer.

Tilbur grabs another mug of something off a table nearby. I didn't notice I'd drained the last one. This new drink is hot, and tastes good, but I don't know what it is. I just want to sleep.

"I'd like to head to bed."

Tilbur shakes his head. "Not until you can stand on your feet. We need to thoroughly warm you up before we leave you to doze off in bed."

I try to stand, but that's a bad idea. I feel like I could fall right into the fire.

"I lost my armor and sword."

No one says anything to that at first, but then Roran glances at the others and comes in close before saying, "We know, Draydon. I'm sorry. We'll try to get it all back, but we're short on people. If Tilbur's men catch them, we'll get it right away. Otherwise, it might not be till you take the throne."

I don't like it, but he's right. Not much else we can do. Whether I can trust these two or not, doesn't make a difference. In the end, I just have to accept it.

"I'll need a new sword and some new armor."

Tilbur gives a slight bow of his head. "I'll take care of that, Draydon. You focus on healing."

I wrap the blanket around myself and crawl towards a chair. I think I'm fairly warm now, but I just need some time. Once I'm seated, I ask for food, and it's not long before I have stew to eat and hot tea to wash it down.

"Tilbur," I call out. He looked like he was about to leave, but I hope he's still here.

"Yes, Draydon?" He comes around and crouches in front of me. I always feel so small around him. Now that I know what's being said about him, and now that I can see more clearly what's going on with him and Roran, I despise the man, but he can still give me the answers I need.

"Tilbur, when I was with Farnum, he used my sword to try to cut through my armor." Tilbur's eyebrows shoot up, and I raise a hand. "He wanted to see if the sword which could cut through anything could cut through the armor that can stop anything."

Tilbur leans forward. "Did it?" The look on his face is intense. "I have often wondered that. Your father wondered that too, but never wanted to risk damaging the armor."

"Same here." I take a moment and talk through all that happened, the details of it, trying my best to explain how the sword penetrated the armor, but didn't at the same time. And also about how the sword didn't kill me, and even the blows, although they hurt, didn't do any damage. When I finish, I ask, "Why did all that happen?"

"Hmm…" Tilbur begins. "That's interesting." His eyes drift around the room like he's trying to grab hold of a thought. "I wouldn't have expected the sword to turn on him so quickly. Most people should be able to use it for a few hours, perhaps even in a battle, without worrying that it'll turn on them." He frowns. "But… the armor. I think that's the difference." He looks at me. "The armor is tied to your father. Did you know that?"

I shake my head.

He continues. "It was tied to the royal line, the second in line for the throne, actually. It shifts around a bit, though, and men have had to give it up at times. But at the Battle of Reber's Gate, your father rescued a Spellcaster, and the woman rewarded him by tying it to your father— specifically to his line."

"With Spellcasters, there's always a catch."

Tilbur nods. "Yes, there is. Although I think this Spellcaster meant well, it's still not a good thing. The armor is meant to protect the second in line to the throne, so there will always remain someone who can rule. So now, your second cannot take your armor. Which is good for you, but not necessarily for the Kingdom."

"So, what does that have to do with what happened with Farnum?"

"Well, enchanted items have a… personality, if you will. They develop loyalties, and that can be good or bad. Your sword and your armor, I suspect, have a strong loyalty to you, and perhaps to each other. When Farnum tried to use your sword to attack your armor, I'm guessing they found their bond with one another in turning against him. You say it tried to kill him after it killed Bilt, right?"

"Yes."

"Then I believe that's what happened."

"And me? Why didn't the sword kill me?"

"I'm not sure. I don't think it's because you can't be injured by the sword. I doubt its loyalty to you will extend that far. I suspect it has more to do with the sword's hatred for Farnum, after what he tried to do. It likely wouldn't kill you because Farnum wielded it. But…" he says and shakes his head. "I'm just guessing. Enchanted items are never to be fully trusted."

I slowly nod and examine Tilbur. I don't want to say it, but I do. "Bilt. You mentioned Bilt."

"What about him?"

"I never told you his name."

Tilbur nods. "I know him. Or, I guess, knew him."

"How?"

"Meeting with Farnum."

"You met with him in person?"

"A few times over the years. Parthun and Farnum had an agreement not to bother one another. But now and then their paths crossed, and I was the one to discuss matters with the man. Bilt was often there. He looks dumb—and he certainly isn't, or wasn't, the brightest—but he was tough and loyal to Farnum. I wouldn't want to have faced him without my sword."

My suspicion isn't eased, but I let it go. Tilbur and Roran can't be trusted.

I will have to rely on Phil, Yeorg, and Clarice.

24

•

Draydon and the Traitors

That's the third time I've walked into a room to see Roran and Tilbur talking quietly together. When they see me, they stop and separate, always coming up with some unimportant matter to discuss. When I ask them what they're talking about, they simply tell me they're discussing security matters, from guards to interactions with the public and everything in between.

I can't believe I trusted these two. I wish Ellcia was here. I feel like I should send both these guys away, but I don't know if it's the right thing to do. I just need someone I can trust completely to talk it over with.

It's been three days since my kidnapping and rescue. And three days since I've been able to trust either of them.

Fortunately, I think I have an ally on the way.

"How long until he arrives?" I ask Tilbur.

"Clarice says Lord Hillbin should be here just after the lunch hour. He'll have to move slowly through the city. The Portly Lord has been a well-loved leader in this area for many years. I expect the people will gather to see his return, and since there's a Royal in the city putting forward a claim on the throne, he'll likely have to stop now and then to declare his position on the matter."

"Thank you, Tilbur."

I have no doubt Hillbin can be trusted. He's a man loyal to the throne and the royal line. The last time we met, he protected us as best he could and did not betray us.

Two hours later, I hear the cheers of the people as Lord Hillbin approaches. A crowd has formed in my throne room. Lord Vickor is here, of course. He's here a lot. And so are the leading businesspeople of the city and other minor Nobles. I hadn't expected them to assemble, but they all seem to think this is the place to be right now.

In a few minutes, I get it. Lord Hillbin enters the palace… well… I guess it was his home just a short while ago… and it hits me why they're all here to witness his approach to… me.

If he refuses to recognize me as the rightful heir to the throne, I don't really know what will happen, but it will seriously discredit me. I didn't know this before, but Hillbin is an extremely influential Lord. In fact, he's one of the oldest, as many of the elderly Lords were killed in the rebellion. If he doesn't support me… well… that's a problem.

On top of all that, he's a powerful influence in the lives of all these men and women assembled before me. If he turns his back on me, they'll all regret supporting me.

Why is this all so difficult? And why do I deal with so much doubt?

I hear him in the other room. For a small man, he has a powerful voice. When it was just a few of us, he spoke softly and moved quickly, giving the impression of a friendly, kind, informal friend. But when the doors open today, his shortness does nothing to suggest anything but power.

Lord Hillbin enters the room, moving with grace and authority. His short, round frame has earned him the title of the Portly Lord, but I kind of feel like he would not be one to mess with on the battlefield. His expression, while happy, suggests a serious focus.

I almost feel like standing in his presence, but I catch myself. If I give way to any Nobleman at this point, I might lose all respect.

Hillbin moves to the center of the room and stops. He stares at me for an uncomfortably long time, his expression not changing. I think perhaps I should say something, but Tilbur and Roran have assured me that I should never speak first in a situation such as this, so I wait.

After a few more agonizingly long minutes, he turns to Clarice, who stands not far from me on my right. Hillbin then smiles at his head steward and nods.

"It is my pleasure, oh future King Draydon," Clarice begins, which is interesting. No one has introduced me like that before. I wonder what this means since Clarice is Hillbin's head steward. "... to introduce to his Royal Majesty, Lord Hillbin, the Portly Lord, Lord of Haner, and close friend of King Hartor."

Wow. I remember that now. He told me he was one of the few people who called King Hartor... Harty? I think. A strange nickname, but I guess it works.

Lord Hillbin then bows, and politely asks, "Prince Draydon, may I speak in your presence?"

Now, that's overkill. He actually has just been introduced, and he should be the next one to speak.

"I welcome it, Lord Hillbin, friend of King Hartor."

"Thank you, Your Majesty. I wish, before I say anything else, to declare in your presence and in the presence of this most Noble company, that I, Lord Hillbin, do now offer you, my future King, my love, my loyalty, and my fealty. As I stood by King Hartor and General Geran, your father, I hope to stand by you." Hillbin then bows again, which is quite the comical sight considering his portly build.

At this, I can't help but smile. I knew he was loyal to the throne, but... I guess I just tend to assume that everyone's going to turn on me. I don't think that's a good attitude to have as I move forward.

"Thank you, Lord Hillbin. Your presence brings joy to my heart, and your words and your vow are a great comfort to me. And may I ask your forgiveness?"

The crowd starts to murmur, and I hear a gasp or two. Roran and Tilbur encouraged me to say this, although I don't know why I bother doing anything they suggest. Who knows what their motives are?

"I cannot fathom what there might be about which you might seek my forgiveness, but Your Majesty, I will certainly hear your confession."

"I wish to ask you for forgiveness for taking your residence in your absence. I did not wish to assume your kindness, but I needed a palace and hoped this would be acceptable to you."

Lord Hillbin chuckles at this. "I see you have the wisdom and grace of your Father and your uncle, King Hartor. If this is how you lead now, you will be a fine King!" The crowd smiles at this and relaxes. "Your Majesty, there is certainly nothing to forgive. If I were here, I would have offered it willingly. But if it is weighing on your conscience, then I freely offer all my forgiveness and express my desire to give you even more!"

I laugh, mostly out of relief, and then make an announcement that refreshments will be served in the receiving room. We make our way out there, and Lord Hillbin comes right up to me, offering some informal words about this and that. It's all small talk. Noble talk. Just words, but I know I'll have plenty of time to speak with him shortly.

We spend the next hour chatting with various people. It's one of the many parts of this Nobility thing that I hate. Roran seems to thrive in it, but I see Tilbur would rather be anywhere else. Likely thinking through how he wants to beat someone up.

When it's time for the boring stuff to finally end, Clarice announces everyone should leave. He does it nicer than that, but I'm just tired of talking to people about useless stuff. Lords and Ladies… I mean… they do a lot of real stuff… not just talk. They accomplish much and these are generous people, but then when it comes to times like this, all we do is tell one another, "Hey, I'm important enough to be in this room!"

I move off into one of the side rooms. Actually, the nice one where Tilbur and Roran warmed me up after my kidnapping. Hillbin and I each find a seat with no one else in the room, and he just stares at me and smiles.

Finally, when he speaks, he speaks more like the man I met a few months ago. "Prince Draydon, it is so good to see you again. I never imagined all this coming about, but I'm pleased. You handle yourself well, and you carry yourself with the bearing of a King. I think you might end up being the perfect mix of King Hartor's integrity and General's Geran's leadership."

"Thank you, Lord Hillbin…"

"Please, in private, call me by my first name, no titles. I will not posture here."

Wow. I like this guy. "Then please call me Draydon in private."

"Draydon…" Hillbin begins. "You went by Caric when I met you last. I'm glad to see you've taken up your given name."

"I didn't want to, but if I'm taking the throne, I have to throw away my old life and be the person I was born to be."

"Very wise," Hillbin says with another smile. "I hate to do this, but if it is acceptable to you, Draydon, I suggest we take a moment to get down to business."

I nod. I don't know what this means, but I'm anxious to hear what's been going on in Sevord.

"As you likely know, I left Parthun's court and came directly here. Word has reached the castle, of course, of your claim to the throne. Your letter was read to Parthun in the presence of the Nobles, and the army is on the move."

That part scares me, but then again, it's kind of what I demanded. I'm hoping this is a good thing.

He continues. "When your letter was read, Parthun nearly killed the messenger, but he could not act in such a way as the Nobles would never have allowed it. Everyone, loyal or not, must at least show support for you in public, or else it would be to declare themselves traitors to the royal line."

"Even Parthun?" I ask.

Hillbin nods. "Even Parthun. And he did. Once he calmed himself down, he gave a great display of joy over the matter of a living heir to the throne who could carry on the royal line, but then shared how grieved he was that he would not be able to honor and love the people as their King. He spent a bit of time trying to discredit you and even suggested that he send his most trusted soldiers to you right away to act as your guards."

My eyebrows shoot up at hearing this. "Has he sent soldiers?"

Hillbin shakes his head. "No, no, no, don't worry, Your Majesty. The Nobles are split, obviously. About half support you, and the other half either support him or are too afraid to stand against him. But every Noble present, loyal or not, knows for certain that sending soldiers is a bad idea. Those who are loyal know the soldiers will be a threat to you. Those who are not loyal know that the soldiers will be taken as a threat. So, we all overruled him on that matter."

"How do you overrule a King?" I ask. I've often wondered about this kind of thing.

"Oh, it's not that we vote or anything. The Nobles merely begin to question his decision and recommend a different choice. It is understood right away that this declares a Noble's disapproval. If the King does not listen to them on matters, they will simply make life difficult for him in each of their realms. For instance, in my area, taxes will simply be late or slow in arriving at the castle, or the men delivering the taxes might even meet up with thieves and the taxes may be lost. The Lords overseeing the farming communities throughout the area will suddenly inform the King that entire crops have been lost. And the Lords overseeing the military or with influence in that area will suddenly announce that their soldiers are unavailable. The soldiers themselves all bear a dual loyalty—first to the King, second to their Noble. If their Noble is displeased, the soldiers will also be displeased."

"So, it's pressure. If you don't like someone, you put pressure on the entire system."

"True! To add to that, a King must have the support of the Nobles to even take the throne. When Parthun took the throne, he merely claimed it. The Nobles are all displeased over that. They should have been given the opportunity to affirm his rule once he took the throne."

"Tell me more of what's been going on."

Hillbin leans back in the chair, making himself look even smaller and begins. He tells me of how shortly after the announcement was read to Parthun, Captain Granel arrived. He read his letter and demanded that Parthun accompany him immediately. Parthun, of course, played his games and refused, but in a polite manner. He explained that he could not possibly leave immediately without putting some important matters in place in Sevord. To do anything else, he said, would be disloyal.

It turns out shortly after that, Granel had to flee the castle, and about a third of the army joined with him once the order was given. They are on their way. The rest of the army has either gone home, or remains loyal to Parthun, or is perhaps afraid of Parthun. And just about every soldier, loyal or not, is discouraged.

"And General Lirnal?"

"He's safe, at least he was when I left. Your letter made it clear that he was not to be harmed, and the Nobles will hold Parthun to that. We can only hope that their pressure and your threat will be enough to bring General Lirnal here safely."

"When will the army arrive?"

"I expect, based on their movement, they will reach this area sometime in the next week to ten days. They are trying to move fast, but armies rarely move quickly. Granel will stay with his soldiers, so you won't expect to see him until the rest arrive."

"And how do we pay for this army?" I ask. Paying for stuff has been a constant pressure on me since arriving in Haner. The money Lord Yune's estate sent is helpful, for sure, but it's certainly not enough to support a third of an army.

"Don't worry about that, Draydon. I think you'll find the Lords who are loyal to the throne will send money, food, supplies, and more. Your army will grow. If the day comes that you need it, you'll have plenty of support."

"Enough to fight for the throne, if needed?"

Hillbin frowns. He takes a moment before he answers, and when he speaks, he shakes his head, and the words come out slowly. "I'm sorry, Draydon, that I don't know."

"I will assume command of the armies of Sevord when Captain Granel arrives," Tilbur announces. "Captain Roran, of course, could do this, but I recommend keeping him close by and allowing me to serve with Captain Granel as we both have more experience with military command."

The last thing I want is for the man I distrust the most in my court to take charge of my armies. Granel should arrive tomorrow; Tilbur tells me his scouts have reported that this will be the case.

So far, this past week has been business as usual, although it's been nice to have Hillbin by my side. He's an intelligent man, quick to figure out issues before they happen and always willing to offer a solution. Just his presence helps me to see why good Kings always surround themselves with wise Nobles.

But Tilbur… he's become increasingly untrustworthy over the last number of days. Clarice reports that there have been no new rumors of Tilbur's involvement with Farnum, but the old ones continue to circulate. He also tells me that Roran has been seen out in the city, speaking with guards and soldiers, but when I questioned him about it, he was evasive and grew angry.

And now Tilbur wants to run my army. "No, Captain Granel will remain in charge."

Both Tilbur and Roran shake their heads. "If you do this," Tilbur says, "it will send a message to the army that you do not care about them. If you just let them sit out there, then you've announced to them that you just want them to act as a shield. You are not claiming them as your own."

"Then why don't I take charge of the army?" I ask. "I can do that. I don't have to sit in here and talk to Nobles and stand outside and talk to people on the street. It will, perhaps, declare that I'm more like my father, General Geran."

Tilbur scowls. "Draydon, what's going on? You fight me on everything. You challenge every word I say. You act like you don't trust me. Is there a reason not to trust me?"

I don't answer at first. I have no desire to lie to him. But perhaps now's the time to call him on his actions.

I glance over at Roran. He's armed. So is Tilbur. I'm wearing my new sword and armor. I have been practicing with it every day, but I don't like the feel and weight of the blade. It's a good weapon, solid and close to the same length as my own sword, and I'm a strong fighter, but if I call them on their treachery and they attack… can I survive? Maybe against Roran, but not against Tilbur. And certainly not against both.

But… it's time to take the risk.

"I don't trust you anymore, Tilbur. I haven't for a long time. You worked against me with Farnum! I know you did! You were seen with him at various times before I met with him. I think you set up the kidnapping and allowed them to slip past your guard." Turning to Roran, I add, "And you have been working with Tilbur. He's practically raised you, and you still resent me for taking your throne."

"We have been loyal!" Tilbur growls.

"Will you swear that on the Raker?" I demand.

Tilbur clenches his fists and shakes his head. "It won't work. Not on me."

"Why not?"

Tilbur takes a deep breath as if to calm himself, but it doesn't seem to help much. "Draydon… I lie!"

I just shake my head at that. I have no idea how to respond.

"I lie!" Tilbur continues. "I lie all the time! It's what I've been doing for the last nearly twelve years! I lie to Parthun. I lie to Corter. I lie to the people. I lie, and I lie, and I lie, and I lie! The Raker determines truth, but it's based on the heart of the speaker. It doesn't matter what I say when holding that statue! If I say my name is Tilbur or even that the sky is blue, it will see a heart of lies in me and kill me! I am too corrupt to endure a test of purity!”

I find myself clenching my fists, but I nearly laugh. “How convenient, Tilbur!” Turning to Roran, I ask, “And you?”

Roran sets his jaw and stares me down. “No. I won’t do it. I won’t be tested like this. I have been true to you, Draydon, and I won’t submit to an enchantment—even in this way. Never again!”

“Then I can’t trust either of you at all. Not even in the slightest!”

Both men stare at me. Roran’s mouth hangs open, and Tilbur’s face is beet red. I watch his jaw muscles flex as he grinds his teeth.

“How dare you!” Tilbur screams.

He slams his fist down on the table, and I jump out of my seat. Both men are on their feet in an instant, and I draw my sword. “Guards!” I call out, and Phil runs in with another four men. “Arrest Captain Tilbur and Captain Roran!” I order.

I watch Tilbur closely. He nearly reaches for his sword, but he hesitates. When they reach him and set about binding his hands behind his back, I fear what might happen if he decides to fight back. He dwarfs all the men. But then he turns to me, his eyes filled with hate.

I glance at Roran and see the same look is in his eyes.

“Throw them in the cells, but do not let a word of this go out to the people or the Nobles,” I say. I’m hoping I can keep this quiet for a time. The last thing I need is for the people to know we’re having this kind of problem. If Parthun’s influence can reach even my two closest family members, certainly no one will trust me to rule this Kingdom.

"You're making a mistake, Draydon," Roran spits. "How could you…"

"Get them out of here!" I holler, and the men lead them away.

When they're gone, I ask for some privacy. I find myself in a soft chair by the fire, and the tears begin to flow.

What a mess I'm in.

I'm so, so very lost.

25

Draydon and the Portly Lord

Hillbin sits across from me, examining my face.

I think we've managed to keep the whole thing with Tilbur and Roran a secret from most people, which is good, I think, but it's hard to keep that a secret from Hillbin in his own house. I suspect I have more here who are loyal to me than to Tilbur, but I have to keep watch.

"Draydon, will you tell me how this all came about? How you came to arrest your cousin and uncle?"

"Certainly," I say with confidence. I lay it all out for him. The rumors, the reactions they would give, the lack of clear answers from Tilbur, what Farnum said, and more. Finally, I explain how it all came out.

When I'm finished, he merely nods. "I see."

"I have to admit, Hillbin, I expected more of a response than that."

Hillbin smiles. "I am just taking it all in." He draws in a deep breath before he says anything. When he does speak, he speaks slowly. "Draydon, let me ask you a question. Let's just pretend for a moment that Parthun stands in your throne room, not too far from you. He does not have a weapon, and he's scared of what you might do to him. You have in your hand a dagger and are about to go arrest him. But let's just say that before you can make your move, a lion walks in and sits down between the two of you. In this story, the lion talks, and he announces, 'I'll protect King Parthun from Prince Draydon.' Now, Draydon, you need to get past the lion and reach Parthun. Tell me your strategy."

Irritation builds within me. I feel like he's treating me like a child, but I stop myself and focus in on his question. I know he's wise, so I take the time to try to figure it out.

"Well, I think I have two options."

"What are they, Draydon?"

"Option number one, kill the Lion."

"Good, but remember something, Draydon. It's a Lion. Not many men can kill such a creature, especially with only a dagger."

"Option number two is to somehow get past the Lion."

"And how might you do that?"

I think for a bit. "I'd have to get it out of the room. If I could do that, I could close the door, lock it out, and then I could tie up Parthun."

"Excellent. Now, Draydon, let's just say that you and Parthun are in a room. You are unarmed, for the sake of the story, and he has the dagger. He's about to attack, but then Roran and Tilbur walk in and take their stand between you, loudly declaring that they will protect you. Roran and Tilbur are both armed with swords and knives. I don't know about Prince Roran, but Tilbur is a vicious fighter. I have heard stories that would make you wonder if they could possibly be true. Tell me, if Parthun is to get to you, what are his options?"

I shake my head. "It's different. Roran and Tilbur are not loyal to me."

"Humor me, if you please, Draydon. Let's just say for the sake of the story that they are loyal to you. What must Parthun do?"

"The same. Either kill them or get them out of the room."

He nods. "King Parthun and the man who calls himself Lord Farnum are much the same. They're both devious, cruel, manipulative men. They have attained their positions and power through lies, extortion, and murder. Men such as they enjoy conflict. They will cause pain for no other reason than to know they have hurt someone."

I want to tell him to be quiet and leave the room, but I hold my tongue. I have to take the chance that I can trust Hillbin, and that he might have something helpful to say.

I see the sadness in his eyes as he says, "Conflict is an easy way to destroy trust among friends." Hillbin slowly takes in a breath and says, "Did you know that General Geran, as loved and respected as his name is, was suspected of being a part of the rebellion?"

I nod. I had heard that. Some of the rebels struggled with me because of that rumor.

"I can tell you right away, having known both General Geran and King Hartor, that this rumor is anything but true. But tell me, who was the Lion in the story for King Hartor?"

"I assume my father, General Geran. He was likely the one who protected King Hartor the most."

"True. He was a loyal friend, but a dangerous enemy. Few people dared stand against General Geran. If you think Tilbur is dangerous… he cowered before your father. Geran could be ruthless if you threatened Hartor. Absolutely ruthless. He once hunted a band of assassins down across the Talic for two and a half months in the middle of winter.

He would not stop until every last one of them was dead. Your father was certainly the Lion, and if anything, a Lion would appear weak next to that man."

Hillbin shakes his head, "But just before the rebellion, rumors began to spread. They suggested that Geran had grown tired of serving under such a weak King. The rumors hinted that Geran, the General who led the people to victory at Reber's Gate, wanted the throne. Then rumors spread that Geran was about to make his move for the throne, and Hartor was afraid of him."

"It wasn't true!" I say, anger welling up inside. I don't actually remember my father much, but I can't stand the thought that it might be.

"Of course not, Draydon. I was there and saw them talking, laughing, enjoying each other's company. They were close, those two. Very close. Your father was not driven by power, but had an intense love of loyalty. But… what better way to destroy trust than rumors?"

I shake my head and am about to tell him this is different when he says, "Both Parthun and Farnum use this tactic a lot. They spread rumors. And rumors are only effective if people believe them. Some people will believe ridiculous rumors. Others will need a bit of truth snuck in with the rumors. Tilbur likely did meet with Farnum, so there's your element of truth. But the goal of a rumor is not truth. The goal is to divide. And now, your two lions have been removed."

Fear grips me, but I don't know what to do about it. I still don't trust them.

"But I heard these rumors from Clarice! I thought I could trust them all!"

Hillbin smiles. "Clarice is good at what he does. He hears the rumors and passes them on to me. I am glad he did the same for you in my absence. However, Clarice doesn't interpret the rumors or filter them, he merely passes them along. It's your job to filter through them, Your Majesty." He pauses for a moment before he says, "Let me tell you the rumors I have heard of you."

My eyebrows shoot up, and my heart races.

Hillbin takes a deep breath, and his eyes drift to the ceiling. "I have heard that you are false, Draydon. I have heard that Tilbur merely found a young man who looks like General Geran. I have also heard that you killed your friend Rulf when he questioned you. I have even heard that you blackmailed Roran into abdicating and have now forced him to support you. I have also heard that, despite the fact that the Lady Ellcia thinks you are in love with her, you are actually in a relationship with Lieutenant Phil's daughter, Laanna."

I lean forward in my chair. "But none of that's true!"

"Of course not." He laughs, but I can see it's not at me. "That's not the point of a rumor, is it? It's not to spread truth. The purpose of a rumor is not even to spread lies. The purpose is to spread division. And as the old proverb goes, 'A house divided against itself cannot stand.' When you hear a rumor, you must first ask if what you've heard lines up with what you know of the person. Second, is there a reason why someone might spread such rumors?"

I stop and think that through. What do I know of Roran? He's been trustworthy. He's sworn allegiance to me. He's stood by me, even though I'm taking the life he wants to live. And Tilbur, despite how he's treated me growing up, he did it to protect me. And he protected Roran and Rulf. And he's now stood by me...

I gasp. "What have I done?"

Hilbin leans forward. "You believed the word of a liar over the word of honorable men. You acted the fool, Draydon. You fell for Parthun's lies. You have been deceived, and you did exactly what Parthun and Farnum wanted. You removed the lions protecting you. Removed both lions from the room." Before I can think of anything to say, he adds, "Both these men have laid their lives at your feet, and you have tossed aside their gift, declaring it worthless."

"What do I do?"

Hillbin leans forward. "Humble yourself. Don't do what Parthun would do and hold to lies. Don't cling to your pride. Do what Parthun would never do. Beg forgiveness."

I run through the palace. I think Hillbin is behind me, but he's short and round. I doubt he'll keep up.

The four men who arrested Tilbur and Roran are guarding their cells. I have refused to allow anyone else to have contact with them.

When I get to the small prison we've created in the palace, I rush inside. The guards react at first, but when they see it's me, they give me a bow.

"Open the door!" I order. "Let them out!"

The doors open, and I rush in before Roran and Tilbur can move. They're both on the floor, sitting with their backs to the wall. Neither one stands. I see the anger on their faces. No… the betrayal. Not their betrayal, but mine.

I don't know where to begin. "I… I'm sorry. I'm sorry to both of you. I heard rumors of you, Tilbur, that you were meeting with Farnum, and it destroyed my trust in you. Then, Roran, Farnum told me that you were working with Tilbur, and I no longer trusted you. I…" I stop and hang my head. "I'm so sorry. I have no excuse. I let Parthun and Farnum's rumors control me. I walked into their trap and rejected the two of you."

Roran's expression hasn't changed. He sits there and just stares at me like he wants nothing more than for me to leave.

But Tilbur, surprisingly, stands. "Prince Draydon," he says. "I am angry that you doubted me and threw me in prison." He lets out a sigh. "But I know what it is like to be manipulated by Parthun. I grew up with that man's lies floating in my head. The anger and rage I feel every day comes from that man, feeding my rage, feeding my hatred. He's a wicked man." Tilbur shakes his head and says, "I am angry, but I... understand."

Roran remains on the floor for another moment. I see him close his eyes and shake his head, but then he stands. "Caric... Draydon, I've lost everything. And even things I didn't lose in the enchantment, I can never have. I've accepted that. I really have. But to set that aside and to give my life to you... only to have you reject me, not trust me, throw me in a cell." He shakes his head again, and I think for a moment that I've destroyed everything between us, but he calms down. "I can't serve you if you don't trust me."

"I trust you, Roran." By this point, the tears stream down my face. I turn to Tilbur and say, "I trust you, Tilbur. I just... forgot my way. I grew suspicious, proud, untrusting, and angry. I'm sorry. I'm not a very good King."

At that, Roran smiles. "No, you're not."

My shoulders slump, and I feel like giving up.

"But, Draydon," he continues, "I think you will be one day. We just have to stop letting Parthun divide us."

"Agreed," I say. "I won't let it happen again." To both of them I ask, "Can we try again? I will trust the two of you."

A smile slowly grows on Roran's face, and he nods. "I'm in."

Tilbur steps forward and puts his large hand on my shoulder. "You have my loyalty, whether you throw me in prison or not. If you want all the details of all I'm doing, just say so. I am used to doing much of my work covertly, so I rarely tell anyone everything that I'm up to. But I can change that."

"No, how about you just tell me more of what you're up to, not everything."

Tilbur nods. "Agreed."

I turn to the guards and order them not to speak of this. If I didn't want people to know there was division in the palace, I certainly don't want them knowing I fell to Parthun's tactics. Nor do I want to spread word that might make people doubt Roran and Tilbur.

I feel like a fool, but I stand with my friends. Despite my actions, I have a cousin and an uncle who remain by my side.

The first day of Spring, the day Parthun has been ordered to arrive, is only weeks away. I don't know how this will all turn out, but it's going to happen soon.

26

Ellcia and the Gramma

Gramma wants to show us where she lives," Marleet hisses. "She's very excited about it. I think it'll mean a lot if we take the time to go."

It's strange to see Marleet with these two. I don't even know their names, but they're from Grimmer. They treat Marleet like they truly are her grandparents, and she just clings to them like they're family. I found it irritating at first, but then I began to realize the problem wasn't them. It was me. I see what they have—Marleet with her Gramma and Grampa—and I'm jealous.

I've never had that kind of thing. Well, at least not since I was really little. I barely remember my parents, and I have no memory of grandparents. Granel told me our grandparents were killed in Parthun's rebellion alongside our parents.

I wish I knew what it was like to have people dote over me like the way these two treat Marleet.

They want me to call them Gramma and Grampa. I thanked them for that, but didn't feel comfortable with it. Now, since I said I wouldn't but everyone else calls them that, I don't know what to call them. Instead, I just act awkward whenever I should use their name.

I wish Draydon were here. He understands me. We could be awkward together.

It's been nearly three weeks since Hemot left, and three weeks since the kidnapping attempt. I still struggle with the fear and some nightmares, but I'm doing better. We've tried to keep up security, though. That's been annoying in one sense, but it makes me feel a lot better.

We reach their house. It's small, has a bit of a smell of cooking—not a nice smell—but it's clean. I can see why they're so proud of it. Having grown up as a servant and since then, living on the run, I know how precious it is to have a space of your own.

They offer us tea, and we both drink it. Denner and Billot, along with Frellson, who's become more and more of my own personal guard, stand outside. The wind is cold today, and I want to invite them in, but there's no room for three grown men in addition to the four of us. In fact, Marleet and I sit in the only place where someone can sit, on the edge of Gramma and Grampa's bed, while they stand and lean against the wall.

Despite my jealousy, I see why Marleet loves them so much. They tell me a bit about the time they spent together at Prince Roran's return. They tell me how they protected Marleet because they saw she was in trouble. They had no idea she was Nobleborn, but when they found out, it didn't surprise them. It turns out they've heard of a lot of Nobleborn who have left the Nobility for a time. It's common enough for Nobleborn children to wander through the country in disguise. They seem to feel this is normal for Nobles, which makes me wonder if my parents ever did anything like that.

After Marleet was taken back into the Royal Court, they had returned quickly to Grimmer along with just about everyone else. A younger man they knew had come with a horse-drawn wagon, and they rode in the back as far as Port, then walked the rest of the way on foot.

I come to find out they're actually related to Hella. Gramma is an aunt or a cousin or… I don't know. It's really hard to figure out that kind of thing. They start to talk about how they're related, and the next thing I know, they've mentioned pretty much everyone they know, and I have no idea who is related to whom or how.

After about an hour, I know it's time to leave. I'd prefer to stay. Gramma is kind of beyond sweet and kind… sweeter than I think anyone on the planet. And Grampa… he just keeps making these little comments that make me laugh! I can't help it. He knows it, too, so he waits for me to take a sip of my tea and then drops another one of them. I've spit out more tea than I've taken in! The front of my shirt is now damp and, unfortunately, so is Gramma's dress.

But the work we have to do in organizing and leading… it's a lot. People come to us for all sorts of matters. Some of the issues can be passed along to others, but when it comes to some stuff like judgments, really big decisions, disputes, and more, we have to deal with it. We also have to keep a constant eye on all matters, or the people tend to just… not take care of things.

I mention it's time to leave, and Gramma's face falls. I feel guilty and almost start to explain that we'll stay longer, but we just can't. It's time to go.

"Well, my Lady," Grampa says in his best attempt at speaking formally, which is not very formal, "Gramma and me… we gonna walk you back to your little hall there by the sea." Before I can react in any way at all, he raises his hands and says, "No, don't you try tellin' us you don't need it. Ladies like yourselves got guards and soldiers and all, I get that, but you need more. We family. You need us to stand with you, and you need to know we here for you. Even

Nobles like yourselves need… um… you know." He shifts on his feet, and his face fills with embarrassment.

Gramma smiles and finishes what he was going to say. "Even Nobles need to know they loved, my Lady. So, let us walk you back."

I smile. That's exactly what we need. Nordin and Hella are like family. In fact, in a way, I feel like Hella is the mom I wish I had. But it's nice to have grandparents as well.

We step out of their little house, and the wind hits hard, knocking my hood back. I turn to make sure the others are still with me, and a sharp pain in my neck and the sound of something zipping past my head causes me to duck.

Someone slams into me, and I see Marleet go down under the weight of one of her guards, but what I can't look away from is the crossbow bolt stuck in Gramma's chest as she slowly drops to the ground.

The men—four of them—kneel before me. Hands tied behind their backs, blindfolded and gagged. Nordin, Frellson, and Denner managed to get information out of them. I don't know how, but I'm guessing from looking at the men that they weren't gentle.

It turns out the healer in this area, here in Freond, is quite good. Apparently, farming accidents can be serious, and it's not the first time she's worked on someone with a serious chest wound. I hear the arrow came out quickly, and there's no sign of poison.

Marleet's there with Gramma now, along with Grampa. The last message I heard, though, is they still don't know if Gramma will make it.

And now, I have to do something about these four men.

It turns out they were sent by someone they call Lord Farnum. I feared perhaps he was someone in the castle, but it turns out he might be the Lord of the City of Rainer. They call that the City of Thieves, so if this man, Farnum, is the Lord of it, he's likely corrupt. Maybe not even a real Lord. I've heard of men and women who have taken power and claimed the title.

And so, this Lord Farnum sent these four men with orders to put a crossbow bolt in my neck. Not in my chest. Not in my head. In my neck. Very specific. And very deadly. If I hadn't moved at that moment, I'd be gone, but then again, Gramma would be okay.

I gingerly touch the bandage on my neck where the bolt grazed the skin. It's fairly deep, and they had to stitch it up. That's the first time anyone has sewn a cut closed on me. I hope it's the last. I didn't take well to it.

The men had fired twice. One missed entirely, the other grazed my neck and then… well. The other shot is why we're here.

And now… I have to decide their fate.

"Frippolee?"

The older man comes forward and gives a bow. "Yes, my Lady."

"What are the punishments in Freond for murder or attempted murder?"

"It is the same, my Lady."

"And that is?" I ask.

"Hanging, my Lady. They must be hung in the square. It is the law."

I close my eyes. I was afraid of that. If that's the law, then I have no choice. But… I still have to order it. And that's what I can't bring myself to do.

I look down at the men. I can't order it, but then again, I really, really, really want to. They shot Gramma. Who does that? Do they even feel guilty?

Nordin assures me they do not.

"Frippolee, is there any question that they were the men? Any doubt?"

He shakes his head. "No, my Lady. The shots came from a small warehouse. No one else was in the building at the time, nor did anyone enter or exit. Two of the men had crossbows, and when they were captured, one of the men told us you'd die whether we stopped them or not. Even without the confession, there is no doubt."

I clench my fists and try to calm my shaking. This is one of the reasons I never wanted to be a Royal.

"And if I don't order their deaths?"

Fripolee's eyes focus on me, and for the first time, I see doubt in his eyes when it comes to my leadership. "My Lady… if you don't…" He pauses and takes a deep breath. "I don't really know, exactly. It's just never been done. The law requires it, so there's no way to change it without changing the law, but even if you did, it would not apply to these men as they committed the crime under the previous law. I…" He shakes his head. "I suspect, my Lady, you are struggling to order the men to death, correct? You feel guilty?"

I nod.

"I understand. I have only had to order a death once, and it was difficult. Very difficult. But there is no other option. The law does not allow for their punishment to be removed or even stayed, and if you protected them, you would be guilty of taking part in their action. You would be an accomplice to the attempted murder of Gramma."

I smile. Not because of the situation, but simply because everyone, even Frippolee, calls them Gramma and Grampa. It turns out they were even well known in the farming communities. They've traveled a lot over the years and are loved everywhere.

"The gallows have already been set up, my Lady. You actually do not have the authority to refuse. Murder always bears the penalty of death."

And that's where I'm struggling. Because... Parthun... unless there is a way to pardon his crimes, Draydon will have to order his hanging. And that's what I don't want. As much as I hate the man, I would rather he be left in a cell. But the law of Sevord won't allow Parthun to live any more than the law of Freond will allow these men to live.

"Take them," I order. It's all I can say, and Frellson and his soldiers drag the men to their feet.

I don't go with them. First, there is a security concern, but second, I've seen a hanging once. I didn't mean to, but I had to buy some supplies from the market for Tereese in the castle kitchens. And Parthun liked his hangings. I still can't forget what I saw. Nor can I forget the cheers of the people.

We live in a brutal world. I know Draydon and I can make a difference, but it will never be enough. There will always be more cruelty.

27

Draydon and the Army

I stand on the wall facing west, back toward the cliffs, Switcher Pass, and Sevord City. It's still cold, but it's a pleasant chill. The Talic does not warm up as early in the spring as the coastal regions, but I'm happy to feel a less bitter wind. In the sun, some of the snow is even melting, which creates ice in the morning after the cold night, but at least we're moving in the right direction.

My mind drifts back to the last time I was here. Well, not here, but down below, moving through the guardhouse to get out of the city. At that time, I had Ellcia and Hemot at my side. Now, it's Roran and Tilbur. The one a boy I had grown up thinking didn't even have the capacity for a full conversation, and the other I grew up believing was my true enemy.

I smile. As much as I care about Roran and Tilbur, I'd still prefer having Ellcia by my side. But, for now, she's where she needs to be, and I'm where I need to be.

Gillan is with us as well. He's a guard, loyal to the throne, and willing to take a risk for the Kingdom. The first time I met him, both of us were committed to seeing Roran take the throne. Now, we're both committed to seeing me on that same throne.

The army, led by Captain Granel, spreads out before us. They're already setting up tents, and it won't be long before Captain Granel and his Lieutenants show up at the gate to report to me.

I feel nervous, actually. It's one thing to claim the throne and speak to Nobles, but to stand here knowing thousands of soldiers wish to offer their allegiance to me… well… that's another matter.

Tilbur has coached me through everything. My first thought was that I should head out there right away, but Tilbur explained the procedure was for the soldiers to approach the city first. Their presence here is either peaceful or not, and they are required to declare their intentions upon arrival.

Three soldiers on horseback leave the army and begin the short ride toward us. They take the road as the Talic is not the easiest ground to move across.

When they reach the sealed gate, I recognize the man in the lead. His face is twisted and marked, scarred from the tragedy that took his and Ellcia's parents in the rebellion nearly twelve years ago. Ellcia's brother, Captain Granel, rides forward a little ahead of the two others and stops.

The silence is broken by Gillan's loud voice as he calls out, "What business have you at Haner? Do you come in peace or war?"

"We come in peace, my friend," Captain Granel calls back. "We come in response to our future King's orders in the hopes that we might offer ourselves as loyal servants to the throne. My name is Captain Granel."

Gillan nods to me. I guess that means the formality is over, and I turn and move to the stairs. Once I reach the ground, I call out, "Open the gates," and they slowly pull back, revealing Granel and the other two soldiers on the other side.

When the gate's fully open, I step forward, and all three men dismount. Tilbur told me to only take one or maybe two steps past the wall, and that's what I do as the men approach. Reaching me, they drop to their knees, and Captain Granel says, "Prince Draydon, Son of Geran, future King of Sevord, I offer you my loyalty, my love, and my fealty."

The two men behind him offer the same oath, and I invite them to stand. When they do, the two men in the back are smiling, and I find myself smiling as well.

"It is good to see you again, Captain."

"And you too, Your Majesty. I have to apologize, however, for holding you prisoner the last time we spoke."

My smile grows larger. "Consider it something we will one day laugh about!" I point to the army. "Have you come in response to my orders?"

"We have, Your Majesty."

"Then I wish to meet with the troops and assume command of the loyal armies of Sevord by appointing Captain Tilbur to oversee the army."

"Of course, Your Majesty."

The smiles on the faces of the men behind Granel grow. I had wondered if they would take offense at such a move, but Tilbur seems to be right. They're pleased with it. Granel, however, is hard to read. His expression doesn't change much, but from what I've seen, he's a good man.

Tilbur calls out to Gillan and within seconds, men bring horses forward. It'll be Roran, Tilbur, myself, and our guards heading out with these three.

When we reach the troops, I'm amazed to see their smiles. I think that royalty typically doesn't smile back at people, at least with a genuine smile, but I just let loose, offering huge grins, waving at people. Anyone I recognize gets a specific wave. I can't remember most of their names, but I do recognize the guards who stood sentry outside of the section I lived in while in the caves, along with a few others.

I was actually afraid I would see some of the disloyal soldiers who worked with Frindor, but as far as I can tell, none of them are here. Of course, there are a lot of soldiers.

When we reach the center of the camp, I catch sight of the command tent. It stands on a bit of a hill and is quite large and fancy. Granel, as he gives his tour, points it out and explains that once I put him in charge of the army and commanded him to come to me, he claimed Frindor's command tent.

I smile at that. I don't really like Frindor, for many reasons. When I take the throne, he'll certainly lose his rank.

"Captain Granel, before I receive your report, I would like to address the soldiers."

He nods at me, and I'm about to dismount, but Tilbur hisses, "No, Draydon, stay on your horse. Gives you more height and more authority."

I turn my horse around. I'm not actually good on horseback. Tilbur's been teaching me, but I'm a slow learner with this. I do my best to make it look like I know what I'm doing as the soldiers gather around.

When I speak, I have to holler. There's a steady wind blowing across the Talic, and we're outside. There are also thousands of men and women here. I'm told they'll spread my words around to those who can't hear.

I do my best to cover the things Tilbur told me should be said. I thank them for their loyalty and offer my lifelong gratitude. I speak about Parthun and commit to claiming the throne and restoring peace and freedom in our nation. I cover a few more things and declare the army under the direct command of Tilbur. And I point out Captain Granel's extreme loyalty, despite Parthun's attempts to discredit him and even take his life.

When I'm finished, every soldier drops to his knees and offers me his or her vow of fealty, to which I respond by offering my commitment to love and care for the nation, serving with humility.

My horse nearly throws me from the saddle when we're finished, as the entire army cheers. I'm not surprised. I thought maybe we were under attack.

Before I'm done, the crowd parts… no, not "parts". Men and women dive out of the way as if their lives depend on it. When I see Traltor and Nareesa racing towards us, I know lives do depend on the soldiers moving out of the way.

They're both huge. Really huge. Traltor is descended from giants, and that's not in question. He's big, strong, kind of ugly… well… I mean, he's a giant-man. He's not just ugly, he's… giantish. So, maybe handsome according to giant standards, but according to human standards… um…

As for Nareesa, his wife, she looks almost like a child next to him, but she's still much taller than any man I've ever met. The story is that she's fully human, but no one believes it. I mean… I've seen her throw grown men. And not just a little way. I've seen her throw them like they're nothing but a toy in the hand of a child.

I brace myself. They're good people. Loyal, kind at times, and faithful beyond question, but they're not polite. All you can do is expect them to do the unexpected.

When they reach me, Traltor wraps his large arms around me and gives me a big hug. I watch my horse run out of harm's way as Nareesa comes around and embraces me as well. Traltor begins to cry, which creates a lot of moisture, and Nareesa strokes my hair like I'm her pet.

"Oh, Draydon, we are soooo thrilled you are here! We've been soooo worried about you," Nareesa says in an attempt to speak in a calming, motherly manner. Unfortunately, the tone of voice sounds more like she's planning on eating me than anything else.

"Put him down, Traltor, Nareesa!" Tilbur hollers.

I have to admit, it's brave of him to speak that way. These two could kill him without breaking a sweat.

Traltor turns to Tilbur and just sneezes at him. As much as I find it disgusting, the selfish part of me is grateful Traltor didn't do that while facing me.

The giant man slowly sets me down, and Tilbur begins to chew them out, but I stop him. "Wait." Turning to the giants, I announce loudly, "Traltor and Nareesa, you have been loyal to the throne, and your son has been a good friend, guide, and protector to me. In addition to this, Nareesa once saved my life. As such, when you come to me, Traltor and Nareesa, I welcome your hugs." I can't believe I just said that, but I did. I remember the advice to offer friendship in response to loyalty. "I just ask that you be more gentle."

Traltor looks embarrassed but pleased, while Nareesa screams out in her aggressive way, "Whoa! That sounds great, Draydon!" as she ruffles my hair. Unfortunately, she's not gentle, and I find myself checking my head to make sure I still have hair up there.

When we head into the tent to receive Granel's report, Traltor and Nareesa join us. Tilbur tries to stop them, but they just laugh and come in anyway. I'm glad they're loyal. They would be a horrific enemy.

As we gather around a table in the center of the tent, I begin to wonder about Traltor and Nareesa. Something is nagging at the back of my mind.

Before Granel can begin, it hits me. They're a significant threat! Not to me, but to Parthun. And as devious and wicked as Parthun is, he's certainly intelligent. He won't miss this one matter. I don't know whether Parthun was involved in the theft of my armor and sword, but that's a major win for Parthun's cause. He could easily kill Traltor if he gets a hold of that sword. But whether he has the sword or not, he'll definitely do something about them because Traltor and Nareesa… they could march right into Parthun's camp and kill him, and no one could stop them.

Parthun won't ignore that matter. This is something I have to consider…

"Your Majesty," Granel begins. "The situation in Sevord City and in the nation is grim."

That's not exactly what I had hoped to hear, but it's not at all surprising. "Yes, Captain, it is."

Granel is about to continue when the flap to the tent opens, and an old man walks in. "Your Majesty," he says with a large grin.

"Berin!" Despite just hearing things are not good in Sevord, I can't help but grin like a fool. "You came! I wondered if you would join Captain Granel."

"Aye," Berin says as he wanders to the table. "I wouldn't miss this, although I didn't enjoy the journey. I'm getting a little old for adventures.

I laugh at that. Berin might be old, but he's far from weak or frail. "Did Hob come as well?"

He shakes his head. "No, those in the castle, for the most part, remained. I doubt Hob could leave without risking his life. And he might not understand all that's going on."

I remember we're in a meeting and turn back to Granel, apologize, and then ask him to continue.

"Thank you, Your Majesty," Granel says. "When I received your letter, Captain Frindor was in the city. I had to be careful, as many of his soldiers are loyal to him, and I did not wish to start a war right then. Parthun has been spreading lies and rumors, turning the army against you, Your Majesty, and against all those who are loyal to the throne, such as me. His lies are effective, and many have been deceived into questioning your right to rule. The rumors even suggest the nation is just about to be disappointed and betrayed by another young Royal. Most of the army is now disillusioned. He has spun everything from Prince Roran's abdication to your fleeing of the castle as proof that no one so young could ever be anything but selfish and unreliable."

I frown at all this. I had hoped we could approach this more directly and handle it with more maturity and trust, but it can never be so with Parthun on the throne. Hillbin is right. Rumors and lies are for the purpose of dividing. And a divided nation will never stand.

"With your letter in hand, Your Majesty, I took command of much of the army, those who would obey my orders at least, and approached the King with Traltor by my side to demand that he accompany me to Haner. As is his way, he had a dozen reasons why he could never leave Sevord City immediately without failing in his duties to the people. While he did this, nearly two hundred soldiers filed into the throne room."

Much of this I already know. I've spoken with Hillbin many times over the recent days about all that he knows of the situation in Sevord.

"At that point, he could not threaten my life, of course, because I had a letter from you and because the Nobles were present, but it was clear I would not live long if I remained. He would find some justification for my death. I left the castle, and on my way out, Traltor and I had to fight off two attempts on our lives. I believe Frindor was behind it all, as some of the men Traltor killed were men who report directly to him. The army set out that day to come to you, declaring our loyalty to the throne."

"And the rest of the army?" I ask. "Those who stood with you in the mountains? Those who were loyal all along?"

Captain Granel shakes his head. "Parthun's rumors have been effective. His words are subtle. They are always well chosen to deceive and corrupt the mind. Many soldiers have simply left—gone home. They are discouraged and angry. Parthun has spun Prince Roran's abdication to be an act of cruelty to the people, and presented himself as the stable, trustworthy option. I believe if it comes to war, many will side with you, but many will side with him and many more will simply walk away." He shakes his head. "I'm sorry, Your Majesty, but I fear when the day comes that you take your throne, you will have a divided Kingdom."

"I expected as much. A man like Parthun will not tolerate unity, unless it is under his control. But we will find peace and learn to trust one another again."

I thank Granel, then ask a question on my mind. "And have you heard of your sister, the Lady Ellcia?"

Granel shakes his head. "I have heard many things about her, and many things about you, but it is difficult to sort out the truth from the lies. Much of what is said are Parthun's poisoned words. From what I have learned, my sister, along with the Lady Marleet, Hemot, and others, have formed a fleet of ships and a sizable force of armed soldiers. Her standing army is nothing compared to what you see here, but enough to cause concern in the capital. Since they have declared their loyalty to the throne and to the rightful heir of Sevord, Parthun is unable to move directly against them at this point, but it will not be long."

"A fleet of ships and an army?" I'm surprised at that. When I left, they had one warship, a transport, and five fishing vessels. That's hardly a fleet, especially when only one is prepared to fight. As for the army... I had hoped... wow... that's great news.

"It is difficult to know for sure, but I believe they have somewhere around a half dozen warships, if not more, and perhaps over thirty civilian ships, many of which have been equipped for battle on some level or another. It turns out the fishing villages up and down the coast have allied themselves with Lady Ellcia's forces, and a group down in the southern coast has begun to form, also in support of the throne."

I had hoped Ellcia and the others would be able to spread the word. I do want to hear some of the rumors, but if they're anything like what's been spread about me, I think it's best if I not poison my mind with Parthun's words.

"If my sources are accurate, I believe Parthun is now unwilling to send any ships out alone, as they never come back. But he is also unwilling to send his entire fleet out to deal with them as they are proclaiming support for you, Your Majesty, which is technically the legal position that all citizens of Sevord and the Talic are required to hold. In fact, Parthun himself has declared support for a rightful heir to the throne, but he has suggested there may be more to the matter than anyone knows."

"And what does that mean?" I ask.

"He is a murderer, a liar, and a manipulator, Your Majesty. He is, I believe, simply trying to put doubt in people's minds."

I'm thrilled to hear that Ellcia is doing well—safe and certainly far better than I'd imagined—but I can't focus on that right now. I need to ensure the transfer of power has gone well. "And one more question, Captain. This one requires a great deal of openness, but I wish to know not the answer you think you should give, but the answer that is fully true."

"Of course, Your Majesty. Ask anything."

"I have just recently placed you in full authority over the armies of Sevord, and now I have just placed you and the armies under Captain Tilbur. How are you handling this?"

Captain Granel shakes his head. "I am absolutely thrilled, Your Majesty. Captain Tilbur is a loyal, strong leader. I am hopeful of spending time with him and to learn from him. I don't need to be in charge, Your Majesty. I lead as my act of service to the Kingdom. There is no difficulty for me in giving up authority to Captain Tilbur."

I nod. "Good. Then I will leave Captain Tilbur with you, and I will return to the city. I hope to see you at the Palace at some point, along with many of your officers."

I turn and leave, mounting my horse, and making my way through the army with Roran and our guards. When we're most of the way back, waving at soldiers and thanking them for their loyalty, I find myself laughing.

"What's so funny?" Roran asks.

"When we entered the tent, Traltor and Nareesa… they were… quiet. It's just funny because I can't imagine them ever being quiet."

Roran adds his own laugh. "You didn't look at them?"

I shake my head in reply.

"When we entered Granel's tent, they took a seat by the side, snuggled up next to one another, and fell asleep within minutes. My guess is Granel is going to have a hard time waking them and getting them out of his command tent."

We both laugh and continue on our way. It's scary to think of what's ahead, but it feels good to have our army with us.

28

Ellcia and the South

My Lady? Are you sure you're okay?" Frellson asks. I'm not really comfortable on horseback, so I'm not surprised at the question. I expect I look as awkward as I feel. "I'm okay, Lieutenant. I just haven't ridden much. I'll get used to it."

Marleet rides beside me on her own horse. She, at least, looks like she knows a little of what she's doing. Apparently, she rode a horse out of Haner. It wasn't much, but it was enough to get over this… whatever I'm dealing with.

I'm sure I'm going to fall off. Again. I don't want to do that. It hurt the last two times I hit the ground.

"Don't worry, my Lady," Hella says as she approaches. "By the time we get to Sevord, you'll be an expert in that saddle."

I frown, despite the encouragement. "Hella?"

"Yes, my Lady?"

"Did you just catch up to me on foot? I'm on horseback, and you're on foot, and now you're about to pass me? Am I that slow?"

Hella laughs and replies, "Yes, my Lady. But don't worry. We won't leave you behind."

I hear her giggle as she picks up her speed and moves past us along the road leading south. I think that's one of the many reasons why I love Hella so much. She and Nordin are so smart and wise, but also so much fun.

I twist in the saddle to catch a good look behind, and Marleet frowns at me. The last time I tried this, I ended up on the ground. The horse nearly stepped on my face. But I need to get a handle on this. I also need to know that everyone else is setting out okay.

I don't expect this journey will be quick—in fact, I expect we'll be weeks—but we have to head south. I need to reach Sevord City, then we have to deal with whatever mess we face there. Assuming we survive that, then we need to make it all the way to Haner by the first day of Spring.

I had assumed we'd only travel with the army that I've built—we're up to nearly seven thousand—but it turns out everyone wanted to come, aside from a few people who have to remain to care for livestock and those too ill to travel. Not even a security force has remained behind. Nordin tells me the peoples north of here, though they are not part of Sevord, are friendly toward the Northern Tribes.

Gramma and Grampa are among those staying behind. Gramma is still too weak to travel, although she's recovering well considering she nearly died. Grampa, of course, is staying back to care for her. I know they're both disappointed. They informed me they feel they are missing out on, in their own words, "The most biggest event done in our nation in our own entire livings."

I can't say they're wrong. This is big. It's kind of turning into a bit of a war for the nation, to wrestle control from a tyrant who should never sit on the throne. As far as I know, nothing like this has happened since Draydon's ancestors established the monarchy, and that was something like seven or eight hundred years ago.

I slowly bring myself around to face forward again, careful to keep my balance. Marleet gives me a thumbs up, and I'm truly proud of myself for not falling.

The road is wide in this area, but that's not always the case. There is, however, plenty of beach, which is not the best to walk on, and there's the forest to my left. It's packed full of soldiers, scouting out ahead and keeping us all safe.

Seven thousand soldiers…

It's more than I had hoped, actually. The northern villages do not have a huge population, so I expected to have less than a thousand. But they've surprised me. A lot of people live up in this area, and pretty much all of them want Parthun gone.

In addition to our foot soldiers and small cavalry, the fleet is slowly moving south, visible in the distance out in the ocean. We're up to eight ships, including the two destroyers we just captured. I think that means we now have two-thirds of the entire fleet, so… we pretty much rule the sea now. Especially considering the fleet of fishing vessels we've acquired, which is a big deal considering each one is fact, maneuverable, and manned by some of the most dangerous fighters in the kingdom: fishermen.

And then, whatever Hemot can muster from the southern coast, assuming he's well received…

I stop that line of thinking. I'm not struggling as much as Marleet is with worry, but Hemot is certainly on my mind all the time. I hope he's safe. And I hope he can meet us with his own little army at Sevord. If he doesn't, our whole campaign might come to a quick end!

My butt still hurts.

Nearly two weeks of travel in this saddle, and I still hurt. The insides of my legs are no longer raw, which I'm happy about, but they don't feel good. At least they're not blistered anymore. But my butt and my back and my shoulders. All of it just aches. All the time.

I'm told that the sore butt-thing is just something I have to live with until I get used to it. The back and shoulders, however, I'm able to deal with a bit each night when Nordin and Frellson spar with me or when Marleet and I spar. I'm getting pretty good with my sword, although I can't match Marleet when she's using her enchanted blade. We've kept what it can do quiet from everyone. I trust most of the people in our group, but even trustworthy people talk and spread information. If the wrong person hears about it, it'll get stolen.

I'm told I'll see the tallest spires of the castle soon. We should be near to the city by noon today, but our scouts tell us the city is shut up tight against our arrival. We haven't sent any messengers ahead, and no one has come to us yet, although one of our scouts was killed late yesterday. The crossbow bolt punched right through his chainmail.

I'm still steaming over that one. There was nothing said. They weren't arguing. My scouts didn't even know Parthun's men were there. The bolt just took the man down, and then the remaining scout, while taking cover, saw three soldiers ride away.

It was cowardly and cruel. But then again, that's just like Parthun.

Marleet is beaming beside me. She's doing a bit better than I am in the saddle. Not that her extra experience helps her now, she's just less sore.

But the big thing that keeps her going is the message we received early this morning. One of Nordin's fishing vessels drew close enough to shore to relay a message. A large force, a little smaller than our own, is moving up the coast, south of the city.

Hemot's frigate, the Geran, is escorting the force coming from the south, and when our vessels approached his ship, Relin was on board. Hemot was safe, successful, and is now riding with the people. Like our army—we have thousands of others with us, those who have no intention of fighting—Hemot's army appears to have a large group of families and even flocks of sheep. That's probably good, too, as we're growing short on food.

Over the next two hours, Sevord comes into view. We have no more run-ins with Parthun's scouts, although we are keeping our own scouts much closer to the army and far better defended now. I've sent two thousand soldiers ahead to circle around the city through the forests. Hemot is supposed to do the same, and the goal is for them to meet up and cut off all routes to and from the city.

On the west side, the ocean, Nordin's ships have maneuvered into position. They face six warships in total, all close to the harbor. The report that came to me was Parthun had one Royal Warship, two destroyers, and three frigates. That's against our one Royal Warship, three destroyers, and four frigates, along with over twenty fishing boats.

Nordin has managed to put a cannon on two of the larger fishing boats, which is helpful, but kind of scary. I watched when they tested it out. It nearly capsized the boat, so I hope it doesn't come to a battle on the sea.

"My Lady," Frellson calls as he approaches. Nordin has put him in charge of much of the army. He's still trying to be my personal bodyguard, however, which is a little strange because he's never around. Denner and Billot keep an eye on me, along with a couple men named Rickle and Yirp. Rickle is one of Nordin's men from Nimville, and Yirp is his son. He's my age, which is weird, because he has no fighting experience, and I'm actually a better swordsman than he is, but he's big, looks tough, and plays the part well.

"Yes, Lieutenant?" I call out.

He's on horseback, riding like he was born in the saddle. On his face is a large grin. "My Lady, we have found a couple who live in a house not far into the forest. They have good news for us."

"Bring them to me!" I order.

He smiles at me and hesitates, so I ask, "Is there something else?"

"My Lady, they will give you a report on Parthun, but I have also learned something else. About Prince Draydon."

My hands shake. I hope the smile means it's good news. I haven't heard anything—anything at all—since he left. Nothing to confirm if he's alive.

"Word has spread throughout this region that Prince Draydon has made a claim for the throne, and that he is in Haner, awaiting Parthun's arrival."

I nearly fall out of the saddle. It's the first confirmation I've had that Draydon's actually alive. Until this point, I've just had to move forward assuming he made it through the Northern Pass, but I had no real reason to believe it. I just had to… hope.

A laugh escapes my lips, and I climb down out of the saddle and twirl around. I feel my face go hot, and I know it's beat red. This isn't the way a Lady is supposed to act, but Frellson just smiles. I think he's happy for me.

"I'll return in a short while with the couple, my Lady," he says and heads off to the east.

Ten minutes later, they stand before me. Not only am I still smiling, but it feels good to be out of the saddle. I do my best to stand in a way that doesn't suggest my back aches, or every movement hurts my butt, but the grin on my face is genuine. "Thank you for meeting with me."

They bow to me. I'd say they're in their twenties. Perhaps just married. Her belly is swollen. I've never been good at recognizing this kind of thing, but I think she's likely just about to give birth.

"My name is Lady Ellcia. I am in charge of these armies, loyal to Prince Draydon, the Crown Prince. We are here to ensure the usurper to the throne, Parthun, son of Trevolay, does not disobey Prince Draydon's orders, and to offer support and loyalty to the future King of Sevord and the Talic." I nearly break out in a grin. I practiced that little spiel a lot, and it came out perfectly. I can't believe I find so much joy in that!

"My Lady," the man says. I see the fear in his eyes, and his young wife steps just slightly behind him. I can't help but notice his hand goes down protectively over her belly.

I'm shocked that he's scared of me. No one has ever been scared of... me! But then I look around. In every direction, soldiers march or ride, others work to set up tents. Thousands of them... and they all report to me. To add to this, I have about a dozen soldiers standing behind me, all with hands on the hilts of their swords.

Add to the fact that I'm a seventeen-year-old girl with six week's growth of hair on her head, sticking up in every direction, dressed in armor and wearing a sword at my hip... there's so much here that's both confusing and terrifying.

I raise my hands, and both the man and woman flinch. "You're not in danger here. I only require honesty from you. That's it. Even if your news is not what I want to hear, if you're honest, then I am your friend."

The man nods, but I can see he doesn't believe me. I guess that doesn't matter. As long as he tells me what he can, I can show him he's safe.

"My Lady Ellcia," he begins, then bows again as he eyes the soldiers standing by me. "My Lady, I…" He gulps, and pulls his wife in closer.

"Young man!"

I turn to see Hella approach. Yes, she's the one I need right now.

In a stern voice, she says, "Young man! Listen closely! You are speaking to a Noblewoman, so first, stand up straight!" The man straightens his posture, and the woman does the best she can to stand straight, supporting herself with a hand on her lower back. "Second, this is not just any Noblewoman, but we expect she will one day be our Queen, so stand straighter!" The man and woman each stretch as tall and straight as they can. "And third," at this, Hella's voice softens, "she is kind, compassionate, and honest. You have nothing to fear, that is, if you respond to her properly. She needs information, and we believe you have it. Please speak clearly and quickly."

"I'm sorry, my Lady," the man says to Hella.

"I am not Nobleborn!" Hella hollers, quite in contrast to the kind, gentle voice a moment ago.

"I'm sorry… woman!" the man says. I see the struggle in his eyes. He's really not sure what to do or say, but Hella appears satisfied. Turning back to me, he bows again and says, "My Lady, please tell me what it is you wish to know."

"I'm told you have some news for me. We have not yet spoken with anyone in the city, and certainly not in the castle. Tell me what you have seen."

"My Lady," the man says again, offering yet another bow. Frustration and impatience boil up in me. I would rather just hear what I need to hear, not listen to this man call me "my Lady" over and over again. I don't really care for the bowing, either. "My Lady," he says yet again, "two days ago, a large army left Sevord City, heading east toward the pass."

"Do you know how many?"

He shakes his head. "No, my Lady. Many."

"Thank you. Is there anything else you can tell me?"

He shifts on his feet a bit and then says, "My Lady, I saw King… um…"

"It is fine to call him King, as that is the position he holds for the time being."

"Yes, my Lady, thank you. While out hunting yesterday afternoon, I saw King Parthun."

I frown. "Outside the city?"

"Yes, my Lady."

That's interesting. So, he didn't go with the army, which left two days before we arrived. I don't know if that's good news or bad news. "What was he doing?" I can't imagine what Parthun might have been up to. Unless he had a large force with him, I'd think he'd stay behind the walls. He's a bit of a coward.

"He was…" The man shifts on his feet and looks at his wife. She gives him a nod, and he continues. "I don't mean to presume upon the Royal Family, my Lady. It is always a mystery as to what they might be up to."

"Tell me what you saw."

"I think, my Lady, he was fleeing."

"Fleeing?" I try to wrap my mind around that. "You mean… fleeing the castle?"

"Yes, my Lady."

"Which direction?"

"East, my Lady. Toward Switcher Pass. He had a force of around a hundred or maybe two hundred soldiers with him. They moved fast. I…" He looks again at his wife. "He looked…"

"Yes?"

"He looked terrified, my Lady."

A smile breaks out on my face. I never expected to scare Parthun. Especially considering he has the castle and all. We only have, with Hemot's forces, somewhere around ten thousand troops.

I turn back to the city and examine it for a moment as my thoughts come together. I don't see any way our forces could capture the city. If we had catapults, we could likely get inside, but we don't. And even so, the army would… My smile grows larger, and a laugh slips out. That's it.

Turning back to the man, I say, "Thank you, my friends. This is helpful information."

They each bow, but neither one leaves. I'm thinking I have to say something specifically to dismiss them, although I don't know what that is other than, "Go away" or "You may leave," both of which sound rude. But then the man steps forward.

"My Lady?"

"Yes?"

"I… well… my Lady, if you are the future Queen, um…" He looks back to his wife, and she nods vigorously. "Would you… bless our child?"

I stare at him for a moment. I can't actually make sense of what he just said.

Doing my best to look like this is normal for me, I slowly look around. Who can I ask… Hella… she's not far away, but she looks as confused as I feel. Frellson… he's within shouting distance, but he's busy. Marleet… she's approaching on horseback. I think she's likely heading to meet Hemot.

"Thank you for your request," I say. "Please remain here. I will return in just a moment. I must speak with a member of my court."

I move toward Marleet and flag her down. She has Denner and Billot with her, and my two guards, Rickle and Yirp, follow close behind me. "Marleet?" I whisper.

"Yes?" she replies, matching the volume of my voice.

"The couple over there, she's pregnant, and... um... they asked me to bless their child."

"Okay," Marleet says. "What's the problem?"

I frown. Sometimes Marleet can be quite unhelpful. "I don't know what that means."

She shakes her head. "I don't know what that means either."

A growl forms in my throat. Sometimes...

I calm myself. I'm guessing Denner's hearing must be quite good, because he moves a little closer and smiles. "My Lady, may I speak?"

"Of course, Denner."

He dismounts and comes in close, keeping his voice low. "This is something few people speak about these days, but it is an old tradition. One of the duties of the Queen of Sevord has always been to bless children, specifically before they are born. It is typically done only among the Nobles, but when the Queen moves among the people, much of her time is spent in blessings. Such a thing has not been done in many years, of course, as we have had no Queen since Her Majesty, Queen Shalsee was killed. You have not likely had to worry about it until now since it is not a tradition much outside Sevord City, and certainly not among the Northern Tribes."

"But... I'm not Queen."

He gives me a strange look and smiles. "Well, my Lady, if you plan on marrying Prince Draydon, you'll have to get used to this sometime."

I glance back at the couple and see the looks of hope on their faces. Turning back to Denner, I ask, "How do I do it?"

When I return to the couple, I smile and say, "I would be honored to offer you my blessing."

Huge smiles break out on their faces, and the man jumps with joy while the woman tries to—unsuccessfully. Moving over to them, I place my hand on the woman's belly, and in my most formal voice, call out, "May your child grow to be strong, kind, and intelligent. And may this child be a true and loyal citizen of our great nation." I then lean toward the woman's belly and, in a quiet voice, say, "And you, child, have two wonderful parents who love you. May you grow up in a home filled with love."

The couple thank me and then head off. I feel honored to have done that, but I hope it doesn't happen too much in the next couple of days. We have a lot to do.

I turn around and take in the situation with the city again. The smile from before, the one that came when I understood what was going on, has returned. To my left, off to the south, I see a procession coming forward, led by Hemot. At the sight of him, Marleet lets out a squeal and runs forward, with Denner and Billot trailing behind.

Two forces... the soldiers from the southern coast, and the forces from the northern coast... ten thousand soldiers...

That's more than I can command. Besides, I'm not a soldier. And I'm not a military leader. Marleet isn't either, and Hemot is... well... Hemot.

Frellson is too young to hold them together. I see him struggle with the responsibilities Nordin's placed upon him.

Nordin or Relin. Those are my two options to lead the forces from here. But I know Nordin's much happier at sea. He's already told me he doesn't think he can handle a hike across the Talic. "Hella!"

She steps forward and bows. "My Lady."

"I wish to send a letter to Captain Nordin and Captain Relin."

"Yes, my Lady." She gives another bow and then rushes off. A few minutes later, she has parchment and is ready to write. I dictate my letters, one to Relin and one to Nordin, stating that I am pulling Relin from the Geran, and he is to report to me immediately. And Nordin is to assign a new Captain to Relin's ship.

With Relin back, running this army is going to be a whole lot easier.

Hella rushes off to see the letters delivered out to the fleet as Hemot and Marleet come up. Hemot approaches and bows awkwardly to me. I still don't like that, but I guess it's necessary.

"It's good to see you, Duke Hemot."

He smiles. "You too, Ellcia!" Marleet elbows him, and he corrects himself. "You too, Lady Ellcia."

"All went well?"

He nods. "We were well received by most. Some of the villages were skeptical of me, but when Relin came forward, there was usually at least one or two of the older men or women who recognized him. We have close to four thousand soldiers."

"That's better than I had heard," I say. "In total, that gives us around eleven thousand troops." I wave for Lieutenant Frellson to come close, and when he arrives, my face breaks out in a huge grin. "I have some good news."

They each wait expectantly as I collect my thoughts. Parthun's escape is good news in many ways.

"I just received a report that Parthun fled the castle yesterday with somewhere around one hundred to two hundred troops."

Hemot frowns, and Marleet shakes her head, but it's Marleet who speaks first. "So, we won't likely catch him."

"No," I say with a smile, "but this is good news."

"How?" Hemot asks.

I can see Frellson is pleased as well. He gets it. "This is good news," I begin, "because it tells us a few things. First, Parthun is scared of us. I don't think with eleven thousand soldiers that we could take the city—not if it's properly defended. We don't have anything to bring down the walls, so we would need to find some other way to get into the city. We could attack from the ocean, of course, but then we have to get through what's left of the fleet."

"How does this help us?" Marleet asks.

"Because," I say, "Parthun's a coward." Frellson nods as he understands, but Marleet and Hemot just shake their heads, so I continue. "If Parthun thought he would be safe in the city, he would never have fled with a couple hundred soldiers. This means the city is not well defended. I'm guessing either his entire army chose to follow Draydon, or he's sent what he has out to fight against Draydon, leaving the city empty of soldiers. Either way, I think there's going to be little resistance for us."

Hemot nods slowly, as though he's not really comfortable with it all. "How do we know for sure?"

"That's the easy part!" I say with a smile. "We ask them."

29

Ellcia and the Nobles

About an hour later, Frellson and three other soldiers ride toward the gates of Sevord. I've sent with him a copy of the letter signed by Draydon and the rest of us, declaring Draydon's claim for the throne. I've also sent a copy of the letter assigning me authority to act in his name. And I've sent a letter demanding the gates be opened, for all soldiers to surrender to their proper Prince, swearing fealty to him, and for the fleet to surrender to Captain Nordin of the Nimville.

I'm confident that Frellson will be safe. If anyone harms him, there will be a reckoning. I think that's pretty clear. But my concern is, most of the soldiers who remain are likely loyal to Parthun. And the Nobles… they'll be a problem. They won't want to submit to me, for one thing, and for another, I expect those Nobles who have remained are here only because Parthun has forced them to. Which means, on one level or another, Parthun controls them.

We watch Frellson and his soldiers approach the gate. When they come well within firing range of the wall—which terrifies me—they stop and wait. It looks to me like Frellson is hollering back and forth to the soldiers on the wall. I don't know how he feels about it, but it's stressing me out a lot!

By the time the gate opens, I think somewhere around two hours have passed. I know I'm bored and frustrated. I expect Frellson and his men are all out angry. Then again, it does take a while for messages to go from the wall to the palace, then for Nobles to talk it through. They're never quick.

Four people on horseback approach Lieutenant Frellson. To his credit, he bows to each in a respectful manner, which reminds me that if I speak with them, even though I'm annoyed at how long they've made me wait, I have to remember respect. I guess it's not the waiting that's the problem. I'm just hungry. I find as a Noblewoman, I spend a lot of time not-eating.

They speak for a moment, Frellson bows again, and then he turns to lead them in our direction. From this distance, I can't see who they are, but then again, I likely won't know them. As a servant, I rarely ever looked at a Noble's face. I doubt they ever looked at mine.

Nordin isn't here, but he gave me a lot of great advice. I just have to keep it all in mind.

How they approach me will tell me a lot about what they think of us. That is the moment when I find out where I truly stand in their eyes. Who speaks first is a big part of it, but then the bigger issue is whether they dismount. When Roran dismounted before Parthun, it was a sure sign that something was wrong. Roran should never have done that until Parthun bowed.

If these two speak before dismounting, then they will not recognize my authority.

As they draw close, I see only two are Nobles, a woman and a man. The other two are soldiers, likely a personal guard for each Noble.

Despite the cold, my hands sweat. I'm bundled up enough to know that my shaking is not from the temperature. I've had to play the part of Nobility for a long time now, but this is the first time I've really had to do so in front of true Nobility—aside from Marleet and Hemot... and I guess Draydon... and Roran... but this feels different.

We've positioned ourselves in such a way that it's clear who's in charge. Marleet and Hemot stand back a short distance, in positions of honor, but not with me. Behind them stand soldiers along with others along the sides. It's a show of strength, but it also leaves me out in a position where no one should doubt that I'm the one they're here to speak with.

I stand confident. It's a combination of what I've learned from Marleet as to how Noblewomen stand and how I've seen soldiers like Frellson stand. I have no intention of being merely a politician. They need to know I can handle myself with my blade.

They reach me, and I wait. This is the moment... how will they react?

The soldiers don't move from their saddles. That's no surprise. They will follow their Nobles.

But the Nobleman and Noblewoman... they just stare at me at first. Neither of them speaks, which is confusing. Either they're waiting for me to speak, or they're trying to decide how to respond.

Nordin advised me to be patient. This whole interaction will be a challenge for them—likely one which they've debated back and forth as to how they should act. I feel frustration grow inside, but I know a big part of it is the hunger.

Wow! I just can't stop thinking about food! I haven't eaten since early this morning, and it's been busy ever since. I just want a bite of something!

Finally, the Nobleman dismounts, and his guard follows immediately. I see a flash of rage cross the Noblewoman's face, but she follows his example, her guard climbing down right after her.

So, they are divided. I still don't know if they respect me—even the Nobleman could be acting more out of fear or trying to walk carefully.

I examine their faces. I don't recognize the man at all, but the woman… I think there's something about her scowl that I remember.

I wait, and after another moment, the man bows. The woman does as well, but her bow is barely more than a nod.

The Nobleman smiles and says, "Lady Ellcia, I presume?"

I give a slight bow of my own—not one of submission, but one of respect. "Yes, I am the Lady Ellcia, representative of the Crown Prince Draydon. And you are?"

"My name is Lord Vdain, and this is Lady Finnipa. We are each Nobles of the Court. We welcome you to Sevord City, but we are unsure as to why a Lady might bring an army to Sevord City on behalf of the Crown Prince."

"That is understandable," I say, although as it comes out of my mouth, I'm not sure it is. "The Crown Prince has been under threat of death from Parthun, Son of Trevolay, for months now. I do not believe that Sevord City stands with the heir to the throne but stands in rebellion to our future King." I lean forward just a little and ask, "Are you… in rebellion… to his Royal Highness?"

The man's face drains of color, and even the woman, despite her scowl, hesitates at the question. I could stretch this out—which is the way of Nobles—but I have no interest in doing so. I want this city. And I want it now.

I'm also rather hungry.

"Lady Ellcia, why would you ask such a question?" the man asks, obviously upset. "Of course we are loyal to the throne!"

Lady Finnipa speaks up at this point, "We are certainly loyal, Lady Ellcia. We would never dream of acting in rebellion to the one who sits on the throne of Sevord."

I frown at Finnipa. "Careful," I say, "the man who sits on the throne of Sevord stands accused of killing King Hartor, other members of the royal family, and of trying to kill Prince Draydon. He has also sent kidnappers to the north to kidnap me, Prince Draydon's representative. If you are loyal to Parthun, I declare you now a traitor to the throne and a traitor to Prince Draydon!"

The woman gasps, and I hear swords drawn behind me. Finnipa's guard goes for his sword, but Vdain's guard merely places his hand on the hilt of his own blade.

Lord Vdain steps forward and offers a smile, not an arrogant grin, but as if he's trying to bring peace to the moment. "I apologize, Lady Ellcia. These are… difficult times. We ask for your patience. It is not simple to know how to navigate our way through these challenging matters."

"On that, we agree, Lord Vdain." I raise my hand, and I hear the soldiers behind me put their swords away. Finnipa nods to the man behind her. He sheaths his sword but remains at the ready.

Nordin told me I can take one of two approaches. I can be friendly and pleasant, or I can be direct and authoritative. If I want to be a politician, I can be pleasant. But if I want this city in my control, I need to be firm.

"I do not wish to spend a great amount of time talking back and forth. I am not much of a politician. I wish to be direct." I stop because Vdain is smiling at me. "Is something funny, Lord Vdain?"

He shakes his head and laughs. "No, Lady Ellcia, there is nothing to worry about. I smile because I knew your father, Lord Rathar."

That stops me. "And what about that makes you smile?"

His eyes bore into me, but I don't see any disrespect there. "Your father and I were not friends, Lady Ellcia. I will not pretend it to be so. We disagreed on just about everything. He was close friends with General Geran, and the two of them were warriors. I, on the other hand," and he pauses while he points to his plump body and adds a laugh, "am not a fighter. I am used to fine dining and comfortable chairs." His smile grows, and he gives another bow. "Despite the fact that we never agreed, I respected your father. He was intelligent and focused. His arguments were persuasive and solid." Vdain takes a small step forward and says, "I see him in you. Your brother, Captain Granel, is not the only one who received Lord Rather's fire."

"I trust that's a good thing?" I ask.

He nods. "As much as he and I argued, I know he was a good man. I envied him, actually. He stood strong under any amount of pressure."

I notice a flash of something in his eyes. Regret, maybe. A quick glance at Finnipa shows none of that. She looks like she's just biting her tongue to keep herself from saying all sorts of things.

"I am glad he was able to stand strong under pressure. But today I am the one who is putting on the pressure." I pause and stare at each of them for a moment. "Here are the terms. I do not believe you have an army behind that wall. I think there is nothing more than the soldiers I can see from here. You have a portion of your navy left, but the majority of it has already declared their fealty to Prince Draydon. In fact, I expect all the loyal Nobility has already gone to Haner to see Prince Draydon crowned, and I think there are only disloyal Nobles, and those who have bowed to pressure, remaining."

I let that sink in for a moment before I continue. "So, I think there are two options for you. Option number one is you will open the gates and send word to all your soldiers that you have surrendered. You will send word to the Navy to surrender to Captain Nordin of the Royal Warship, Nimville. My army will then enter the city and require oaths of fealty from every Noble and every soldier. Finally, I will appoint a caretaker of the city to see to its needs until the newly crowned King Draydon returns to sit on his throne."

By the time I finish, the mouths of both Nobles are wide open, and the strong arms of their personal guards hang limply at their sides. Neither Noble speaks at first, but then finally, Finnapa manages to ask in a weak voice, "And if we refuse?"

"Do you mean, if you refuse to submit to Prince Draydon's representative?"

I let that hang in the air before I continue. I know she can't answer that. If she does refuse to submit to Draydon, I can arrest her on the spot. And if she denies my authority, Draydon will arrest her upon his return to the city. So, instead, I merely answer. "If you refuse Prince Draydon's wishes, Lady Finnipa, then I will order Captain Nordin to demolish your fleet, and destroy any buildings he deems to be a threat at the port. I will then appoint a force to remain here surrounding the city, and the rest of the army will move to the shore for the Navy to transport to the docks to allow entrance to the city. When they reach the castle, they will breach the walls, and any Nobles not quick to swear oaths to Prince Draydon will die before they have a chance to explain their hesitation." I step closer to them and scream, "This city belongs to Prince Draydon! You and the traitor Parthon have held it from the rightful heir for too long! I intend to be at his coronation at Haner and if I have to step over your lifeless bodies to be there, so be it!"

I hear Marleet whisper behind me, "Whoa," and I do my best to calm down. That was far more than I intended. And I... I can't believe I said that. Although... I am very hungry. And, now that I just found out that Draydon is definitely alive and well in Haner, I can't wait to get there. But, back to what I just said, I hate the thought of anyone dying, let alone at my command.

"Oh," Lord Vdain says quietly, then louder adds, "You are definitely Lord Rather's daughter." He lets out a nervous chuckle before he bows low and says, "Please, let us return to the city to confer with the other Nobles."

I shake my head. "No."

Lady Finnipa looks at me like I'm insane. "No? What do you mean, 'No'?"

Unfortunately, this wasn't exactly part of the plan. We expected they would ask to confer with the other Nobles, and I was supposed to allow them. But I've changed my mind.

"I think, Lady Finippa, if you have reached your age and are unfamiliar with the word 'no', then you will need to grow up quickly. I mean, no. No, you will not return to the city. Tell me, how many Nobles are left behind to rule the city in Parthun's absence?"

Vdain bows and says, "Four, my Lady, including us."

"A strange number to leave behind," I reply. "Very strange. It's a number that does not allow for much disagreement, as there is no one to break a tie." I find that interesting, but not surprising. Pathun left them in charge of the city but did not leave them a situation in which anyone could properly lead. "You will send word to the other two Nobles that they are to come at once to meet with me. I will require your oaths of fealty here in the field before the city, in sight of the soldiers on the wall. Then you will order the gates to open, and we will enter. If you refuse, I will allow you to reenter the city. That should offer you the time you need to put your affairs in order while my soldiers force their way in, and you await your execution, as I will not give you a second chance." I let my eyes bore into his like he did to me a moment ago and add, "And when my soldiers find you, Lord Vdain, they will execute you and have the mess cleaned up before I enter the city."

Again... I can't believe I said that, but it's out now. In the future, I probably shouldn't deal with people when I'm hungry.

Lady Finnipa's face fills with rage, but she calms herself down, while Lord Vdain appears... well... he looks like he has accepted my words. It's not like they have any other choice.

"Yes, my Lady. But if we send our guards back, will you guarantee our safety?"

"If you do not act in any treasonous manner, then you are guaranteed your safety, as far as I can offer it. But if you act against Prince Draydon or his goals, then you have no hope of safety."

"That is all we ask, my Lady. Will you provide me with parchment and a quill so I might write a letter to the others?"

I order it brought, and it's not long before the letter is written. I almost ask to see it, but Marleet warns me not to look at it. That would be to suggest that I believe Lord Vdain and Lady Finnipa are intentionally trying to engage in treason, and as much as I think each of them would, it's probably better to take this chance.

The letter is sent off and within another two hours, the gates open, and two more Nobles exit, another man and a woman. When they arrive, they bow to me, then dismount, and the man stands by Finnipa and the woman by Vdain. Ahh... it makes sense, they were left as two couples. I can't help but think that would complicate the leadership of the city even more.

I think I recognize Finnipa's husband. He used to yell at me if his room didn't smell right after a good cleaning. I never figured out what the right smell was supposed to be.

"Welcome," I say. "Are you aware of who I am and why you are here?"

They bow, and the two new Nobles say, "Yes, my Lady."

"And what is your answer?"

They hesitate for a moment, and I notice four men approach from north of the city—Relin is among them. It's good to see him, and I'll be happy to hand authority of the army over to him. Out of the corner of my eye, I watch Frellson go to meet him. I want to concentrate on the Nobles, but I see from Relin's expression that not only has he arrived, but he has good news.

Relin comes close to me, and I say, "Welcome back, Captain Relin. How is our Navy?"

"Excellent, my Lady. We have just gained six ships."

My mouth drops open. "Where from?"

"The six ships remaining in rebellion to Prince Draydon, my Lady. Captain Nordin sent word to them, along with letters from the Crown Prince. It did not take long for them to see wisdom and to remember their loyalty. The Captains of the six ships have all sworn fealty to Prince Draydon on the deck of the Nimville, and their crews were in the process when I left them."

"That is good news," I say, but I can see there's more. "Continue, please, Captain Relin."

He bows, "Yes, my Lady. Before I landed, I saw that our ships had begun to dock, and I expect by now we control the Port. If you'd like, we can start ferrying soldiers around the wall and into the city."

I glance at the Nobles. Any confidence or arrogance present a moment before is now gone.

To Relin, I order, "Take command of Prince Draydon's coastal army. If the eastern gate of the city is not open within the hour, begin to ferry your soldiers through the Port. You will have no need of further orders from me, as you will be free to begin your attack."

"Yes, my Lady," Relin says and moves off.

I turn to the Nobles. "I will give you no more chances. This is the final time I will ask. Will you swear fealty to the rightful King and lead his armies to his castle?"

A few minutes later, I have their sworn oaths, and Relin is ready to lead four thousand soldiers through the streets of Sevord and to the castle. He has insisted that I allow him to secure the city before I enter, so for now… I wait.

I think this is the first time in my life that I've ridden into the castle courtyard on horseback, and it's entirely different. Only royalty or returning victors typically enter the city this way, and I'm certainly not royalty.

I guess maybe I'm the victor.

The people have mostly watched me from within buildings, peering out through windows, although some have stood in dark alleys. I'd love to stop and convince them that they're safe, that I'm actually entering the city on behalf of the Crown Prince, but that's not possible. I'll let Draydon figure that part out. I just want the city firmly under his control before I head east to meet him at Haner.

I almost laugh at the thought of it all.

Here I am, a girl who's grown up in the castle as a servant. I've cleaned the toilets, scraped dirt off the floor with my own fingernails, and polished silver statues and even cutlery with my own spit—that part I haven't told anyone about. The Nobles who walk behind me… in the past, they would have left me shaking in fear. Now, I find them annoying.

At the castle gates, the entire senior staff has assembled. There's one I look for right away. Tereese. There she is, standing with her three assistants. The rest of her workers are likely preparing a feast.

Oh… a feast! I hadn't thought of that! I sure could use a hot meal that's not eaten by the side of a campfire!

I dismount just before the main doors leading into the castle—doors I have never used before, at least as far as I can remember. People like me have not had reason to come and go through the Noble Entrance.

As I enter, Relin meets me in the entrance hall with a frown on his face. "I'm sorry, my Lady. I request that ya remain here for just a little longer."

"What's going on, Captain?"

He shakes his head. "My soldiers have found over thirty men hiding in shadows, tucked away in various closets, and hidden behind curtains."

I frown. "That seems odd. Why are they hiding?"

He holds up a crossbow in one hand, and a knife in the other. I get it. Assassins. So, the threat in the castle is still real.

"I might be able to help find a few more," Marleet says, stepping forward.

I give her a nod, but before she goes with Relin, I ask him, "Will she be safe?"

"Of course, my Lady."

"Also," I say, "what Lady Marleet shows you must be kept secret. Those you speak with must not share what they learn with anyone."

He bows to me. "Yes, my Lady."

They head off, and I wait. The room has around twenty soldiers, all standing guard. Down the hallways I see even more. It makes me smile. Aside from a few possible threats, the palace is ours!

The problem with waiting right now, however, is that I'm still hungry. When I'm not moving, my mind goes to food.

When Marleet and Relin return, I'm pleased to hear they found no one in the secret passages. That suggests Parthun likely doesn't know about them, which means the castle is that much safer.

We head to the throne room, and I'm pleased to see that Relin has already ordered a chair set up for me at the base of the stairs leading to the throne. I stare at the throne for a moment, and my face breaks out in a grin. I picture Draydon up there, and I almost start to laugh. We're so close!

So much effort, fighting so hard to see the right person on the throne. First Roran… and now Draydon.

We are so close!

The four Nobles take their place to the right of my seat—I guess that'll be my left—and I sit. This has all gone smoothly so far. Now it's time to get things moving here.

Before I can say anything, however, Lord Vdain asks, "My Lady Ellcia, thank you for the privilege of being here."

"You're welcome, Lord Vdain." I figure that means he wants something, so I wait.

Smiling at me, he bows and asks, "I am only curious, that is all, but I have a question. Why does the Crown Prince remain at Haner and not come directly to Sevord City?"

"Because, Lord Vdain, the usurper to the throne, Parthun, has been trying to kill Prince Draydon for quite some time. We do not believe Prince Draydon would be safe anywhere near here until Parthun is removed."

It's very interesting to me that Lord Vdain does not disagree with me, nor do any of the others. They have sworn fealty to Draydon. I hope they can be trusted to keep their vows.

"Captain Relin!"

"Yes, my Lady," Relin says, approaching me. "What are yar orders?"

"Is the castle secure?"

"Yes, I believe it is, my Lady. At least most of it is. We continue to search out further areas."

"Good. Then I wish for you to go to the dungeons and release Rulfor, Son of Traltor. I also wish for you to confirm that General Lirnal is no longer in the dungeon. He should have been taken to Haner. Finally, when in the dungeon, I wish for you to check Tilbur's pit to see if Denner and Billot, Lord Yune's guards, are still in there."

"Yes, my Lady."

"I also wish for you to bring Hob to me, if he is still in the castle, and for you to send soldiers to retrieve Berin from his cottage outside the city. The Lady Marleet can give you directions."

"Yes, my Lady. I know of Berin's cottage. I have been there a few times in my younger days."

"And," I say... unsure if I should continue. I don't mind giving orders to help things move along for Draydon and for the Kingdom, but I really don't want to be selfish.

"Yes, my Lady?" Relin asks.

I decide to go for it. "I wish for a feast. I'm hungry." There... I said it. It feels good to order that. I know Tereese is likely putting one together for me, but... I'm really hungry! "I also wish to have a personal staff while I am here for sending out messages and orders. I don't want to be questioning who is loyal and who I can send."

He bows and smiles. "Of course, my Lady."

Wow. I feel selfish and controlling for asking for those things, but I have a lot to do in a short amount of time. I still need to get to Haner. I can't imagine everything's going to go well with Parthun's arrival. I fear Draydon is going to need my army.

Hob stands before me.

Well, he's sitting at the moment. Before that, he stood. Before that, he rolled. In fact, he rolled his way into the throne room. Relin almost hit him for his disrespect of the room, but I don't actually mind. Hob is certainly not sane, but he's loyal. And he's been an enormous help to us.

Despite the fact that he irritates me, I'll let Hob away with just about anything. He's a good man, right down to his core.

"My Lady," Relin begins, "we were able to find three out of the six. Lieutenant Hob, Denner and Billot."

I frown at that. "The others?"

"As you see, we have good news with Denner and Billot. But the prison guards tell me that General Lirnal was taken from them just two days ago when Parthun fled the castle."

I'm actually happy about that in one sense, because it means Parthun is obeying Draydon's orders, at least to an extent. But I did want to release him myself.

I glance at Marleet. She stands to my left with Denner and Billot behind her. They remain hunched over and give the impression that they are unsteady on their feet. Tilbur's pit has long been thought to be a death sentence, although it's actually functioned as a means of escape from the castle. Even though they were not in there, we'd like to maintain the illusion, as Tilbur's Pit may be useful for Draydon in the future. So, we pretended to rescue them.

"And Rulfor?"

"He was there until shortly after General Lirnal was released, my Lady."

I frown at that. "What do you mean?"

"Well, my Lady, you know he has giant blood, correct?"

"Yes, I know that, Captain."

"It turns out he simply climbed out of the pit and walked out of the prison. The guards tried to stop him, of course, but he just… pushed past them."

I stifle a laugh at that. I'm not surprised. "And where did he go?"

"He left, my Lady. They tried to stop him at the gates to the castle, then again at the gates to the city, but he overpowered them at each point. Not violently. He just… walked out while some of the soldiers hacked at him with their swords, and others clung to his legs, dragging on the ground behind him. Since the city is so short on soldiers, they decided to simply let him go. There's not much that can be done to stop someone like him, and Lord Vdain ordered the soldiers to focus on defense."

I nod to Vdain. "That was wise, Lord Vdain."

He smiles and gives me a respectful bow.

"And that only leaves Berin," I say to Captain Relin. "Have you found out if he is at his cottage?"

He shakes his head. "No, my Lady, the men I sent will not likely be back for a couple more hours at least. But I questioned Hob, and he believes his brother went with Captain Granel to Haner."

"Did he tell you this?" I ask Hob.

Hob shakes his head in a dramatic fashion. "No, Lady Trip, I just guessed it."

"That's not my name, Hob," I say with a smile. "Remember, that's the name Berin gave me when I needed to disguise myself as his apprentice."

Hob furrows his brow and looks at me like I just don't understand. "Well, Lady Trip, if he named you 'Trip', would that not mean your name is… Trip?"

"No… Hob…" I begin, already feeling the familiar frustration I experience every time I interact with him. "He… I mean… he can't just rename me."

"But you said he did!" Hob shakes his head. "My Lady Trip, you just said Berin gave you that name! You said it. You can't take it back. No, no, no, no no!"

"No, I mean…" I bury my face in my hands. If Hob wasn't such a good man at heart, I think I'd just move on to other things. "Hob, I now give myself a new name. I give myself the name, Lady Ellcia."

He smiles and stands up straight. "Yes, Lady Ellcia!"

I roll my eyes, but then ask, "Tell me about your brother. What makes you think he went to Haner with Captain Granel?"

Hob turns his head on a bit of an angle and leans forward. Opening his eyes really wide, he shouts, "I DON'T KNOW! I JUST THINK THAT'S WHAT HE'D DO!"

"Okay," I reply, grinding my teeth, "thank you for your time, Hob." As an afterthought, I add, "When we head to Haner ourselves, you are welcome to come with us."

He smiles, and without another word, walks out of the throne room. I don't think I'll ever get used to that man. But… I remind myself of both his loyalty and his pain. He might be mad, but I suspect if I went through what he went through, it might have broken me as well.

Once I've finished with a lot of the business of the castle, I head to the main dining hall. I've been in that room many times before, of course, but never to eat. But eating is exactly what I intend to do!

When the smell hits me, I nearly start to run. I feel Marleet's grip on my arm, and when I turn to her, she hisses, "Slow down! You're a Lady, remember?"

I enter, and Lord Vdain and Lady Finnipa are already there, seated near the one end. Their spouses are with them, and Nordin and Hella sit next to them, with Relin on the other side of them. At the end, next to Vdain and Finnipa, is my seat. It's pretty fancy, and I feel awkward knowing I'm the guest of honor. I assume that's where Parthun would have sat as recently as a couple days ago, and that's the only thing that makes me feel okay with sitting in the seat. It feels like a great way to move the Kingdom on from his wicked rule.

The only problem is the rest of the seats. Marleet is, by far, the highest ranking Noble in the room. In fact, it's only Draydon's orders that put me higher than her. But it appears that Vdain and Finnipa have chosen to place themselves next to me.

I'm about to order them to move, when Marleet whispers, "Let it go. I'll sit with Hella."

We take our seats, and I ask Nordin to offer a moment of gratitude for the meal. I see Vdain and Finnipa wish to make speeches, but I wave my hand. "We eat first!" If I don't get eating, the growls from my stomach will drown out their useless words, anyway.

Lady Finnipa scowls at me, but she seems to accept it. Lord Vdain doesn't seem to mind. I've grown to like him very quickly. I think he's ultimately loyal, just not very strong. It's too easy for him to fall to the pressure of a man like Parthun.

The first course comes out, and a large plate is set before me. I'm not really sure what I'm looking at, but it smells so good. I see Tereese smile at me from the side of the room, and I smile back. I think I see a tear run down her cheek. I know she's one of the ones who has fought so hard to see Parthun removed, although she's had to do it in secret.

I cut into the meat, and I can hardly contain myself. I want to just start shoveling it in. I'm so hungry, and it smells so good. Not even Finnipa's slow, arrogant words as she bores Hella with some boring story about a boring dress can't spoil the excitement I feel at the thought of getting this food into me.

It's half-way up to my mouth… now almost at my lips… my mouth is open.

A snarl pulls me away, and I look up in time to see Relin climb up onto the table. Time seems to stop as he crawls down the table towards me, knocking dishes and cups and food every which way, his movements like a blur from his nearly inhuman speed.

When he reaches me, he knocks the fork out of my hand, causing rage to flood my heart, but then he crashes into me, knocking me backwards, and smashing my chair underneath us both. My head hits the floor, and I see stars for a moment, but then my entire body is wrenched to the side, and Relin's on top of me, his face still filled with rage.

Nordin appears above him, and I'm about to cry for help, when he comes down on top of me as well, crushing me under his enormous bulk. I twist and push and pull, but I can't do much. A moment later, they've shoved me under the table.

Marleet's beside me, arms wrapped around me, but she's covered in blood. Relin and Nordin are gone now, so I check her over. "Where is it?" I hiss. "Where is it?"

"Where's what?" Marleet's crying, and I'm afraid she's going to start to panic.

"Where are you injured? Where's the blood coming from?"

"It's yours!" Marleet cries between tears.

That's when I notice the pain. I look at my left arm to see a crossbow bolt. In shock, I lift my arm to see the other half of the arrow protrude out of the underside of my arm. I start to scream. The pain is just too much. Marleet's holding me, saying something, but I don't understand her words. I begin to pass out and feel myself sliding back, Marleet doing her best to catch me.

I awake to Marleet leaning over me. My head hurts, so does my arm. I'm… I'm not sure where I am.

"Ellcia? Can you hear me?"

"Of course I can. You're only inches from my nose."

Marleet pulls back. "Sorry, your eyes are kind of unfocused."

"What happened?"

"You were shot. Relin got to you in time to push you out of the way, but the bolt lodged in your arm. They got it out."

"Why does my head hurt?" It feels like my brain's trying to break through my skull.

"That'll be from when you hit your head. You came down pretty hard when Relin knocked you back. He saw the assassin up in the rafters just in time. If he hadn't, you'd be dead."

I sit up and immediately wish I hadn't. Taking a deep breath, I force myself to remain in a seated position. My head starts to clear a bit, and I can think, but it still hurts. My arm actually doesn't hurt anywhere near as bad.

I try to twist around and get my feet on the ground, but I cry out. Yep, there's the pain in the arm. That's not good.

"They say it's going to heal well, but you'll have a nasty scar." Marleet shakes her head. "No, sorry, two scars. One on one side of the arm, another on the other." She shrugs and adds, "I guess you'll be wearing long sleeves all the time from now on."

I smile as best I can. "Depends how it looks. I might like it. It'll remind me of the cost of all this. It might be like the scar on my neck from the last attempt on my life." I lift my good arm and put my hand on Marleet's shoulder. "It's all worth it. Even this part. It's worth it. And we're nearly there."

She smiles at me, and I see a bit of relief in her eyes. I know what it's like to lose hope, and I think it's my job to keep it alive.

"Did they catch the guy?"

She nods. "Relin and his soldiers caught him within minutes, along with another two men and three women, all armed. One of them even had poison in a pouch. I know Tereese's kitchen is too tight to allow anyone to slip poison into the food, but I'm guessing if that woman with the poison could have gotten close to your meal, you'd be gone. At least an arrow… well… I'm sure it hurts, but we can pull it out."

"What have they done with them? The assassins, I mean."

"Relin had them interrogated, and they're in the prison."

"What did we learn?" My head aches, but I have to keep moving forward.

"I'll let Relin explain it to you."

That makes sense. I get up with Marleet's help, and she helps me dress. When I'm ready, I make my way out of my room and find an entire apartment. I'm not sure at first where we are, but Marleet tells me it's her family's quarters.

I'm impressed. She lives in luxury. I remember cleaning this place over the years, and always thinking it was one of the nicest apartments in the castle.

I hesitate at that. The only apartment I don't think I've ever seen is the King's apartments. Even Parthun wasn't arrogant enough to claim those quarters as his own—at least while he remained Regent. I assume it's even nicer than what I see around me, but it's hard to know for sure until I see them.

When we exit through the main doors, I find Denner and Billot waiting along with around thirty soldiers. Everyone looks relieved, and they lead me through the corridors to the throne room. Once there, Relin is summoned and gives me his full report.

It turns out they were under the command of a Noble, remaining here to disrupt and to kill whoever was in charge. Once I was dead, they were ordered to move on to the next one in charge. Then the next. Then the next.

"Lady Finnipa, I assume?" I ask. I start to roll my eyes at the thought of how obvious it is that she's the one, but I catch myself. That kind of thing hurts my head.

"No, my Lady," Relin says. "It was Lord Vdain."

My mouth drops open. He was, by far, the more peaceful of the two. How could he be the one who's arranging all the murders?

"There must be some mistake," I blurt out.

He shakes his head. "I'm sorry, my Lady. Four of those we captured confessed to taking orders directly from Lord Vdain, and when we searched his quarters, we found not only extra weapons, but the same poison carried by the one assassin, along with a signed order from General Corter for him to engage in these activities."

I shake my head. Corter… he truly is a fool. To leave such evidence behind allows Parthun to keep his hands clean and to hang Corter if the need arises. I guess if nothing else, we now have evidence to convict Corter. One less traitor to have to worry about when Draydon takes the throne.

"Keep the letter in a safe place. We will need it in time to come. And Lord Vdain now? Where is he?"

"Tied up and under guard in a cell down the hall, my Lady."

"Do I have the authority to sentence him, Captain?" I don't know what my limits are.

"I'm not sure, my Lady. But either way, it would be best to keep him alive at this point. I recommend you imprison him until trial by the new King."

I like that option. I don't want to break the law by sentencing a Noble if that's something only to be done by a Royal, which I suspect it is, nor do I actually want to sentence him. I expect the penalty is death.

"Put him in the prison. Do not give him any extra privileges. And confine his wife to her quarters. I also want Lady Finnipa and her husband interrogated, but I don't want them injured. At this point, aside from her obnoxious personality, I have no real reason to suspect her."

"Yes, my Lady. It will be done."

Before he leaves, I order, "Please bring in more soldiers. I want another sweep of the entire castle, and I want them to remain. Work with the Lady Marleet on this matter, again, keeping certain matters, of which we spoke earlier, secret. And don't forget to check the rafters."

He bows low to me, and I can see the regret in his eyes. I feel a little bad for reminding him of that, but they need to be more thorough. It'll only take one crossbow bolt.

"Two more things, Captain," I add. "First, I also want you to send two thousand soldiers into Switcher Pass to secure the area before we travel through. I want to ensure no assassins are left hiding in trees or caves."

"Yes, my Lady."

"And second…" At this point, I smile. "Captain Relin, you are doing a fantastic job."

"Thank you, my Lady." He gives me a large grin, bows one more time, and then leaves.

I turn to one of my attendants. "Please, bring me a meal. Right away!"

30

Ellcia and Switcher Pass

’m glad my headache’s gone, at least," I whisper to
Marleet.

The city lies behind us, and we have a long trek
ahead. We figure we’ll be at least five days, if all goes well,
just getting through Switcher Pass, then another five to get
to Haner after that. The first of day of spring is twelve days
away, so we’ll be cutting it close.

Very close.

"What about your arm?" Marleet asks, also in a
whisper. Apparently, it’s bad for Nobles to show weakness.
We’re supposed to be strong and stoic and… I don’t know.
We’re just not supposed to complain.

"It hurts. A lot. And it’s itchy. But the healers say it’s
clean, and I don’t have anything to worry about. They say I’ll
be able to use it more as the days go on. But for right now,
every step of my horse causes pain to shoot up into my
shoulder."

I twist in the saddle and look behind—something I
couldn’t do very well only a matter of weeks ago—and look
out over the city. I appointed Nordin and Hella as Regents.
Come to think of it, I guess I was functioning as a Regent

while in the castle. Now, that's strange. I was actually Regent Ellcia for a little bit…

But while we await Draydon's return to the city, Nordin and Hella will do well. They are honest and kind, but never back down if they know what's right. The only problem is they're both hands-on people. Hella loves organizing people and running a kitchen. That might drive Tereese up the wall. And Nordin loves to be out at sea and ordering soldiers and workers around.

All of that will be difficult. If they're not careful, they might forget to actually sit in the throne room and… lead.

"They'll do fine," Marleet says, obviously noticing my look back at the city. "We just have to hope that they allow other people to do the work, that's all."

Frellson rides toward me with another report. I think Captain Relin is about a day's ride ahead, so I don't expect to see him for a while. Hemot's with him, which means Marleet is worried, but she's trying not to think about it.

"What news do you have for me?" I ask Frellson.

"My Lady, the soldiers have found dozens of men and women in the forests, hiding in caves, and camouflaged throughout the trees and undergrowth. We continue to sweep the area, but we have lost over fifty so far."

I close my eyes and shake my head. Fifty! That's fifty men and women who won't return home. Fifty men and women who answer to me… and my orders have cost them their lives.

It's hard to think this is worth it when the guilt and horror at the loss of life hits me like this. But, under Parthun's rule, entire towns have been wiped out. People have been executed for any number of reasons. While living in the castle, we saw none of it, heard none of it. Parthun, despite ignoring me and treating me like I was a nobody, seemed like a decent man.

But the cost of life with that man on the throne is far greater than fifty men and women. Sadly, I doubt this fifty will be the last of those who have to lay down their lives to see that man removed.

"Continue your sweeps," I order. "We not only have to get every last one of Parthun's men to protect ourselves, but we need them all dealt with before we return. It'll only take one arrow to end Prince Draydon's reign before it fully begins."

"Yes, my Lady." He bows his head to me, then rides off. I'm grateful to that man. Nordin was right about him. He's loyal, competent, and strong. We've needed him.

I duck behind a fallen tree, pulling Marleet down next to me. Denner and Billot refuse to leave our side, despite Marleet's orders for them to join the fight. They're excellent leaders, both of them, but their commitment to Marleet's safety comes first, and they stubbornly refuse to budge from it.

I hear screams and poke my head up just a for a second. Arrows fly every which way, and fires burn. We've been four days since leaving the castle. Aside from capturing over two dozen more assassins in the pass, it's been fairly uneventful. We've reached the largest of the villages in Switcher Pass. The others were empty—I assumed all the people were either at Haner or they had congregated in the main village.

We thought that until we found the bodies of the villagers. But at that point, it was too late. We were already at the main village, and Parthun's soldiers streamed out of the huts and houses of the village.

"Frellson!" I call out. "Circle around and cut them off!"

"Yes, my Lady," he replies, then turns to some of his soldiers, passing along the orders. A moment later, he's crawled up next to me, keeping his head low while he speaks. "Much of our forces are well ahead of us. We thought the area was secure—and I think it appeared so. The villagers must have been killed within the last few hours. I think these soldiers have been lying in wait for a long time. And there's a lot of them!"

"How many?" I ask.

He shakes his head. "It's difficult to know at this point, my Lady. I would say at least a thousand, if not more."

I nearly choke on hearing that. I'm not sure we have that many ourselves in this area. Frellson blew the horn, calling all those within hearing to come to our aid, but we're spread out throughout the pass. Help might not arrive in time.

Frellson, Denner, and Billot leap to their feet, drawing their swords, and I twist around. Six men and women charge out of the forest at us, all big, scary, and angry.

I jump up and draw my sword. With the weight of the blade, I had grown used to using two arms, but these days, with my left arm injured, I've had to practice with only one. Now's the moment of truth. Now's the moment to see if I can fight without my left arm.

I deflect the blade coming at me and find an opening with the woman in front right away, driving my sword at her chest. The impact knocks her back. It doesn't penetrate her armor, but instead slides to the side and drives into a crack between the breastplate and shoulder armor. She jerks back, and I take my opportunity, disarming her, and kicking her in the belly.

As she stumbles back, two more come at me, both men, both large. I bring my sword up, but Marleet moves past me in a blur, taking out the men with her enchanted blade, and then moving on to come to the aid of our friends.

When they're all down, Frellson grabs me by my arm and drags me away from the village, while Billot grabs Marleet, with Denner taking up position in front.

"Let me go!" I order. "I can fight!"

"No, my Lady," Frellson replies.

"That's an order, Lieutenant!"

He shakes his head as we crash through the underbrush. He's not a big guy, not like Nordin, but there's no way I can overpower him. But I'm in charge! He'd better listen to my orders!

"Let me go now!"

He yanks hard on my arm, and I crash down behind a large boulder. A moment later, Marleet lands beside me.

"I'm sorry, my Lady," Frellson says, "in this situation, I am obligated to get you out of danger. I know you can fight, but you are our leader. Your life must be protected at all costs!"

He calls out to fifty of our soldiers as they reach the area, ready to join in, and orders them—ALL of them—to stand guard over us. I'm irritated by this, but Marleet puts her hand on my arm and shakes her head. "This is the way of things, Ellcia. We all have a part to play. Remember that. Yours is to lead and to stay alive. Your death would cost more to this army than a thousand soldiers at this point."

"No!" I holler. "My life is not worth more than a thousand!"

She grimaces at me. "I don't mean it like that. I mean, if you die right now, the soldiers… they'll lose hope. In fact, they might even go on a rampage—that's happened before—or they'll disband, and Draydon won't have our support! You have to stay down now if we are to be the help Draydon needs."

"But they're dying out there!" I've begun to cry. I can't leave them to sacrifice themselves like this.

Denner comes down close to me at this point while Billot orders the soldiers, my new guard, into position. "Please, my Lady. You must. This is the price good leaders pay."

"What do you mean?"

"For a wicked man like Parthun," he says, "sending people to die means nothing to him. It's a means to get what he wants. But for leaders such as yourself, you must continue because your part to play in this is to lead. There are times when your leadership requires you to allow others to sacrifice. If you were wicked like Parthun, it would be easy, but because you have a good heart, it is agony. Your price that you pay must be to suffer with the horror that other people have died at your command."

I stare at him with my mouth open. I can't think of anything to say. The men guarding me have begun to fight. I can't see who, but they are dying for me now. "But... I can't live with that!"

He shakes his head. "You have no choice, my Lady. When you stepped in as a representative of Prince Draydon, you took this weight on your shoulders. You must carry it. Their lives include a choice at every moment—do they serve, or do they run? Your life includes a choice at every moment—do you lead, or do you run?" He glances over his shoulder at the sounds of the other men. "The price you pay, my Lady, is to carry the pain of their death for the rest of your life. It is the price good leaders pay."

I look into his eyes and see two things. I see that he's telling the truth, and I also see that he knows what he's talking about.

Those eyes tell the story of the weight he carries. Denner has ordered men to their death.

"I must leave you now. The soldiers need me."

He spins around and jumps into action. It's just Marleet and me alone in here. It's not quite a cave, more like a bit of an overhang, but enough that I feel somewhat protected.

Marleet pushes me back, then does what I don't expect. She steps out in front of me, draws her sword, and takes her stand. I feel sick to my stomach. I know Parthun's men are coming after me. I know I'm the one they want. If they kill me, they hurt Draydon. If they capture me, they can use me against him.

But Marleet… do I really have to let her sacrifice herself for me?

The only peace I have at this is that Marleet's sword will probably make her the best protection I can have… and keep her safe.

The fighting goes on for a while. I peer out past Marleet and past the rock now and then. We've lost a lot of our soldiers, but more have come to replace them. Before I can look too long, Marleet pushes me back. "Stop it, Ellcia! You're going to get yourself killed!"

Denner's right. This is hard. I think it would be easier to die for them than to let them die for me. I know Draydon would feel the same way.

Maybe that's a good sign… it means the nation is not going to be in the hands of a man like Parthun. Draydon will hate to send people to their death. Every life is precious to him.

I hear a new voice. Someone's coming, but… not just anyone. The voice is familiar.

I hear him. His voice makes it through the clanging of swords and the screams of pain. "Oooooohhhh… this is going to be fun!"

It's Hob. That's definitely Hob.

I peer around Marleet again. She tries to push me back, but she's leaning out as well, just as curious as I am.

Hob's arrival has changed everything. In the first few seconds after he shows up, four men fall. He just… rolls and slides and spins around… and men drop. I hear horses, and Captain Relin and Hemot arrive, along with a lot of soldiers. They trample some, kill others… it's brutal, and I can't watch.

I pull back as they finish the fight, not wanting to see it. The only peace I have is that it's now over. When they call me to come out, Marleet peers around, holding me back with one hand before she'll release me. She's small, though, and after a moment or two, I just push past her.

We come out to find the scene of… I don't even want to think about it. It's horrific. Men, women… dozens, maybe hundreds, dead. When I look into the distance, I see many bodies throughout the area.

Relin hasn't stopped. He's not fighting anymore, but he's sending soldiers in all directions to make sure it's over. I don't hear anymore fighting, but the trees grow thick in this area. I doubt I'd hear much.

"Nooooo!!"

I spin around at the sound of Marleet's scream. My first thought is Hemot. He just arrived, and I can't bear the thought of losing him. He's been a friend as long as I can remember.

She's on the ground, leaning over someone, but Hemot's standing behind her. Billot's there as well.

The tears begin to stream down my face before I even know for sure who it is, but I can't hide from this.

I come up behind Marleet, crouch down, and put my arm around her shoulder. She shakes Denner as if he might respond, but I know there's no hope. Not for him. Not anymore.

A moment later, I'm holding my friend, doing my best to soothe her as she sobs. Hemot comes in close and wraps his arms around us both. He wasn't close with Denner, but he grieves for Marleet.

I examine Billot. He looks lost. His eyes are unfocused, his hands hang limply at his side. His sword lays at his feet. Denner was like a big brother to him. They'd served Lord Yune together for decades.

Relin's coming toward me, and I leave Marleet in the care of Hemot. I want to run and scream and cry, but the only thing I can do is lead.

"Report," I say in a scratchy, shaky voice.

"My Lady," Relin replies, "reports are still coming in, but it appears that Parthun left a large force here. They've been hiding in underground bunkers and waiting for us. I'm told by one of the men we quickly interrogated that when Parthun came through, he took around a thousand of the soldiers who were lying in wait. We only faced those who remained. I can't know for sure yet, but I believe we've lost close to two thousand of our own, perhaps more."

I close my eyes. This is a dark day.

But I remind myself, this is why we are doing this. Parthun must be removed. At this point, just about any cost is worth it to wrench the throne from that snake.

I slowly ride out of the trees, leaving the forest and the cliffs behind me. Ahead, spread across the Talic Region, are thousands of my soldiers. Behind are thousands more, still back in Switcher Pass.

The archers have taken up position, keeping an eye out for the Shaloomd, which have already started to circle. I glance up and do a quick count. I'd say there are over thirty up there now. Perhaps more.

The final count of those we lost in the attack ended up much higher than Relin first estimated. Over four thousand fell in that battle in Switcher Pass, leaving us with around six thousand. Far less than I expected to give to Draydon to support his ascension to the throne, and that's four thousand more deaths on my conscience.

Denner was right. This is brutal.

I glance at Marleet. She hasn't taken Denner's death well. Neither has Billot. I didn't know this before, but Denner actually served my parents for a time when he was around my age. Then, due to a set of circumstances I don't understand—there's much about the ways of Nobility that make no sense to me—he was transferred to Marleet's family.

I look ahead but close my eyes for a moment.

Switcher Pass took its toll on us. So has this entire journey. I also don't think Parthun's given up his fight for the throne, but at the rate we're moving, I think we should reach Haner in five days, or maybe early on the sixth. We should arrive just in time for the coronation.

If all goes well.

31

Draydon and the Speeches

The Shaloomd have gathered, along with vultures, crows, ravens, and countless other birds. Somehow, they know. Somehow, they are aware that the day is nearly here.

I stare out at Frindor's army from the southern wall of Haner and do my best to maintain my courage. I want to scream and cry and run. Frindor's soldiers cover the ground like sand on the seashore. And they know they have the advantage. I have never seen a true battle before, but I can tell the difference between the way they move and the way my men move.

My men are shaking in their boots. Frindor's men are ready to claim victory. And it's no wonder. We're hopelessly outmatched.

I had picked the first day of spring, thinking that sounded both like it gave enough time, but also because I always loved spring. I thought it was such a beautiful time of year. Now, here we are on the first day of spring, and rather than receiving the kingdom, I face an army ready to kill me.

They've sent their demand for my head. I feel sick to my stomach at the thought, but they actually asked for my head. Just my head. They want it. My head! Detached from my body!

Who… who would ask for such a thing?

Again. I want to scream and cry and run.

"Maintain your courage, My Prince," Tilbur says to me quietly. "We have not lost. We still draw breath. I have faced greater odds and emerged victorious."

"You have?" I stare up at him in wonder. There are few people I actually have to look up to. Tilbur is one of them. But now, as I think about this man facing off against greater odds than we face now, I find myself overcome with awe. "You really have?"

Tilbur takes another look out at the army before us. "Well, perhaps not. Reber's Gate was quite the challenge, but…"

He stops. I don't like that. "But what?"

"But, truthfully, the odds weren't this bad. And… we had General Geran."

I know he's right. I know I can't possibly live up to my dad in this situation, but we will fight hard. And I've made use of every single person I've found with any sense of strategy or understanding of war. I'm still unprepared, but we're just about as ready as we can get. "What would my father have done in this situation?"

Tilbur shakes his head. "I learned just about everything I could from Geran. Truly, I did." He turns to me and gives me one of his rare smiles. "But no matter how much I learned, I could never predict what he'd do." His hand comes down on my shoulder, the weight of that bulky arm pushing me down. "You're a lot like him, Draydon. You'll get us through."

I smile at that compliment, but I don't really feel like there's much truth to it.

Turning back to the south, I shake my head. Again… there's a lot of them. One of my suggestions was to take our stand in the city. I mean… pull our armies into Haner and fight from behind the wall. In my opinion, that would give us the best shot since Frindor would have to breach the wall before he could get to us.

Sadly, that idea was thrown out. It turns out if we come into the city, Frindor can surround the walls and simply wait us out. All the soldiers will eat so much food and require so much space, we'll run out of patience before Frindor does. On top of that, it will send a message to the people of Haner that we will not protect them, but we will put them in danger. Finally, it will convince the nation that I am a coward who won't face his enemies.

But… despite all that… I still think that's better than dying. Unfortunately, no one else agrees.

Now the Nobles… they can hide behind the walls. They arrived about a day before Frindor's soldiers reached us. Some wanted to run right away, heading north to Morgin City or to their estates in the north of the Talic Region, but despite the fact that they wanted to, they stayed. Tilbur explained that Frindor's soldiers could be patrolling the entire area, and everyone knows by now that Frindor is far from honorable.

Out of the Nobles who have arrived, many are loyal. And, unfortunately, many just fear they'll suffer if they do not attend. Lord Yune and Lady Aldora, along with Lord Hillbin, seem to be doing an okay job of keeping the Nobles calm, but there's a question of whether I will emerge victorious. Looking out over the enemy, I don't blame them for doubting their chances.

But what's worse than all of this is not those who fear, but those who are certainly not loyal. I know each disloyal Noble will turn on me in an instant.

But for me, right now, I have to face Frindor out on the fields of the Talic Region. Apparently, the time I'm spending on the wall right now is expected. I'm supposed to observe the enemy as I make up my strategy. Observing, of course, is something I can do. But creating a strategy? Oh no, that's something I don't know the first thing about.

The best I have is to put Traltor and Nareesa on the front lines. I don't know about Nareesa, but I'm not too concerned about Traltor. He seems to have the skin common to giant men that protects him from arrows and swords and spears. He's also incredibly strong. I think he might help turn the tide of this battle.

Nareesa, however, concerns me. Since she won't tell me what her limits are, I have to just take guesses. Her skin isn't that flabby, grayish color like Traltor or Rulf's. In fact, her skin looks almost like mine, and my skin won't stop a crossbow bolt. Not at all. She's strong—strong enough that it convinces me she definitely has giant blood in her, or at least some kind of enchantment, but can she be injured? I don't want to send her to the front lines if she can simply be killed by the first arrow shot. Considering her height, she's certainly a big target.

But she stubbornly won't tell me if her skin can stop an arrow. She... just... won't. And no one apparently knows. Or is willing to say.

Still, she and Traltor are on the front lines.

We've set up traps and a strong defensive line. I was afraid I would have to lead the charge, but it appears that we won't be taking that approach this time. We're going to wait for Frindor's troops to come to us.

It's funny, actually. General Corter is in charge of the troops standing against us, but no one even mentions him. Frindor's the real threat. Corter is likely to run at the first sign of defeat. I'm told he's as incompetent as any coward.

So, in that sense, we are equal. Corter, over that army, is incompetent, but has a strong leader under him, Frindor, who can move them forward. With us, I am over this army, and I am incompetent, but I have a strong leader,

Tilbur, who can move the army forward. I also have Granel, and countless others who have stood strong against Parthun's cruelty and wickedness.

Perhaps we have a chance. If we can even the odds.

I head down from the wall. Tomorrow, the battle is set to begin.

The sun hasn't yet shown its face, and for that I am grateful. The darkness is the only thing that prevents the day of battle from taking place.

I blink away the dry eyes, the tiredness, the exhaustion. No one else looks like they wish they were still in bed. I guess it's just me.

I take a moment and consider each of the ones in front of me gathered around the table. These are my Captains and my Lieutenants. I'm supposed to inspire them this morning, at least that's what Tilbur tells me. But how do I inspire others when any one of them would be a better person to lead this campaign? And any one of them could die today.

I examine Lieutenant Phil. He's big. Muscular, but… well… he's been a tavern owner for many years… kind of… well, he's not thin. I'll just say that. But he's been a soldier, and this is not the first battle he's faced.

Next to him stands Laanna, also a Lieutenant now. She's never seen battle before, but she's competent with a sword, and has been a good adviser over the recent weeks. She's also a quick learner and an even faster thinker— enough that she's able to lead well, even in areas she knows little about.

Then there's Lieutenant Gillan. The lead guard over the western gate of Haner. I pulled him in because he's loyal and because of his experience in war. He's offered a lot of great direction.

Next to Gillan stands Terr, with Gerr on the other side of him, two more Lieutenants. They're both solid fighters, and even Terr's missing arm and Gerr's missing leg doesn't seem to slow either of them down.

Back behind Gerr and Terr, sit Traltor and Nareesa. They're... picking their nails. And each other's nails. I know they are loyal, and strong, and brave. And I will count on them. I tried to offer them the rank of Lieutenant, but ranks mean nothing to them. Nothing at all.

Off to the side, a little ways back, stands Berin—or Lieutenant Berin. He wears a solemn expression. I know he hates war. We all do. Even those of us in this tent who have not seen war, hate it.

Next to Berin, of course, I have Roran, my Second Captain. He's my closest friend in the room, and I can't imagine facing this day without him.

And Granel, my Third Captain. His damaged face shows little to no emotion or expression of any kind. But, he's wise, and trustworthy, and honest, and... only a fool would ignore both his skill and ability and the love the men in the army have for him. He will lead well today, of that I have no doubt.

Finally, I have Tilbur. That man used to terrify me. In fact, he still does, in a way. He's built like a troll: tall, strong, and he looks like he's about to eat me. Even his mostly bald head adds to the effect of how tough he looks.

"Are we ready?"

"Yes, Your Majesty," Tilbur replies. Everyone else remains silent. They report to Tilbur. Tilbur reports to me.

"Excellent, First Captain," I reply.

As I stare at the men and women, despite my fear and nervousness, and tiredness, I can't help but smile. And from that point, I begin my speech.

"My friends," I say, the grin overtaking my face, "I am so proud to be here with each of you. To know that everyone in this tent at this moment is loyal to the throne and committed to the right is almost more than I can handle. And to understand that outside this tent, thousands of soldiers stand loyal to the throne, loyal to you, loyal to me, makes me want to shout for joy, and weep in humility.

"We are facing odds that appear impossible. We all know that. We know that our seventeen thousand troops face over twice that number today. The fact that you remain here and so do all the men and women outside this tent when we face such a threat is not only a testament to your loyalty, but to your courage, commitment, and faithfulness.

"My pride in you, my friends, is almost more than I can bear. And it is this very thing that helps to remind me that when I take the throne, and I will take the throne, when I sit on that throne, I will continue to serve the people of Sevord and the Talic with humility, always remembering that is I who serve you, not the other way around.

"Today, we will embark on the beginning of many such battles. Not all of them will involve swords and shields and armor, but they will all be costly, and they will all be a testament to the value of what we fight for. We fight not just for duty, but for honor and for freedom for all our people.

"So, my friends, be of good courage, and stand strong. And today we will see victory!"

Everyone cheers when I finish, and my smile grows. I worked hard on that speech. I'm supposed to give another speech to the soldiers outside, but this is the one I feared the most.

When they stop their cheering, and the room goes silent, I'm about to go over the plan for the day, when Traltor snickers, and quietly says, "You said duty…"

He and Nareesa break into laughter, and I stare at them in horror. At such a moment… how could they… they're like little children!

I glance at Tilbur for support, but he's fighting down a grin. Phil has his hands over his face, but his shoulder's shake. Roran loses it, laughing louder than Traltor. Gerr and Terr have almost fallen to the floor, holding each other up and wiping the tears from their eyes as they laugh. Only Gillan remains steady, but I see… I see it in his eyes. He's just doing all he can not to laugh.

I realize at that moment that I have two choices. Either put them all in their places and tell them to grow up, or laugh along with them. I don't want to be the grumpy King, so I let a smile slip onto my face. In another moment, I'm laughing with them all.

It's childish, silly, and ridiculous, but we laugh.

One thing's for sure, we need this. We need to laugh. And, I think, those outside the tent will hear our laughter and perhaps that's what they need to hear as well. Too much suffering, too much loss, too much fear.

We need to laugh.

When we finish, I just smile at them and order, "To your stations!"

We file out of the tent, and I smile at the soldiers nearby, hoping that our laughter mixed with confidence— even joy—might help. Captain Tilbur takes up his place near the center of the army to direct everyone. I'll be joining him soon.

Laanna stations herself near Tilbur, but closer to the front. She has a knack for quick decisions, and we placed her over the archers. Her position allows for her to send orders quickly to the different squadrons of archers, moving them back and forth to support the front lines.

The others move to the troops they oversee, reporting directly to either Captain Granel or Captain Roran. Roran and Granel report directly to Tilbur.

Everyone else reports to Tilbur, that is, except for Traltor and Nareesa. Their orders are a little different. They're not leaders… not really. I'm told they've never been leaders. They just kind of do their own thing. If you can get them to understand and follow their orders, then you get to benefit from their loyalty. If not… you just hope they don't do too much damage. I'm told their hearts are in the right place, even if their actions aren't always.

They take up position on the far west side of our front lines. Their orders are to remain there until the moment Frindor's troops charge. I hope they do.

I move through the troops on horseback to the front lines. It's not good for me to remain this close to Frindor's army, especially since I don't have my enchanted armor, but I must speak with the soldiers.

When I get to the front, they quiet down. They know why I'm here. Traltor and Nareesa take their positions not far away. They're my protection out here, but I asked that they not stand close, as I'll look like a child. That's not the impression I want to give.

Once I'm ready, I call out, "Loyal people of Sevord and the Talic, this is the day! This is the day when we face those who threaten to own our nation. This is the day when we face those who wish to see cruelty, malice, deceit, and rumor rule our lands. And this is the day we rise victorious! For if we fail, we leave our children to a fate under the reign of a cruel tyrant, a usurper to the throne, a murderer! And that is something no one here is willing to do. But when we stand, we raise our hopes high, and when we triumph, our future is secure. Today, you fight not for me, but for you. You fight for freedom. And you fight for truth!"

No one says anything when I finish. I think they're expecting more, but that's all I have. After far too long, Nareesa cheers, and the rest of the people join in, banging their swords against their shields.

I immediately move back through the army, meeting my guards and making my way to Tilbur. I greet everyone I pass as best I can.

The sun is just poking up at this point. I would have liked to face Frindor with the sun at our back, but Frindor's too smart for that. Instead, we positioned ourselves just west of the city, forcing Frindor to come at us either from the south or north. Since the north would require him to move entirely around behind us, the south was the obvious choice.

When I reach Tilbur, I step up on the platform he had built for leading the war effort. If the front lines fall, we'll have to pull back, but for now, we're out of reach of any archer.

Reports come in every ten minutes or so as the sun comes up. We're keeping a close eye on everything.

As for the enemy, Frindor informed us yesterday that we had until this morning at dawn to send my head. Truthfully, I keep expecting someone to come up behind me and start sawing it off. I assume at least some are thinking it, even if no one's actually doing it.

But I have to remind myself that these men and women aren't standing with me because they fear me. They stand with me because they are loyal to the throne. They love the throne of Sevord, and they hate the usurper who sits upon it.

Their loyalty drives them to lay down their lives for me, as I am willing to lay down my life for them and for the throne. Hard to believe it was less than a year ago that I didn't even know who I truly was, nor was I willing to sit on that throne. I still don't love the idea of being King, but I love these people, and I love this nation.

When the sun is about half-way peeking up over the mountains to the east, which is around mid-morning, I see movement in the enemy camp. Soldiers shifting around, troops moving along their front lines, then I see Frindor come out front. He's about to give his speech to rally to troops.

"Now, My Prince," Tilbur whispers.

I signal to Traltor, and he steps out past our front line and bellows out to the enemy, "Brothers and Sisters, hear me!"

I blink a few times. He's facing away from me, and the volume almost hurts my ears. I doubt there are many in Frindor's army who can't hear him. It also means Frindor will have to wait until Traltor is finished to give his speech.

"You all know me! Or you know of me! I'm Traltor, son of Nush. I have fought for the Royal line for well over a hundred years. I was there with many of you at the Battle of Reber's Gate. I saw my brothers and sisters die by the swords and the clubs and the spears of the Rebers. You know what we fought for. We did not fight merely to conquer, like Talic Wolves, seeking to devour. We did not fight merely to steal, like Shaloomd, swooping down to rob us of all we hold dear. We fought to protect our land, our freedom, and our way of life! We fought to hold back the barbarian hordes as they sought to take our families, our homes, our land, our very lives."

My mouth hangs open. He should have given the speech to our troops! He has a way with words. I have never seen this side of him, and Rulf certainly didn't get this quality from his dad. In the short pause, I see Frindor turn to his troops. It looks like he's about to start his speech, likely hoping to hold back the damage done by Traltor's words.

"But now, what do you fight for?" Traltor calls out, his booming voice echoing across the still morning air of the Talic and forcing Frindor to wait until he finishes. "Do you fight for freedom? No! You fight against freedom. Do you fight for your rightful King? No! You fight for the usurper who has seized the throne, imprisoning General Lirnal and attempting to murder Prince Draydon! Do you fight to protect your lands? Your way of life? Your families? Your lives? No! You fight to keep on the throne the very man who threatens your families and all that you are! You stand as traitors to the throne, traitors with Parthun, traitors with those who killed King Hartor and General Geran. You stand against General Geran's son, the rightful heir to the throne!"

He pauses for another moment, and Frindor raises his arms and waves them. I assume he's speaking, but his voice doesn't carry this far.

After a few more seconds, Traltor speaks up again, but this time, his voice raises in volume and intensity. He sounds angry, yet filled with hope. "I… I stand with Prince Draydon. I stand with the rightful heir to the throne. I stand with those who seek to fulfill their duty!"

Traltor's shoulder's shake with this part, and Nareesa punches him in the side. I glance at Tilbur, and he slowly shakes his head, but there's the faintest hint of a smile on his face.

Frindor appears to be trying to start his speech again, but Traltor hollers out, "Leave your traitorous ways, my friends! Renew your loyalty this day to your true King. Throw away your rebellion, your hatred, your stubbornness, and come to Prince Draydon. He is kind and gracious. Come to him! Ask him for forgiveness and pledge your loyalty and your fealty to him. He will welcome you with open arms as he has welcomed me." He then reaches out and gently puts his arm around Nareesa in a loving manner, and calls out, "As he has welcomed us!"

Tilbur smiles at me. "Geran always told me, never underestimate Traltor."

I'm in shock. That man… that giant… he's something else! "Is Nareesa a good speaker like him?"

Tilbur's smile grows larger. "I believe her version of this speech was something like, 'Hey, dumb-dumbs! Stop it!'"

I have to admit. That's somewhat underwhelming, but I do like the simple clarity of such an approach.

I examine Frindor's men. They shift on their feet; they look around. No one can come to us, unfortunately, as Frindor will order them shot before they get too far. But their hesitation will hinder their ability to fight.

Frindor's mad. I can see it. He turns to his men and starts to yell at them… I think. It looks like he's really trying to either scold them or do his best to overcome the damage done by Traltor.

Traltor, however, is not finished. He leads our armies in a cheer. Then another. Then another. Soon, we're all caught up in the excitement, and I'm cheering along with everyone else. Our cheers come out in a rhythmic shout. Again, and again, and again. Over and over, we shout, scream, stomp our feet.

Frindor stops, then starts, then stops. It's not long before he drops his speech and then tries to get people to shout their own cheer, but nothing works. Their spirits are broken. Traltor did it. No one on that side is ready to fight anymore.

At least not the common soldiers, but I see enough officers ordering their soldiers forward that Frindor's troops begin to advance. They're not at a run yet, but Tilbur says they will be soon enough.

The battle has begun.

32

Draydon and the Battle

Closer and closer they come. My heart races, my legs feel like jelly. I want to turn and run away, but I can't. Well, I can run. I certainly *can* run! But for the sake of my soldiers, I can't.

"Hold the line!" Tilbur hollers. He signals to Traltor and Nareesa, and they take off running to the east along the front lines. I watch as Frindor rearranges his troops accordingly. This is the test. It gives us the answer to what we're wondering.

"They have something," Tilbur says matter of factly. I don't know how he figured it out, but I guess he can see from Frindor's response that there's a special focus on Traltor and Nareesa. It's not just because they're a threat—they are that, for sure, but it's more.

When Traltor and Nareesa come to a halt, Tilbur gives them their next signal, letting them know they need to move a lot during the battle. This isn't good. Aside from the matter of crushing their morale, Rulf's parents are our greatest weapons.

The enemy has reached the half-way point, and they break into a run, charging our defenses. Laanna calls for her archers to ready themselves, adjusting them accordingly for Frindor's troops, and they prepare.

When the soldiers reach two-thirds of the way across, they hit our first defense: pits. Down they go through the thin boards, sticks and grass covering the deep holes. Dozens, no, hundreds, drop out of sight. The pits themselves are not so deep as to kill a man, but with countless soldiers dropping on top of you...

I don't want to think about it. It's a horrible way to die.

The soldiers continue to run, unable to stop as those behind them push them on, but when the pits are filled, they push on past. In a few more steps, they reach our second defense: spikes. They trip and stumble over boards and levers that when stepped upon, raise spikes up just enough to cut into ankles and shins.

They stumble and fall, and trip over one another. Hundreds go down, some trampled by those coming behind, others getting to their feet and carrying on. Many who make it past that point will be far too injured to be too much of a threat, and few, if any, horses will carry on.

As expected, Frindor orders his soldiers to circle around to the west and east. We have traps in that direction as well, and they work beautifully, but now we're on to the next defense: archers.

Laanna has already ordered hundreds of archers to respond to the shift in the enemy's attack, but she was well prepared for that already, as we had assumed this adjustment. She calls out her orders, and the archers let loose, focusing on those attempting to come around and attack our flank, but not ignoring those in the middle, either.

I close my eyes.

The battle has only begun, and I have witnessed far too much death already. I begin to wonder if I can make it through the rest of this fight without opening my eyes even once, but that possibility comes crashing down as Tilbur elbows me.

"Keep those eyes open!" he hisses. "The soldiers nearby will draw strength from your resolve. Don't give in to the fear."

"But those are my men and women dying out there!" I reply in a whisper. "Frindor may be ordering them forward, but they're my people. Even on Parthun's side, they're my people! I'm ordering their deaths! How can I do this?"

Tilbur puts his hand on my shoulder, and I see compassion in his eyes. He understands. I'm shocked by that. He's always seemed so heartless. Loyal, yes. Strong, yes. Wise, yes. But heartless, absolutely.

"There is nothing good in war, Draydon," he explains to me. "Nothing. Sometimes the end of it means peace for a while, but war is never a good thing. It is a wickedness that often forces itself into our lives. These men and women die because of that wickedness. Not because of you. Remember that!" He then pushes me forward a bit, toward the battle. "Now, focus!"

Laanna's archers have done their job well, thinning out the ranks. Between the defensive traps and the arrows, Frindor has lost a lot of soldiers. But that was the easy part. Even I know that.

The enemy soldiers, driven by the orders of their officers, crash into our front lines. Our spearmen hold strong, and the archers continue to shower down their arrows, but Frindor's archers are not far away.

Tilbur signals to Roran who watches the eastern flank, and he signals to Nareesa who, along with Traltor, wreak havoc among the soldiers attacking from that direction. Nareesa calls out to Traltor, and he nods before the two of them charge out into Frindor's ranks. When they reach the enemy archers, they run through their midst, making an arc back towards the west.

I find myself both horrified and thrilled. I'm thrilled that the enemy faces such resistance, moving us toward victory, but I'm horrified to see so much death.

Tilbur's right. There is nothing good in war.

Traltor and Nareesa continue through the enemy archers, slashing, tossing, kicking, punching. I am pleased to see that arrows do bounce off Nareesa's skin, not just Traltor, but I see her flinch which each shot. No doubt she has giant blood, but I expect it's farther back than her husband's.

Reaching the other end of the army, they stop and fight in that area. I look back. Frindor's sending out orders, and his troops are trying to recover.

I keep an eye on Rulf's parents. We're all concerned for them, as we strongly suspect Frindor has some strategy for their demise.

I see two men with crossbows on horseback, riding west near Frindor's front lines. The fact that they're on horseback is not unusual. Frindor himself is in the saddle, but these two men... the way they ride... something's up.

I point to them, and Tilbur smacks my hand down. "Never physically point to something in the enemy camp, Your Majesty! You give them an advantage."

I rub my forearm. Tilbur wasn't gentle. He seems to go back and forth between calling me Draydon when he's being kind or caring, but then speaks formally when he wants to be focused.

"Do you see those two on horseback?" I ask.

He nods. "I saw them move east earlier when Traltor and Nareesa crossed to the other side."

"Are they the threat we fear?"

He nods. "I think so. Let's test it to make sure."

Tilbur signals to Granel on the west side, who then signals to Nareesa. She, once again, calls to Traltor, and the two take off running to the east, circling around, crushing, slashing, kicking, punching, throwing, and more.

I look back at the two men on horseback. Sure enough, they've turned around, and they're now making their way to the east. "We have our answer."

Tilbur nods again. "Whatever we do, we have to keep those men away from our giantfolk."

I wish, at that moment, we had Rulf here with us. He's difficult, although in a different way than his parents, but he's strong, like his parents. It would be good to have his strength and support in this battle.

The morning continues with more bloodshed, more death, more destruction, more loss. Traltor and Nareesa run back and forth across the front lines, killing countless soldiers along the way. I have had to force myself to see Frindor's troops merely as soldiers. As enemy combatants. Otherwise, it'll tear me apart. I've had two or three moments when I've almost called out for a surrender, unwilling to continue resisting at this price, but Tilbur has helped me remain strong.

The only way to bring down this tyrant is through courage and sacrifice. I just wish these men and women didn't have to be the ones who paid the price.

"We have turned the tide," Tilbur announces, pulling me away from my focus on the western flank.

"What do you mean?"

He points with his chin at the enemy. I don't really see it at first, until he tells me to look around at our army.

I do and see that we've suffered very few casualties. In fact, our front lines remain largely unbroken. Laanna's archers are doing a great job, the spearmen are holding strong, and the soldiers behind the spearmen, those under Lieutenant Berin's command, have had little to do. Most of our soldiers have seen no action at all.

The enemy, however, has suffered great losses. The discouragement they feel seems to have taken the fight right out of their hearts, and I think… it's hard to believe, but I think we've brought them down to close to our own numbers. At this rate, we will overpower them in very little time. If all continues as it is…

Tilbur growls, and I tense up. We both see it at the same time.

I've been so focused on the army in front of me, I forgot to watch the surrounding regions. From the south, moving at a fast pace, another army approaches.

"Who is it?" I ask.

Tilbur shakes his head. "There are only three options. It could be the Rebers. If so, we're really in trouble. I don't know who they'll side with, but I'm pretty sure it's not you. They are vicious fighters."

"Second option?"

"Leito."

"But they're loyal to us!"

"Yes, they are. Hopefully, it's them."

"And the third option?"

He frowns, watching them closely as they approach. "The third option is the worst." He slowly shakes his head and leans forward a little, as if that will give him a better view of the armies in the distance. Finally, he nods. "Yes, it's them."

"Who?"

"They're from Rainer. It's Farnum."

"Farnum has an army?"

Tilbur nods. "He certainly does. He didn't during Hartor's time, but he has thrived under Parthun's reign."

"How can you tell it's them?"

"Colors," Tilbur explains. "Those are Farnum's colors."

"But Lord Dimtor. Wouldn't he try to stop Farnum? He's pledged himself to me."

"He might have. I think you actually gave Dimtor a bit of courage. But if he did take a stand, he's likely dead now. Either way, that's definitely Farnum, and he is not on our side. If he's still able to use your sword and armor, he himself will be quite the force, let alone his troops."

"How many?" I do my best to figure it out, but it's just a sea of soldiers.

"I'd say ten thousand."

"Ten thou—" I catch myself and lower my voice. "How did he get so many?"

"Rainer is a big city. And he likely hired mercenaries from Reber or elsewhere."

I briefly hope we can find some reinforcements. Maybe Milter will come. Maybe the troops who went home from Sevord City out of discouragement will show up. But I can't count on any of that. "How long before they arrive?"

Tilbur examines the approaching army once again and then says, "An hour. Maybe less."

"Then we need to make some serious advancements in this battle in the next hour."

We push hard, even gaining some ground. Our defensive traps are either full or have been removed by Frindor's troops, so we push on without them. It's not long before Frindor's pulling his soldier's back, and our own soldiers, those not yet engaged in the battle, cheer the front lines on.

I'm beginning to think the reinforcements won't stand a chance when Farnum's troops arrive, and everything changes. The arrival of a massive army such as he's brought, nearly as many troops as Frindor has left, changes the morale of both our troops, and of the enemy.

The cheer of my troops from a moment ago now ends, and Frindor's troops cheer away, giving the enemy forces a push and enthusiasm and drive that they have not shown until this moment. They surge forward, breaking our line of spearmen in minutes, and our swordsmen, under Berin's command, engage immediately. Laanna scrambles to adjust her archers, but reports inform me she's dangerously low on arrows.

Our archers are prepared to draw their swords when the time comes, but I've ordered them to pull back when they're out of arrows. They've fought from the beginning. They'll need a rest.

Our spearmen, those still alive, come back while others replace them, and Berin orders his swordsmen to push on, but it's still not enough. The effort breaks our entire front lines, and Tilbur and I are forced to pull back and relocate to continue to lead the battle.

Farnum's troops circle around to the east, coming up on Roran's flank, and troops move in to support him. We're now facing a full-on attack on two sides.

I remember at that moment our need to keep an eye on Traltor and Nareesa and turn back just in time to see what I hoped never to see. Traltor stumbles back and forth. Something's not right. The enemy around him jabs him with spears, but I know that's not it.

Nareesa steps close and knocks soldiers away as she grabs Traltor, doing her best to support his massive bulk. My eyes land on a man… one of the men I saw earlier on horseback with crossbows. He's on foot at this point, but he aims for Nareesa. I call out a warning, but there's no way she can hear me.

A bolt lodges in the back of her neck, and she jerks forward. A moment later, she has it ripped out, but I see her stumble, just like her husband. Traltor goes down, but Nareesa barely notices. She begins to wave her hands in the air like she's warding off enemies no one else can see, then drops to her knees.

I don't know if she falls on her own, or if the enemy brings her down, but there's no sign of either now as the enemy surges around them.

"Fall back!" Tilbur orders, then grabs my arm before I can respond.

"How did they find arrows to pierce Traltor and Nareesa's skin?"

"Don't know, Your Majesty," Tilbur shouts. "That's something to figure out later."

We pull back and regroup. My soldiers have a chance here to take a second stand, and they do just that. I look around, selfishly, to make sure my friends are okay. I see Laanna. She's… on her feet, but… an arrow is stuck through her right arm—that was her good arm! Someone's working on it while she continues to shout orders. Roran, Phil, Granel… I look around and manage to set my eyes on everyone.

Tilbur shouts orders. I know I'm supposed to do that as well, but I don't really know what to say, so I just pay close attention to the kinds of orders he makes.

I grip the railing around our secondary command post, leaning forward as if that'll help. Frindor's men fight like their lives depend on it. It's as if the new arrivals have whipped them into a frenzy, and our soldiers can barely hold the line. Tilbur orders reinforcements, and I see some of the Lieutenants pulling back their troops and replacing them with others.

My heart races, and I can barely think straight. We had been doing so well, now we're fighting for our lives, and I'm not sure how we can hold.

Frindor brings his troops around to our western flank, and Captain Granel responds quickly. He reinforces the troops, making use of Laanna's western archers, and sends in spearmen. General Lirnal spoke well of Granel, but it's a real privilege to see him in action!

The troops fight well, but with the attack coming on three sides, I feel like we're being squeezed. My breathing quickens, and panic floods my heart. The soldiers around us no longer remain still. They had stood steady for hours, only shifting themselves to keep moving. Now, they turn, they move, they adjust, they draw their swords, then sheath them.

We're in trouble. I can see it around me, but even if I couldn't, Tilbur's expression says it all. He's not scared, he's just… angrier.

The reports come in. With most of them, I don't know what to do with the information I hear. I just nod and thank the men who come. But these reports… casualty lists… I think we've lost close to a thousand. A thousand lives… gone.

I signal to Laanna to send more archers to the western front, and Tilbur sends more spearmen to the east. To the south, the enemy breaks against our lines, again and again. I see the areas where Traltor and Nareesa went down. Enemy soldiers reach that point and move up and over a large object. It makes me sick to think of who that is under their boots.

Another cheer goes up from the enemy camp. I didn't see it at first, but… oh no…

Tilbur clenches his fists and slams them down on the railing. I can't see how many there are, but another force comes at us from the southwest. They come up and over the countless hills throughout the Talic, swarming across the land.

"How many do you think?" I ask Tilbur.

"Too many!" he hisses, but after a moment, he says, "I'm sorry, Your Majesty. I would suspect that's another one to two thousand. It is difficult to know for sure.

A horn blows from the enemy side, and for a moment, hope floods my heart, thinking perhaps they're pulling back to regroup. We could use the time and the breather to adjust our strategy. But my hope falls when Tilbur shakes his head and growls, "Parthun you snake!"

He's arrived. He's finally here. He hasn't just sent others to do his fighting. He's come too. Which means, if we can turn this around, I can finally remove him.

But if we can't take care of his army, it doesn't matter if he's here or not. We're done.

"Out!" Tilbur orders, pushing me back.

I glance around as we move off the platform. The western front has broken. The spearmen have fallen or have been pushed back, and it's sword to sword.

I drop down out of our command platform and move a little east with Tilbur. We're boxed in here, but he orders the troops not yet engaged to spread out and around the western and eastern forces attacking us. It gives the enemy a little more to focus on, and I can see it eases up the pressure on our soldiers.

Movement to the south catches my eyes. I see Traltor back up on his knees, but then he collapses again. He's alive! Whatever was on that arrow, though, seems to have knocked him out. I hope Nareesa is the same—only unconscious.

The pressure continues around us. We're still around the platform, but down a little lower so we can't be easily targeted. I keep an eye out for my Lieutenants. So far, I can see most of them, but Laanna and Roran are out of sight.

Someone slams into me, and I crash down on the ground. The snow has turned to slush this morning, and it creeps through my armor and clothing almost immediately. I push the guy off me, and scramble back to my feet to find others pushing through. No, not pushing through. The enemy is pushing them back.

Another two men stumble into me, and I see someone stumble into Tilbur. He calls my name, but by the time I get to my feet, I have to draw my sword.

The battle has reached me!

33

Draydon and Frindor

I swing wildly at first before I remember my training. The moment I do, I have the upper hand. Tilbur explained that few soldiers have any serious training in swordplay. Most just volunteer or are conscripted.

Some of these soldiers will have served as guards, but most are cobblers or tavern owners or farmers or countless other trades or professions. They know how to handle a sword, but have had little to no actual training or practice.

I easily fend off those coming at me. The occasional one gives me some more trouble, but that's rare. I do, however, wish I had my own sword, not this one. And my armor. As much as I don't like the damage my sword can do, it would make every fight so much quicker.

Someone new comes at me and from the first moment our swords touch, I recognize that I'm outclassed. The guy is fast, and it's all I can do to keep his blade away from my neck. I parry, then try to get past his defenses, but have to pull back again right away.

He knocks my sword off to the right, and before I can pull back, he lunges for me. I freeze for just a second, but in a blur, a large shape takes him down.

I fend off another attack from a woman who's extremely unskilled and looks nearly as scared as I feel, and then push back a young man who looks like he could be her brother. I yell at them to abandon their rebellion and stand with their true King, and they... simply step back, lower their swords... and, as strange as it is, apologize.

"Stand with my soldiers! Fight for Sevord, not against it!" I order, and they... do.

I turn to see what had happened to the man I had fought only a moment ago, the man who outskilled me by far. Tilbur stands above the man's body, fighting off two enemy soldiers at the same time.

A large group of Frindor's soldiers come at us, but an even larger group of my own forces rushes in, fighting them back. I get a moment's relief, and I actually catch sight of Frindor and General Corter.

The General stands with his sword drawn, a look of terror on his face, spinning around, facing everyone as if he or she might be his foe. He appears to be surrounded by his own soldiers, but he... he looks like a terrified cat that just fell in a pool of water. He doesn't know which way to run, he just knows he wants to run.

But Frindor... he not only looks confident, but his eyes are on me. It's as if he cannot see anything in this world aside from his target. In his eyes, I see nothing but hatred. Nothing but rage. Nothing but murder.

I know one thing for sure: he's coming for me. Not just his army. He is. It won't be long before I face that man. And if I thought anyone I'd faced until this point was hard to fight, Frindor is going to be far worse.

"This way," Tilbur orders and drags me along.

I go with him. I don't know what else to do. This is just a mess. I feel like I should stand with my soldiers, but I really don't know. I could go anywhere here and have to stand with them.

"Where are we going?"

"Back!" Tilbur replies.

I dig my heels in. "That's not an answer!"

"The battle's lost," Tilbur hisses under his breath. I can barely hear him. "We have to get you out of here so we can regroup. We'll build again and find an opportunity to take down Parthun when he's vulnerable."

"We're leaving?" My voice comes out in just a whisper. I can't believe this… I can't do this.

"No other choice!"

I frown at him and pull my arm out of his hand. "Yes, there is another choice. And I'm taking it. I'm staying here."

He spins me around and points back at the battle, just a few strides away. Through clenched teeth, he growls, "Do you see that? Do you see all that? That's thousands of men and women fighting to keep you alive. The battle is lost. Most just don't know it yet. If you stay, you'll die! For them, you need to flee! So, come on!"

He grabs me again, and I pull my arm out of his hands one more time. "No!" I grab his arm and point with my other hand back at the battle. "Do you see that? Do you see all those soldiers? That's thousands of men and women fighting to put me on the throne. Not just to keep me alive, but to keep the kingdom alive!"

"The kingdom won't live if you don't live!"

"And if I can't take the throne today, I won't ever sit on it!"

I stare him down. For a big, intimidating guy, I know a couple of things about Tilbur for sure. He's loyal, and on some level, he cares for me. After a moment, his face softens to a point of resignation.

He nods at me and gives me a halfhearted smile. "You're just like your father."

Despite our situation, that makes me smile.

We both turn back to the battle and move forward. I don't see Frindor at the moment. That kind of scares me. At least when I know where he is, I can be prepared. I fear he's going to jump out at me at any moment.

But all that's forgotten when in a few seconds, I'm engaged in the battle.

We fight hard. I notice that my soldiers fight harder when I'm around. They're protective of me, but I think they want to see me fight.

I'm grateful for the daily practice over the months leading up to today, and really grateful that Tilbur is a brutally hard teacher. He had me sweating every time, gasping for air. And now, while my soldiers gasp for air, I'm still going strong. And that seems to inspire them.

A sense of peace washes over me, despite the terrible situation. I want to scream and run away, but at the same time, I know I'm doing what's right. I'm fighting for the freedom of my people. I'm even fighting for the people siding with Parthun as I know they're siding with him either because of his lies or fear.

We push forward and start to gain some ground. We're outnumbered, but I won't give up. And neither will anyone else. We will stand and take this throne back for the people!

I jump up and bring my sword down hard on an enemy soldier's shield. The man stumbles back, dropping his sword in the process. He scrambles out of the way and even when he gets his weapon, the fight's gone out of him. He gets to his feet and slips off through the crowd, only to be replaced by another two.

But the joy of driving one more enemy away isn't what I'm focused on. With my extra height and the occasional jump during battle, I can see over the heads of others. And I saw it. Another army. This one is huge, pouring over the hills of the Talic. If we were outmatched before, we're about to be crushed.

As if just seeing them isn't enough, Frindor's men cheer. I hear the cries, "Victory for King Parthun! Long live King Parthun!"

My arm grows tired, but still I fight on. I catch a glimpse now and then of Tilbur. He fights like an animal, using everything: sword, fists, feet, head. He just goes from punching to kicking to slashing to head-butting. Now and then he picks up a shield, but not to protect himself. Instead, he uses it to bash soldier's across the head or to throw at approaching threats.

The cheer goes up from the enemy again along with, "Victory for King Parthun! Reinforcements have arrived!"

Some of our soldiers pull back, so I cry out, "Do not lose heart! We fight for freedom and loyalty! Fight for the throne of Sevord!"

It's the best I can come up with at this moment. I'm so scatterbrained with all the attacks and my attempts to defend myself that I'm not even sure what I said.

My soldiers surge forward with a newfound energy, and we push back the enemy a little more. When I have a moment, I jump up just a little to catch sight of the approaching army. They're nearly here.

"Tilbur!" I call out.

"Yes," Tilbur replies. He told me in the midst of actual combat, we should never use titles.

"Another army…" I ward off an attack, "… approaching…" I duck and then bring my sword up under an enemy's guard, "… from the southwest."

"I see them!"

Out of the corner of my eye, I see Traltor again. He's back on his feet, and as he slowly twists around, I see Nareesa beside him. I fight a bit more, and then glance back at them when I have a moment. They may be on their feet, which is great and all, but they're not fighting. They appear to be asleep. Whatever Frindor did to them, it knocked them out good.

Speaking of Frindor, that's when I see him.

And not just him, but dozens of new soldiers. They swarm around me, and I do my best to fight them off, but no one engages. At least not with me.

In fact, they avoid me, pulling out and around as if they're scared I might hurt them. I can't imagine I'm that good with the sword, but then I see why.

I'm alone. No Tilbur. No loyal soldiers. No one.

No, not no one. I'm surrounded by a wall of soldiers—most facing outwards, keeping my friends away. The only one in this circle with me… is Frindor.

He still has the look of hate and anger, but along with it is the largest smile I've seen in a long time. It's a hungry smile. It's a smile that says he's about to get what he wants, and his drawn sword lets me know exactly what that is.

"I'm not one for lots of words, Draydon."

I shake my head. "Me neither."

He charges, and I face off against a man whom I think might be able to best Tilbur. He's fast. Every jab feels like he hopes to skewer me, and each swing lands like he expects it to cleave me in two.

If I had my own sword and armor, this man would be dead already, but as it stands, I can barely hold my own.

I feel my arms weaken, doing my best to slide his attacks off to the side, rather than simply block them. Even with the cold wind, I've been sweating for a while, but now I begin to gasp for air. Frindor, however, looks like he's not even breathing heavy.

The look in his eyes changes, and the rage grows. He increases his attack, driving down my defenses. I hear Tilbur hollering for me in the background, and ordering everyone he can to break through the line to get to me, but I can't concentrate on that. It's all I can do to parry each attack.

But then the moment comes. I feel a pain in my hand as he brings his sword in, but I manage to keep hold of the grip. It's not enough, though, because he swings his sword hard and connects with my blade, driving it off to the right, then comes back, slashing at my side where the armor is weakest.

I stumble back, and he drives his sword through the break in my armor.

I feel it go in.

I hit the ground hard. The pain... oh, the pain is intense! I don't think I've ever felt anything like this. Even when I was stabbed with knives while wearing my enchanted armor. I felt it... but it was not like this. Nothing like this.

I can't help but cry out, and tears stream down my face.

"Ahh... is the young little Prince upset now?" Frindor asks with a wicked grin. "All your dreams of sitting on that throne are coming to an end this very day."

I want to come up with something witty to say, but I just can't. All I can do is ask, "Why? Why betray the throne?"

His smile disappears, and the rage returns. "Well, Caric, or Draydon, let me tell you why! It was your dad. It was him I hated. Hartor was one thing. I could put up with him, but your father... always so intense... always so focused. I wanted to learn from him and become an officer, but he didn't think I had it in me. In fact, he caught me spreading rumors about another officer. I had to do it. That other man stood in my way. Geran declared me unfit for service at that very moment. When he was killed later that day, I joined the rebels, spread the rumor that he was involved in it, and set my focus on destroying the throne."

I shake my head. So, he's the one who tried to discredit my father. "But Parthun… you want him on the throne?"

He shakes his head. "No, but I also know that out of all the sons of Trevolay, he's the last one Geran would want sitting there. So… I put up with Parthun and will continue to, knowing Geran is not only dead, but that I've killed his only son."

I grab my sword from the spot where it lays and fight with all my strength to stand. The battle is so loud all around me, but it still feels far away.

Frindor laughs, and I don't blame him. I must look like a pathetic opponent. I manage to stand as straight as I can, but I'm still hunched over on my left side where Frindor stabbed me. I can still lift my sword, so I step up and try to attack, but he easily knocks my blade aside. I don't have the strength to hold it anymore, and it hits the ground, followed by me, shortly after.

"Ahh, tears! That's an appropriate response, Draydon. Tell me, why are you crying? Is it the pain?" With that, he comes up and kicks me in the side.

If I thought it hurt before, it was nothing like this. The pain I feel now makes all other pain I've ever felt like nothing more than an irritation.

I almost black out, but I'm disappointed to find my eyes stay open. When I catch my breath again, all I can do is cry.

It's not the pain, though, that causes the tears. It's Ellcia. Someone will tell her. I'm sure of it. She might just hear in a rumor, but she'll hear. And… I don't want her to hurt.

Frindor laughs. "And here you lay, a servant pretending to be a Prince, about to die by my hand."

"No, Frindor," I manage in a growl. "I'm not dying a servant, nor am I dying a Prince. I will die, that I think is true, but I will die with the heart of a King!"

He opens his mouth to respond, but appears at first to be left speechless. After a moment, he looks around as if he's suddenly remembering there's a war going on. "I'm sorry Draydon, whether you fancy yourself a King or not, I have to finish this. You're not the only one I plan on killing today." With a mocking bow, he adds, "So, your Majesty, it's time to say my goodbye."

I decide not to close my eyes. I'm going to face him. Even though I can't even pick up my blade to defend myself, I will look him in the eye until the end. It's the only defiance I have left against his and Parthun's cruelty.

The circle of soldiers around us surges. I have a brief moment of hope that it's Tilbur, that he's managed to break through, but when I do my best to twist my neck enough to see back that way, the wall of soldiers remains solid.

I quickly turn back to Frindor. I will stare him down.

He comes at me with a large grin on his face, raises his sword, and I watch as it comes down, but just at the last second, someone slams into his side, and he stumbles away.

At first, I think it's a boy. Small, fast, short hair, higher voice, but then I hear her scream, "Get away from him!"

I nearly cry out her name. She found me! Ellcia… she found me!

She attacks the man fast and hard, each swing not only driven by skill, but passion. Frindor's face fills with fear at first, but he gets his feet under himself and charges. A moment later, she's on the defensive.

As he easily pushes her back, he has a big smile on his face, shaking his head as if he's been given a gift. "My next stop, Lady Ellcia, was to come for you, and Lady Marleet, and the one they now call the Coastal Duke." He steps up his attack, and Ellcia trips backwards on the ground. Knocking her sword aside, he places the tip of his blade at her throat. "But now you've saved me the trouble. I'm guessing Yune's daughter and the Milterite are here somewhere. That will simplify my work."

I roll just a little, groaning as I do. Grabbing some of the thick grass sticking up through the brown and red slush, I pull myself as best as I can.

"Ahh, your Prince comes to save you," Frindor says with a laugh. "Hurry up now. You might as well die in each other's arms."

"Draydon!" Ellcia calls, not moving more than her eyes and mouth. The blade pushes in against her skin. I fear Frindor could shift just a little, and it would all be over.

I struggle more and get a bit farther, finally reaching her side. I wrap my arms around her, and Frindor laughs, pulling back the blade just a bit. It's enough for Ellcia to come in and grab hold of me, and in a moment, we're both weeping.

"You found me," I whisper. I can't manage anymore volume than that. "You found me."

"I did," she says through tears. "I brought an army. For you."

I smile. "Thanks."

It seems silly at a moment like this, but I'll take it. I'll take whatever she has to give.

"Enough of all this!" Frindor says with yet another laugh. "Time to die, Princeling."

I see the shadow of his raised arm, and the movement out of the corner of my eye, but I just keep my eyes fixed on Ellcia. I had wanted to stare Frindor down, but this is better. I'll die like this, and I'll die a happy man.

I run my hand through her hair… it's spikey, and there's a wound, maybe a couple weeks old, on her neck. But her smile… I have her back now. That's all I need.

I hear a grunt from Frindor as he swings the blade down, but once again, his sword doesn't reach us. This time, however, I hear a cry of pain. We both look up to see Frindor in the air. His sword is… bent! And his face… filled with horror. The large man across from him, the one holding him, stinks. I remember that smell. I'll never forget it.

One word escapes my lips. Only one can I get out at this moment. "Rulf."

I pull Ellcia's face into my chest and bury my own in her short hair as Rulf deals with Frindor. I've seen what he can do when he's angry against a man who might threaten to hurt the ones he loves, and I don't care to ever witness it again. I try to block out the sounds and simply smell Ellcia's hair.

She smells like… she's been traveling. But it's the best thing I've ever smelled in my life.

"Draydon… girl… you can get up now."

"It's Ellcia," I say in a croak, and he shakes his head.

"I thought the other one was Ellcia. The boy."

"No, you didn't, Rulf!" she scolds, and I see that little smile, just the corner of Rulf's lips, curling up.

He pulls Ellcia to her feet but stops when he sees me. "You're hurt," he says in that way Rulf has of saying just a little less than he needs to.

Tilbur appears at my side, and I twist around to see what's going on around me, doing my best to avoid Frindor's broken body. The soldiers who made up Frindor's shield around me are gone. I don't know who dealt with them, but I'm glad they did.

The others around are not fighting. They're standing guard. I think… for me. I'm not sure I'm thinking straight.

Tilbur brings a waterskin to my mouth, but I shake my head. He gives me a look that I interpret to mean this isn't an option, and I do my best to swallow as much as I can.

"Report," I say to Tilbur, but he shakes his head.

"You're out of the battle now. You focus on recovery."

I shake my head in the same manner he did. "No. I'm the Crown Prince. This is my battle. Report, Captain!"

A grin breaks out on his face, and he pulls back and salutes before he says, "The latest arrivals were Lady Ellcia's troops. Parthun's army thought they were reinforcements for them, so were not prepared when her troops reached them. From what I can see, Lady Ellcia herself fought harder than most of them, doing her best to break through to you. I'm glad she found you. If she hadn't..." He pauses a moment before saying, "The battle continues, and I'll have to attend to it shortly, but most of the enemy troops, from what I can see, have either surrendered or are fleeing."

I nod. "Thank you, Captain. Please, see to the rest of the battle for me."

"Yes, Sir!"

He turns to Rulf and orders, "Rulfor! You will see to Prince Draydon to ensure his safety. That is your number one task. Everything else is secondary."

Rulf grunts his reply, but before Tilbur can leave, he asks, "Roran?"

"Last I saw," Tilbur replies, "he was holding his own on the eastern front. I will see to him."

A man and a woman rush up, and from their dress, I assume they're healers. They set to work on my wound, checking Ellcia quickly to see if she's injured as well.

Rulf stares down their necks as they work, which makes each one quite uncomfortable, but I know he won't be happy unless he can fulfill his duties with as much intensity as possible.

The pain comes in waves, but I ask Ellcia to bring me up to speed. She rushes through it all. Most of it I had hoped would turn out that way, but for her to own the fleet and Sevord City was too much to expect. I'm blown away by it. It also turns out they came across Rulf, wandering through the Talic Region. He was heading this way, but unsure of where exactly to go. While she explains it all to me, the big guy just stands there, stinking and grunting, not adding anything to the conversation.

When they have me patched up, a stretcher is brought, and two large men pick me up, one on each end, and carry me. Rulf walks in front, eyeing everyone we pass, and Ellcia walks beside me.

When we get to one of the higher hills in the area on the way to the city, I ask them to carry me to the top, and when they do, I get them to turn around so I can see the battle. Tilbur was right. The battle is finished. I see a few skirmishes here and there, but many soldiers are on their knees, some with their hands on their heads.

"Set me down!" I order. "I can't go back to the city. Not yet. Not until it's finished."

We call soldiers to us and send word by those who say they can run fast. In a little while. I have word back. Parthun has been captured, along with Corter. Corter was actually riding towards Leito when they found him. I can't imagine what he planned on doing there. They're loyal to me.

Most enemy soldiers have surrendered. We have won, and all is well.

When Tilbur arrives to give more detail, I order him to offer amnesty to all Parthun's men on the condition that they swear fealty to me and give their word that they forever reject Parthun as King. I insist that Parthun not be brought to me, though. I won't give him the honor of speaking to him on the battlefield where so many of my people died so he could maintain his cruelty.

Instead, I order him, Corter, and all his Captains bound and brought to me at my palace in Haner.

He bows, but before he can leave, I ask, "And Farnum?"

"I wondered, Your Majesty, if you would ask about him."

I nod. I want to know about him, but also my sword and armor.

He shakes his head. "He escaped. I have sent soldiers to search for him, but it will be tricky to find him and even harder to capture him.

I dismiss Tilbur and wait on the hilltop while he receives oaths of fealty. They may give it to any officer, and between my troops and Ellcia's, we have many. So, it doesn't take long, maybe only a couple of hours. When they're finished, I send word that I'm ready to enter the city.

I don't want to be carried in on a stretcher, but I can't walk right now—at least well enough—and I don't feel like being dragged. We enter the southern gate, even though I've mainly used the western gate as of late, because it's the most direct route to my palace.

We cross through into the city to loud cheers. I make a point not to acknowledge Parthun, although I see him bound behind me when I glance back. It's exciting to recognize some of the people standing at the sides of the street. They cheer, they jump up and down, and there is a general celebration.

I feel sick to my stomach, however, because I see the looks on many faces. Anxious. Worried. It's not just a victory, it came at a cost. Many of their husbands or wives or sons or daughters fought out there today. And many won't ever come home. Their families just don't know it yet. I don't even know yet who has lived and who has died.

I hear them boo and shout and curse Parthun. I decide to let it happen. I think he needs a bit of that.

We weave our way through the city, past countless people. The Nobles are all at the palace already, although it's far too small to accommodate them all.

When we reach the gates to my palace, or Lord Hillbin's residence, I wave for the men carrying me to stop. I swing my legs off the side, and Ellcia helps me to my feet.

As soon as I'm upright, I know I've made a mistake. The whole world spins. I fear I'll fall on Ellcia, but in a few moments, everything settles.

I raise my hand, and the crowd goes quiet.

"My friends," I begin, but I'm surprised at how quiet my voice is. I see Parthun back there in the procession, but I still haven't looked directly at him. "Today, my friends, truth and loyalty have won. You have won. And the man behind the lies and death and murder of so many of our loved ones, comes before us in chains."

The people cheer. I love the sound of it, but it's a little loud for me right now. I wish they would whisper their cheers.

When they calm down again, I call out, "I will now enter my palace here in Haner and see to the traitor, but please, I invite you to return in two hours for my coronation."

They cheer again, and I wave, smile, and roll back onto my stretcher. I'm glad the men carrying it are strong, because they've managed well for the entire trip so far.

34

———•———

Draydon and Parthun

We enter the palace and find another crowd. I wave at them but direct the men to take me down the hallway away from them. I'll leave Parthun and everyone else to Tilbur for now.

We find a quiet room, and the healers and Ellcia help get my armor and shirt off, while Clarice takes care of getting me some warm food and plenty of water. I'm certainly not up for sitting on the throne or even getting crowned King at the moment.

The healers work on my wound some more, cleaning it, trying to stop the bleeding, and bandage it up again. I don't look at it, but Ellcia's expression lets me know it looks pretty horrible.

I smile at her, and aside from when she looks at where Frindor's sword cut me, she just beams back at me.

"We made it," I say.

She nods slowly. "We did. I can't believe it, but we did."

There's so much to tell her, and so much I want to hear, but I feel the pressure of all that lies before us. "I can't wait until this is all over, and we can just talk. Maybe we can sit on that roof of that old, abandoned warehouse near the harbor while we catch up."

Her face breaks out in a large grin, and she lets out a laugh. "The first nice day when we get back to Sevord!"

"Deal!"

I smile back and add, "So, that's how long your hair grows in two and a half months."

She runs her hand through it and smiles back. She looks perfect to me.

When they're finished cleaning me up, and I've had some hot stew and another big drink of water, Clarice ushers everyone out and helps me dress in something more appropriate for the next leg of the journey.

I don't like someone else dressing me, but I don't really have the strength to do it myself. When we finish, a knock on the door interrupts us.

"Come!"

The door opens and Tilbur and Roran walk in. I try to get up, but it takes me a bit, and they have to help. "Congratulations on a battle well fought!" Tilbur announces.

"You too!"

I surprise him with a hug—a slow one—followed by another for Roran. Somehow, despite what all has happened today, this seems right.

"You ready?"

I nod. "But I want it to happen as we planned."

I move through some back hallways, kept clear by some of Tilbur's soldiers, and enter the throne room from a side door. The moment I step out, the Nobles cheer, although they are far less exuberant than the common people. I know it's genuine, but I think refined people struggle to show too much excitement.

I take the throne at the head of the room. There is a process for all of this, Tilbur tells me, but I have decided to shake it up a bit.

I wave for silence, and Tilbur pushes Parthun forward, knocking him to his knees near the center of the room, but slightly off to the side. Captain Tilbur then takes his place just behind the man.

"Thank you, Captain."

I turn toward the door, but Parthun speaks up. "Your Majesty!" he calls out in a loud voice. "I thank you for the privilege of an audience, but I do not know why I might be in chains. I have kept the Kingdom for you, unaware that you might still be alive…"

"Captain Tilbur?" I call out, interrupting Parthun.

"Yes, Your Majesty."

"Did the traitor Parthun know I was alive while he sat on my throne?"

"Yes, Your Majesty. In fact, he sent me to kill you."

At that, I hear a gasp among the Nobles. I like putting on this bit of theater before I officially claim the throne.

"Then," I continue, "it would be logical to assume that Parthun was not keeping the throne for me but trying to kill me in order to keep the throne for himself. Is my logic sound?"

"Yes, Your Majesty."

Parthun's face screws up in a look of terror and frustration, and then declares, "Your Majesty, you would not take the word of a man who…"

I raise my hand and say, "Captain Tilbur?"

"Yes, Your Majesty."

"Did the traitor Parthun bring General Lirnal with him?"

"Yes, Your Majesty," Tilbur replies, then asks, "Would you like me to bring him before you?"

"I would."

Tilbur waves to the back of the room, and four soldiers bring Lirnal forward. It's been months since I've seen him, and even then, I was just getting to know him. But the man I see before me, struggling to stay on his feet, is almost unrecognizable.

His face is bruised and bloody—those are fresh woods. He's lost a shocking amount of weight, and he has far more gray in his hair than he did the last time I saw him. I want to cry, but I hold it in.

"General Lirnal?"

"Yes, Your Majesty." His voice comes out in a croak, but I see the smile. This is what he wanted, no doubt about it.

"I understand I cannot restore your rank and declare you innocent of all crimes until I have been crowned King, but I declare that the instant the crown touches my head, you are absolved of all suspicion, and you are immediately appointed first General of the Sevordine Armies. You will not need a further declaration from me. The crown on my head will be your appointment."

"Thank you, Your Majesty."

"And General?"

"Yes, Your Majesty."

"Thank you for your service to the kingdom. I recognize every cut and every bruise and every scar as your gift to the throne, and proof of your loyalty. You have made the Royal Line proud. My hope is to one day live up to your honor."

At that, he begins to cry. I know I shouldn't do it as I have a lot to cover, but I can't help myself. I struggle out of my throne and make my way to him, wrapping my arms around him. We both weep on each other's shoulders, and I whisper, "I know what you did in the dungeons. I know your sacrifice and how you remained there to keep the peace, so I might take the throne. I know. I can't thank you enough."

He squeezes me as tightly as he can, and when I pull back, I order Clarice to assist him. He can barely walk. Neither can I, but Roran comes and assists me. As I return,

I give a smile to Ellcia and catch a glimpse of Marleet and Hemot. Oh, how I've missed all three of them.

When I settle back on my throne, Parthun speaks up again. "Your Majesty. See, I have brought General Lirnal as you ordered and…"

I interrupt yet again with, "Captain Tilbur?"

"Yes, Your Majesty."

"Did you see the injuries and wounds on General Lirnal?"

"Yes, Your Majesty."

"In your experience, Captain Tilbur, were those wounds inflicted recently?"

"Yes, Your Majesty."

"So, my orders for General Lirnal to be brought to me unharmed were not followed."

"No, Your Majesty. The traitor Parthun certainly did not obey you in this respect."

"Thank you, Captain Tilbur."

"Ahh, your Majesty," Parthun calls out, "but it was Captain Tilbur here who inflicted most of the injuries back at the castle."

I nod. "Captain Tilbur, if you have acted improperly toward another officer, who in the Sevordine Armies would be responsible for addressing that matter with you?"

"The first General, Your Majesty."

I nod. "Then let it be so. You will report to General Lirnal shortly after my coronation to see if he wishes to press charges."

Tilbur smiles and bows. "Yes, Your Majesty."

Parthun frowns. I did not believe it would be wise to merely take the throne until I addressed a few matters regarding Parthun. Fortunately, he is acting exactly as I suspected, desperately trying to talk his way out of everything and blame everyone else.

"Your Majesty," Parthun calls out again. "I have only acted out of integrity over the last twelve years, and Captain Tilbur's slander a moment ago is unfounded. It is merely his word against mine. Seeing as he has a history of brutality, it is obvious he is not to be trusted."

I wait for it. It's coming… I know it…

Parthun leans forward a little and adds, "I would recommend, Your Majesty, that you turn to the Nobility at this time. If over half can speak to my honor, and no proof can be provided, then by law, I must be absolved of all accusations."

Many Nobles tense up. The moment has arrived. It comes down to this.

I cannot rule without the support of the Nobles, and at the moment, they fear Parthun too much. Despite his chains, he truly is a venomous snake. Many will suffer if I can't take away his poison.

Turning to the Nobles, they all bow to me. They will expect me to ask for them to speak to this matter, but also ask for their support, but I have something else in mind.

"My friends," I say. I glance around the room. Ellcia is with the Nobles. She just beams at me. I catch the eye of Marleet, and she bounces a little on her feet and waves. Hemot, standing on one side of her, does his best to look serious and focused, but he only looks like he's ready to crack. On the other side of Marleet stand Lord Yune and Lady Aldora, with Lord Hillbin and Lord Vickor.

So many I can count on, but I know Parthun holds power over many more.

And this… is… the moment.

"My friends," I say again. "I wish to offer you something. Something I do not offer lightly." The expressions on the faces of the Nobles turn to suspicion. "I know from the way I speak, it might sound like I am about to bribe you, but I am certainly not. I actually wish to do something else. I wish to free you."

Now I truly have their attention. Some appear hopeful. Others appear offended. Both Tilbur and Hillbin worked with me on the choice of words, so I follow their advice carefully.

"I wish to offer you amnesty. If there are misdeeds or improper choices, I offer you amnesty. If word comes out in the future about what you have done before this day, I will ignore it. I do this because I suspect that the traitor Parthun has sway over many of you, controlling you because of the possibility of disgrace. But I will promise you now that I will not allow this to happen. Amnesty is offered and will not be removed, regardless of your response to my next question. You have my word on that."

The entire room relaxes as if all the problems have just suddenly fallen away. I glance at Parthun, and I can see I've just taken his final move away.

"My friends," I call out. "How many of you wish to step forward to attest to Parthun's integrity? There will be no consequences for you from me to offer him your support, nor will there be any from me if you do not."

No one moves at first, then I see two Nobles take a half-step forward, but then pull back quickly.

I turn back to Parthun. "No one, traitor. No one to stand with you in your time of need. Perhaps that might cause you to rethink your choices?"

"Your Majesty," Parthun calls out. He's desperate now. I can see it in his eyes. "I have prepared Sevord City specifically for your return. If you would only return with me to the city, I will show you how loyal I have been. I have even kept the crown in Sevord City rather than risk it on the journey, allowing you to…"

Breaking with the pattern a bit, I call out this time, "Lady Ellcia!"

"Yes, Your Majesty," she replies.

"Tell me of Sevord City."

"Yes, Your Majesty. As per your orders, I moved through that area, but it was in my heart to do more than just come meet with you, so I captured the city from the traitor Parthun as a gift to you on your coronation."

"Captured?" Parthun spits out. "Captured? That is absurd, Your Majesty. There was no need!"

"Actually, Your Majesty, I am glad I did," Ellcia says with conviction. "The city was walled up, and what was left of Parthun's fleet stood guard at the harbor. We managed to enter, but we found the castle filled with assassins. In fact, if his Majesty has noticed, my left arm is injured from where I was struck with a crossbow bolt from one of the assassins left in the castle. We captured dozens. If you had returned to the castle before we swept it clean, it is my opinion that you would have been killed immediately."

"Your Majesty," Parthun says with a laugh and a shake of his head, "I think you'll find..."

"Captain Tilbur!"

"Yes, Your Majesty."

"When Parthun's troops, under the command of the late Captain Frindor, approached the city, they made a demand of the people of Haner, did they not?"

"Yes, Your Majesty."

"What did they demand, Captain Tilbur?"

"Your head, Your Majesty."

The Nobles gasp.

"Just my head, Captain Tilbur?"

"Yes, Your Majesty. They seemed to think they wanted it separate from your body."

"Hmm..." I say, "Now, that's concerning."

Parthun waves that away as if it's nothing. "Oh, Your Majesty, I cannot be held responsible for any of that, for I was not yet there. I would never have..."

"Captain Tilbur."

"Yes, Your Majesty."

"I am, Captain, as you know, so new to this ruling thing. As such, I sometimes fail to understand how people wish to communicate."

"Yes, Your Majesty, that can be a problem."

"Perhaps, Captain," I say, "you could help me."

"Yes, Your Majesty."

"If Parthun's troops communicate through severed heads, as gruesome as that is, would it not be wise to assume the best way to proceed is to also communicate in the same manner?"

Parthun's eyes go wide and nearly pop out of his head. He glances at the Nobles, but no one meets his eyes.

"Of course, Your Majesty," Tilbur replies.

"Thank you, Captain Tilbur. Then, in this case, it is my judgment that if the traitor Parthun, son of Trevolay, speaks again in my court without my permission, then you are to sever his head from his body as a message to all those who wish to betray the throne of Sevord."

The Captain draws his sword and comes around to the side of Parthun. Tilbur's smile grows by the minute, and Parthun shrinks before him.

Turning to the Nobles, I ask, "Do I, Draydon, son of General Geran, next in line to the throne, have the support of the Nobles to take my place as your King?"

The Nobles, every one of them, bows to me.

"Then I ask for your oaths of fealty to me now, and I will be crowned immediately after."

They each offer their oaths, which takes far longer than I would have thought as most are wordier than the average person, and then we head out. Typically, I can be crowned anywhere, but I want to be crowned in front of the people. And I have something special in mind.

When we step out, the Nobles file into the crowd, and I stand in front. I wave for Ellcia to stand by me. I don't want to go through this without her. She's still in her armor and traveling clothes, so she likely doesn't look like a Noble to anyone else, but she does to me.

I call out for Lord Hillbin, and he comes forward. Tilbur tells me that whenever a new King has been named, different Nobles have requested the right to place the crown on his head, which always gives them a certain amount of status and power. I don't care about that with Hillbin. He not only deserves the honor, but he's someone who won't likely abuse any power this gives him.

He comes forward, and I know just about everyone is wondering what I'm going to do for a crown. The official crown is apparently back in Sevord City, but I never intended to be crowned with it anyway.

I raise my hand, and the crowd goes silent. "My friends, I am about to be crowned your King, and I am grateful to be crowned here in Haner, as this is the first of the major cities to welcome me as their own. As such, I did not want to be crowned with the royal crown as kept in Sevord, but I have commissioned a new crown, which I intend to wear here in Haner and the rest of the Talic, anytime I am in this area of our great nation."

I can see the people are pleased, and I wave for Ennen, the blacksmith, the first in Haner to swear fealty to me. He comes forward, carrying something in a cloth. I haven't actually seen it yet. My request was that it be made light, and not from gold or silver, but something that declares that I am of the people.

He hands me the bundle, and I pull back the cloth, anxious to see it. When it is out of its wrapping, my mouth drops open. It's made of brass: thin, light, and woven together. It looks like it might actually be comfortable, and I smile at Ennen, putting my hand on his shoulder, thanking him.

I hold the crown up high and call out, "The crown of Ennen, the Blacksmith, is the one I will be crowned with. I have named this crown the Crown of the People. Know that every time I wear it, it declares that I serve the People of Sevord and the Talic, that you are mine, and I am yours!" Turning to Hillbin, I call out for the people to hear, "I wish to be crowned by the Lord of this City, Lord Hillbin. This will serve as a constant reminder of his loyalty and love for the kingdom, and a constant declaration that those who serve and honor, those who show loyalty, those who are true to our people, will always be honored."

I hand the crown to Hillbin, and immediately notice the problem. I didn't think this one through. Seeing as he's so... short and portly... well... I actually have to kneel before him so he can get it on my head.

When it sets down, I feel a sense of such... thankfulness. But something else as well. Tears stream down my face as I feel so humbled, so low, so small. How can someone like me rule a nation like this?

As I turn back to the people, I realize I can't.

I certainly can't.

That's why I have Ellcia by my side. And Roran. And Tilbur, and Marleet, and Lord Yune, and... even Hemot.

I raise my hands high as the people cheer so loud I think my ears are going to burst.

35

Draydon and the Future

I sit on my throne, surrounded by select Nobles such as Lord Hillbin, Lord Yune, Lady Aldora, and Lord Vickor. Vickor does not actually rank high enough to be here for this, but seeing as he was the first Lord in the City to swear fealty to me, it seems appropriate that he be brought in.

Marleet and Hemot are here, and Ellcia sits not far from me. I've already squashed the expectation of a wedding today—or anytime soon. I'm confident I want to spend the rest of my life with Ellcia, but... I'm seventeen. That's no age to be married.

I also have my officers present. They all survived, although not without injuries. Phil took a sword blade to his side, in a similar spot to me. It's not life-threatening, but I know it hurts. Laanna actually took an arrow through her right arm, but it's been removed. She's lost her cheerful approach to everything, which is a little strange. I guess an injury on each arm will do that for most people.

Roran came through without injury. He fought hard and inspired the troops. Gerr, Terr, and Gillan are all well, with only minor scrapes, cuts, and bruises.

Granel, however, was in quite the accident. He fought like a wild man throughout the battle, but his left leg is broken just below the knee. He does not look happy about it, but I'm told he'll be fine.

Traltor and Nareesa are well. It turns out Frindor used enchanted crossbow bolts, dipped in a sleeping potion of sorts. It was all he could find to deal with a giant. I'm just glad Farnum didn't reach them. He could have killed them with little trouble, assuming my blade didn't turn on him.

I'm grateful they're okay, and that Rulf is with them out on the battlefield, catching up. Having him out there is good. Rulf hasn't bathed since he escaped the dungeons, and Traltor and Nareesa are not ideal people to have in a meeting.

I look over at General Lirnal… Uncle Lirnal. He sits next to Tilbur and is smiling, although I see he's not entirely here. We've fed him and given him plenty of water, but it'll be a long time before he's back up to his old self.

My side aches. A lot! Every movement, even turning my head, affects it. I just want someone to knock me out and wake me up when it's all better, but that's not going to happen.

I've received reports on the state of the nation, and we have drafted up letters to go throughout the country, announcing my ascension to the throne and Parthun's arrest. We will also have a trial for Parthun, but it turns out that must happen in Sevord City.

I've already received reports on the battle, but I want more information on something specific. Aside from the officers loyal to Parthun, everyone else has offered oaths of fealty to me. Parthun's officers themselves, however, have shown a little more resistance. I'll leave them to Tilbur and Lirnal and Roran to figure out. Those three are my officers, and that puts that responsibility on their plates.

"Captain Tilbur?"

"Yes, King Draydon."

Wow. That's going to take some getting used to. "Do you have any word on Farnum?"

He knows what I'm asking. Farnum's only part of the concern. The bigger issue is my armor and sword. Those two items could take a man like Farnum and turn him into a greater threat than Parthun ever was.

"I'm sorry, Your Majesty. We believe he fled the battle once Lady Ellcia's troops arrived. At this point, we assume he has moved south to Rainer."

"Send soldiers to find out," I order.

He gives a slight bow. "Already done, Your Majesty." He smiles and says, "But I have something else for you in the meantime."

"What might that be, Captain?"

He reaches behind him and pulls out a sheathed blade. I recognize it immediately, and everyone in the room smiles. "The King's Sword…" I say under my breath.

I take it from him, but I need his help strapping it on. I don't have the strength to do it myself at the moment.

Once it's on, I slowly draw it, and everyone gasps. It's truly beautiful. A real work of art. The blade is black—a deep, shining black that both reflects the light and absorbs every bit of it. It's as if my eyes slide off it. I know the sword has many talents, most of which I haven't learned yet, but the one thing everyone does know about it is that by simply drawing it, all enchantments on me are canceled.

I don't feel any different, so I suspect that means I had no enchantments to worry about. And now that they've seen me draw it, they know I'm under no one else's power.

"I will teach you how to use it," Tilbur says. "Your father, General Geran, was well acquainted with its abilities. Despite the rules to the contrary, he taught me a great deal."

"I look forward to that, Uncle Tilbur," I reply. I don't think I've ever called him that, but I think maybe it's helpful to remember we're family.

I sheath the blade and sit down again. Just that short time on my feet is enough to leave me gasping for air. This is going to be a rough start to my rule.

Lord Yune stands, and I invite him to speak. "Your Majestyyyy. Once againnnn I wish to tell youuuu how happy we arrrre to have you as our new Kingggg. But I wish to aaaask. What are your next stepssss?"

I smile. I don't know much about ruling. Nor do I know much about what the days, months, and years ahead will look like, but I do know a bit of this.

"I have three immediate goals. First, I will heal here in Haner while we work to put the Kingdom back together. Second, I will head to Sevord to establish my rule in the Capital."

"And after thaaaat, Your Majestyyyy?"

"We will remove Farnum, freeing Rainer from his tyranny, and then there's something else."

"And that issss, Your Majestyyyy?"

"Trolls."

He doesn't say anything to that, just stares at me.

"Prince Roran and I learned something in our travels. The trolls—the Reber Trolls—they are men, perhaps women as well, and maybe even children. They are enchanted folk. They terrorize our lands, but they have been cursed to do so. I wish to free them, and to find out what it is that holds them."

I smile at Ellcia. We have a lot to do for the Kingdom, but I'm not just going to rule. I'm going to be the King who frees the Trolls.

$$\cdot - \bullet - \cdot$$

Epilogue

Three years later…

My horse steps to the right as Ellcia comes up next to me. I never liked her horse. He has a bad temper. At least he's good to her. They seem to have a bond.

"You ready to do this?" I ask.

She smiles at me and slowly nods. "I've been ready for this for about a year. I'm a little sick of sitting in the throne room and overseeing meetings. I'd kind of like to get out there again. I'd like to take some risks that don't involve the possibility of assassins."

"Yeah," Hemot says with a laugh, "but the last time we were out there, we had assassins on our tail continually."

"I don't think any of us have an assassin-free life ahead of us," Marleet pipes in.

I laugh. "That's for sure."

I turn my horse around and look back to the castle stables. Tilbur's coming with a big frown on his face. He's not happy. In a way, that's familiar, but he's been smiling so much the last six or eight months that I hate to see the frown again.

"I'm sorry, Captain," I say before he can tell me what's bothering him. Well, tell me again. "This is something I have to do."

"I know, Your Majesty, but that doesn't mean I have to be happy about it."

"No, I guess not." I smile at Tilbur, not to annoy him or because I'm happy to see him upset, but because he's become like a father to me since I've taken the throne. Lirnal and I are close, of course, but Tilbur… I never expected to be so close to that man.

"Seems like a bad idea," Rulf says, adding a grunt.

"Oh, it's okay, sweetheart," Yinni says. She stands just a little shorter than he does and is built like Rulf's mom. Tall and thin, easily hiding her giant blood, but I wouldn't want to mess with her.

"Don't worry, Draynee. Rulfy will be good. I'll keep him in line."

I still don't know where Yinni came from. She's sweet and kind, but like most people with giant blood, she struggles to understand what she can and can't do. I don't think anyone should call me Draynee. Ever. But, ever since Rulf's mom found Yinni for Rulf as a possible future wife—which is weird… I mean, who tracks down a wife for her son like that? Nareesa just disappeared for a month and came back with Yinni. And now they're engaged. Apparently, giant folk have a three-year engagement—to the day—so they still won't be married for a while, but it's just so… strange!

Anyway, ever since Yinni arrived, she and Rulf are inseparable and when Rulf grunts, Yinni interprets. The strangest part about it is… I think she's usually wrong in what she thinks Rulf means.

A new voice pipes up. "The soldiers are ready, Your Majesty."

I thank Frellson and look over my friends. We're just missing Roran. He should be out here shortly, and then we can head out. We have a lot to do. I need to get my sword and armor back from Farnum and remove that man from Rainer, and I need to deal with the trolls.

The trolls… they're going to be tricky. I have a few ideas on where to start, but… I definitely want my sword for the whole experience. Well… actually, I have my sword, the King's sword, strapped to my waist. I'm just wondering if my father's sword wants to come back to me, or does it now belong to Roran? Or Lirnal?

"Are you sure, Your Majesty?" Tilbur asks me, pulling me away from my thoughts.

"Yes, Tilbur. I'm very sure. The people of Rainer need to be free, and the King must play his part in their freedom. And the enchanted people, those condemned to live as trolls, they need to be free as well. After three years, the Kingdom is firmly in my grasp, so now's the time to free these people."

I turn and, without another word, head out across the castle courtyard. It's time to cross the Talic once again.

To Be Continued…

If you enjoyed this series, please take the time to leave a review!

Pronunciation Guide

Now, you might think that I have tried to create a proper pronunciation guide, but I don't know how to do that. I could look it up, but not only do I not understand diacritical markings, but I think most people don't. So… I made a pronunciation guide that makes sense to me with the capital letters pointing out the emphasis.
And here it is.

Berin	BARE-rinn
Caric	CARE-ick
Corter	CORE-ter
Draydon	DRAY-dunn
Ellcia	ell-CEE-ah
Farnum	FAR-num
Frindor	FRIN-door
Frippolee	FRIPP-oh-lee
Granel	GRA-nell
Gratter	GRA-terr
Haner	HAY-ner
Hartor	HAR-terr
Hella	HELL-ah
Hemot	HEM-mot
Hillbin	HILL-binn
Leito	LAY-toh
Lirnal	LIR-nall
Marleet	mar-LEET
Morgin	MOR-ginn

Nordin	NOR-dinn
Parthun	PAR-thunn
Rainer	RAY-nerr
Reber	REE-berr
Relin	RELL-linn
Shaloomd	sha-LOOM-d
Shalsee	SHALL-see
Shawn	AWE-some
Talic	TAL-ick
Tallia	TAL-lee-ah
Tilbur	TILL-burr
Trevolay	TREV-oh-lay

CHECK OUT THESE BOOKS BY
Shawn P. B. Robinson

Adult Fiction (Sci-fi & Fantasy)

The Ridge Series (3 books)
ADA: An Anthology of Short Stories

YA Fiction (Fantasy)

The Sevordine Chronicles (5 Books)

Books for Younger Readers

Annalynn the Canadian Spy Series (6 Books)
Jerry the Squirrel (4 Books)
Arestana Series (3 Books)
Activity Books (2 Books)

www.shawnpbrobinson.com/books